KARMA KILLER

Nobody's perfect… & karma is calling.

Anathema Morgan

Dedicated to every life lost to mindless violence, every life lost to some lowlife behind a gun, every life lost to the monsters driven by the monsters before them.

Dedicated to...

The twelve lost in Monterey Park, California, on January 21st, 2023.

The twenty-two lost in Uvalde, Texas, on May 24th, 2022.

The ten lost in Buffalo, New York, on May 14th, 2022.

The ten lost in Boulder, Colorado, on March 22nd, 2021.

The twenty-three lost in El Paso, Texas, on August 3rd, 2019.

The thirteen lost in Virginia Beach, Virginia, on May 31st, 2019.

The thirteen lost in Thousand Oaks, California, on November 7th, 2018.

The eleven lost in Pittsburgh, Pennsylvania, on October 27th, 2018.

The ten lost in Santa Fe, Texas, on May 18th, 2018.

The seventeen lost in Parkland, Florida, on February 14th, 2018.

The twenty-seven lost in Sutherland Springs, Texas, on November 5th, 2017.

The sixty-one lost in Paradise, Nevada, on October 1st, 2017.

The fifty lost in Orlando, Florida, on June 12th, 2016.

The sixteen lost in San Bernardino, California, on December 2nd, 2015.

Dedicated to the families of the victims as well, and to the victims and families of every other shooting I could not list – Sandy Hook,

Columbine, Aurora, Virginia Tech, the list goes on and on...

I know there is no way to heal or recompensate, but I can strive to help any way I can...
And encourage future generations to be BETTER.

*Man is least himself when he talks in his own person.
Give him a mask, and he will tell you the truth.*

—Oscar Wilde

CYCLE ONE

A Twelve-Step Guide to Finding Your Final Girl

/// October 21ˢᵗ, 3 AM. Ten days until Halloween.

"Fuck Michael, marry Jason, kill Freddy."

Olivia leans against the hood of Laurie Thompson's car, disregarding the clear expense invested in the machine. Laurie gives her a warning glance, cigarette smoke threading through her lips. The night sky looms over their high school's parking lot, lending those beneath an ominous, peculiar sort of embrace that Lake Leer's populace has learned to tolerate or fear. Or both.

Laurie takes another couple drags of her cigarette before she bothers to grant her companion a response. "You've done it, Olivia. You've turned me off of 'Fuck, Marry, Kill'. You want a ribbon?"

"I would rather have a little gold star, myself," Olivia jokes. At any other time, her passion for cheerleading and her ditzy demeanor would be irritatingly obvious. Here, fresh from a night of partying and debauchery, her messy blonde hair is tangled in dangling strings, and her immodest clothes are stained with the odorous detritus of alcohol. "What, don't like horror movies?"

Laurie chuckles, their lifelong residence *perfect* for such a flick, she thinks. A little Colorado mountain town with a sinister, alliterative name, foggy forests that stretch on for miles and hide away long-abandoned mines, a disconcerting number of disappeared children and violent murders over the years...

"Nah," Laurie says, kicking a pebble towards the school. "No, I'd give myself nightmares."

"Aww," Olivia mocks, a mischievous grin forming on her drunken face. "Little Laurie scared of ghosts?"

"No," Laurie objects, kicking Olivia in the ankle. The cheerleader jumps, a slight giggle escaping her. "Not ghosts," Laurie continues. "But this town has had a lot of serial killers. Remember that one guy a few years ago that was obsessed with making kids into orphans?"

Olivia shakes her head. "I got better things to do than read about deranged murderers. Like party!" She giggles, her head swaying back. "Drink, fuck... Hey, speaking of which, when are you and Billy gonna go at it? You've been giving each other *so many* eyes..."

"Well, I've only got two, don't I?" Laurie snorts, and Olivia breaks into giggles again. "I don't know, we'll see how drunk we are when we get home. Nick is probably fucking his date in there, though."

"You think?"

"He's not going to have many other opportunities, is he?" Laurie snickers, running a finger along the roof of her resplendent car, lonesome in the lot. It had been a gift from her parents two years ago, on her sixteenth birthday, a fact she found herself reticent to share with most anyone. "His date... uh, Violet, right?"

"Violet," Olivia confirms.

"Yeah, Violet. Doesn't put out a whole lot, does she? I mean, the nerd's probably never even done it before. Doubt he's gonna get her this drunk again, is he?"

"True," Olivia smirks. "She's never partying again after this, that's for sure. Can't wait to see our little wallflower all over the Internet... oh, it's gonna be priceless."

"Oh my God, did they take—" Laurie begins, but her face goes white and her tongue goes numb, and not for the words she had planned to say.

No, it is for the screams that burst out inside the school.

The gym seems formless, dark, cold, an empty void... a million symptoms of Violet Vance's inebriated lack of comprehension. Her eyelids threaten to come crashing down permanently with every blink, every movement of her limbs weighed down with metaphorical boulders. She has never drunk alcohol before in her life, and she is quite certain she will never do so again. She hadn't even meant to, really.

She realizes, with no small level of anxiety and inner turbulence, that she feels like she might faint. This, however, is a bad place to sleep. Not surrounded by these... vultures.

One of the three boys steps into frame, a silhouette in the lightless school gymnasium. Why Billy and Laurie and their friends wanted to hang *here* of all places, Violet had no idea. She knew they had done it before. Perhaps it was just the thrill of it all. Maybe they liked doing things they weren't supposed to... Scratch that, she *knew* they loved breaking the rules.

Did she want to be here? She was leaning against the idea more and more every passing second. The question grows quieter in volume as time crawls forward, but it screams and screams to make up for its gradual declination. Even so, nothing pierces the drunken fog. She can feel a little drool escaping the corner of her mouth. Sexy.

She can't see Nicholas very well in this light, in this haze, but she knows his straw-colored hair when she sees it. It makes her think of a particularly sandy mop. He and his two friends — Billy, Laurie's boyfriend, and... some redneck named Harrison, she thinks — have been talking and trading misogynistic jokes for the better part of half an hour, a collection of empty beer cans in their wake.

"Hey, Violet, you still awake?" Nick asks, a tone that many might mistake for concern. At this point, she has come to the conclusion that she was an idiot to ever fall for it. She's known for years that these boys are real jerks, to put it one way, and yet her loneliness had taken the wheel tonight.

This is the last time she goes out of her way to earn the social respect and admiration of her peers.

"Mhm," Violet groans out, the syllables stilted. She tries again.

"Yes." It's more of a croak, and even worse than her initial attempt. Violet shuts up.

Nick chuckles. "Damn, you've had a lot to drink. Are you okay?"

"Sure I am," Violet tries, the sentence halfway coherent.

"Good, because I remembered teasing you at the club, and, well..." He crouches down, running a hand through his hair, the shy hesitation almost authentic. "Well, I just wouldn't want you to think that wasn't *going* anywhere..."

Violet frowns, invisibly doubting in the dark. "I..."

"Man, are you really fucking around with the bimbo's head?" Billy shouts out from the corner, the gym echoing as he hops down from the benches. "We got her *pissed,* Nick. She's free game."

Violet groans uneasily. She doesn't like how that sounds.

Nick breaks his disguise with a chuckle, standing to meet Billy. Harrison lags behind as he lets out one of his stupid guffaws, the sort of laugh you can only find in a redneck mountain town. "You go through all the trouble of wasting the shit out of her, and you still haven't fucked her? Weak, man." Harrison has always had a way with words, Violet mentally remarks, but the dry humor is a poor distraction from her thumping heart. The alcohol would serve that purpose better if it hadn't been giving her such a violent migraine.

"Well, why don't you have a go, then?" Nick asks, clearly exasperated. "We'll take turns."

Something darts through the dim, a shadow in the moonlight. Violet tilts her head, whimpers meekly. They take no notice. The shape has disappeared as quickly as it came. Violet wonders if it's a trick of the light, a hallucination, maybe. Does excess alcohol cause those? She has no idea. For all her book smarts, she has never put much research into inebriation.

"Take turns?" Billy mocks. "Nick, look at her. She won't even be *awake* that long."

Violet should be concerned with her impending fate, whatever that is — worried for the depraved things they speak of. But her heart thumps not for them, not for her... rather, it fears for the chill in the air. The moon gleams through the gym's high windows, casting celestial rectangles on the floor. For a few more seconds, all is still. She was seeing things.

"Then all at once, why not? You saw her in the bathroom, I'm sure the little bitch isn't gonna complain." Nick's suggestion is met with agreement and childish snickers, the kind born only of an empty well of empathy and far too much alcohol.

She watches her date and his fri— no, this was a bad idea, he's not a date, she needs to stop calling him that, and—

Violet loses her train of thought, stolen away with another dart of the encroaching figure... a *shape,* briefly leaving lithe silhouettes under the moon's light. Violet tries to speak, but her lips stall. She is paralyzed, uncertain. She knows not who will be worse — man or stalker.

"Are you sure we won't get, like, gay and stuff doing that?" Harrison asks, in a tone that suggests he is somehow completely serious. Even someone as meatheaded as Billy sighs in disappointment, giving Harrison a good sock in the jaw.

A rustle near the emergency exit, a little *click* of a lock. Violet can feel the sweat that runs down her forehead, bits of her hair snared in the edge of her mouth.

"You're a stupid shit, Harry," Billy says, with all the condescending air a weary father might grant their troublesome toddler. Harrison frowns, rubbing his petulant jaw.

"Look, man, it's just something my dad says—" Harrison begins, before the air cracks with the snap of a crossbow prod.

Violet jumps with a shriek as a crossbow bolt burrows through Harrison's cheeks, blood spilling under the moon. Harrison's mouth helplessly flaps in a guttural imitation of speech, dumbly shredding the flesh behind his bloody teeth with every attempt.

No one even has time to panic before a gloved hand lunges into sight, dainty fingers possessing impossible strength. The assailant rips the bolt from Harrison's cheeks, his tongue tearing loose, torn through the gory mess that remains of his face. As he struggles to scream, the killer, small and buried beneath a leather jacket, emerges from the shadows. The bloody bolt now pierces the boy's chest with the murderer's guidance, one, two, three times.

Harrison's mouth spits blood, rivulets running down his chin. The killer turns their glare to the other two boys, too drunk to react as fast as they typically might, too paralyzed by the grisly act to think as fast as they typically wouldn't. Under the light of the moon, Violet can make out some sort of Japanese kabuki mask, of all things. Harrison's brain, historically slow, finally realizes he has perished, and the body drops.

The kabuki killer lifts up the bloody quarrel, crimson bathed in lunar light, the dead boy's torn tongue looking vaguely like some grisly kebob. The killer stares the two surviving boys dead in the eyes, her own shining violet. Finally, they speak, with a predatory click of their tongue. The voice is deep and graveled, but it is distinctly female.

"What's the matter with him?" she asks with a twirl of the bolt, granting the murder all the levity of a black comedy. "Cat got his tongue?"

Nick eyes the emergency door, his ticket to any possible escape, a crazed serial killer between the two adolescents and their survival. He stammers, but he cannot formulate a word. The killer dejectedly shakes her head as the boys fail to answer, throwing the bolt and its skewered tongue to the floor. In her other hand, she lets the shaft of some sort of hunter's axe slide down her palm, letting the head just barely tap the floor. It has yet to shed blood, and Violet knows not where it could have possibly come from.

Billy's fight-or-flight complex seems to finally come to a conclusion. He charges, drawing the switchblade he always carries from his belt. He tries to tackle his attacker, but she barely stumbles as the blade plunges into her stomach. She makes no noise of pain, her breaths taking no more than a single hitch.

Billy gasps in shock, trying to push the blade in further. The killer does not budge, meeting him eye-to-eye. His right hand squeezes her shoulder, the dark shirt beneath staining with blood. Billy looks up at her and whimpers for the first time in his forsaken life.

One of her gloved hands grabs hold of his throat. She pushes him back, her grip the only thing keeping him on his feet. "Guilty," she declares, the word biting.

Billy thrashes, unable to pull free of her grip. Nick backs away, clearly not one for heroism, but he slips and lands headfirst on the cold tile. The killer barely gives him a glance.

"H-hey!" Billy shouts, his feeble attempts at freedom pathetic in her hold. "Guilty? What does that even mean?! You're the one killing people, you crazy bitch!" His voice is unable to accurately capture the depths of his fright.

"You don't even remember my voice, do you?" she asks, pulling his face close to her mask. "You don't remember me at all."

"N... n... n-no, I... I—"

The killer lets out one airy chuckle. "Shame. Guilty."

"G-guilty of *what?!* Let go of me, let go!"

The emergency escape door starts to shake. It visibly quivers as Laurie and Olivia do their best to open it outside, but their best is not nearly good enough. The two girls begin to scream for Billy, but the killer owns his attention, choosing to finally acknowledge his question.

She tilts her head towards Violet, paralyzed and approaching a complete breakdown. The girl wants nothing more than to run, run far away, but all she manages to do is slump onto her side, hitting the cold tile with a mix of a sob and a whine. "You wanted her to pleasure you, did you not?" the killer scoffs, one of her fingers running along Billy's cheekbone. "Well, then. Allow me."

She finally lets go of his throat, her boot stomping onto his foot. He screams as it cracks under the pressure, her free hand tearing the switchblade out of her stomach. She buries his blade between his thighs, his next wail the loudest yet. Nick tries to scramble to his feet, encouraged by the demented display, but Billy is aware of nothing more than pain. He falls to his knees as blood pools between them, his voice temporarily reaching its peak.

"You look better on your knees," the killer says coldly, both hands wrapping around the axe's handle. Violet tries to crawl, her limbs failing her with every attempt. She looks back in transfixed terror as the executioner's axe comes swinging down, lopping Billy's head off with a ghastly geyser of blood. His last screams are cut short, pieces of him painting the floor with sickly sounds.

The emergency door trembles under the force of some heavy object, the latest attempt at rescue by the girls outside. Violet can barely make out Laurie's cries for Billy, anguished and beyond desperate. Nick's feet rapidly approach Violet, away from the madwoman.

"Oh, *Nicky!*" the killer says in singsong, leveling the axe in her hands, blood dripping down her mask and shirt.

Before she knows what's even happening, Violet feels Nick's panicked hands taking grip of her clothes, wrenching her up. She knows not what to do but sob, too exhausted to struggle, forced to stand by the tearful delinquent. He pins her swaying body in front of him, her heart trying to thud its way out of her chest as she stares the killer in her gleeful violet eyes.

The double doors to the rest of the school are too far, he knows that, so he will throw the sheep to the wolf. Violet tries to struggle, specks of vomit coating her lips. She whimpers pathetically, but it is the best she can manage.

"S-stay back! Fuck off!" Nick yells, and Violet doesn't know if he's dumb enough to believe the woman will actually listen. The killer lumbers forward, absently dragging the axe's head across the floor.

"Oh, Nicholas..." she coos. "Sacrifice won't ease your sentence."

He hesitates, and then he decides to give Violet to the killer. Violet screams as he throws her, the head of the killer's axe narrowly missing her shoulder. It nails Nick in the face behind her, something she knows by the sudden squeal of pain. He hits the floor, mutilated and bleeding, as the killer grabs the cuff of Violet's shirt. Violet lets a hopeless whimper escape her, her wavering eyes just inches from the murderer's.

She cringes under the looming mask, sobbing, preparing for the worst. The seconds are slow, painfully so, crawling by like days. The axe lowers, back to the killer's side, and Violet hopes it will be over fast.

"Innocent."

Violet blinks, her heart skipping a beat. She looks up at the killer, speechless. The killer gently lets go of Violet's shirt. She stumbles, but the killer lightly steadies her shoulder with unexpected compassion. Violet's sobs fade away as she grants her masked savior a glance of confusion. She meekly grunts some sound, something meant to sound like "What?"

"Innocent," the killer says, her tone different, almost warm. "Run."

Violet is paralyzed. She is frozen. Surely this is some sort of twisted game, some—

"Run!"

She doesn't know how she does it, but she finds it within her to stay upright. Violet's heavy legs operate on their own determined will, carrying her away at the killer's command.

As she runs for the far doors, the last thing she hears is Nick's strangled screams, the axe shattering bone. The doors slam shut to the sound of the killer claiming her next.

"Did you call the fucking police?!" Olivia screams, the only noise louder than the baseball bat battering the door.

"Yes! Get the fucking door down!" Laurie responds, barely able to speak in the frenzy they call fear. She runs a sweating hand through her hair, giving the steel door a kick. It hurts her foot more than her obstacle. "Fuck!"

Thud. Thud. Thud. Thud.

"This isn't working!" Olivia says dejectedly. "Why would they lock it? It wasn't locked when we got here!" She gives the door another fruitless slap with the bat, but it somehow accomplishes even less than the dozens of attempts before it. The head of the bat splinters and cracks with the latest assault, forever an underachiever.

"Should I go around to the front? Maybe it'll be easier to knock down, or get in, or I can find a window or something—"

"You're hyperventilating!" Olivia shouts, not far from such a thing herself.

"Of course I'm fucking hyperventilating!" Laurie scoffs. "Why are the police so damned *slow* in this stupid fucking town?!"

"Maybe they don't get enough tax money," Olivia moans, uselessly smacking the door with the pathetic remains of her bat.

"Why the *hell* are you talking about taxes right now?!"

"I'm coping!" Olivia snaps. She draws the bat back, preparing for another futile battering, before suddenly freezing.

"What are you doing?" Laurie hisses. "Hit the—"

Olivia shushes her, raising a finger to her lips and tilting her head towards the door. Laurie shuts up, panting, her heart seemingly louder than a freight train.

Thump, thump, thump, thump, thump...

No. Not her heart. Footsteps. Fast ones.

Then a scream, a voice unnaturally high. Nick's, maybe, if he was stressed, yeah—

"Help! Oh God, *help!*" The door rattles, shaking with sputtering stress.

The two girls' struggle begins anew. Laurie kicks at the door again, ignoring her throbbing ankle, the third blow knocking her onto her back with the desperate force of it. The world spins around her as she hits the pavement, rising vomit threatening her throat.

Then she hears the lock click. "God, help, Liv, help!" The door creaks open, just a smidge. A bloodied arm emerges into the stiff winter air, desperate for a savior.

Laurie lifts her swimming head, watching the scene with rising horror. The realization hits her, another shriek stalling at her lips as Olivia grabs hold of Nick's tainted hand. He has never once called her Liv.

Olivia tugs, clearly met with significant resistance, the arm almost withdrawing completely. "Come on, Nick!" she screams. "Open the door!" She grabs the door handle, tries to wrench it open, but something holds it back. Nick screams.

No. Not Nick. The voice isn't quite right.

"Olivia!" Laurie squeals.

Whatever strength that has been putting Olivia through her paces vanishes. The arm jerks free, but it is just that – an arm. Olivia tumbles back, the door slamming shut again as abruptly as it had opened. Nick's detached arm flops into Olivia's hands, dressing the pavement in a tapestry of pooling blood. Olivia cries out in mortified horror, throwing the limb away. It lands without spectacle, tears running down Olivia's pale cheeks.

"Oh, my *God!*" she wails, jumping to her feet as panic seizes the reins.

A hand punches through the steel door, gloved and somehow uninjured by the feat, fingers grabbing hold of Olivia's face. She lets out another bloodcurdling scream as Laurie gets to her feet, only to immediately slip on a puddle. She tastes the asphalt again as the hand drags Olivia forward, pinning her to the door. She tries to pull free of its grip, but whoever it is proves their impossible strength, leaving Olivia more likely to tear her face off than break free.

"Help!" she screams. "Oh, Christ, *help—*"

"He can't hear you," the killer's voice growls, fingers squeezing spiderweb cracks into the cheerleader's skin. Laurie pulls herself up by the hood of her car, but she isn't fast enough, too breathless to shout for help. Rivers of blood run down Olivia's face, trailing onto her clothes and clogging up her throat. She writhes in useless protest, screaming through blood, but the hand is pulling her against the door, *crushing—*

The first *crack* rings through the sky, Olivia's skull granting its first concession, then another, and soon they overpower her protests, gloved fingers wringing free crimson, and then—

Snap.

The sound is like a muffled gunshot, Olivia's head twisting sideways. One eye lolls out of her crushed, brutalized head before her body hits the floor.

Laurie barely has time to finally scream.

The door breaks free of its frame, wrenching loose with a horrid, metallic groan. It drops like a guillotine, crushing Olivia's mangled body with a grotesque *squelch.* The killer behind it is unusually tall, yet small in stock. A hunter's axe dangles from one hand, a leather jacket over her stained shirt. Her baggy jeans and her large boots are dressed in the blood of four. Untidy, supple silver hair sits striking in the night.

But none of it compares to the scarred kabuki mask. The design is unique, unforgettable — the thinnest lines drawn down the sides, little carved nicks above and below the eyes, a painted tear under the right eye, one long gash scarring the left cheek. The eyes beneath the mask's slits are hollow, lifeless in their violet shade, though she knows someone — some monstrous thing — watches her through them.

"Guilty," she declares of Laurie Thompson, Olivia's body crunching as the killer steps onto the door.

"Wh—" Laurie sputters. "What the fuck are you?"

The woman tilts her head, considers, her axe tasting the pavement. Finally, she speaks.

"Call me Karma."

The voice is raspy, like it crawled out of a grave, but still possessing a feminine tinge. It lilts with the introduction, some sadistic pleasure in her words. Laurie shivers at the sound, her palms frozen numb as she slowly drags herself away, eyes fixated on the Karma Killer.

What little remains of Olivia's skull cracks like an egg as Karma steps into the lot. Laurie winces, the noise eliciting a few tears. "Oh!" Karma exclaims perkily, like a distracted child. "I almost forgot!"

Karma turns to lean into the darkness, and for a moment Laurie considers escape, but the killer is too quick. She returns, Olivia's body eliciting its last whimpers as her killer vacates the doorway. "I brought you something," she says.

Laurie shrieks, slumping down against her car, as Karma waves around Billy Grant's decapitated, dripping head.

Karma chuckles — the sound sends shivers up Laurie's spine, even as her brain starts to overtake her fear, if only just. She has heard Karma's voice before. The revelation hits her like a bundle of bricks, but she struggles to think of where, fails to place it. And every time her dead boyfriend's head spills blood onto the lot, the subject tucks itself away once again.

"Oh, *God,*" is all Laurie can manage.

"Hi! I'm Billy!" Karma chirps, waving Billy's head around like some sort of tarnished puppet. "I'm a cheating bastard that drugs girls as a cheap substitute for consent while my girlfriend mocks my victims from the sidelines!"

"Stop..." Laurie whimpers, hands bunching together.

"Oh, but that's right," Karma says, shaking the head to make its jaw flap open and shut. "I forgot! Laurie's a heartless, remorseless *bitch*, the kind that ruins people's lives for a laugh and a few likes on the Internet! Wow, at least I know I'm not going to Hell alone..."

"Shut up!" Laurie screams, stunned by her own courage.

And Karma *laughs*, oh, how she laughs, Laurie's bravery some kind of joke to her. And why shouldn't it be? Laurie knows at this point the woman is somehow superhuman, tearing through a steel door like that. Worse than that, Laurie realizes, she's a superhuman with an insane grudge. She's known her whole life that Lake Leer attracted this sort of person, but she had never dreamed some such reaper would come to claim *her*.

And yet, here she is.

Karma subdues her laughter, mumbling to herself. "Oh, that's hilarious." She tosses the head to Laurie, drenching her clothes. Laurie jumps, yelps, throws the head aside just as quickly as she catches it. She almost regrets her panicked reaction as it hits the ground, rolling down the pavement like an abandoned volleyball.

"Here's the funniest thing, though, *Thompson,*" Karma hisses, leaning down, no ounce of soul in her burning eyes. "*No one* is coming to save you."

She pauses, and Laurie, for a second, freezes with her. Karma looks towards the streets, and Laurie can just barely hear them too — police sirens, far off, but bound to be there within a few minutes.

That's not fast enough.

Karma lets out of a huff of palpable annoyance, turning her attention back to her captive audience. "Shit, looks like I was wrong on that count," she growls. "Alright, looks like I'm going to have to kill you now. Horrible knowing you!"

Laurie spits out her wasteful protests as Karma grabs hold of her shirt with her free hand, preparing her axe in the other. She lifts her axe aloft, slamming the girl against of her own car, about to execute—

As Laurie hits the hood of her car, the keys in her jean's back pocket crunch against her skin, the car alarm setting off with the mistaken click of a button. The sound is merely alarming to Laurie, but it appears downright deafening to her captor. Karma lets out a roar of pain, releasing her grip as she instinctively reaches up to cover her ears.

Laurie takes a breath of relief. Determined not to make it her last one, she acts before her brain does, her feet kicking out with as much force as they can muster. They plant themselves in the center of the stunned Karma's chest, lacking enough strength to topple the goliath. Thankfully, Olivia's corpse and the remains of the door do that for her. Karma slips, landing on her back, buying Laurie a precious few seconds.

Laurie takes them, rolling off the car and onto the street, somehow managing to land on her feet. She tears open the driver's door, locking it as soon as she's in, rushing to start up the engine. Karma stands with a wretched groan, clutching her head with one hand. The car stalls.

"Start, you *motherfucker!*" Laurie screams, determined not to let this goddamned car be the death of her.

A gloved hand smashes through the passenger window, bits of glass blemishing her skin with shallow cuts. Laurie grits her teeth, the car's engine finally getting itself together. Laurie screams, but she is not so sure it is out of fear this time. No, it is out of fury.

"Get *off !*" Laurie shouts, the car tilting a little from Karma's strength as the killer tries to wrench the passenger door loose. Laurie hits the gas.

The car lurches forward, Karma's arm ringing with a nasty *crack* as the mask disappears from sight. The killer's hand holds on, the car stopping twice, the passenger door groaning as it starts to bend under her strength. "Go to Hell!" Laurie screams, slamming the car alarm again. It shrieks like a siren, and Karma's broken hand loses its hold. Laurie hits the engine once more, the car finally escaping the parking lot, the vehicle's triumphant roar overpowering Karma's howls of frustration.

Laurie turns, her car pulling out of the lot just as several police cars make their way down the street. Probably Lake Leer's entire department, that. She looks back at the school, panting, little rivers of blood running down her cheek.

The killer has vanished.

Laurie settles back into her seat, measuring her breaths as she starts the radio. Anything, anything, she didn't care what came on, just anything.

Loud noises. Karma can't handle loud noises, for whatever reason. Remember that. She held a grudge. She would be back, for a crime Laurie likely committed, but she had no idea—

She blinks. The voice. The voice comes to her, and she is grateful the road ahead of her lays neglected tonight, for she cannot focus and contemplate the realization at once.

Kora Lynch.

"Well, I'll be damned," Laurie breathes, and she lets out a weary chuckle when she realizes how fitting that phrase feels now.

Run.

BZZT! BZZT! BZZT! BZZT!

Run!

BZZT! BZZT! BZZT! BZ—

Violet silences the alarm clock in an instant. She opens one eye, heart still racing, the dream fresh on her frazzled mind. She had gotten too drunk, far too drunk, and it had all seemed so *real,* but here she was in her bedroom — the giant, worn plushies in one corner, the half-empty dresser in another. Curtains perpetually jail the windows, the early birds chirping outside.

Her stress slowly submits, her hand sliding down the bedside table, fingers running across a lighter—

She opens her eyes, and her heart resumes its marathon.

She sits up slowly, sweat a second layer beneath the clothes she had worn to the club last night, with Nick and Billy and—

Oh, God.

A lighter she's never owned before lies on her bedside table, soaked in blood and lying beside several photos. With anxious hesitation, she picks up the photographs, examining them with rising nausea. She recognizes them all, and the memories return, taking her hostage.

She had taken the drink, and Nick had said it wasn't all that much, just a bit of wine, and then she was falling over—

There is the first, her drunken visage crowded into a bathroom stall, eyes drifting to dreams unknown, drooling mouth crooked, her shirt halfway down—

And then they had her twirl, and then they had her undress, and she had giggled and let the clothes drop, because she couldn't see through the haze, she didn't know any better—

There are more, five or six, and why they hadn't used a phone camera, she didn't know. Maybe they didn't want some sort of paper trail. Hell, she knew the school had a darkroom for the photography students, and she knew Nick was one of them.

Despite herself, she shuffles through the photos, warding off sickening guilt. With each photo she loses articles of clothing, losing any remaining traces of sobriety and dignity, and—

Innocent.

She pauses, blood tainting the edges of the last two, the most explicit.

Run!

Violet picks up the lighter, the Karma Killer's parting gift. Her chest briefly lies inert, her heart clenched in a vice grip.

Come on, a pretty girl like you has to show off more often, don't you think?

In a moment of startling venom, she doesn't feel bad for the brutality... for the boys' deaths.

Innocent.

She jumps to her feet, startling herself as she nearly knocks over her bedside lamp. The window groans in meek protest as Violet yanks it open, offering it the bloody lighter and the stack of photos. Violet breathes as every last nightmarish memory flakes off in flame, a whisper in the wind.

The next day is dull, to say the least — but, as Violet reflects, a shootout would probably be remarkably dull compared to the weekend she had just survived. School drags on like it always does, the only sign of a change the lockdown of the gym, something Violet finds particularly curious. Her mother and father dote over her like they always do that morning, out of habit and not out of insight, counting the calories of her cereal, giving her at least three hugs each before she leaves the house, imploring her not to attend any more parties. Violet agrees, but this time, she actually means it.

Biology is dull, English is half as tedious. Algebra 3-4 is substantially worse than both, the only thing since that night to allow her some mediocre sleep. Violet longs for lunch, just so she can go find some solitary corner, lose herself in another book and pretend she isn't mere feet away from the sight of a mass murder — a romance, the kind she never reads, but thrillers hit a little too close to home right now. Every class ebbs with a malevolent atmosphere, her every move accompanied with an extra twitch of a finger or a sudden jump at every noise. Violet wonders if she's beginning to truly discover paranoia firsthand.

She daydreams in history, watching her classmates, the whiteboard seeming to track her inattentiveness with a silent glare. She sighs as the teacher drones on and on and on, the words no use as a distraction. She asks questions, and students raise their hands. Violet would normally be one of them, but she doesn't currently have it in her. She knows she'll pass the class no matter what she does.

An odd silver-haired girl answers the next one, a silent type that Violet has seen a few times in the halls. She is also, admittedly, the star of a few... steamy daydreams. Still, Violet doesn't know her name, and right now, she doesn't particularly care. She rests her cheek on her history textbook, listening to her heart thud against the table. *Then again, how common was silver hair anyway?*

"Whitechapel, ma'am," the girl answers, the answer to an evasive question. In truth, Violet would've ignored the answer, too — if it wasn't for the way the silver-haired girl's voice *rasps.*

"Thank you, Kora," the teacher says, a whisper outside Violet's tunnel vision. Kora turns her head, sees Violet staring, gives her an awkward smile. Violet blushes, and for once not out of childish embarrassment. Her heart thuds against the desk again, doubly quick.

She sits with her head buried in her arms, two desks away from the unmasked Karma Killer.

CYCLE TWO

Lifestyles of the Lonely & the Lynched

/// **October 11ᵗʰ, one week ago. Twenty days until Halloween.**

"I know who you really are, Kora... know you like no one else does."

Kora stiffens with the words, her fragile hands squeezing Laurie's tight. They keep their slow dance steady, though Kora can't quite explain how she's managing it. She has never danced before. She's not sure she will ever dance again, in all honesty.

"You do?" Kora whispers, holding back any number of cheeky responses. She decides not to make a joke about how she's probably just one more slandering or beating away from picking up an axe and adding to Colorado's least favorite statistic. After all, it's taken her so long to get this dance, and you don't endear yourself to most people with that kind of humor. Besides, it's more exaggeration than reality.

Laurie pulls her close, their chests together, and Kora fails to stop herself from shuddering. She watches her dance partner with captive eyes. The wavy, immaculate blonde hair, the sparkling blue eyes, the perfect red of her lips, her ample...

Ample red dress. Yeah. The perfect amount of... red.

Laurie clears her throat, and Kora snaps her eyes upward. "Mhm. I know you're sort of soft inside... I know you've got a kind soul, even if you like to hide it beneath all the cute little nervous jokes..."

Kora blinks, grants herself a small smile. "I... suppose. If you wanna get all mushy, I mean. Like, I think you could compare me to a good cupcake, y'know? Really soft and creamy on the... uh..."

She trails off, already regretting the metaphor. Laurie, thankfully, ignores that comment as she leans closer, trailing lipstick up Kora's neck. "You just know all the right things to say, Kora. All the things that make me feel okay... and I hope I can make you feel a little less alone. A little less scared."

Kora laughs, gasping as Laurie's teeth longingly graze at her neck. She tries not to break down completely yet. "I, uh... wow, you really do know me. Better than I thought, really. More observant than you look."

Laurie giggles in a way that fills Kora's chest with embarrassing butterflies, her breaths seducing shivers from Kora's skin. Her teeth tease Kora's ear, almost biting down. "You don't have to be scared, Kora. You don't have to hide a thing from me. I'll stay with you... You won't lose me, not like..." She trails off, inhaling gently.

"Like..." Kora whispers. "I... how do you know so much? This is a little bit weird. Do I have a Wikipedia entry I don't know about, or some weird cult following, or..." She shuts up as Laurie's delicate fingers trail down her spine, descending...

"But," Kora continues, "I'll admit knowing my whole life story and all my inner fears is... uh, okay, it's definitely weird, but it skips a lot of the awkward talking and revelations, y'know? Like, we can just, know each other, and—"

"Shut up and kiss me," Laurie murmurs, her other hand tilting Kora's chin downward.

"I—" Kora blinks. "Yes, ma'am?"

Laurie leans in, closing her brilliant blue eyes, their lips finally meeting, after so—

"Lynch!"

And just like that, the scene is shattered, her elaborate fantasy taking its leave. Kora's knee slams into her desk with a surprised jolt, a bog-standard high school classroom escorting reality back to its unwilling subject. Her notes for some earlier class tumble onto the ground. As she wearily blinks, trying to remember what real life feels like again, several snickering students exit the classroom with the welcoming screech of the bell.

"Detention's up, kiddo," Mrs. Day says from her desk, barely looking up from the homework she's grading. "I don't suppose you were daydreaming about your late English assignments?"

Kora grumbles and leans over her desk, fetching the fallen notebook, her mind wandering to Laurie once more. "Anatomy?" she tries, hastily stowing her things in her backpack.

Mrs. Day, a slightly plump woman with glasses that seem to survey your soul itself, gives Kora her distinctive, unamused glare. In the silence that follows, a horrified Kora desperately hopes the clinically stoic teacher hadn't caught her joke. The student gives her teacher a nervous, winning smile. Those two adjectives don't work well in combination, she immediately decides.

Mrs. Day watches her shove the last of her belongings into her backpack — her half-eaten lunch, her beaten and fading sketchbook, her pens (half of them out of ink). "Kora," she says, "I know it's probably too much to hope you finished the weekend's assignment."

"It's only Monday," Kora says, slinging the backpack over her shoulder.

"*Last* weekend, Kora."

"Oh," Kora mutters. "Yeah, uh, that's a negative."

Kora expects her to go off on another one of her speeches, one to remind Kora that she is a brilliant 16-year-old girl, one that could easily be pulling straight-As in honors courses if she really tried. This is admittedly true, but Kora vehemently shakes her head whenever this sort of thing is brought up, because the idea of moving even further up the "locker-dwelling nerds" totem pole is not altogether appealing.

Mrs. Day thankfully doesn't. Maybe she sees Kora is having a weird day (read: engaged in a territorial dispute with her brain over an army of teenage, hormonal impulses), or maybe she's just overwhelmed with the mound of ungraded homework that sits on her desk. Either way, Kora doesn't complain.

Instead, Mrs. Day just gently smiles and says, "Just try to get on top of it again, okay?"

"Okay," Kora agrees noncommittally, exiting the classroom in a hurry and mourning her wasted lunch hour.

"And, Kora," Mrs. Day calls, prompting the student to turn her head. "I don't want to see you in detention again, okay? Dropping water balloons on students' heads isn't as funny as you seem to think it is."

"It was kind of funny," Kora murmurs.

Mrs. Day gives her a reproachful look. Kora smiles nervously. "I mean, *only* kind of funny. You know, not funny enough to do again... or, uh, ever, at all, anymore."

Mrs. Day shakes her head, adjusting her glasses. "Alright, kiddo.

Get to class."

"Okay," Kora mumbles, taking her leave.

Kora regrets rushing through the crowded school hallways when she realizes there was no reason to hurry. The *teacher,* of all people, is late to his own class again — a typical occurrence for their psychology tutor, honestly, so she probably should've expected it. As per unspoken tradition, the mixed-grade psych students are milling about outside the door. Must be locked, Kora assumes.

As she tugs off her deafening headphones, mournfully disposing of the indie folk she so adores, she finally hears the boy who has probably been shouting at her back for some time. "Hey, *Lynch!*"

She recognizes Skyler Simmons' voice in an instant, his relaxed, androgynous lilt a perfect match for the boy's effeminate looks. She turns on a dime, giving Skyler a relatively unsurprised look as he comes to a weary stop before her. He awkwardly wraps his arms around her tall frame, ignorant of the many disgruntled students having to weave around them in the corridor. "L— Kora! Have I mentioned you look *fabulous* today?"

Kora blinks, looking down to meet his eyes. She practically had to do that with everyone. "What do you need, Sky?"

"Oh, come on, can't I compliment my good friend—"

Kora blinks again, going out of her way to make the action passive aggressive this time around. Sky nods, chuckling, his curly brown hair bouncing against his shoulders. "Alright, you got me, I—"

"Homework?" Kora asks.

"Yeah, you know, I might need a little help again—"

Kora rolls her eyes, wrapping an arm around his shoulders to drag him beside a closet door, freeing them from the tide of the crowd. As soon as they are out of general eyesight, she holds out her hand. "Give it here."

He hands over a couple of battered papers that look like they've survived Gettysburg. Knowing him, whatever they've been through was likely much worse than that. She presses the empty sheet against the wall, taking out a pen to start filling out the answers with apathetic ease.

Sky leans against the wall, the attempted definition of suave. "So, what have you been up to, Kora?"

"Guess," she says dryly, eyes fixated on her sloppy handwriting, messier still when she's mimicking his.

"Lusting over Laurie Thompson?" he says coyly.

She nearly tears a hole in his paper with a startled jolt of her pen. *"What?"*

"Look, Dennis from, uh, from art club, he was in detention with you earlier. You were totally daydreaming, dude, right? You even started saying shit—"

Kora's cheeks flush with embarrassment, something damnably conspicuous on her pale complexion. "Don't! Shut up. Which one is Dennis again?"

"The one that looks like a weasel," Sky says brightly.

"Great," Kora deadpans, as if that's any help at all. "Tell him if he keeps talking shit, I'll stab him in the dick with this pen."

Sky rubs his chin thoughtfully. "He'd probably be into that."

"Look, I don't want to know. Okay? I'm not interested in weasel fetishes."

"You have to phrase it like that? That's crass." Sky shakes his head. "You know, maybe you should get out there, Kora. Make your move."

"What?" Kora exclaims, actually turning to face him for once. The school janitor ambles towards the closet, nearly tripping over his mop. "Shut up," she hisses, returning to Sky's homework.

"Hey, what're you doing on the wall there?" the janitor squints, his words slower than a tortoise's approach.

"Graffiti," Kora says, without even turning around. The janitor doesn't even think this over, giving them both a hearty chuckle as he unlocks the closet and steps into it.

Sky stares, utterly perplexed. "Did he really just—"

"He's going blind," Kora explains.

"Blind?"

"And senile," she adds. "Look, he doesn't care."

"Right," he says. "Anyways, I stand by what I said. Quit being a sissy. Go ask her out or something!"

"Laurie?" Kora scoffs in disbelief. "Sky, I swear, I will draw dicks all over your homework."

He rolls his eyes. "Come on, Kora, don't be like that. Think about it! She's hot as hell, and you'd probably get to meet all her friends! You don't have friends. You need friends."

"I don't need friends."

"Kora, you're like the biggest loser at Leer High right now." He thinks for a moment. "Other than Violet and Lyn."

"Never talked to them."

"See?" Sky exclaims in disbelief. "You're not even herding up with the rest of the losers! Just think about it. Laurie, cheerleaders, parties..."

"Don't care about any of that," Kora says, and it's only 95% a lie. "Besides, she's a senior. And a cheerleader. And popular. Feels a little—"

"Don't you *dare* say out of your league," Sky groans.

"What, am I that pretty?" Kora chuckles.

"No, no, I just don't want to sit here while you recite shitty film clichés," Sky dismisses. "They're bad excuses, too. Laurie is cool, man. Her friends probably are too, but I don't really know them. Look, I'm serious, you look so mopey all the time. You're so quiet all the time, you've got no friends—"

"I said I don't need friends," Kora interjects. "Besides, aren't you my friend?"

Sky bites his lip. "You might call me that, but I just figured myself as some guy in art club who gets you to do his homework."

Kora frowns. "Fair." It's a simple statement, but it's better than admitting that he's right about far too many things. The fucker probably is the closest thing she has to a 'connection' here, and he's honestly annoying. A really talkative annoyance.

Still, she's not going for it. She's not stupid. She turns and hands him his crinkled stack of homework, desperate to get him to go away and let her forget this conversation ever happened.

"I'm just saying, Kora," Sky says coyly. "Imagine how great the sex would be." He winks, spins on his heel, disappears around the corner.

With those words, the army of teenage hormones upon the battlefield of her brain shoots her common sense and logic dead.

She's going for it. She's stupid. Kora runs for the nearest bathroom.

Sky bounds back down the hallway to catch his friend Tony, another closeted member of the art club. Sky smacks his shoulder, good nature in his grin. "Dude, I think I did it!"

"What? Did what?" Tony asks, meeting his friend with a dramatic sigh.

"Kora, the silver haired girl who shows up to art club sometimes? I think she's actually gonna go ask out Laurie. Can't believe I managed that one with our resident brooder, honestly."

"Ah, I see, shipping again," Tony says, plainly uninterested. "Skyler Simmons, you really ought to get a life... Wait. Laurie's a lesbian?"

Sky's good cheer vanishes, his grin frozen halfway. "Is she not? The dumb blonde cheerleader, right? Gay? Got caught fingering a girl in the broom closet?"

Tony shakes his head, starting to break into laughter. "You idiot," he chortles. "That's Olivia, not Laurie!"

"Oh." Sky blinks. "Shit. Well, that's—"

The psychology teacher bustles down the hallway, huffing and puffing like a train out of order. Mr. Ward surveys his gathered students, his goliath brows bunching together as he opens the door to class. "What're you all hanging around out here for? The door's unlocked." He steps inside. "Hurry up, then!"

Sky looks around the crowd in disbelief, his previous train of thought already AWOL. "Alright, look," he groans. "Which one of you assholes got here first?"

One boy tries to disappear into the crowd, guiltily clearing his throat.

Drops of water slide down the bathroom mirror, Kora's soaked hands running over her face. She coughs as she lifts her head, more out of anxiety than any real malady. She is nothing if not judgmental.

Her hair? Conceptually, it's wonderful — soft, long enough to dance beside her elbows, possessing just enough curl to bounce with her step... but then, it's also a dark silver. She had never quite figured out how that happened. Her eyes were a sort of amber, which she supposed would be nice, if they were just a tad brighter. Kora's face is okay... In fact, she can't find any complaints for that one. Lips are a bit small, but nothing you can do there.

She steps back, examines her clothes. Flannels? Yes, that just screams sophisticated. *Everyone* in Lake Leer wore flannels. Her jeans are too baggy to really show off much of anything, not that she'd honestly know if there was anything to flaunt. Her backpack, laying askew in the corner, looks as if it was dragged out of a trash compactor.

Kora frowns, leaning over the sink. She looks over her T-shirt, the artwork and logo promoting an obscure indie band that, on Kora's careful reflection, really makes her look like some sort of hipster. Oh God, she looks like she's an incel, doesn't she? She moans in rising dread, pulling down the front of her top a little. Nope. With cleavage, she just looks like a slut. Or a dope fiend. Or a slutty dope fiend.

Perhaps Laurie is the type to long for a slutty dope fiend?

This is hopeless. She tugs the shirt back to its original position, deciding the lesbian hipster look is, somehow, her best option. She pokes her sides, gladly noting that the flannel at least hides how damn skinny she is. Maybe Laurie won't immediately laugh her off if she doesn't realize she's talking to a skeleton.

"I am fucking doomed," Kora sighs, the words echoing in the empty room.

The next couple classes are an exercise in interminable tension.

In biology, her penultimate period, Kora focuses herself on much more important matters. She decides she wants to get the whole mess over with today, lest her mental soldiers of logic regroup and carpet bomb the teenage hormones. They were good at doing that relatively fast, and with their victory, she'd probably start throwing up everywhere. Avoiding that is a greater motivation than anything Sky could come up with.

She bounces her heel all through biology, every anxious jerk of her knee seemingly doubling the length of the current minute. She ponders with enough focus to look productive, knowing Laurie stays at school an extra period for her cheerleading practice. Kora could catch her on the way there, or... yeah, she could. Hopefully. She didn't want a public spectacle for when this goes horribly wrong.

When her last class finally sets her loose, she is the very definition of speed, if not of grace. She trips a couple times, but she keeps sprinting, her heart beating fast enough to make her think she's charging right into a dragon's lair. Seriously, what is it with the human brain and deciding things like asking a girl out warranted a fight-or-flight reflex?

Kora's, however, seems to lean towards a fight — a feeble and laughable fight, but a fight. Fear and anxiety shift into adrenaline as she drifts towards the school gym. As she heads out onto the campus grounds, she can hear the first drops of rain coming down, a commonality in this town. Maybe it'd give her good luck. Kora loved rain.

That's stupid. She's being stupid, her fight-or-flight is well beyond stupid, and the dumbest thing she's done all year is buying a word of Sky's bullshit.

By the time she stops debating just what level of stupid she's being, Kora realizes she has found her building. She steps into the hallway, the rain pattering outside, and finds the signs that point towards the gym. She's never really had to go here much, only during pep rallies. She's put off taking PE as long as possible, after all. If she was in the same grade as Laurie, on the other hand, she'd have been eager to find her way into a locker room.

The halls are mostly empty, save the occasional cheerleader or debate team member heading off to their respective destinations. Kora treads along slowly, scanning the hallways, and upon her like lightning, there she is — Laurie Thompson.

The legions of logic in her head are quickly beginning to regroup. Undeterred (mostly), Kora moves before she can change her mind, feeling like a ghost in her own melodramatic body. "Uh, hi— hello?" she speaks, her voice sounding as if it's coming from far, far away.

Laurie turns, the look on her face not exactly one of "Oh, hey, I'm glad to see you!" No, the expression communicates something like "What do you want?" What she actually says isn't much better.

"Hi?" Laurie asks, with all the air of someone who's been approached by a muddy, diseased puppy. "Who are you?" She adjusts the backpack on her shoulder, already dressed in her cheerleader outfit. Kora struggles to remember the script she'd come up with in Bio, distracted by Laurie's damned legs... outfit. Her outfit. Her lovely... Ugh.

"Uh," Kora stammers, already forgetting the first line.

Laurie raises an eyebrow. "Oh!" she exclaims. "Wait! You're

Carrie, right?"

Oh, right. Name. "Kora," she corrects. She mentally bins the script.

"Kori," Laurie repeats with a nod.

"Well, uh, close, uh, close enough," Kora decides. "I'm from, uh, art... uh, culinary class?"

"I don't take culinary."

"Right," Kora stutters, remembering too late that they don't share any classes whatsoever. "Anyways, I sort of just, well, uh, wanted to ask, a thing... something. A question. I want to ask one, I mean."

"Well, you might want to hurry it up a little," Laurie shrugs. "I got practice in like, five minutes."

"Right, yeah, sorry, I'm just... I just want to, uh..." Kora can hear the God she doesn't believe in laughing at her from the heavens.

"Cat got your tongue?" Laurie asks impatiently.

"No, sorry, I—" Kora's heart launches itself off a cliff. "I am, maybe, kind of, sort of, trying to ask you out. On like, a date. You know. I don't... Just. Yeah."

In this moment, she decides she's going to murder Sky later. Go all *Shining* with it. Bastard.

The seconds crawl on like drunken turtles. Laurie's face imparts a reaction faster than her lips do, but it's not a good one. No, she looks incredulous. *Offended,* even? Kora is pretty sure that's not supposed to happen.

"You know what," Kora stammers, backing up as the last insolent teenage hormone is shot dead. "I think I'll just—"

"No, you stop right there," Laurie snaps, stepping forward. Kora has a feeling she's not going in for a kiss, but she stops anyways, a deer in headlights at heart.

If it's leading up to a kiss, it's going to be a particularly rough one. Laurie shoves Kora against the hallway's wall, planting one palm besides the taller girl's head. "Who the *hell...*" she begins, looking more than a little outraged, "...is telling people that I'm a fucking *lesbian?*"

Kora opens her mouth, ready to throw Sky under the bus in an instant, before she remembers he actually said no such thing. "I..." she hesitates, shrinking under Laurie's gaze. "Well, I guess I just... assumed? Is it that big a deal, or—"

"Yes, it's a big deal!" she hisses, clearly trying to keep her voice low. "Look, I know *you* wouldn't understand, Lynch, but I actually have *friends.* Hell, I have a boyfriend!"

"Oh," Kora mouths, realizing she has made a *massive* mistake. "Wait, you know my last name but not my first?"

Laurie ably ignores her irrelevant question. "A boyfriend, Lynch, a *boyfriend,* because I'm not some degenerate. I can't say I'm that surprised to see you're into that, but don't drag me down with you. I'm actually kind of valued in this school, in this town."

Kora flinches. "Right, I'm sorry, I'll just—"

"You haven't even spoken to me before now, anyways," Laurie scoffs. "Where'd these thoughts come from? You some kind of pervert? Have you been watching me or something? How disturbing is that?"

Kora doesn't say a word, focusing more on trying not to break down and cry, or something equally humiliating. Laurie pulls a pen from her purse, carelessly scrawling something on Kora's cheek. Before today, Kora would've liked to think she'd fight back against people like this, but the adrenaline has vaporized and she has frozen, so she just stands immobile in her pathetic weakness.

"Here," Laurie says, an air of mock politeness in her tone as she finishes with Kora's cheek. "There's a couple phone numbers for you. Other local fags." Kora cringes, wondering when she'll get used to being called that. "Just in case you get lonely."

"I..." Kora tries, but she knows nothing's coming out. She's wishing she hadn't, for that matter.

"Oh, shut up," Laurie says, turning around. "Happy Halloween, freak." She sweeps Kora off her feet as she turns away, bouncing the girl off the wall and onto the floor. Laurie skips away towards the gym, chuckling mirthfully under her breath.

Kora slumps against the floor with a groan, feeling something in her backpack crack under her. She swears under her breath as she hears the slam of the gym doors echo down the corridor, finally allowing herself a tear or two.

Meanwhile, inside the gym, Laurie pulls out her phone, finding Billy Grant in her contacts.

Friday the 13th. Halloween. Scream. Nightmare on Elm Street. Texas Chainsaw Massacre. I Spit On Your Grave. Silent Night, Deadly Night. Child's Play 3. Henry: Portrait of a Serial Killer. Kora spills the large stack of DVDs across her desk, making room. Little bigger than a closet, it's all draped in dark, the sun stubbornly slinking through her shades. Her bed, a tangled mess of sheets and blankets, is covered in autobiographies on mass killers, macabre drawings, and stacks of shirts and jeans.

The desk itself, even without the extensive collection of slasher films, is equally cluttered. Pens, more sketches, dirty dishes and snack wrappers, an ancient television that has to be from the early 2000s, an old desk lamp that tends to flicker every so often. She drops her backpack on the desk, her chair creaking with age as she sits.

Kora sniffles, angrily wiping at her face with one sleeve, cheeks still stained with tears. She is home now, but that fact provides little comfort, for the building has never quite lived up to the word. She opens up her backpack, the contents soaked. Her eyes widen as she realizes what she must've broken in her little fall. She yanks out the remains of a cheap, shattered water bottle, cringing at the backpack's soaked interior.

"Fuck!" Kora hisses, scrambling to pull out her sketchbook. Of course, it's far too late for that — it's been wet for an hour now, water soaked into the pages. She pulls out her drenched keepsake, sketches blurred and torn, the ink in her latest design spreading across the page like tears. "Fuck!" she repeats, throwing the sketchbook across the room. "Damn it!" It uselessly bounces off the wall, landing on the floor with a wet flop.

She buries her face in her arms, letting the rest of her backpack's contents soak, knowing it's far too late to save any of it anyways. Kora sits there for what only feels like minutes, her weary eyes taking the rest they are so rarely given. Downstairs, she can faintly hear the thump of heavy boots, her father home from work. Brilliant. She doesn't move, exhausted and bitter. Endlessly bitter.

Nothing's fair, nothing's right.

There is a slow knock against her door, She lazily opens one eye, seeing that the sunlight outside has abandoned her. Of course. Her father never returns before nightfall. Otherwise, he might actually see his own daughter for once. No, she must've dozed off.

He cracks open the door, leaving her squinting into the light of the hall. There he stands, a distant look in his misty eyes, the gray of what hair he has left just barely in sight. His head nearly scrapes against the ceiling, his own height likely responsible for his daughter's. "Did you make dinner?" he asks, the service something he has come to expect.

"No," Kora mutters, keeping her marked cheek out of sight. She'll have to bandage it up later or something, just so he doesn't notice.

He nods, looking at the mess in her room for just a moment. "You okay? What'd you do to your sketchbook?"

"I just dropped it."

"Be careful with that," her father chides. "Your mother gave that to you."

"I know," Kora says bitterly. "I'll make dinner in a moment, Dad. I was just thinking. I just forgot."

"Well, don't forget," he says, his voice monotone. "We both need to eat."

"Of course."

"And, Kora? No more detentions. School phoned me. This is the third time in a month."

Kora sighs. "Yes, sir."

"I know you're better than that. And I know we shouldn't have to talk about that again."

She turns her face away, nodding slowly. "Won't have to."

"Good." He closes the door, leaving her in darkness.

After midnight, she goes out for her evening walk.

It is a nightly habit of Kora's, these lonely wanders. In a town like Lake Leer, one could only regard this as a Bad Idea. It's the sort of town that swallows you up when the sun isn't looking, the kind where the crumbling stones of every beaten building seem to be burying something beneath. It's the sort of town where mysterious disappearances are commonplace and overlooked, the police too incompetent and too apathetic to really make any mark. It's the sort of town that seems to house a beating heart, and the titular lake the town was built around could be a gate straight to Hell.

Call her morbid, but to Kora, it was nothing if not serene.

Lake Leer was named as such because of the colossal lake it surrounds, high up in the mountains, far from what would conventionally be seen as 'civilization'. It's sort of like having a fountain in the center of town, but in this case, it's the lake, one often seen as haunted. Even if you didn't believe any of the urban legends, it still possesses a decorated history — one littered with deranged killers, collapsing mines, a miasmic fog in the air, and spite seeping through every crack in the streets.

If there's one thing dumber than wandering Lake Leer at night, it's following the lakeside trail, given that there was absolutely no security or lighting in the area. Lonely wanderers there at night often found themselves victims to traffickers, stolen away in the dead of night. But to Kora, a lonely teenager with a troubled mind, it has only ever soothed. She loves the sight of the moon reflecting over the rippling water, the pleasant breeze that grazes along skin, the knowledge that she will be completely unbothered and alone, if only for a while.

At least, that's how it usually goes.

Tonight, she drifts down an all-but-hidden path, the hill she descends leading to the rocky shores of the lake. It's like a bowl, almost, the lake below her, the town above. The music ebbs and flows in her ears, earbuds soundtracking her night with some band nobody knows — her usual.

You keep me up all night, every single reflection a bitter bite / Not a single song I could sing, not a single word I could write...

Kora hangs onto the words, onto the soundscape, the negligence of her surroundings proving her undoing. She only notices the car behind her as its headlights shine over the crest of the hill, barely grazing the grass her feet carry her over. Kora hesitates, heart pounding. No one ever comes down this trail, especially not in a vehicle. She pulls out her earbuds, glad for the hoodie hiding her face. The rain that has battered her down the last fifteen minutes suddenly has a voice, omnipresent and ominous.

Kora hears the car's engine idle, familiar voices drifting down the hill as the headlights dim. The first boy embraces the rain, exiting the driver's seat. He is one of the rare few taller than her, black haired, well built. He is dressed more like a biker than a student, but she knows he attends her school. She's seen him before... Billy... Billy something...

"Kora Lynch?" Billy asks as his two friends exit the car, one of them shielding his face from the weather. Kora's heart catches up with the scene and starts pounding, her breath catching in her throat.

"Y... yes?" she replies weakly, unknowingly condemning herself.

Billy chuckles, steps forward. "Good to meet you," he says personably, punching her square in the jaw.

The earbuds fly off into the storm, the faint music vanishing with them. The punch briefly knocks her right out of reality, and by the time Kora begins to actually feel the pain, she's already slipping. She tumbles backwards, nearly biting off her tongue as her back slams against the hill. Before she knows it, she is rolling down the decline, every bounce wringing a new ache out of her body. She finally comes to a stop at the shore of the lake, lips tasting the wet sand.

The boys cackle above her, footsteps slowly descending. Kora whimpers, tears indistinguishable from the rain running down her face. She tries to sit up, injured arm pushing past her pain. She grits her teeth, the taste of iron fresh on her tongue.

Billy and his two hyenas slide down the final slope of the hill, snickering amongst themselves. He adjusts his jacket, traces of Kora's blood staining his knuckles. "Sorry I had to do that," he says. "I'm Billy. I'm Laurie's boyfriend."

Of course he is. Fucking cheerleaders and their bad boys. Kora meekly raises her head, rubbing her cheek. "Look, I... I don't want any trouble, all right? Can we... can we just..." He doesn't acknowledge her.

"This is Nick," Billy says, jerking his head towards the smaller, impish arts student on his left. "And this is Harrison," he says, gesturing to the sandy-haired redneck on his right. "We just thought we might introduce ourselves."

"Just... just listen to me," Kora hisses, blood running down her chin. "I didn't... I didn't know she was... Look, just-" She puts her weight on her painless arm, clumps of wet sand settling between her fingers.

"Nuh-uh-uh," Billy chides, raising his foot and savagely stomping on Kora's hand. She chokes out a startled scream, the bone snapping beneath his heel. The pain flares up through her arm, crawling like ice, and Harrison's boot comes in to catch her in the chin. Kora falls onto her side, all too aware she's sobbing. "Nick," Billy orders. "Check her jacket."

Nick grabs hold of her as Billy presses his boot down on her knee, quashing any resistance with ease. Nick grabs her by the hair, dragging her up enough to rip off her hoodie. She shivers, exposed in the cold, her T-shirt already soaking through. Nick drops her, casting her aside without a thought.

Nick searches her hoodie's pockets, discovering her cell phone. Kora's eyes widen as he tosses it to Billy. The bigger boy chuckles, looking down at Kora. "You won't need this, right? Or did you actually plan on calling those numbers on your cheek?"

"No!" Kora exclaims. Billy grins and hurls the phone behind him. It lands with a splash, far into the lake. She whimpers, her first thought somehow that of "my dad's going to kill me". The second one is a little more rational.

These boys might *actually* kill her.

Billy tosses the hoodie into the sand, and she tries to prop herself up on her elbows, get to her feet. Billy grabs her by the hair and drags her to the water, the two of them wading in knee-deep. Kora tries to slap and scream, but one hand is broken and no one seems to hear her cries for help.

"Shut up!" Billy spits, kicking her in the chest. She nearly blacks out with pain, hitting the shallow end of the lake with a tumultuous splash. The water laps against her nose, some of it seeping into her nostrils. She sputters sickly, grimly glad that it's at least freshwater.

Billy crouches down, resting his elbows on his knees, the water lightly tinged with crimson. "So," he says. "Kora, what have we learned about hitting on other people's girls?"

Kora's teeth chatter in the cold, her head spinning with the retreat of reason. She coughs for breath, giving Billy a venomous look. Before she knows what she's saying, before she realizes she's hit her limit, she makes the glare pleasant in comparison to her words. "That I wish I could've left hickeys all over your slut of a girlfriend."

He chuckles airily, although the surprise in his eyes betrays his demeanor. "And you're better?"

"Yeah," Kora coughs. "People don't talk about me taking three dicks in the locker room after a football game." Honestly, she doesn't know if there's any truth to that particular rumor. She has always doubted it, really. Right now, however? She doesn't give a fuck.

"Wrong answer," Billy growls, seizing her by the hair and plunging her head beneath the waves. The lake swallows her, the girl's legs and arms instinctually kicking in panicked protest. Nick and Harrison wade in to pin her down, the suffocating depths rushing around her, moonlight barely peeking through the lake's surface.

She thrashes and thrashes, the panic in her chest overwhelming. She can't breathe, she's going to die here, she might actually die here, and her last words were going to be cheeky slut shaming, and if that isn't one way to cap off her stupid, invisible life, she doesn't know what is—

The lake laughs, the waves whispering woe.

And just when it's all about to go black, just when she can see lights and spots in her peripheral, when she thinks it's all going to fade away, when she can swear hands are reaching from the sand to pull her under, faces forming in the lake bed below—

And there is one word, only one word to reach her sunken ears, and it is spite beyond description.

Survive.

Billy wrenches her free, air filling her lungs as her ears pop with her own gasps of breath. The boys are laughing, but she barely hears them, blood and water running down her body, the freezing air a sweet sensation.

And in the distance, Kora swears she sees a figure sinking beneath the waves, below the moon.

Before Kora can comprehend the surreal slideshow, the primal hallucinations, whatever was in this blasted lake, Billy's fist slams into her face, one, two, three times. She dangles above the lake, held aloft by her captors, trails of spit and blood mingling with her matted hair.

"She didn't learn her lesson, boys," Billy says, grabbing her by the shoulders and lifting her up to her battered feet. "Let's teach." The hyenas cackle as they drag Kora up the slope, the girl too close to unconsciousness to really put up a fight.

The world is a blur, sight an intermittent privilege, the hum of the car doing little to awaken her from her haze. She is thrown into the back seat, one of the boys settling besides her — Nick, judging by Billy's barks, words she can't bring herself to make out.

The engine roars and brings them into motion. Kora doesn't know where they're going. She doesn't know much of anything. Reality feels like a ruse, and when Nick's hand pushes her cheek against the glass of the car window, she doesn't have the energy to writhe.

His hand gropes and probes, and with what seems like a blink, her shirt and her jeans are torn, ripped up, ripped *off* — but Billy's saying something, something like "no more", something like "no time for that". And Nick's depraved hand retreats, fingers reluctantly withdrawn from her exposed bra.

And before Kora knows it, the car comes to a stop. Billy tugs open the door supporting his victim, grabbing her by the neck before she can land against the pavement. She finds it in herself to ball her fist as he drags her out in her underwear, but he slams her head into the car door. She goes limp once again, blood running down her chest.

Nick is on the phone, the only phrase she catches being "we're here". Her heads lolls backwards as Billy starts marching her beaten body again, dragging her through the cold rain. Some sort of establishment lies before them, tainted by the scent of alcohol. A neon sign welcomes them to what Kora reads as *Lizzie's Liquor.*

The three boys drag her to a back alley, the door before them some sort of employee entrance. With another blink, it opens wide, Kora's weary brain unable to process the two women behind it. She tries to gurgle out some sort of "help", but she chokes on the words. Billy says something like "make her look like a criminal", and the women reluctantly nod, giving each other doubtful looks.

And then she's passed off into the women's arms, freezing in her underwear. The last thing she remembers is being dragged into some searingly white bathroom, the women's lips dancing as Kora slumps against the wall. Kora paints her bare thighs with vomit, and the darkness takes her.

CYCLE THREE

Good to Know That If I Ever Need Attention, All I Have to Do is Die

/// **October 12th, the day after. Nineteen days until Halloween.**

"Let me get this straight, Ms. Lynch. You were assaulted and undressed by three of your fellow students, who then abandoned you at... hm, Lizzie's Liquor, where we found you?"

"Yes," Kora hisses through her teeth, clinging to the flea-bitten blanket that the police had provided her. "Yes, that's *exactly* what happened."

She meets the police captain with bloodshot eyes, amazed her skull isn't cracking under the pressure of her migraine. He is a thin, balding man, his sunken eyes calculating, his voice like sandpaper. He leans against the steel table, making no attempt to distract her from the reality set upon her — the reality that she's being questioned in an interrogation room for a crime she certainly didn't commit.

She was beginning to wish she had drowned in that damn lake.

From what little bleary glimpses she's caught of the rising sun today, she can guess that school might be starting now. She has no way of telling for sure, the only view of the lightening sky outside being the barred window on one wall. All she knew was that the sun had barely been peeking over the horizon when she was dragged out of the bar an hour ago and thrown into a police car, barely conscious.

Kora has always hated police, especially the ones in this damned town, and they really aren't doing anything here to change that opinion.

The police captain, Mr. Lumis, meets her eyes with evident disbelief. "I don't mean to cast your story into doubt, Ms. Lynch. That said, you were in a state of significant undress and undoubtedly intoxicated at a lesbian bar infamous for... reckless patrons, let's say..."

"And as I told you when you tested me," Kora nervously retorts, "I don't know how it... I don't know how I could have been drunk. I didn't have anything to drink that night, I've *never* had anything to drink in my life. I've never even had sex before, and you're accusing me of, what, sleeping and drinking with those two girls you found me with? Are you serious?"

"Ms. Lynch," Lumis repeats, her last name a stunning summary of the last twenty-four hours. "The two women you were with, they explicitly described you engaging in... actions of a sexual nature with another woman."

"What?" Kora mumbles, her heart trying to wrench itself free of her rib cage. "I don't even know them! I couldn't even tell you their names! Have you even found this person I supposedly slept with?"

"That doesn't necessarily disprove anything, Ms. Lynch," Lumis responds dryly, his tone without sympathy.

"Yeah?" Kora chuckles, anxiously gesturing to her blooming black eye. "What about this?" She points to her right hand, the fingers still shattered and dressed in gauze. "Or the *broken hand?* Am I just really fucking kinky or something? Is that your claim?"

"I am not making any decisive judgments," Lumis says calmly, his conscience seemingly finding no guilt in blatant lies. "I am merely recognizing the... distinct possibility."

"And yet it sounds an awful lot like judgment, Mr. Lumis," she says, imitating his insufferable voice as she recites his name. "Sounds an awful lot like you don't care about the facts of the case."

"And *you*, Ms. Lynch, are not helping *your* case when you speak with such a tone."

"I don't think I have a case," Kora scoffs, leaning back in her cold chair. "I don't think I have an argument you'll accept, and I'm not sure why I'm even trying."

"Ms. Lynch, I would appreciate it if you didn't engage me with such hostility."

"And I merely want to acknowledge the facts of the situation," Kora says, trying not to stammer as she takes charge of the conversation. Would ruin the moment, that.

Lumis leans back in his seat, scratching his chin as he works to maintain his poker face.

Kora seizes the opportunity. "You can charge me now instead of properly investigating the case, but it wouldn't look good on your record if you get it wrong, would it? Not much for the police to do in such a small town, and if you screw up such a minor case, how can you be trusted to handle the murderers and kidnappers that come around monthly?

"Sure, you found me in a bar, but I told you my side of the story, and I think the depth of my injuries confirms everything I've said. Besides, go ask Lizzie herself, or the employees on shift that night. Go ask literally anyone other than the two women who I was found with. I doubt they'll remember letting me in."

Lumis raises an eyebrow.

"I can't deny having been in the bar, but I definitely didn't go there by choice," Kora persists. "As for your 'eyewitnesses'? As far as I could tell, they were good pals of Billy's. He probably paid them off to say what they did. I can't prove that, but I don't know why else they would lie. Either way, you could arrest me for being in the wrong place at the wrong time, you have the power. But I think, respectfully speaking... you should be finding some more evidence before you jump to any rash conclusions. You know, just for the sake of doing your *job.*"

Lumis blinks, and though he manages to maintain his stoic demeanor, Kora can't help but smirk. His silence says it all, filling in the blanks his impenetrable composure presents. She steadies her breathing, knowing she's right, gleefully pleased that *he* knows it.

Eventually, he begrudgingly breaks the silence. "I will call your father, have him take you off our hands."

"Thank you," Kora says shortly.

"Of course," he breathes stonily. He drums his fingers on the table, lost in thought, eventually gesturing towards the door. "You will be returning here in a week, following more investigation into your case. We'll decide on any charges then. Just stay out of trouble in the meantime, yes?"

"That was the plan," Kora murmurs, cradling her shattered hand as she stands.

Lumis rests his palm on the door handle, meeting Kora's eyes once more. "Good. Let's hope that will be the last time we speak."

Cooking oil spits and sputters out of the frying pan in protest as a one-handed Kora attempts to maneuver some tongs with a newfound lack of finesse. Burgers are about the only meal she could think to make with her broken hand, short of just shoving something simple in the oven, because her father certainly wasn't offering to take care of the two of them for once in his life. He sits at his precious recliner, watching the television intently — some true crime CSI bullshit, same as every night.

The living room and the kitchen form one room, the difference between them only visible via the contrast of carpet and tile. It's a crowded house, the kitchen barely twice as wide as the fridge beside her. The stovetop is stuffed far too close to the sink, the nearby kitchen island leaving room for a savaged cutting board and barely a sliver of tile to walk. It's not much to work with, but she's made do for years. After all, Kora's lived here her whole life, and her father hasn't set foot in this room since her mother passed.

They haven't really talked much since he picked her up from the police station. He had asked her what had happened, and she had recounted the story — in as little detail as possible, mind you, skipping basically everything to do with the adolescent infatuation that led to this mess in the first place. He had merely sighed irritably, leaving her to spend the rest of the drive trying to drown out his abysmal country music. He hadn't punished her or anything, and he'd even brought her home instead of making her go to school that day like she thought he might.

Kora turns off the heat and slowly transfers the burgers on a plate, relieved to be in a state of proper dress again. The oversized hoodie is a comfort against her battered body, her baggy T-shirt functioning like a security blanket might for a frightened child. She turns to her father as she dumps the frying pan into the sink, despondently realizing how hard that will be to clean with one hand. She leaves it to soak for now, clearing her throat.

"Dad," Kora murmurs, and he grunts attentively in response. She places two of the patties between buns for him, wishing she didn't have to bribe him with food to get his attention. "Would I... maybe be able to skip school tomorrow?"

"Why would you need to?" Dad replies, fixated on the television. "You said the police didn't charge you."

"Just... stress, and my body's still hurting," Kora says, dressing his burgers with cheese and condiments. It's a little slower than usual. "That Lumis guy really wouldn't let off."

"Lumis?"

"Yes," Kora answers, looking over her shoulder. "Why? You know him?"

"Used to," her father replies. "Don't pay him any mind. You won't get put away. He's had it out for me since I was younger, and I imagine he let that grudge get the best of him."

Kora brings him his meal, nearly slipping on a pile of garbage by his chair. "Really? What did you do to make him hate you so much?"

He smiles lightly, the expression something that comes once in a blue moon. "Oh, you know. Youthful abandon, getting away with murder. Nothing unusual."

Kora doesn't quite get the joke, but she chuckles nonetheless. "Well, that's good to know. I thought I might've been in actual trouble. Still, I really think I should let my body heal a little."

"Your grades are slipping, Kora," Dad says, taking his food off her hands. "You're cooking just fine. I don't see why you can't handle sitting through a few classes."

Kora bites her tongue, eager to point out that he wouldn't make a damn meal for himself even if she shattered her back. "Dad... those, you know, those kids I mentioned, that beat me up in the first place? I'm not eager to go back to school so soon after. I'll run into them in the halls, and like—"

"It's a school," he says nonchalantly. "There will be tons of adults around, security. No one's going to beat you up in a school hallway. You'll be fine."

"I would just like a break. I'm really stressed right now, okay?"

"It's high school. That's normal. If you weren't averaging Cs and Ds, I might let you. Unfortunately, you are, and you can't afford to miss another day."

"Dad..."

"No," he says. Kora bows her head in defeat, infuriated shivers running up her spine. "That's final. You will be fine, so long as you don't take any more midnight walks."

"Yeah," Kora murmurs, turning back to the kitchen. "Yeah, I guess so."

Come morning, it only takes an hour for Kora to conclusively decide that she will not, in fact, be fine.

She wakes up from her regularly scheduled nightmares to a screeching alarm clock and a rushed breakfast. Kora darts out of the house with a chunk of toast protruding from her lips, swallowing it down as she takes off for school, her splint pressed to her chest in the autumn air.

Lake Leer is tiny. There's only one high school in the entire damn town, and that school doesn't even have a bus service. Half the town is close enough to walk, after all, and the other merely has to make a short drive around a lake. Kora is lucky enough to be a walker, and she is immensely grateful for that. Her father driving her every morning would easily lead to some form of patricide.

The Lynch family lives just down the street, so she arrives at her prison of a school in no more than ten minutes. Short of breath and freezing half to death, she starts down the school's hallways, as early as she usually is. She always shows up about an hour ahead of time, mainly because she would rather be here than sit silently with her father all morning, even with homicidal bullies roaming the halls.

Making her way to her usual early hours haunt, Kora approaches the history classroom, home to the closeted art club outside class periods. She refers to them as "closeted" because very few students, if any, admit to being part of its membership — a tradition stemming from an incident two years ago, wherein some weirdo covered every inch of the principal's office in drawings of genitalia. No one publicly admits to being part of the club now, because it's one easy ticket to getting harassed and bullied, or for being seen as having some peculiar fixation on genitalia. Or both.

It's hypocritical, Kora thinks. She's never heard the sports teams or the senior boys talk about anything *but* female genitalia.

Kora shoulders open the art classroom's door, about half the club's membership sitting around tables, doodling and idly chatting. This is typical, with the club normally preferring casual socializing over structured activities. Kora wouldn't exactly consider herself one of the 'friend group', but they allowed her to sit there and occasionally make some snarky comment, so they are the few students that remain in her good graces.

Olivia Kemp approaches Kora as she enters, the ditzy cheerleader flashing her a convincing smile. At least, it would be convincing if Kora didn't know who Olivia ran with.

Kora remembers far too late that Olivia heads the art club, making this a conversation she cannot avoid.

"What are *you* doing here?" Olivia hisses, her displeasure apparent, one flawlessly-manicured hand running through her long, sweeping hair.

Kora stops in her tracks, a little surprised to see Olivia acknowledging her existence at all, much less with such palpable disgust. She's best friends with Laurie, but as far as Kora's aware, Olivia's been caught fingering girls under their desks before, so she's not exactly sure why she'd be bothered by Kora's whole... lesbian deal.

Then again, Kora doesn't know why she's attempting to find excuses for the behavior of Laurie and her friends. They are vultures eager for humiliation, through and through.

"I'm... I always come here," Kora says quietly, anxiously gazing across the room. She so desperately does not want a fuss, does not want everyone focused on her black eye, her bandaged cheek or her shattered hand. She does not want to be the beating post again, so she just mentally begs Olivia to keep it down.

Unfortunately, Olivia is clearly not proficient in desperate telepathy. "Yeah, I know. But that was *before* you got caught getting blackout drunk and jailbaiting women in bathroom stalls."

Kora widens her eyes, fixing upon Olivia the fiercest death glare she can muster, but it's a small classroom. Eyes are already turning onto the latest spectacle, and Kora almost wishes the ground would swallow her, sink its teeth in and drag her under, take her away from this downright apocalyptic scene.

"I—" Kora stammers, her throat so dry it hurts. "Look, I don't know what you heard, but it's not true. Let's not make a big deal of it, okay?"

"Make a big deal of it?" Olivia smirks. "How do you think I heard about it? It's *already* a big deal, Lynch. It's all over the news. Not a lot goes on in this town, you realize that?"

Kora's heart abandons its marathon, instead electing to plummet in horror, sink down through the earth. She can only imagine the look on her face must be absolutely *priceless.* She glances towards Sky and his two friends, trying to silently beg for help. He's been watching the whole thing, but he doesn't say a word. He just stares, her mouth wide open in shock.

Paralyzed. That's the word. She's paralyzed.

"I... I, uh... I..." She can't find any words. Fuck. Fuck. Fuck. Why couldn't she just drop dead out of shame? She feels as if she might.

"Look, what a girl does in her own time is her own business," Olivia says, initially sounding the most rational she's been all semester. "But this art club already has something of a... reputation, and the last thing I need is some pervert giving us the wrong sort of attention. So shoo, Lynch. Get out of here."

Kora wants to, honestly. She wants to flee with her tail between her legs, back off like the bitch she's always been. She can feel tears welling up in her eyes, and the last thing she wants to do is start sobbing like a baby in front of the only people who have actually sort of tolerated her. She manages to stem the tide, giving Sky one more pleading look. He knows her the best.

Come on, Sky. All the homework you had me do for you. Sure, it's not much of a basis for friendship, but... we bantered, right? Gotta count for something.

He turns his head, whispers in his friend's ear — Tony, she thinks. The other boy snickers a little. Sky doesn't vouch for her. The silence speaks for him.

"Fuck *off,* Lynch," Olivia snaps, tapping her foot impatiently.

Kora flinches, giving Olivia a wounded glance as she darts out of the classroom. She runs, tugging her hood over her head, sweeping her silver hair under it the best she can. There's too damn much of it, though, and people passing by recognize her, she knows they do, the way they glance, their judging eyes, a relentless cackle of hyenas closing in—

Kora bursts into the nearest women's restroom, locking herself into a stall as she falls to the cold tile. She breaks and lets out one choked sob, louder than she would like, burying her face in her knees. She digs her nails into her arm, the stabbing sensation a suitable distraction.

The minutes drag on like hours, and the more she panics and overthinks, the more she has to know. Kora tears open her new backpack, a hand-me-down from her cousin, and tugs out her cheap, piece of shit laptop. Bitterly, Kora wishes she had her phone, for something just a little bit more mobile than the clunky brick of a computer she now has to carry around.

Kora logs in, immediately pulling up Lake Leer's local news site.

It's something she never checks, for reasons Olivia herself elaborated — outside of your monthly batch of knife murders, nothing happens in this fucking town. She has to correct several typos, her fingers shaking so badly they click all the wrong keys. She opens the list of today's stories, finding her own criminal face on the front page.

High schooler found engaging in sexual activities with two adult women at notorious lesbian bar, interrogated by police.

The horror rises in her throat like vomit, the dread stealing every breath she manages. She clicks on the article proper, skimming the text. It's the best she can do in her blind panic. *Kora Lynch, 16...* They put her fucking name in there. They put her fucking name in there, and they—

And the article goes on and on, attributing the black eye and the broken hand to nothing more than adolescent fetishizing, decrying the youth's penchant for destructive relationships and reckless abandon.

Only a talentless hack could write this shit.

The laptop clatters to the bathroom floor as Kora realizes the rising sickness is more than just her world falling apart. She leans over the toilet, her breakfast coming up with violent ferocity.

The minutes turn to hours, the hours turn to days.

Kora's week portentously kicks off when she finally emerges from the bathroom, glassy eyes aching, only to find *faggot* spray-painted in blood red on her locker. It's still fresh, the smell hanging in the air, the slander painting her with its contemptuous odor. Kora snarls at nobody in particular, deciding to forget her books and simply walk away.

She passes Billy and his gang in the halls, the hood over her head failing to hide her silver hair. She was going to need to cut it at this rate. They snicker as she passes, but they don't touch her. For once, it seems her father was right.

"What are you hiding your face for, Lynch?" Harrison yells behind her, and Kora freezes, like he's raised a hand to her face. "Maybe some dyke will find the black eye attractive!"

He breaks into some nasally guffaw, as if he actually thinks he's funny. Kora forces herself to keep walking.

The first couple classes go by without a hitch. Kora lays her backpack on her desk and buries her face in it, bouncing her leg in a more erratic rhythm than usual, feeling less like a student and more like some entrenched, paranoid soldier. At one point, a classmate passes her by, and she jerks up in prepared panic, nearly knocking her desk over. She gets a few glances, but thankfully that goes mostly unnoticed.

Kora considers telling Mrs. Day her story, the *actual* story. She's about the only teacher who's been consistently kind to her, and the only one that seems to actually listen to what Kora has to say. At the end of English, Kora wearily trudges halfway up to Mrs. Day's desk. The teacher gives her a look, one borne of concern, but it also immediately confirms that her teacher has seen the news. Kora smiles awkwardly and spins on her heel, leaving the classroom as fast as she is able while still looking halfway natural.

"Kora!" Mrs. Day calls. Kora pretends not to hear her.

No one talks to her. No one says a word. This isn't new, but she's never been quite this vulnerable, never so exposed. She's waiting for someone to break the silence. Kora hides her face all through biology, gritting her teeth and tapping her fingers against her backpack. She tries to steel herself for whatever will come next, even as she knows it won't do a damn thing.

Kora figures she'd come off paranoid to just about anyone else, but she finds it well beyond justified. Last year, some kid got caught trying to sleep with a teacher for better grades — they were reported *by* the teacher, actually — and they never got the end of it. That wasn't even getting into the stories about unfortunate souls like Jackie Winters, who were all but ghosts in the school's storied, graffiti-covered walls. What Kora had supposedly done was miles worse than any of those stories.

And in Lake Leer, a town so forgotten and remote, so distant from entertainment opportunities and cultural hotspots, the slumbering herd becomes wolves given the smallest opportunity for excitement.

Her psychology teacher holds her back after his class, making it clear that he expected her not to engage in any deviant behavior in his classroom, or for that matter, the school. Kora stares at the floor and nods her head, drowning him out as she draws mental images in the indented tile. It's not him she's worried about. The day is almost over already, time flying by like nothing.

Kora's waiting for the torches and the pitchforks, and they're taking their sweet time. That just makes it worse.

The day ends without any other incidents, and Kora does her best to keep it that way, making a beeline off campus. Right before she exits the gates, a hand settles on her shoulder, and Kora spins around like a pinned bunny.

It's just the principal. *Just* the principal. Shit.

"Yes?" Kora swallows, meeting Principal Moore's eyes. The balding, rotund, bespectacled man is actually shorter than her, like most, so it's a little awkward. "School's over, I'm just—"

"I know, Kora, you're not in trouble," he instantly reassures. "I'm sorry if that was your impression."

"Sort of," Kora admits, looking around the crowded school courtyard. Students disperse and head home around them, others gathering in packs. Satisfied that she's safe from any heckling, at least for now, she returns her attention to Principal Moore, giving him an anxious smile. She doesn't much like the guy, in all honesty. He's nice, in the "hello, fellow students" kind of way, that fake sort of friendly that adults like to employ to make you think they understand you and what you're going through.

They never seem to realize how easy it is to see through that whole act.

"I apologize, Kora," Principal Moore smiles. "Well, the school board heard about your... your incident. We had to, you know, what with all your injuries—"

Oh, great. So there really is no one in this town that somehow missed Billy's little setup. Kora could almost shoot herself on the spot.

"Anyways," Principal Moore clears his throat. "Until the police decide what really happened there, we're... I'm not going to be making any judgments, Kora, so you don't need to worry. You aren't in trouble with the school, this is not our jurisdiction. But, your mental health *is* my concern, on the other hand, so—"

"Isn't that for my father to handle?" Kora says shortly, knowing the only potential caretakers more useless than her old man would be employed by Leer High.

"Them too, really," Principal Moore nods, his voice nauseatingly chummy. "But, well, you spend so much time at school, you know, all teenagers do, so it falls to us too. We have a school counselor, and I'd ask you to have a couple visits in the next two weeks, just so we can see how you're doing—"

"I don't need a counselor. It's a black eye and a broken hand.

Mentally, I'm just fine."

"With all due respect, Kora, you don't look fine. That, and I'm afraid I must insist that you speak to a counselor, at least a couple times. School policy. If you don't wish to after that, you won't have to."

"Fine," Kora says, tugging away from him and disappearing into the crowd.

Rather unfortunately, the reaper man doesn't come for Kora that night. He merely sends a brick flying through her window.

She wakes up to her window shattering, a couple hours before her alarm clock is assigned to free her of her night terrors. No, the sound of cracking glass does that this morning, the brick flying just over her head and putting a massive dent in her bedroom wall.

The sudden, bludgeoning crunch wrenches a scream out of the sleeping teenager, knocking her out of her usual early morning lethargy. Outside, a car engine tears away, tires squealing as it speeds down the street. Kora sits up in a hurry, clutching her blanket to her chest, the brick vacating itself from the fresh hole in her wall and slamming onto her desk.

Whore is painted on the brick in a sickeningly bright yellow.

Kora is only a half hour early to school that day. Her father bustles out the door earlier than she does, beelining towards the police station to report the brick incident. He is boiling over with rage when he leaves the house, slamming the door shut with enough force to shake the damn building. Kora is more than a little terrified by the display of emotion, something he so rarely gives, especially when it comes to anything involving her. Then again, maybe he's just upset about the damage to his property.

The bathroom proves to be her new morning haunt, her backpack thrown to the counter as she examines herself in the mirror. She brushes one hand through her hair, its idiosyncrasy something she's always loved, but she would take being able to disappear over an eye-catching color.

Kora gingerly pokes at her black eye. It's slowly healing, but it's taking far too fucking long. Her hand itches in her splint, and she has half a mind to tear it off, damn the consequences. She idly turns her head as the bathroom door opens, wishing she hadn't been brave enough to forgo the stall.

She doesn't recognize the student that enters, a girl with beautiful, flowing dark hair — a tangled mess, honestly, but it's an alluring match for the ratty old T-shirt and flannel. Everyone in this fucking town dresses exactly the same, Kora thinks, and not for the first time.

The stranger runs her hands under a tap and wipes off her face, her figure almost uncomfortably thin. She turns and sees Kora, glazed green eyes narrowing slightly. She adopts a bit of a smirk. "Hey, I recognize you." Her voice is smoky, all but monotone.

Kora shifts uncomfortably, moving to grab her backpack. "Look, whatever the joke of the day is going to be, I'd rather not hear it."

"Joke?" the girl asks slowly, her reaction speed clearly not up to par. "Oh. No, I wasn't going to make a joke. Actually, I think you're pretty cool."

Kora raises an eyebrow. "Okay, this is a little more creative than most of the shit people put me through, I'll give you that much."

The girl frowns and lethargically shakes her head, drawing closer, in a sort of... how the hell could Kora even describe it? Some sort of strut? Her voice takes a different tone, but Kora can't honestly tell exactly what she's going for. "I'm serious. You're a little out there, little crazy. It's cool. I mean, to sneak into a bar underage and just get beat the hell up in the name of crazy sex? It's so cool, dude. You're really wearing that bad girl vibe, you know?"

"Uh... thanks?" Kora raises an eyebrow, her back against the wall. She's not sure how she ended up there. She doesn't really care, honestly, because she can only look this girl up and down and question if she's stoned.

"Who are you, even?" Kora asks, the girl leaning in close... very close.

"Mabel," she responds, her chest just inches from Kora's.

"Mabel Alexander. Nice to meet you, beautiful."

And then it clicks. Mabel's trying to hit on her.

This woman is *definitely* on drugs.

"Listen, I have class in like... twenty minutes," Kora says weakly, only to shut up as Mabel's hands run along her flannel's collar. High or not, Mabel is admittedly rather gorgeous, the butterflies that usually belong to Laurie alone making their way to the forefront.

"Look, I, uh, I didn't actually..." Kora begins, trying to figure out the best way to tell Mabel that she had had no sex that night, or any other, for that matter. One of Mabel's nails runs over Kora's collarbone, touching bare skin for just a second, and Kora gasps as she shivers. Suddenly, Kora's regiment of adolescent hormones dig out of their graves and shoot rational thought dead.

"I, uh, didn't actually intend on making it to class anyways," Kora finishes, her heart silently screaming at her brain to quit being a hormonal dumbass. Her brain responds with the mental equivalent of blowing a raspberry.

Mabel's smirk widens, her breath definitely smelling faintly of weed. Strangely enough, it's not a turn-off — if anything, Mabel's relaxed confidence just encourages the oft-ignored pariah. "Good. Me neither." Mabel leans in, standing on tiptoe, and before Kora really catches up with reality, she is having her first kiss.

Somehow, the act is a lot... wetter than Kora thought it would be. It's also a million times better than she thought it would be. She tries her best to return it competently, all rational thought obliterated with a mental sledgehammer, but Mabel is luckily able to make up for her inexperience.

"God," Mabel murmurs between kisses. "Can't believe Laurie passed you up." She makes some sort of... sound in her throat, lips running down skin, her teeth nibbling at Kora's neck. Kora finally hears her own panting, so plainly desperate, so nice to have the loneliness lifted, if even temporarily, and...

And she isn't sure whether her heart is beating so fast because of the beautiful girl on her neck, or if it's because Laurie's name entered the equation. "You know Laurie?" she breathes, the words vocalized before she even thinks to say them.

"Yeah," Mabel confirms, her teeth tugging on the front of Kora's shirt teasingly, the taller girl's heart skipping a beat. "She's a... friend."

She's a friend. No, no, no, no no no no no no—

And just like that, the lightness in her chest is that much heavier. Of course, it all makes sense now. Maybe Mabel is just some horny stoner. It wouldn't be thoroughly unusual. Unfortunately, she's more likely putting Kora in a rather compromising position so that Laurie or someone else can "accidentally" walk in and take pictures or some shit, and—

And speaking of compromising images, Kora jumps as she feels Mabel's nails graze her hips, hands so close to undoing her jeans. Mabel looks up at her, concern drawing lucidity out of her eyes. "Sorry, did I scare you?"

When did Mabel even get on her knees? Kora's eyes dart to the bathroom door, expecting someone to burst in, expecting someone to come in and laugh—

Or maybe Mabel will really go through with it, and maybe she'll start spreading stories, exaggerate details, or maybe she'll turn Kora down at the last second, laugh in her face-

"Kora?" Mabel asks, and Kora can't help but think that she genuinely sounds concerned.

Or maybe she's just an excellent actor.

Kora lurches forward, fight-or-flight kicking in, knocking Mabel aside as she seizes her backpack. "Sorry," she says, trying not to trample the baffled girl as she bolts out of the bathroom.

"What an interesting lady," Mabel remarks.

Day three arrives, and the reaper is thankfully out of bricks.

Kora arrives at school two minutes before her first class. Somehow, indulging her father's attempts at understanding her was much more appealing than whatever hazing she'll endure today. By the time he headed to work, she reluctantly slung her backpack over her shoulder and took off to school, eager for her weekend, if only for a couple days of respite. She's fooling herself, though, and she knows it — if they're slinging bricks through her window, the weekend will provide her no sanctuary.

Her history class today requires a computer lab, which she gleefully takes advantage of by avoiding her assignments. The school never checks the browser history, for whatever reason, so she takes a computer in the corner of the room and starts looking up Mabel Alexander.

She finds Mabel's social media pretty quickly — with such a small town, it's easy to narrow down if you've got the right girl or not — and Kora's heart sinks with immediate displeasure as she sees the usual suspects cluttering Mabel's friends list. Some of them, at least — Laurie and Olivia. She seems to be outside Billy's friend group, a fact Kora finds slightly reassuring. Mabel definitely wasn't one of the women at the bar, either, so...

Still, Kora sighs, it was for the best that she got out of there quickly. It was only a shame she couldn't get much of an idea of who Mabel actually was from her profiles. The girl seemed fairly withdrawn, and all she can divine from these stoned selfies and bong galleries is nothing she didn't already know.

Reluctantly closing one of Mabel's sexier, huskier selfies with a bit of a huff, one eye watching her prowling teacher, Kora checks her school email. She doesn't have any genuine interest in whatever the school may or may not announce, she's just a slave to muscle memory. She skims one email from the school counselor, informing her of her appointment dates. Kora bites her lip, quickly backing out of the email.

There is one more message, one immediately peculiar, as the sending address is not that of a school email. She raises her eyebrow slightly, the sender's name nothing more than nonsensical gibberish. The topic is simply *Something you might like* with a stupid little winky face. Kora warily clicks on the email, her morbid curiosity trouncing her better judgment.

It's pictures of naked women, which she normally wouldn't complain about. No, the major problem is they are all covered in literal *shit.*

Kora gags, thankfully able to exit the tab before she runs for the classroom's trash can.

Kora spends the next class period in the nurse's office, a mandate she never asked for, but something she graciously accepts. The nurse checks her for fever, asks her some questions that sound suspiciously relevant to her mental state, and then has her lay down with a vomit bag until lunch rolls around.

This school is fucking lucky she doesn't have much of a temper, she muses, as she heads out to go find some quiet, lonely corner. Kora just wants to eat in peace.

Of course, life is nothing if not vindictive.

As she passes through the school courtyard, head held low, her hood once again fails to hide her silver hair.

"Hey, Lynch!" a familiar voice jeers, hand grabbing her shoulder. "Where you off to? Got more women to pimp yourself off to?"

Kora shrugs the hand away, turning around and giving Nick the most imposing "fuck right off" glare she can manage. Clearly, it's not enough. Harrison is behind him, snorting and stuffing his face with potato chips. Billy is absent, for some reason unknown to her, but Kora considers that a boon.

"Don't think she's talking to us, Nick," Harrison says, smiling like a complete idiot. "We were trying to be friendly, Lynch."

"Do you usually make friends with the people you humiliate?" Kora asks, any emotion in her voice long gone. The typical panic isn't even there anymore, really — it's been replaced with stormy irritation, a wearied resignation to whatever comes next.

Nick smiles. "We didn't do a thing. You know that. Everyone knows that."

"Don't care about the bullshit story you guys spun up," Kora says, turning around. "Bye."

"What, gonna go cry to mommy and daddy?" Harrison shouts, smacking Nick on the shoulder, clearly trying to impress his friend with his sixth-grader insults.

"No, course she isn't," Nick remarks, sliding his hands into his pockets. "Don't you remember? Her mommy got *murdered.*" He says the last word in singsong.

Kora stops in her tracks, spinning on her heel. "Funny. I thought you guys gave up on those jokes in junior high. I was so excited that you finally had new material."

"Eh, probably for the best," Nick shrugs. "With how much of a freakshow you've been lately, I'd half expect you to go begging for a taste of mommy, you know what I'm saying?"

He smirks as Kora stiffens, her cheeks flaring up. "Look, she's embarrassed," Harrison grins. "You must be on to something!"

No, she's not embarrassed. The heat in her face is rising, her healthy hand clenching into a fist. "Shut up, Nick," she growls, faintly aware of the audience gathering around them.

"Ooh, that really got her," Nick announces, clearly having the time of his life. "No, you're right, Lynch, I'm sorry. I just figured you'll take it in bed or in a grave, even, knowing how sick you are—"

He barely gets that last word out as Kora decks him in the jaw. Her full strength doesn't amount to much, but the sheer surprise of the action ensures that Nick hits the ground. Students gasp and shout in surprise as Kora pounces on the boy, fist coming down to knock out a tooth.

"Holy shit, she's gone crazy!" Harrison yells, and Kora realizes with the third punch that they set this up, she's playing right into their hands, now the heat will be off them and *she'll* look like the monster, and now she's losing her mind, and they'll put her behind bars, and—

She lets her bloody knuckles go in for another beating, the rising panic not enough to overcome her anger. This was the last time *anyone* would talk about her mother like that—

Harrison grabs her, clearly trying to tug her off, but she jerks her elbow back and nails him in the balls. He falls over with a startled squeal of pain like the pig he is. She manages to batter Nick another couple times, his body thrashing helplessly under her, before two teachers dart out of the crowd and seize her arms. Their shouts and demands fade with the wind, Kora Lynch seeing red.

Leer High's favorite outcast doesn't regret a single blow.

"Have you lost your mind?" Dad shouts, slamming his fist into the table.

Kora anxiously fiddles with the cuff of her sleeve. "No."

"You *pummeled* a boy into the ground, Kora!"

"He did it first."

"So you say!"

Kora meets his eyes for the first time tonight. "So I say? You don't believe me?"

He matches her gaze with his own palpable rage. "I'm not saying you're lying. However, the police are still investigating that night, and you going to town on one of the boys in the middle of school *really* doesn't help your case."

"He was saying some real... bad stuff, Dad, I..."

"That's not an excuse, Kora," he says, failing to keep a level tone. "You are getting yourself in... in trouble I can't *believe*. You are completely out of control, and I don't get why that's so hard to understand—"

"And I don't get why *I'm* so hard to understand!" Kora snaps, slamming the table. Her knuckles still ache with the beating she delivered earlier. "It's not like I *want* to be this way, but you wouldn't know that!"

"I have to work, Kora, and—"

"Oh, shut up," Kora hisses. "The fucking *television* is the only thing of worth to you in this entire goddamn house!"

"Kora," he says, letting her name hang in the air, clearly unsure how to proceed. "I-"

"I need to go on a walk," Kora stands.

"Kora, it's almost midnight—"

"And I need to take a walk." Kora snatches her jacket off of its hook.

"Kora, don't you *dare* step out that door—"

"Then stop me, you tyrant!" Kora shouts, letting the darkness take her.

Kora has no idea how she always ends up back at this lake.

She sits on the shoreline, skipping stones, surveying the spot of which she nearly sunk. Seeing what had come after, she was beginning to wish she hadn't survived.

She skips another stone, putting more force into the throw. The projectile sinks below the waves, swallowed by the moon's reflection. Glassy waves churn against the shore, barely lapping at her feet, their touch the only touch she's beginning to feel she'll know.

She wipes at the snot and the tears, rubbing her face clear, the effort pointless. The next pitiful sobbing session begins, and she buries her face in her knees, squeezing a stone. She can't even listen to some really depressing shit to set the mood, her phone somewhere out there, somewhere beneath the waves.

And Kora thinks for a second, just for a second, of how nice it would be, to wade out there and grab it, sink below, and...

She waits to hear snickering up the hill, for someone to come down and give her another beating. No one comes. Kora is alone, and she's not sure why that's so much worse.

Kora just wishes she could forget, wishes everyone else would forget she ever drew breath.

She skips another stone, the only disturbance to the cold, dead silence.

Kora sniffles, rubbing her nose again, traces of crimson still seeped into her knuckles. She hasn't been able to wash them completely clean. She watches the waves lap up at her feet, kicks off her shoes, wriggles her toes in the wet sand. She lets the water wash them over, shivers a little with each chilling tide.

And the sadness has settled in, just like another pair of clothes, a warm jacket to hold her close. She is not afraid.

Kora stands and steps into the lake, letting it come up to her knees. She shivers as she ventures forward, bending down to collect water in her hand, splashing it over her face. She lets it wipe the snot and grime free, gingerly rubbing at her black eye. The process is far too difficult with one hand, and an irritated Kora rips the splint open.

It falls into the lake, her shattered hand throbbing with pain, like it has a heart of its own. She drenches her palms, running cracked fingers over her face.

For once, she can agree with Nick. Her mother is lucky to be gone, lucky to miss the sight of her daughter despondent, dead in all but body.

Death spared her mother the taste of disappointment, a taste Kora bears on her insolent tongue. Kora hadn't exactly turned out to be anything, had she?

And maybe, just maybe, she's finally realizing what suicidal depression really feels like, what the words really mean. And she doesn't know where it came from, when it had made its home here. She had always thought the wish for death would come like a train, something horrifically obvious, something unbearably loud...

But no, it had just settled over her heart in stony silence, waiting, whispering, and she hadn't even seen when. She hadn't known suicide would be so silent.

Kora wades further into the water, admiring the moon. It is beyond beautiful tonight.

And the words and whispers tell no lies. The police will eventually find some reason to nail her down, put her away her for a crime never committed. Even if they don't, no one will forget all of this. She'll never be left alone again, never be free to blend in with the crowd. There is nowhere to run to, nowhere to hide.

That is the curse of Lake Leer, really. You are born in this town, and you will die in this town.

You will die in this town...

Kora cradles her broken hand, only noticing the water that laps at her chest when her heart freezes up. It soon becomes a comfort, and she stands there for a moment, taking it all in... the sound of the drifting waves, the light of the rising moon, the knife in her twisted hands...

She blinks sluggishly, words of woe whispering so intently. And she cradles the knife in her hands, turns it over, lets the blade tease the skin of her palm, and she has no idea where the blade came from, and it is beautiful, and...

Kora swears she can feel fingers grazing her ankles, the lake ready to tuck her into bed, put her to sleep. And it is beautiful.

And she knows it's all over for her, all hope of a normal life gone, never a face in the crowd again, and nowhere has she known anything but hate, and the knife in her hands is a gift given with reason, the lake free of judgment...

Only in the corner of her mind does she hesitate, inquire what the hell is happening, and it is silenced, dissent dying.

She strengthens her grip around the handle, extending her arm, pulling down the sleeve of her hoodie. Her skin is pale, wet, soaked like her clothes, and it is beautiful...

Kora grits her teeth and sobs, painting crimson in one, jagged master stroke, letting the blood form a painting of its own, and it is beautiful...

And everything feels so much easier, now that the pain is the only thing that's real.

She stumbles a little with the next tide, the cold not enough to wake her from her self-destructive haze. The shadows embrace her where no one else has, blood tainting the water, and she steps forward with an open heart.

Kora curls broken fingers around the knife's handle, drawing another jagged line down her second empty canvas. The pain that sparks in her hand gives her body another kick, her glassy eyes blinking furiously, the moon suffocating her. And then it is gone again, the awareness, the reality, and the pain ebbs, the red running rivers...

And it is...

Too late.

Kora blinks, taking in air, her cold chest rising and slumping, her slowing heart wrenching her thoughts back to reality. And she takes in the air, and she enjoys every exertion of her lungs, the chill in the air, and she realizes what she's done.

She looks down, staggering with the tide, her arms covered in crimson, the pale skin beneath drowning. She lets out the first of her last ragged breaths, letting her lips form a single, broken sob.

"I'm sorry."

Kora has no idea who she's talking to, just the thump of her heart, the moon blurring and shimmering before her eyes. The world shakes and unravels, hands rising from the waves in droves, wrapping around her bleeding arms, and they are pulling her down, and she is sinking lower—

"Mama—"

Fingers tighten around her throat, her next breath her last, her eyes settling upon the kabuki mask bobbing upon the rippling waves.

And it doesn't occur to her to survive, it doesn't occur to her to wonder how such a strange object came before her, and it doesn't occur to her that she won't last another minute.

Kora's hand reaches out for the mask, trails of blood bridging the gap between her arm and the lake, her head so dizzy, the world blurring out of focus.

And Kora falls, meeting dead men within the lake bed, and they take her under, embracing her, and she no longer wonders what it's like to die alone.

The lake laughs, the waves whispering woe.

CYCLE FOUR

Wrathchild

/// Somewhere else. October 15th. Sixteen days until Halloween.

If this world has any mercy, let them forget me. Let them all forget.

She is drowning, she is falling, the emptiness encompassing everything, blood and breath bidding bayartai—

If I had one more chance, I'd find a way, forgo this foul fate, watch you cut me free—

The abyss absorbs, her body a fading memory, and all she knows is that she is aware — not really, somewhere between consciousness and otherwise, a spark snuffed, a light lost—

Take it away, I tore myself out, devoured this heavy heart, where is the end, where is the white light, where—

It's all over, isn't it? If she had a mouth she would laugh, but it's gone and it's oh so dark, there's nothing to be found, and she brought this upon herself—

Hangman's hateful heart belongs to Envy, Lynch's longing Lust belongs to—

It's all over, it's all gone, you threw the key away and buried your eyes stitched shut—

Give it all to me, let your forlorn frame fray, your fate is sealed, but I transcend—

And she sees trees in silhouettes, fear tangled within roots, despondent broken boughs, mangled faces drawing rings, cycles spiraling every year, thousands upon millions of—

And you will wait, and you will weep, and you will wane, and you will never find a home—

And she swings in shame, dead and defiled, just another sunken star among the suicide shadows—

You have brought this upon yourself, you have forged your fate, you have given it all—

And she is alone.

Survive.

And she is frightened.

Survive.

And she is without hope.

Survive.

And so she hangs, an inconsolable imprint in a forest pale and empty.

A forest, lost for you—

Take her hand—

Where are you—

The wind howls, the dead reach out, eager to extinguish—

My severed savior?

And frail fingers intertwine—

Rise—

And Kora Lynch remembers touch, sweet touch.

My Vision of Vengeance.

The dark defers.

Kora falls to her knees, finding impossible breath as her throat unravels, and it is there, and *what the holy hell just—*

"Nothing holy here, Kora Lynda Lynch."

Kora searches for the voice's owner, scanning the otherworldly murk around her. Inverted spires dangle from a hovering sea of murky water above. Bloody red waves rage as aberrant animals dance among them, the world beneath inexplicably dry. Weathered stone statues dot the landscape, a dead field twisting and turning, scorched and scarred. It is dark, but not so much as to stifle sight. A set of ancient stairs lie before her, looking just translucent enough to make Kora feel that they'll disappear the moment she turns away.

Kora has the odd inclination to look down, her throat winding through her fingers. And her body is... well, it has seen better days. She gasps, unsure of what unseen force ensures her placidity. Her flesh writhes as a thousand slithering coils, spinning ribbons of black and purple. They buoy upwards, her skin never static. Her body has abandoned its every feature, any clothing, everything that made Kora distinct erased with these serpentine black coils.

She hesitantly rubs her head, and it feels like it always has, even as strands of this strange fiber curl in the shape of fingers.

Kora breathes, but she feels no heartbeat.

She thinks to contemplate her paradox, but the voice embodies the air once again, a serene hum that paralyzes as easily as it encourages, a menace beneath every word.

"Come to me, child. Up the stairs."

Kora obeys without a second thought, silence in her every step. The fabric of her fingertips unravels and reconnects, detached flecks dancing into the crimson ocean above. She slowly shuffles up the stairs, bits of her fluid feet caught in crevices and painlessly torn free.

The air around her becomes a sort of purple haze, chunks of her cheeks and limbs flaking off like rising embers. Even so, her form never looks any worse for it, new cords and coils forming before she realizes they were ever gone.

The stairs stretch on for a seeming eternity, but her new body shows no sign of fatigue, no wear nor tear. Kora reaches its peak, coming to an elevated, magnificent gazebo, a fountain within trickling dark crimson. She looks over the brim, the water forming a facsimile of blood. She turns to the table overlooking the eldritch landscape, sat atop an attached balcony and fitted with two chairs.

"Sit," the woman commands, pondering the great view below them. Kora does not inquire as she obeys, watching the coiled figure with overt interest. Their forms are startlingly similar, though Kora has, for once, found herself much shorter in height. "Do you know who I am, child?"

Kora realizes with a mental blush that she has no mouth. She helplessly struggles, mute beneath the lord of this world.

"You don't need a mouth to speak to me," the woman says, impatience striving to defy her natural charm. "Humans..."

"Sorry," Kora says internally, the words echoing through the air. "No, I don't know. Am I in Hell?"

"This place been described in such a fashion, but I find that description limited. I am something far greater than your... paranoid, abstract beliefs. So unimaginative, your kind..."

"Then," Kora begins, choosing her words carefully, "where am I?"

"The 'where' does not matter. It rarely does. What matters is your new station, now that you have died."

Kora anxiously rubs her tangling hands together, taking in the endless gravel and twisting roads below them. "So... I am dead."

"Extremely," the woman says dryly. "Drowned, bled out. Only could've been more sure of it if you had someone stomp your skull in, I imagine."

Kora winces at the description. "This isn't quite what I expected."

"Nothing ever is, youngling."

"I don't see anyone else here. Besides us, I mean. Seems like a rather exclusive afterlife."

"That's because it isn't one."

Kora tilts her head. "So I'm alive?"

"No."

"But I'm not in the afterlife. Am I not dead, or—"

"In between."

"How does that even work?" Kora asks. "I'm either alive or dead, right? I can't just be—"

"Humans," the woman sighs. "So slow. I thought your kind already transcended this insipid, asinine mindset ages ago. The theory of the cat in the chamber and all that."

"So... I'm neither dead or alive?" Kora asks with trepidation. The woman's very presence stuns her into bashful reverence.

"Yes. You were dead when I found you... dead and gone, knowing naught but despair. You should be thanking me."

"Thank you," Kora says gently, acting without a thought. "But... why? Who are you?"

There is a pause before the woman graces Kora with an answer. "You can call me Ira."

With the name, she finally stands, black strands taking form, color spreading over them, stitches forming into an eleven foot monarch. Ira turns, a decadent royal cloak and dress to match covering every inch of skin below her neck. She smirks hungrily, her luxuriant, wild hair matching her eyes and lips in their blood red shade. She raises a goblet of wine, black bandages wrapped around her hands.

"Consider me a guardian angel," Ira smiles. "You are the first to take my interest in several years, Kora Lynch. A hopeful light in a sea of treasonous apprentices."

"You don't look like an angel," Kora admits dumbly, taken by Ira's dreadful beauty, her confident visage only bolstered by the raging malice in her eyes.

"No," Ira agrees, propping Kora's chin up with a finger. "I am *so* much more."

Kora shivers under her gaze, blood red eyes piercing her forgone soul. "I... if you have the power to... to keep someone in some limbo between life and death, to... to have all this, wherever we are... what could you possibly want from me? What could I do that you can't? I'm just some stupid kid."

"Oh, nothing," Ira says, her smirk deepening. "Absolutely nothing. Consider this an act of charity, child."

"Charity?"

"Oh, yes," Ira replies, one thumb rising to stroke Kora's cheek. "You know what I see, youngling? I see a soul lost and mangled, a soul beaten under, a soul that's been taking dirt its entire life and never got the chance to make a change."

Kora shifts uncomfortably, her body seeming to fluctuate further under Ira's finger.

"And I can't help but pity you, you see," Ira continues. "I have been alive so long, and I will be alive for longer still. Everything there is to see, I have seen... every possibility for happiness, every ill-advised love, every act of anger and venom..."

She watches Kora with predatory eyes, her expression downright wolfish. "Every chance for retribution, every judgment and righteous *vengeance*... they have belonged to me."

Kora involuntarily whimpers, a chill running down her shifting spine.

"You... didn't get any of this, any of life's beautiful victories," Ira soothes, sympathy a shadow of supposition. "I cannot help but pity you. And to think, the ones who did this to you run free, guiltless, unbound... it must anger you something fiercely."

"I don't feel much of anything right now, really," Kora admits.

"Isn't apathy maddening? To feel nothing? To forget all your passion in an instant?"

Kora watches Ira's manic eyes with growing discomfort.

"Isn't it just heartbreaking," Ira muses, "to realize you will never leave that forest again?"

The forest of fallen failures strikes utmost terror into Kora with the simple recollection. "Please tell me you brought me here for a reason. If you're only here to... to remind me, I don't-"

"To gloat? To dangle your fate in front of your damned eyes?"

Kora doesn't answer, wringing her hands together.

"I'm glad you didn't say that, child," Ira says sincerely, staring across the wastes. "I'm glad you know better than to insult your betters. Then I really would have to make you *wish* for the forest again."

Kora shivers, nodding slowly.

"No, you are here for a reason, youngling," Ira turns back to her, taking a sip of wine. "You are here because I see something in you, something... powerful. I see that need for justice in a world without it. You're one of the few to understand how unfair it really is, how cruel and pathetic the people around you are. How so many villains slip out of grasp, high on innocence lost..."

"So, you're one of the good guys?" Kora asks faintly, knowing that is probably too good to be true. Too good for her, if nothing else.

"There is no such thing, little one. I am not asking you to be a savior, a superhero, an inspiration. Such fantasies are beneath both of us."

"Then what are you asking me to be?"

Ira smiles. "Vengeance. Retribution. Justice. Judgment. *Wrath.*"

Kora shifts uncomfortably. "You want me to... kill people?"

Ira rolls her eyes. "Kill the wicked, of course. But again, you humans... you simplify it so much. There is an art to this pursuit, child. You don't just kill them... you give them what they deserve. Killing is an undeserved mercy, a final judgment. No, you make them suffer, you make them regret, you gift them guilt, dangle that last judgment above them like a carrot on a stick. And then..." Ira smirks, snapping her fingers.

"I..." Kora stammers, her struggle to conceive a fate worse than the forest leaving her desperate to appease. "I don't... I really wish the people that hurt me would get what was coming to them. I really do. But I'm... I'm not the person for the job. I don't have it in me, and... judgment shouldn't be placed on the shoulders of one girl."

"You will have my guidance," Ira says, and the longer Kora sits under this woman, equal parts barbaric and beautiful, the harder it is for Kora to justify disobedience.

"I'm not sure I'm what you need," Kora confesses. "I'm just a girl. I've never even killed someone before. I fucking cried when I accidentally stole a chocolate bar from a gas station."

"That will be handled," Ira says, as if such ingrained morals are mere inconveniences.

"Handled? What the hell are you going to do?"

"What is necessary, young one," Ira growls, and the world around them freezes.

Kora shuts up, squeezing her wrist.

"Kora, Kora," Ira coos, changing tact. "Your mother was murdered, yes?"

Kora stiffens up. "I don't like to talk about it."

"Butchered in her own home, body unrecognizable, police utterly clueless. They never found the killer."

"Please stop..."

"You haven't thought it over your whole life, Kora, so someone must," Ira says lowly. "Do you think it ended with you? The man who killed your mother, he killed dozens. Every day, children lose their parents, mothers lose their children, siblings lose siblings. People kill, they rape, they steal, they desecrate. I am giving you a chance."

Kora sniffles weakly. "I..."

"I am giving you a chance, child. A chance to save others from the fate you suffered. A chance to protect, a chance to fix things where no one else will. These are dirty deeds, but someone needs to pick up the executioner's axe in this world... a world so blindly afraid to make the hard decisions."

"I'm scared," Kora admits.

"And they shall know that feeling," Ira says coldly. "I cannot keep you here. You make your decision now, and it is final. If you aren't willing to do what is necessary, I will have no choice but to return you to the forest I found you in. Maybe the solitude suits you."

"And..." Kora asks, tears embracing the purple haze. "If I take the other option?"

"Then you will have never died. I will return you to the land of the living, this one time. A second chance, something so rare in this world. It is a rather magnificent gift, one offered to very little. I advise taking it."

"The catch?"

"You know it already," Ira answers. "You will punish those who slip out of sight. You will become the sinner's silent stalker, the defiler's dogged devil."

"People like that..." Kora whispers. "People like that aren't scared of anything."

Ira whispers where Kora's ear should be, resting one hand on her faceless cheek. "And you won't just be anything, my little Karma. You will *define* wrath."

Kora shudders in waves, her malicious mistress running chipped nails up her arm.

"What will it be, Kora?" Ira whispers. "Obscurity or rebirth? Death or glory?"

Kora answers, so blissfully unaware of what roads this next word will lead her down.

"Glory."

And the smile that breaks across Ira's face will haunt Kora for the rest of her unlife, take a leading role in her gallery of night terrors. Ira's eyes flare greedily, her tone only now possessing of pleasure.

"That's my girl," Ira says.

And before Kora can begin to formulate a reply, before she can really realize just how she's forever damned herself, Ira tilts her head towards the fountain. "You will be wearing a new face, little Karma. Retrieve it."

Kora swallows, a lump in her throat. She hesitantly eases towards the fountain, crimson water quietly trickling into the basin. Sunken in the sanguine, she sees it again.

Kora reaches into the cold water, violet black courting crimson, strands of her hands unfurling into the water. Her swimming fingers find the scarred kabuki mask, a single tear half-faded under one cheek. It is clear that the artifact is a survivor of a thousand wars.

"What is it?" Kora asks.

"A gift," whispers Ira, resting her hands upon Kora's shoulders. "Put it on."

Kora looks it over, finding nothing to keep it in place, but the mysterious benefactor looming over her shoulder snuffs any hesitation. She presses the mask against her face, and it soon begins to cling to her restless skin of its own accord. Ira slowly turns her subject in a circle, eager to appraise.

Kora shudders, her body tingling with energy, a need to move, to run, a relentless *rush* overtaking her. "How do I look?" The words arrive with more childish desire than she intended, her mind set upon a desperate aspiration to make her new mistress proud.

"Like it was made for you," Ira smiles. "Now, go, my vision of vengeance. Do me proud."

And with that, Ira shoves her servant into the basin. Kora's arms snap out in shock, only for murky appendages to burst from the bowl and wrap around her limbs, holding her under. Her recently reacquired breath abandons her, the mask refusing to leave its new owner.

And she has no regrets. In fact, if she weren't drowning again, she might laugh. It was almost... funny.

The irony, that the woman they'd driven to die was going to be the arbiter of their fates. It was something beautiful.

With her last laugh echoing over blood red skies, she drowns again, pledging to make it the last time.

The moon looms low over Lake Leer, casting its grim reflection across the water.

The waves froth as a writhing body rips free from its depths. Disturbed dirt muddies the water brown, the lake's silence defied with the thrashing below.

The kabuki-masked corpse emerges, dirtied silver hair bursting free of the water. Her glistening mask embraces the night, taking a disbelieving glance at the shore. She feels for the ground, unbroken fingers running through sand as she takes two impossible breaths. The soggy bandage beneath her cheek must've slipped off at some point, but she feels no pulse of pain where it once lay. She flexes her undamaged hand, suffers no bruise around her eye.

She is alive. Despite all sense, she is alive.

Not just alive, either. She feels *good,* better than she ever has, and she takes in the smell of the lake, stronger than it's ever been. She pulls herself free from the rippling waves, shirt clinging to her skin, the lake's whispers a soothing lullaby to her ears.

Kora grins beneath her mask as she wades towards the shore. She feels *incredible.* She glances over her arms, taking in the scars with disbelief, but they are just that — scars. She feels them over in wonder, the wounds looking months old.

No one could survive what she just had, and yet she was here. Whoever this Ira woman was, Kora couldn't even begin to pass it off as some premortem delusion. There was no natural way she could've survived that, period.

And yet Kora feels her heart beating, louder than it ever has before.

She trudges up the hill with restored ease, a purple hue hung over her eyes, coloring her night. The town is quiet. It must be almost morning, Kora thinks, rubbing her pale, cold hands together.

She drags her boots through dirt as she finally reaches the fading trail that leads back to town, lost in her thoughts. The journey takes mere moments, though she really has no idea where she is going. She is not sure she wants to go back to her father like this — hell, she thinks if she goes back to her father after the utter lack of care he's always shown her, *especially* tonight, she might really knock his jaw in—

She stops for a moment, collects her thoughts. Kora shakes her head, pacing on.

Her head is misty, clouded like a drunken whirlwind. Kora stumbles frequently but never falls, the air prickling at her living skin. Eventually, she finds herself in the town proper, identical houses stretching down the road. Kora lives on the other side of the goddamn lake, she realizes, and she immediately decides that she isn't going back home tonight. Not on these weary legs.

She catches laughter from a house across the street, two stories tall. The living room is alight with activity, and Kora creeps forward in dissociative half-interest. She tilts her head and peeks through the narrowly parted curtains, mask inches from the glass. They don't see her, a classic nuclear family, parents and two children.

She focuses more intently on the whispers, the words.

The father was arrested six years ago for drunk driving, ran over their kids' dog. Mother used to slap and spank her kids when they cried as babies, but has since long stopped, likely out of guilt. The boy would often steal toys from his sister when she was an infant, giving no credence to her tears. The girl often sneaks candy from the cupboard in the dead of night. The childrens' sins hover thin, so innocuous in comparison to their progenitors.

Kora narrows her eyes, watching the children run to the table with their bowls of cereal. She stumbles away, panting. How did she know all that, how did she know—

She darts to another house on a hunch, peering at the couple inside, unfolding newspapers and preparing coffee. The husband has been jailed twice for tax evasion, has a habit of abusing his authority at work to get his subordinates to do the more mundane parts of his job, bashed a neighbor's car door in after they leered at his wife...

She glances over at the wife, panic rising as her quivering palm pressures the glass. The woman was an eager gossip in high school until she and her pack accidentally drove a girl to suicide. She lied to her husband about wanting kids, so she intentionally miscarried. She doesn't take sugar in her coffee.

The wife turns her head, a plastic chuckle falling away as she spots the lurker outside. Before she says a word, Kora slips away, head spinning.

I know. I know. I know what you've done, you—

You will have my guidance, her new matron had said. And so Kora did.

A police officer drives by on his way to the station, and Kora retreats to some bushes, watching him pass on by. A deeply racist man (to no surprise), the kind that plants cocaine in a black man's house to jail him for it, and a liar on testimony on top of it...

The car drives by, leaving Kora unseen. She glances back at the house, thinks of the woman responsible for a suicide, her fist clenching with such force that her nails etch stinging grooves into her skin.

Is it personal bias, sympathy for a girl with a story so similar to her own? Is it the fact that she could remove the victim's tormentor without a care in the world? Walk in there, and so easily...

Blood runs down her sleeve, rendering Kora lucid enough to rip the mask off her face. The anger fades to the background, reduced to an ebb, an aching, vengeful need...

Kora stares down at the kabuki mask in horror, and before she knows it, she runs, runs to the only person who just might hide her wicked heart.

Kora urgently knocks on Mabel Alexander's front door, ruing the recollection that her arms are still stained with blood. At least most of it was washed away, and what remains is far from fresh, but still...

She wishes she hadn't let her jacket float away with the lake, her resuscitated heart working itself half to death. Mabel finally opens the door, somehow looking more stoned out of her mind when she's sober. Not an early bird, apparently.

Stole a bong from a dispensary. Took her mother's car on a joyride. Throws rocks through rich people's windows.

Kora shakes her head, trying to silence the voice with willpower alone. "Shut up," she mutters weakly, blushing slightly as she meets Mabel's eyes. The other girl tilts her head, confused.

"Hey, Kora, you chill? You look hurt. Is this about the bathroom thing? If I made you uncomfortable, I'm really sorry."

Kora focuses, crafts some sort of tunnel vision, her head pulsing with pain. *Came onto Kora Lynch in a Leer High restroom... 'friends' with Laurie Thompson...*

She feels like her skull might crack. The whispers narrow, louder, focused.

She does not consider herself a true friend of Laurie, merely her plug. No ill intent. Genuine.

She gasps, letting go of her newfound gift and assuming a look of fright with natural ease. "I got in trouble," she says weakly. "Bad. Can I...?"

"Yeah, uh, here," Mabel says, snatching a leather jacket off her coat hook. Throwing the jacket over Kora's shoulders, Mabel takes her inside, unaware of the lamb's blood that might as well mark her door.

CYCLE FIVE
Karma Kills

/// Lost. October 18th. Thirteen days until Halloween.

Blood trails down the hilt of her knife, the makeshift blade nothing more than an abnormally durable bear tooth. She holds it aloft in grim determination, her test beneath the gods. The blade splays the light of a lamp, spitting scarlet, eager to bolster the woman's whimpered pleads.

The ceiling fan spins above her in mundane silence, not a sound to be heard in the dim living room. The woman tries to crawl away, but the killer is far bigger than her, and the heel of her boot crushes the victim's knee. It crumples in like a tin can, the woman's fitful screams muffled by the industrial-grade tape over her mouth.

"Silence," the killer commands, her tongue acting without direction, her body a distant observation. She rolls the dagger in her palm, side-eyeing the living room window. Two headlights cruise down the street outside. They disappear. Silence. She breathes, already burying remorse.

The woman tries to pull away, and the killer obliterates the last of her knee, grinding bone down to dust. Tears taint the woman's picturesque features, but the killer cannot abide by them. Her own face is wet and weary, guilt-ridden for a crime yet committed. She steps off the woman's ruined leg, crouching down to address the victim properly.

"I apologize," the killer confesses, avoiding Lea Lynch's broken eyes. "I really did love you."

Lea shakes her head, long out of tears, blotches of crimson dotting her purpled skin. She struggles against the tape that binds her hands, but she is tattered and torn, and the killer is in complete control. The murderer contemplates the knife in her hand as the tears run down, genuine and truthful. And no one would know that she had meant it. No one would.

"I really did," the killer chuckles, expecting to be found a liar. "I really, really did."

The killer's hand clenches the hilt of her weapon tight, cracking it in her grip. Her palm shakes, careless, presciently regretful. With one final scream of anguished abhorrence, the knife descends, piercing one angelic amber eye. She rips the blade free, bringing with it chunks of iris, moving in for another stab, and another-

And Lea Lynch's screams end where Kora Lynch's begin, untarnished eyes snapping open to the sanctity of her own shadowy room.

Petty vandalism and theft as a teenager. Stole several cars. Shouted at his wife for failing to miscarry. Raised a hand but didn't carry through.

Kora Lynch isn't exactly sure what she had expected from her father. For him to be nothing more than a dumb teenager and a shitty father wasn't exactly top of the list. That said, when he drove her to school that day, she looked him over for the fourth time since she got her abilities unnatural, uneasy and unconvinced.

Sure, it hurt to know that your father hadn't wanted you around in the first place, but he had always felt... worse than that. *Wrong.* And she had always assumed this gut feeling held a basis in fact, but now...

Maybe her gift was capable of the occasional mistake, maybe it missed things sometimes, but Kora doubted it. Whoever gave it to her, whatever... *thing* Ira was... she didn't seem the type to make mistakes. Not that Kora had any clue what she had witnessed when, well...

She had died. The thought takes grip of her as she joins the horde in the high school hallway, knowing that the feet that drag along tile are those of a corpse's. She is a dead woman breathing, a vengeful revenant, a walking impossibility. A zombie, a ghoul, a wight, a ghost, a wraith.

And yet... she feels nothing has changed, like she stepped into that lake for some secular baptism and emerged better off for it. If it weren't for the scars down her arms, those pinkish-red reminders, she'd believe the whole thing never happened, that she'd dozed off into some fantastical fever dream — the product of a creative mind and far too many slasher movies.

But no, she had died. And what she had seen...

Kora shivers, tugging the sleeves of her flannel over her marked arms, a newfound nervous habit. She had held these powers for a weekend, two days, and she had learned much, too much. She knows of her father's old... wishes, his yearning for a life of his own. She had discovered the depths of the Lake Leer police department's depravity, of the buried burdens of everymen young and old...

She had learned the married couple that lived next door to her made sex tapes and posted them online, and yes, she had felt the masochistic need to confirm this, and yes, she regretted it. They were not pretty people.

The only confirmation of Friday's nightmarish reality was that Kora remembered dying, *really* dying. She remembered meeting some mysterious benefactor from the great beyond, and it was an unavoidable fact that she really did possess a shining spotlight onto every person's greatest sins.

This is a power she wouldn't wish on anybody, much less herself.

And the mask...

The kabuki mask haunts her, a constant companion, a kindred keepsake. Even now, it sits in wait in her backpack, for she cannot seem to find any way to part with it. It is almost like a security blanket, some grounding tether, a certificate of her outlandish survival. She has begun to feel that if she lets the mask stray too far from her person, her body may remember it ought to have bled out, and she may just collapse and die on the spot.

Ira and the dread forest, they are but dreams to her now, distant, hallucinogenic memories. But the mask is real, the mask tests true under touch, the mask is too alluring to ignore... so follow her it does.

It had all been a haze, really, that night. She had ended up at Mabel's somehow, and she had left the afternoon after, dressed in a leather jacket that the girl insisted she kept. Kora was grateful for Mabel's relative innocence, this much she knew. It would be nice to have someone she could potentially call a genuine friend, someone...

Kora frowns. Someone she could confide in. What a foreign concept, especially now that she belongs to some sort of bloodthirsty divine.

She doesn't regret it, she thinks. She will do anything to forsake the forest, anything to fend off the final fade to black... and even so, she has not heard from Ira since that night in the lake. She has seen no signs at all.

That, Kora thinks, is more than enough for her.

She deftly weaves through crowds, a talent she has long mastered, giving every passing student wary glances.

The bespectacled boy on her right? Sells test answers. Truly despicable.

The jock walking across the hall who most certainly isn't compensating for anything? Prone to assaulting people who reject him. Classy.

The dark-haired, pale-skinned girl who really could pass off as a boy with the barest bit of effort? Petty Internet troll. Actually, Kora notes on second glance, that particular student probably *is* a boy. They just don't know it yet. How deeply into someone's subconscious can she spy?

Kora shakes her head and hurries onward, startled by the hand seeking her shoulder. Kora spins, leaving her breath behind her, heart taking off in a momentary flight of panic—

And it's just Mabel. Just Mabel. Lovely, adorable Mabel. Kora fails to reclaim her breath in a different sort of anxiety entirely, the girl raising an eyebrow.

"Hey. You okay, Kora? You've been really weird lately," she asks, tact ever intact.

Kora blinks. "You've known me for, like, four or five days, tops."

"And is all this paranoia your usual? Jumping at small sounds and glaring at people and shit?" Mabel responds, doubt evident in her voice.

"I suppose not," Kora concedes. "Just... bad dreams."

"You still never told me what happened to you Friday night," Mabel says, shouldering her backpack with all the grace of a stoned slug. "You were really cut up, and freaked. Like, really freaked."

"I know, I was there," Kora sighs. "Obviously, I was there. Look, can I tell that story later?"

"You've been saying that a—" Mabel stops and grabs Kora by the shoulder, halting them both in the middle of the hall. Students split in a stream around them to compensate as Mabel squints at Kora's eyes.

"What?" Kora asks. "I'm sorry, I got to get to class."

"You get contacts, dude?" Mabel says, completely missing her point. Nothing unusual there, really — the girl was unobservant and of the shortest attention span at the best of times.

"No?" Kora says, hoping her face looks as confused as she feels. "Mabel, I'm sorry, I do really like hanging, but I gotta—"

"Your eyes weren't purple before," Mabel says, clearly entranced. It's a look of rapt attention Kora would deeply enjoy if she wasn't so bewildered.

Kora stares. "Excuse me?"

"They're—"

"Mabel!" A familiar voice exclaims, sending a chill down Kora's spine. She spins on her heel and makes to get the hell out of there, but she isn't nearly fast enough. *"Kora!"*

"Oh, good, so you *do* know my name," Kora groans, turning to glare Laurie Thompson and Olivia Kemp dead in the eyes.

Apparently Kora's "fuck right off" glare has improved since last week, because Laurie actually hesitates, if only for a moment. The two girls lean in to give Mabel a tight hug, a ceremony that even seems to surprise the recipient herself. Laurie's eyes meet Kora's from over Mabel's shoulder, a wolfish smirk forming on her lips.

It's gone again the instant she pulls away, Laurie's picture-perfect façade in full force. "I didn't know you were humoring... damaged girls like Kora, Mabel," she says, her words as sweet as honey. Kora scowls.

Mabel frowns. "Look, I told you before I'll 'humor' whoever I want outside your group," she says, ably managing to downplay the irritation she clearly feels.

"Is she a buyer?" Olivia asks, clearly holding back from cackling like a hyena. "I didn't know your business was in such shambles, Mabel."

"I've never seen a drug in my life," Kora interjects. Mabel raises an eyebrow, and Kora shrinks back slightly, wondering if that just made her a whole lot lamer for her one defender.

"No, but she's trying to get some pussy, I bet," Laurie says, sending a devilish wink Kora's way. Kora winces quietly. "Did I forget to tell you about that, Mabel?"

Drove away Billy's former girlfriend, Jackie Winters, by spreading stories through the school, falsely accusing Winters of having an STD so she could date Billy herself. Also outed this girl as transgender in the process - Jackie was so relentlessly bullied that she's taking her senior year online. Had a couple hit and run traffic incidents. Kora's eyes narrow, her prior taste in women suddenly on trial, her stomach sick and seething.

"Whatever the drama is, I don't care," Mabel says, looking between the two of them. "I'm tired, I've never cared about the Mean Girls shit, and I just want to, like, get to class and maybe sneak a blunt, so—"

Kora curiously pries a little further, her eyes fixated, reality around her blurring into tides of indistinct motion. *No... did not actually take three dicks in a locker room.*

Goddamnit. Kora would've had a field day if that rumor were true.

"What are you looking at, Lynch?" Laurie scowls, a statement borne of Kora's deadened stare. Kora blinks, wrenching herself away from Laurie's rap sheet. "Didn't I already make it clear that I'm not yours to ogle?"

"I—" Kora begins, and that's where it ends, because she has nothing much to say. Besides her one moment of vindictive wit when Billy was pushing her face into the lake, she's never really been one for clever comebacks. That lone exception had truly come out of nowhere. "I wasn't trying to—"

"God, you're disgusting, Lynch," Laurie scoffs, turning to leave. "At least the black eye healed nicely."

Kora blinks, the motion wetter than usual. Fuck, was *this* going to be the bomb that bursts the dam? Not the dying, the extradimensional visitor, the super powers, but some fucking bully at some stupid fucking high school...

Then again, Kora supposes, it feels a little more grounded than anything else she's been through recently.

"Guys, lay off," Mabel sighs, moving between them and Kora. She gives Mabel a confused glance, knowing the girl is putting any good reputation she had in this school under a guillotine.

Laurie chuckles under her breath, melting into the crowd. Olivia gives Kora a shake of her head, indictment in her tone. "Pervert." Kora scowls at her in frustration, the girl utterly mean-spirited whenever Laurie was around, cruel and petty—

Especially prone to groupthink. Terrorized her longtime childhood friend to gain Laurie's approval. Compulsive liar. Uses peanut butter to get her dog to—

Kora gags, the tears breaking free, but more out of disgust and sickness than humiliation. Olivia's smug smirk wavers and Laurie glances back to examine the spectacle. Mabel's hand reaches out to steady Kora's shoulder, but it barely grazes flannel as she rushes to the bathroom.

Mabel yells her name, the other two girls bursting into juvenile laughter. One student moves in to grab her, maybe to help calm her down, maybe to prolong the persecution. She has no idea. She moves without thinking, giving him a half-hearted shove, more strength behind it than she ever thought she possessed. He flies into the lockers, imprinting them with the shape of his body. The crowd mills around the boy, amazed by her feat of strength, but Kora is already gone.

She bursts into the bathroom seconds later, slamming the door behind her as if the world itself is at her heels. Kora prowls down the stalls and ensures each is empty, nausea rising in her throat. Confident in her solitude, she slumps down against the wall, trying to ease her speeding heart back to a safe pace.

She is scared, so tired of being scared. So sick of feeling hunted, so weary of watching the world for pitchforks and torches.

Her shaking hand subconsciously unzips her backpack. Before she can start fathoming the world through the purple haze, before she can get a grip on her ailing self, the mask is already in her hands, her only stability.

Kora glances at the bathroom door again, listening for footsteps. None, she confirms, her hearing so much better that it had ever been. With simmering anxiety, without a clue why, she flips the scarred kabuki mask around, pressing it to her tear-stained face.

Her breaths steady, her heart slows. Her scarred arms slowly stop shaking, soothed by the mask's privacy, its promise of protection.

Somehow, in some way, it feels good, better. Different. Natural.

And her heart sets off again, gathering speed, marching a marathon, but it is not of discomfort now. Kora slowly rises, listening to her breaths subside, turning to face the mirror.

You'd think she'd look ridiculous — this scrawny, pale, silver-haired girl, dressed like some pathetic hipster, wearing this ancient artifact over her face. Like some sort of veil between her and the world, like some sort of shield to the slander and sin.

She leans over the sink, the mask beneath her dangling hair allowing these moments of peace. Her T-shirt slightly hangs loose from her frail form, displaying the name of some obscure punk band with a name half as long as any of their songs — *Golden Snub-Nosed Monkey Eating Berries.* Pair that with the mask, and she looked like a slasher killer. A *sexy* slasher killer.

"Hello, Lady Voorhees," Kora mutters out loud, surprising

herself with the sultry tone she takes. In response — as if she needs to answer herself — she lets out a weary chuckle, one that sounds so much different than she always had — more confident, more dangerous, more *free.*

Kora glances at the bathroom door, footsteps too far away to be approaching. "Man, it's really convenient no one but me comes in here."

It's strange, she muses, how she's the only person willing to hear Kora Lynch speak. Two years ago, that would've been the last thing she hoped for.

Kora leans forward, her mask just inches from the glass. It has struggled over the years, been beaten past the point of repair in an interminable war with injustice, but... it has its own sort of charm, its own guarantee of survival.

Under the light of the bathroom, she can barely see through the mask's slits. Tilting her head, she finds that a piercing, darkened purple has long overtaken her old amber eyes.

"Well," she ponders, painted purple. "I'll be damned."

Fading flakes of paint depart with the wind, the sign reading *Harding's Hunting* seemingly as chipped and faded as the store it represents. The occasional raindrop lands upon Kora's brow, and she reminds herself to get home soon, lest it start storming. She hovers by the old local hunting store, bouncing on her feet, her unmasked face harboring another raindrop.

She steps inside, checking the clock. 1 PM. She almost has a hard time finding it, every wall stacked high with firearms, camping equipment, fishing rods, and all the miscellaneous items you'd expect from such an establishment. Kora wipes her sneakers off on the welcome mat, the front desk unmanned. She is thoroughly unsurprised, knowing the store sadly doesn't see much traffic, despite how perfect of a place Lake Leer really is for an outdoorsman or a hunter.

That was probably the only great joy her father had ever imparted upon her, hunting. An uncharacteristic enthusiasm possessed that man when he was neck deep in the woods, hunting rifle in hands. It was the one area where they fell in unambiguous agreement, and she often yearns to go treading through those woods in search of prey again, if her lethargic moods ever let her go long enough to manage it.

She approaches the front counter, distracted by a small crossbow on display. Despite her long respite from the hobby, even she has to admit she wouldn't mind trying out that beauty. She shakes away those irrelevant thoughts, anxiously pacing as she rings the bell on the counter.

"Just a second!" Mr. Harding yells from the back room, several scuffles and scrapes escaping into the store proper. It has been a while since she's seen him, but Kora remembers him well from all her visits to his prized store — his jovial voice is a perfect match for his appearance, a bright, bearded old man with a constant smile.

The shuffling does little to soothe, and Kora groans under her breath. "Hey, Mr. Harding!" she says, raising her voice. "It's Kora! Look, I just need to use the bathroom—"

"Kora? Kora Lynch? Isn't it a school day?" he asks, something collapsing in the back room. Kora raises an eyebrow. "What are you doing wandering around?"

"I felt sick, going home early, I just needed to pee," Kora replies, feeling as if she might die if she stands here any longer. "Can I please use the bathroom?"

"Yes, of course, go right ahead," Mr. Harding says with his sun-spitting smile, emerging from the back room with a box of crossbow bolts in his arms. "You know where it is."

His smile hits her like a train, a window to the secretive soul.

Has beaten his wife and child for seven years. Good actor. Put his son into a closet several times over his life. Never been investigated by the police, likely never will be. Mother too scared to report any wrongdoing. Cops too corrupt to ever make a goddamned change. Liar, liar, liar, wears a smile like he's done no wrong, flashes a grin like it makes up for every bloody fist—

"Kora? Are you okay, kiddo?"

Kora blinks, traitorous tears blurring her vision as she takes two steps back, every baited breath bound behind her teeth. No, no, she didn't want to know all this, she didn't want to bear every burden, she didn't want—

Is no one sacred? No one? And this man, this champion of common courtesy, the man she looked up to for *years...* just a fraud behind a fake fucking air of cheer?

"Kora?" Mr. Harding asks, moving around the counter. "Say, what happened to your eyes? Did you get contacts?"

"I'm fine," Kora chokes out, brushing her hair over her eyes. "Contacts... yeah, I'm, uh, I'm going to go use the bathroom."

She darts into the store's restroom before he can respond, tucked away in the corner of the building. She locks the door behind her, pressing the full weight of her back against it, as if he'll chase her with a belt, a belt she knows he's used, a fist she knows he's—

She tugs open her backpack, her anxiety skyrocketing, her pulse well on its way to putting her under. The cramped, unassuming bathroom stares at her in silence, the bare essentials haphazardly crowding her.

She practically throws the backpack across the room, the mask in her hands as Kora falls to her knees, vomiting into the toilet. She spits out the grit of every sin she's had to carry, bringing the mask up to hide her hurt as soon as she's got nothing left to give.

Kora shudders, whimpers, digs her nails into her jeans. The mask shields her face as it always does, holding her close, steadying her, then bringing her to another bitter rise...

And her heart is hurtling again, but now it embraces energy, admires adrenaline, now it's good, now it's better, now *she's* better, and the song begins to play—

Like a long-lost lullaby to her ears, like someone who knows every last thing to say.

Kora's fingers curl around the sink basin, dragging her to her feet. She finds herself before the mirror, facing the music.

Kill him. It's so fucking simple. He's a monster.

"I can't do that," Kora murmurs, resting her masked forehead against the mirror. "I can't just do that on a whim."

But then she'd be complicit. Every beating that follows, every lash of a belt, every shattered scream, all her fault. She can stop it, she has the power. She knows all they try to bury, and she is strong, stronger than she should be, strong enough to *hurt.*

"I can't hurt. I'm already hurting. I can't do that to others."

She can wish it on no one else, and yet she doesn't stop him from bringing it on others. She knows her powers aren't wrong, they never are. She is unwilling to sacrifice a little for the sake of a brighter future, a coward too frightened of the blood on her hands—

"There's no blood on my hands. There won't be."

And yet there already is, she's already made a deal, the Lady Ira holds onto her heartstrings, and with a flick of the wrist, maybe they'll come undone. Besides, where's the harm, the harm to the good people anyways, the ones with hearts and hope? This man has done nothing but take it all, bury that potential down below.

"I... can't. I'm a coward, maybe, but..."

And she's scared, and yet she doesn't see, doesn't acknowledge one simple fact. Her fright will damn that family to endless pain, no end in sight, and she can end it, she can—

"I..."

She is capable, she is strong, she is vindictive, she knows justice, she is all that they'd fear, she just needs to—

"I *can!*" Kora hisses, fist shattering the mirror and caving in the wall beneath. The word came out wrong, and yet...

And yet, it feels so *right*, so satisfying, so... karmic.

Go, my Vision of Vengeance.

"I should..." Kora's fingers curl, cracked bones popping within the aperture.

Do me proud.

"I *must.*"

Karma dislodges her fist from the wall, growling deep, a hunter harboring hatred.

Karma considers herself, the kabuki mask bearing faded scars, but it is still too clean, far too spotless. Her eyes are brighter now, the purple even more palpable, rising with her rage. With her need, her heartbeat, her *wrath.*

Let's dirty up that mask.

She's slipping into a dream, one where she's found the switch to set loose her inner animal, her penned predator, one where she's finally found *herself.* Like she's finally free, Karma prowls, the word a fitting adjective, a matchless name.

She silently positions herself next to the bathroom door, thinking faster than she acts. Karma presses her cheek against the wall, salivating lips waiting by the door's hinges.

She has been in this store dozens of times since she was a child. There is only one camera overlooking the main lobby, and that's all it has ever needed. It's hooked up to a computer in the back room, easily dealt with. If he were out of sight, well... she'd be a ghost.

She steadies her breaths, tasting the air. She can hear him outside, enhanced senses taking in his every motion, catching the smell of his favorite breath mints...

And she shrieks away the silence, playing against him his greatest asset, that of the actor.

"Help! Oh God, help, *help!*"

And like the deer, he runs, heading right for her trap, hand spilling sweat, fingers wrapping around the door handle—

If only you had shown your family this much care, I wouldn't have to do this—

He tears the door open, rushing inside. As soon as he is out of camera view, before he can even turn his head, she lunges out, her ludicrous reflexes an unfair advantage. Her hand clamps over his mouth, her other arm pinning back his flailing limbs. His eyes bulge in fear, his mouth screaming for a savior out of sight.

"Shut up!" Karma growls, her voice like gravel, words going primal. She drags him across the room, pinning his head against the wall.

Don't drag it out, you'll change your mind, do the deed and run, fucking run—

He writhes against her grip, but despite his superior mass, despite every indication that this bony girl shouldn't be able to slam him against the bathroom wall with ease, she does.

Make it fast, make it fast, you fucking animal—

"This is for your wife and son," Karma hisses, her mask warm against his ear.

"Kora, what—"

And before he can plead, before he can find her better nature, she digs fingers into his hair, pulls back, slams forward, pulls back, slams forward, *crack,* pulls back, slams forward, *crack,* pulls back, slams forward, *crack,* pull, slam, *crack,* pull, slam, *crack,* pull, slam, blood, pull, slam, blood, pull, slam, blood—

Karma sees naught but red, chunks of brain and bone and blood dripping between her fingers. Mr. Harding's head finds itself unrecognizable, crimson tides slathering the wall, a flapping chunk of his cheek flopping to the ground with a wet slap. His jaw dangles like a broken puppet, one eye bulging out of its socket. It's almost comedic, really, the mess that she's made, the man that she's just—

She drops the murdered man, his head crumbling into three, remains splattering all over the floor. His body crumples, half of his neck and scoops of his scalp landing in the toilet bowl.

Karma breathes, hot and heavy, her heart serene, her bloody hands shaking with release, an excitement bubbling within her chest and tingling between her legs. She stares into the mirror, the purple in her eyes simmering low, her kabuki mask delightfully dirtied.

Not just that, either, she sees — her shirt has taken a new color, her jeans soaked down to the knees, not an inch of the skin of her hands left unblemished. And yet, it all feels...

When the comfort comes, she shoves it down.

Karma rises, reminds herself to move, retrieves her backpack. She bursts out of the bathroom, nearly knocking the door off its hinges. She darts into the back room, ignoring the racks of supplies, stepping over boxes and doodads as she approaches the computer across the door.

Her heel comes down on the PC case, smashing it like she smashed the man's head, one, two, three, four and five, any security files thoroughly demolished. Shattered computer components are brought down to dust, the case torn to tiny pieces.

She stumbles out of the back room, knowing there will be no police, at least not until he never returns home tonight. Karma takes her time, moving to escape.

She turns, wonders for a moment.

Well, it couldn't hurt. Couldn't hurt *her,* anyway.

She appraises the shelves and cabinets, smashing through a glass display to retrieve a hunting axe. Karma turns it over in her hands, an adaptable tool, easily wielded with either one or two hands. She smirks under her disguise, grabbing the crossbow and slinging it over her shoulder. With a short grunt, she picks up a box of bolts, carrying it in her free hand.

Satisfied, Karma exits the shop through the back entrance, stealing away, steering away from the main road. Where the guilt refuses to relent, the satisfaction sates, steeling her heart and pleasuring her pain as she disappears.

Karma twirls the axe in her palm, liking the feel of her weapon, something safe, something predatory.

Just in case.

CYCLE SIX

Drop Dead Gorgeous

/// **Last-Minute Laundry. October 19th. Twelve days until Halloween.**

Kora Lynch drums her nails against the laundry machine, shielding her face from the windows that overlook the street outside.

Crack—

Another car passes by the laundromat, attracting her paranoid gaze. It cruises by without accusation, and Kora mentally urges the laundry machine to stop taking its sweet time. Three or four other people idle in the building with her, every single one arousing her suspicion. These days, it is a gift easily given.

Crack—

The machine rumbles under her arms. Kora fixes her eyes on the tumbling clothes inside. The blood doesn't seem to be washing out, something she anticipated, dreaded, and presciently rued, all at once. She bites her lip, her clenched fist bouncing against the machine now.

Crack—

"Fuck!" Kora swears under her breath, running hands over her eyes, trying to forget the stench. It's been a whole day, an entire evening's restless tossing and turning. A whole night's worth of trying to wash blood out of her skin, a whole—

Crack—

It's over, so why can she still smell it? Why can she still hear the skull cracking like glass? Why can she still feel every satisfying fucked up murderous pleasurable addictive arousing hateful horrifying—

Crack—

"Shut up!" Kora hisses again, and a nearby customer gives her a startled glance. She smiles awkwardly and buries her face in her arms again.

It's all she can think about, all she's thought about for hours, every crack, every slam, every tearful cry... How his head just shattered like an eggshell in her hand, how the pieces and the blood within brought her to some violent climax...

And the thing was, she would've found that funny in the moment. That sort of metaphor would have earned her a low, morbid chuckle then. Now, it just made her want to dart for the nearest toilet.

Most horrifyingly, she isn't sure if she's scared of herself, or if she's merely frightened of getting caught, discovered, hauled off to jail and thrown in solitary confinement for the rest of her days. Did they give life sentences for one heinous murder? She didn't know.

In seek of distraction, she walks up to the apathetic employee at the front counter. "Excuse me?"

Her heart pounds with unfounded paranoia, sweat nesting beneath her silver hair. If she didn't know any better, she'd think that it was everyone else in the world who could see her sins.

They don't know. They don't know. Nobody's coming for you.

Her body stubbornly ignores sense and reason, opting for blind fear and nightmarish visions of the future.

The man looks up from his magazine, tiredly slumping his shoulders. "Problem with your machine, miss?"

"No, not... exactly," Kora says slowly, not sure how much of her spoken anxiety is real and how much is a mere mimic of her typical behavior — the 'mask of sanity', that's what it was called. "I... so, yesterday, I accidentally cut myself while I was cooking, you know, chopping vegetables... um, I've never exactly had to clean blood out of clothes before, and there's some stains on the sleeve of a shirt, and uh, it's not just coming out, so..."

The man sighs and retrieves a large bottle, sliding it across the counter. "You'll need to use some bleach, ma'am. Feel free, just bring it back when you're done, and don't drink it."

Kora raises an eyebrow. "Why would I drink it?"

"I don't know, I have to say it. Store policy. Dumbass kids keep going around drinking bleach for their TikToks or whatever," the man says. "Good luck with your sleeve."

"Thanks," Kora says, taking the bleach.

Snip. Snip. Snip.

Locks of hair plummet into the bin at Kora's feet, the mirror before her fixed on her guilty gaze. She looks down at the trash can with some sort of sheepish grimace, extending several long strands of hair with an iron grip. *Snip.* She sheds silver.

Snip. Snip. Hide. Hide. Snip. Hide.

Kora doesn't know when she started cutting her hair, really. Somewhere in between another bout of anxious vomiting, true crime documentaries and erratic tears, she had grabbed a pair of scissors and just started chopping. She couldn't watch the bits where they got caught and shipped off to jail anymore. They distressed her to a degree she simply could not escape from.

Snip. Snip. Hide. Snip. Murderer. Snip.

And she wishes she could just cut away the guilt and the anxiety and the fear and the slow decaying rotting inside this easily but she can't and she's *killed* and even when her hands are as clean as they could ever possibly be she can still see the blood on her hands and she sees his face in every mirror and every time she just—

Murderer. Murderer. Murderer. Murderer. Murderer.

Kora drops the scissors, spasming hands grabbing hold of the sink as she starts retching again. Unfortunately, Kora has nothing left to give. Her stomach clenches as she dry heaves, doubled over in sleepless agony.

Kora looks up, eyes red and watering, chewed fingernails digging into the countertop. She rummages through her backpack, cradling the keepsake that has accompanied her in every avenue, even after the... the...

Her skin breaks out in goosebumps again, her panicked hands nearly dropping her stronger face. She takes a more secure grip, tucks it to her chest, breathes in, presses the mask to her face again, a sanctum, her only safety...

Karma breathes, presses her hands against the wall. She stares at the tangled pile of abandoned hair, steadying her breathing, feeling the panic and guilt make way for resentment and resignation. She curls one hand into a fist, the tremors that terrorized her body slowly fading away.

Calm. Calm. Calm. Hate. Hate. Hate. Cleanse. Cleanse.

She takes a deep breath, listening to the titillating little growls that rise in her throat. Karma bends over to fetch her scissors, extending several strands of hair.

Snip. Snip. Snip.

She hums under her breath lightly, some amateur rendition of "One, Two, Freddy's Coming for You". The tune is soothing, serene, synchronizing with every shedding strand. By the time she finishes with the rhyme, Karma leans forward.

She tilts her head, a satisfied purr coming to her lips as she examines the mask she knows so well with keen interest.

The blood is gone.

She didn't wash it off, didn't wipe it clean, it had done so itself. Prepared itself for the next...

Karma frowns, her lighter heart eager to leave that sentence unfinished, begging to leave it at an ellipsis. She grants it that much, malcontent to leave her hands bloodless for now.

With all they've done to you with all the hurt they've slung upon you and you bow out—

They drove you to fucking Die—

Karma breathes, runs her palm over the cheek of her mask, drifts back to tentatively tease her shoulder-length cut. It still curls at the ends, but with its new length, it compares more to a dashing knight than a princess' sweeping locks. If she was dressed in something bulkier than her old T-shirt and jeans, one would very easily see her as just another lumbering redneck in this mask.

Good. The farther from timid Kora, the better. A mask is made to disguise, not accentuate. A mask is made to mold, made for versatility, made to leave a mark...

And by Karma's second life, she would leave a mark.

The house shudders with the slam of the front door, her father home. Brilliant. If only he had been guilty of more, if only he had harbored more hate...

"Kora!" he yells, a rarity. Karma raises an eyebrow, taking a moment to remember the name belongs to her.

"What?" she snaps, tapping her fingers along the counter, her voice taking a deeper pitch under the mask.

"Come down here, Kora! I'm not yelling all the way up the stairs!"

Karma growls, giving herself one more longing glance in the mirror before she tucks the mask away again.

One identity isolated, another assumed.

Kora sprints down the stairs, impishly springing onto the ground floor. Her father hasn't found his weary seat yet, another peculiarity in a night full of them. He stands next to the overburdened dining table, shuffling through papers with heavy eyes. He looks up at her as Kora approaches expectedly.

"What's up?" she asks, hoping the conversation will be interesting enough to keep her mind off the last day or so. This may be the first time in her life she's ever actively desired to speak to her father, now that she thinks of it.

"I've been dealing with the police today," he begins. Kora recoils on reflex, her heart nearly bursting out of her chest before she remembers the whole altercation with Billy's group.

No, they don't know. I mean, I'm sure they know Mr. Harding is gone for good, but they can't know it was me, this is just the earlier bullshit, it's fine—

Kora blinks, managing to maintain an innocent demeanor. "Right."

"We're going to have to see them again this weekend," he continues, his voice hesitant. "For the final conclusion regarding your case, and that, and..."

And for the first time in... well, in *forever,* her father bows his head low, struggling to speak.

"Dad, are you okay?" Kora says, taking on a tone of concern with him for the first time in many years. "I'll be okay, my story will check out with the facts and all that, and—"

"Kora," he raises his hand, silencing her. "It's not that."

Kora's heart sinks low. "Then...?"

"You know Dan... Mr. Harding? From when we used to go hunting?"

Kora's heart promptly tunnels through to the core of the Earth. "Yeah?"

"Kora, he's... they found him murdered. Barely even recognizable. Like..."

Like your mother. He let the words hang unspoken, but she saw them coming. She knew they had been coming.

And he reaches out a hand, tears actually rolling down the old man's face now, and she's never seen him like this, never seen him so *human.* And for once, she wants to take his hand, accept the embrace, steady him where she can...

If only she didn't rent out this red right hand.

She retreats, tears running down her cheeks. He goes to say something, but Kora panics, darting back up the stairs. He doesn't pursue. He knows better than that. She tears her mask out from under her jacket as she retires to her room, teeth grit so hard they hurt.

"You *fucking—*" she explodes, ignorant of the fact that her father can likely hear the shout. She throws the mask across the room with as much force as she can muster, and it hits the wall with a *thump* before flopping onto the floor. Tears fly with it, flung into the dark as she marches over, giving the mask a good kick. It cartwheels up onto her bed, amicably accepting the abuse.

"Dead, he's *dead,* I've hurt my father, I've hurt myself..." She falls to her knees, teary eyes set on the silent mask. "Ira, you fucking *devil,* you fucking *cheat,* you fucking *monster,* what have you done to me?"

She almost expects the mask to light up in answer, prepares for the otherworlder herself to appear in Kora's bedroom and deal with her blaspheming herself, but no one appears. Kora sits alone with the mask, this inanimate object that is somehow tearing her apart in ways no one else had ever managed.

Kora crawls into her bed and tugs a blanket over her shaking body, curling up as the cold catches up to her. She shakes and shudders like she's sick, and she realizes she *is,* her slow mental infection courting physical illness, rendering her worse than she's ever been. She digs her nails into her scarred arms, teeth chattering with rage, with cold, with fear.

And to think she bought Ira's serpent tongue. Trusted her words, believed her crusade for good, for justice-

Or, Kora darkly thinks, she was just a coward, so afraid of that forest.

And with the police closing in, with her social life in permanent shambles, with almost every soul she knows trying to fuck her over, it's only the forest at the end that keeps her from sending the scars upon her arms some soulmates.

We can make this better.

"No," Kora sobs. "I can't... they'll either get me for Billy's shit, or they'll get me for yesterday. I'm done. It's over..."

And it hasn't really sunk in until she's said it, hasn't really registered as reality until she's acknowledged it.

"It's all over," she says, drowning in guilt and fear.

Kora looks over at the mask, hesitant to face its war scars. "You brought me back," Kora whispers, swallowing uneasily. "There had to be a reason."

Save yourself. You still can.

"I just... I need to do something, something good. I helped Mr. Harding's wife and child, but... it just feels so, so..."

Kora sniffles, rubbing her cheek against the sheets. She watches the mask, her only companion, the only thing to see her without judgment.

"I can't say he deserved to get away with that, but I just... I feel so *awful...*"

They say it gets easier.

"I don't want to find out," Kora shudders, her hand curling into a fist. "No more killing... and I'll be okay. They won't find me."

But what about Billy's 'prank'? That police captain has got it out for you. You have no proof you didn't mean to be there, only the appearance of common sense. For him, it might not be enough.

Logic, sweet logic, you could afford to shut the hell up more often.

Kora shudders, biting her lip, reluctantly embracing her better half. It is a warm comfort, nothing new, but she can see the current running underneath the scars, the danger, the passion, the polyrhythmic temper of an acerbic avenger...

"I'm not myself with you."

The mask seems to silently agree.

"With you, I could..." Kora licks her lips nervously, wiping tears from her face. She sits up and shelters the mask in her lap, gingerly stroking it. "I could prove I'm innocent. Get those girls or... or somebody, to confess. I could be home free."

The mask stares up at her, concurring with her conclusions.

Kora tries to steady her heart, attempting that box breathing thing she had read about. She stands and paces in guilty circles, holding the mask to her criminal chest, coming to terms with her forsaken future.

Kora grimly submits to the panic, if only for a moment.

"Fine," she says pensively, running a thumb down its cheek. "Fine, but no killing. Okay?"

If Kora didn't know any better, she'd swear she could feel the mask wink at her in response.

Another scene, another swap.

The night is listful and lonely, Mabel's leather jacket doing little to stymie the cold. The choice in apparel is not so much out of sentiment as it is pure pragmatism — she feels more comfortable with clothes that aren't recognizably Kora's, and abandoning the dainty little flannels for a work night is a given anyways.

She adjusts the jacket as she crawls through brush, smirking under her mask. It is a perfect fit. Karma feels good, hosting hunger, licking her lips in anticipation of the hunt ahead. She follows the main road, staying within the trees. Not for the first time, she is glad the citizens of Lake Leer haven't trampled all over nature's bounty in erecting the town. It hands her a lot of hiding places.

Her boots delicately dance through dirt, the footwear stolen from her father's shoe closet. Like the flannels, muddy sneakers bore no value when it came to intimidation, so they were quickly forgotten. The Doc Martens, on the other hand, were a welcome change.

She creeps up near the edge of the road, her fading jeans hooking on foliage. Karma tries to get a decent view of Lizzie's Liquor across the road, bramble batting at her mask. Karma shoves it aside with an annoyed hiss.

I bet Leatherface doesn't have to deal with this shit.

She efficiently eviscerates twigs with her new hunting axe, eager to try it out on something pumping blood. Her fingers stroke the handle, waiting with an inpatient grip. She makes it through the brush, only for one twig to swing back and thwack her face. Karma recoils, and in one last fit of frustration, she tears the plant loose of the dirt, throwing it aside.

"Fuck's sake," Karma hisses, wishing (not for the last time) that one could deal with nature as easily as you could the damned. She pulls out her dad's old smartphone from her leather jacket, something he had given her as a temporary replacement without much argument after she had told her story. Good thing, too, because her own phone belonged to her lady's lake now. She opens an audio recorder and hits play, tucking the phone into her back pocket. She'd edit it down later.

No killing!

Karma rolls her eyes, casing Lizzie's Liquor. Every so often, a car sails on by, thankfully unaware of the woman in the wild. The building is throbbing with music, as per usual, pulsating lights escaping the windows at irregular intervals. Her eyes skim over the side of the building, peeking into the back lot, a crowded little alleyway wedged in between several small businesses.

It was there the employee entrance of the bar lay, the one where Billy and his crew had handed her off to the two girls, their accomplices... the wicked little whores. And sure as sin, there they indulge in their smoke break, smoke rings twirling to dance upon the stars.

Karma licks her lips, tightens her trembling grip on the axe in anticipation. The two girls watch the road, cars passing with convenient sparsity, clearly chatting about something. One girl stops to squint, freezing on her way to take another drag. Karma raises an eyebrow, belatedly realizing the girl is looking right at her.

Oh, shit.

The dumb bitch must see some white mask lurking in the dark, just watching. A true horror movie scene if Karma had ever seen one (and Lord knows she had), but she had kind of intended on being something of a silent predator. The hum of an engine drifts ever closer, and just as the girl blinks, Karma darts from the bushes, placing the speeding delivery truck between her and her victim.

The girl doesn't see Karma vacate her cover — at least, she thinks she doesn't. Karma follows the truck down the road, her legs aching to keep up, some sort of enhanced speed propelling her. Before it can outrun her, Karma leaps, grabbing onto the top of the truck and pulling herself over.

Karma rolls, kicking off the swerving vehicle before the liquor-guzzling driver can really think twice about the thump above him. She sails through the air, aiming for the roof of Lizzie's Liquor with improvised grace.

Grace answers none of her prayers. She hits the edge of the roof with a whump, slipping and tumbling down the wall. With more pain than she expected, she lands with a flop in a dumpster, her shoulder blade cracking against the lip. Trash caves in around her as she sinks, Karma's body ebbing with invisible bruises.

"Ow."

Karma tilts her head, inhuman hearing granting her insight. One girl speaks from inside the lot, clearly too frightened to investigate, frantically whispering to her constant companion. "I swear, I saw this... this weird Japanese mask in the bushes! Over there!"

"I don't see anything."

"It disappeared when the truck came by!"

"Now you're just making shit up. That sounds like one of those cheap tricks horror movies use to compensate for bad writing."

"But then there was the big noise over there, the crash! You heard the crash!"

"It was probably just the alley cat. Rupert, or whatever you call him. He's always getting into things."

Rupert?

A rebukeful hiss slathers Karma's ear in saliva. Karma nearly jumps out of her skin, scowling at the mangy cat. Rupert appears to be equally unhappy to see her, giving her a wide berth. The clotted brown of his foul fur looks more like the dye of dumpster diving and less like a natural hair color, and he smells like he showers even less than Harrison. Karma turns up her nose in disgust, the superhuman smell currently a curse.

"Shoo!" Karma whispers furiously. "Piss off! Bad cat! Bad Rupert!"

The cat just hisses louder, claws unsheathing as he strikes with considerable courage, ripping new lacerations into the side of Karma's neck.

"Ow!" Karma whispers, trying to find some solid ground in the shifting refuge. "What are you *doing*, you little... Ow! Cut it out, you stupid shit!"

The cat lets out a rather loud meow, some insipid imitation of a battle cry. It lashes out again, claws slashing across Karma's shirt. "I'm going to... Come here!"

Karma finally scrambles to some stability in the pile of rubbish, jumping to tackle the pesty little creature. The cat bolts off like a bullet, leaving behind it a little shriek as it darts into the alleyway. Karma hears the two girls yelp in fright as Rupert runs as far as his little legs can carry him.

Great. Just fucking great. I am the worst serial k...

She feels her weaker half cast down her judgmental gaze.

...Serial investigator of all time.

Karma rolls her eyes again as she leaps out of the dumpster, believing she no longer has any time to waste. She dusts off her jeans, yanks her axe loose of all the rubbish, and darts through the alley with silent speed.

She emerges before her queries, who quickly begin to engage in the enticing act of hyperventilating. They scream out bloody murder when they see her, and Karma raises a finger to her mouth threateningly, waving the axe around in a vaguely intimidating fashion. They shut up immediately, drawing close to each other, eyes practically bulging out of their sockets.

Crybabies, Karma scoffs.

"Hello, girls," she drawls, one eye taking note of the lighter sticking out of the blonde one's purse. She takes it for herself, rolling it around in her palm. "Do you two know why I just *adore* fire?"

They both stare at her, wearing expressions of abject terror and... what looks like complicated confusion. She shrugs, striking the lighter, the flickering flame illuminating her mask.

"Fire..." Karma breathes. "Fire cleanses. Fire is objective, fire is fair, fire is violent *wrath.* It takes one and it takes all without any petty concerns for regret or morality. The strong survive, the weak wither away..." She tilts her head, cupping the dancing flame in her gloved palms, letting her words slow to a crawl. "It is chaos, beautiful chaos... tearing down all that does not compare to it, all that has failed to render it helpless. It is without complexity, and that sort of remorseless drive... Just so hard to find these days, don't you think?"

She snuffs the flame with a smug, unseen smirk, tucking the lighter into her leather jacket. Karma can't help but be proud, really — she had been so excited for the villainous monologues, and for something so spontaneous, she thought she had come up with a rather exciting one. It had *character,* even if it was a tad cliché.

Karma looks expectantly between the two girls, Blondie and... Ginger. Gingerie doesn't roll off the tongue so well, and "Redheadie" was even worse. Karma taps her foot against the pavement impatiently, as if to ask "Well?"

Blondie licks her lips nervously, hesitantly raising her hand. "Miss... miss..."

"Karma," she answers helpfully, gesturing to the mask. "Contract k... investigator."

"Miss Karma," Blondie says, sweating bullets, her eyes a tapestry of terror. "You..."

"Well, spit it out."

"You've... you've got a napkin stuck to your mask. Uh... there... the right cheek..." She gestures helpfully.

Karma blinks, a slow, irritated huff rolling through her body like the storm it shall precede. She quickly finds the traitorous thing, tearing an old, soda-slathered napkin free of her mask, throwing it away with no end of mirth.

Don't kill them, Karma. Just ask the questions and go home.

Karma silently mourns her soiled speech, purple eyes fixing the accomplices of her tormentors in place. "Monday night of last week, Billy Grant, Nicholas Nelson and Harrison... whatever the hell his last name is. You met with them. They brought a girl with them, beaten bloody, well close to death... and handed her off to you."

Karma raises her axe. Taking full advantage of her newfound strength, she seizes both girls and slams them against the alley wall. They squeal out in startled pain as Karma lines them up, lodging the axehead in the wall, blade framing Ginger's neck. She pins the handle tight against both girls' throats, looming over the two of them.

"Now... it's the next part of the story I'm not so clear on. And I don't want any questions, I don't want any pleas. I don't want you to wonder why I care about this, I don't want you to come up with some sob stories about this or that. You will answer my questions, and you will answer them honestly, because I know when someone lies... I can see right through you. Consider my generous mood to be a gift, not a privilege, and act accordingly."

Karma's eyes narrow on Ginger, who has started to cry, shuddering with every brush of the axe against her pale skin. *Spits in the occasional rude customer's drink. Had sex with Blondie in her mother's closet while said mother was sleeping?...Interesting. Public sex... cunnilingus under Blondie's table... Are there any chaste crimes here?*

God, did she pull these two straight out of a hentai? The people you find in lesbian bars...

"H-he just—" Blondie begins, and Karma's head pivots to meet her gaze. "Billy, he just... he messaged me the day before, told us what he was going to do. We didn't want to help, honest! He just... We don't have a lot to live on, I'm living with my mother right now, and..."

"I said no sob stories," Karma growls, debris running down the wall as she pushes the head of the axe in deeper. "Get on with it."

Almost got arrested stealing a vibrator... Oh, for god's sake... Nearly crashed a car because Ginger was eating her out... These two are lucky I don't believe in punishing lust.

"Money... he paid us, bribed us. Just to make sure the girl was there all night and had a shot or two of whiskey, and that was it! We didn't do anything to the girl, we just let her sit there and... did our own thing..."

Orgasmed six times in front of Kora Lynch's unconscious body... Oh, Jesus Christ!

"We... we're sorry," Ginger whimpers. "Please."

"I said no pleading!" Karma snaps, running low on her limited supply of patience. "You didn't touch K... the girl? Just... each other?"

"No, we absolutely didn't!" Blondie interjects, shaking her head furiously. "God, we're not like that!"

Truth. The two girls left Kora alone after bringing her to the bathroom.

Karma breathes a sigh of relief, ignorant of Blondie's nervous shuffling. "And this is all you know?"

Ginger nods. "Everything! We just took the money and left her there, we swear!"

Truth.

Karma steadies herself, reaching into her pocket to turn off her recording.

You have what you need. Run. Get the fuck out of here.

But they've seen her, they'll connect the dots eventually, her hair alone is pretty bloody distinctive, and besides, her tongue is still tingling, her fingers pricking with pins and needles, and *God,* how can one bask in the presence of such rampant lust without lusting herself?

Karma, go! You don't need to murder them! They're just unwitting accomplices, they aren't evil, just stupid and horny! This entire encounter is punishment enough!

"No, it's not," Karma mutters.

"What?" Ginger murmurs, looking at the killer in overwhelmed horror.

Karma! Bad Karma! Bad! Bad, bad, bad, bad! Get the fuck out, get the—

Karma smiles grimly as she curls her fingers around the axe handle. The masked murderer looks between the two girls, scared stiff, their life likely flashing before their eyes. Finally, the judge serves the sentence.

"Complacent accomplices... Guilty," Karma decides, letting the words linger.

"Wha-" Blondie begins, words wrung into wails. Karma's axe screeches forth in a second, tearing a trench through the wall and Ginger's neck. Blondie shrieks as her girlfriend's head twirls through the air in postmortem, gracing the air like a popped cork. Blood sprays against Blondie's face as she loses her voice, bits of severed bone sprouting from the stump. Ginger's body collapses, her last gift a pool of blood at her lover's feet.

Karma turns, twirling the axe as she readies the second execution, her body shivering with excitement, overbearing release running through her skin in waves—

Blondie brandishes a bottle of pepper spray, tears running down her face, and Karma finally realizes why she had been squirming so damn much.

Blondie fires the spray, blinding the killer and sending her stumbling. She ejects an exasperated grunt of pain, swatting at the air with her free hand, stumbling over the corpse's leg.

Blondie makes a run for it, darting out of the alley. Karma reaches out blindly, relying on her superior hearing, making an educated guess—

Her hand snatches the back of Blondie's shirt, and she throws the girl away from the road, granting her no quarter. Vision quickly begins to return to the infuriated killer, her murderous gaze locked upon Blondie.

Blondie moves to use the pepper spray again, but Karma is fast, too fast. Her axe whistles through the air, chopping Blondie's hand clean off, spurts of sweet blood painting Karma's shirt. The killer pays it no heed, lurching forward as Blondie squeals like a startled pig. Karma's fingers lock around the girl's throat, lifting her off her feet.

Blondie kicks and screams, an action rendered blackly comical in the way the stump of her right wrist sprays like a leaky faucet. "Good girl," Karma growls. "Bleed on me, that'll help."

The girl screams for help, Karma's hand tightening around her throat. The music in the bar is far too loud for the girl's breathless pleas to attract any attention. Smiling, Karma slams Blondie into the dumpster, the girl's back cracking under the weight of her superhuman strength, intensifying her screams.

"You need money? Dumpster diving, honey, you'll find something worthwhile!" Karma chuckles mirthfully, pulling the lighter from her jacket and throwing it into the dumpster. The fire takes no time at all to spread its ecstasy, wrinkled burger wrappers and alcohol-tainted napkins set alight in a matter of seconds. Without a moment to even mull over the potential of mercy, Karma slams down the lid, trapping the screaming girl with the burning rubbish.

"Oh, baby, my heart burns at the thought of you, don't you know," Karma croons, tipping the dumpster onto its side with her boot. "Oh, honey, this blaze is burning me up, inferno inciting, oh, don't you know, know, know!"

Blondie slams herself against the scorching lid, her screams violent, desperate, seasoned with the smell of burning skin. It is no use. Karma presses the dumpster against the wall of Lizzie's Liquor, scorching hot lid clamped tight with brick, trapping her victim in her homemade Easy-Bake Oven.

Karma slings her axe over her shoulders, nodding along to the earworm she can't get out of her head. She trudges out of sight, dancing and twirling into darkness, savoring every scream.

"Oh, this hellfire's gonna take my soul, lay me, slay me, soul ready to sow..."

The bloody axe trails behind her, smearing the sand of the shore with stains of scarlet. One boot wearily thumps in front of the other, then again, and again, the Karma Killer making her slow, battered stride. Her dirtied mask hangs from her other hand, no guilt in its eyes, no yearning for repentance.

It cannot mold its shape, it cannot move, cannot change. Even so, Kora still knows it smiles, widening its gruesome grin with every stolen soul.

Kora pants softly, an overwhelming struggle in every sinful step. Her feet toe the lake's soulless water, her right hand letting the axe slip. It plunks beneath the waves, sinking with ample anticlimax.

Kora raises her dead eyes, her body belonging somewhere else, somewhere worse than this. She raises the mask, the light of the moon shining through its narrow eyes. She lets one more tear crawl down her cheek, her body barely withholding an outburst of incriminating emotion.

"You go back to her," Kora whispers, hurling the mask away, returning it to Lake Leer.

Mabel has come to expect these midnight visits from a girl as odd as Kora Lynch. She's also come to expect the girl in some state of emotional distress, but this takes the despondent cake.

Mabel opens the door after the second knock, Kora overcome in tears. She staggers forward, and Mabel wraps her arms around the taller girl without hesitation. Kora buries her face in Mabel's shoulder, her mouth uselessly trying to form words, but she just chokes with every attempt. She shudders and sways against Mabel's chest, unable to breathe.

"Hey, hey, Kora, honey, it's okay, it's okay," Mabel coos, kicking the door close with her foot. "What the hell happened? Kora?"

Kora breaks into a coughing fit, nails digging painful purchase into Mabel's back. She holds on tight, so tight, so afraid to see her disappear, to see the only good thing in this fucked up life fade away in front of her. How could she know anymore?

She stares over Mabel's shoulder with bloodshot eyes, expecting Ira's face in every reflecting surface. "I... I can't..."

"Hey, it's just us. My mom is out, night shift, you know. Come on." Mabel squeezes Kora's free hand, slowly leading her through the living room, steering them over piles of dirty clothes and potato chip bags.

Kora takes reassurance in her only friend's confident grip, quivering, guilty, hopeless. Mabel steers them both down the hall, keeping them in a sort of mobile, tangled hug, an awkward concession that Kora wouldn't give up for anything. Mabel runs a hand through Kora's hair, her marijuana-coated breaths the greatest reassurance Kora knows.

"Está bien, Kora, it's okay, I got you," Mabel soothes softly as she shoulders open her bedroom door, the nature of Kora's predicament a distant concern. She grabs Kora's other trembling hand, interlocks fingers, squeezes. Kora shakes a little less, box breathing.

Mabel leans in, pecks Kora's cheek, lays the two of them into her bed. Thankfully, it's more than big enough for both girls. She lowers her hands to Kora's waist, pulling her close, their chests pressing together as Mabel keeps her in a protective embrace. Her hand stays with Kora's.

Kora lays there for a few minutes, sobbing uncontrollably, some sort of dam spilling open over God knows how long. Mabel strokes her hair with the utmost patience, humming softly and running delicate fingers down her friend's trembling form. Kora finally speaks, her voice overwrought with despair. "I'm... I'm sorry..."

"For what?"

"You..." Kora shudders, burying her face in Mabel's chest. "You don't want to know."

"Is this about the blood stains on your shirt?" Mabel gives her a knowing look, lifts her face up with one hand. "Kora... I forgive you. People terrorizing you isn't your fault."

"I don't like myself right now," Kora whimpers, unable to make any proper confession. To know that Mabel saw such damning evidence and immediately assumed self-defense... It was credibility no one else attributed to the silver-haired pariah. "Putting it lightly."

"I like you right now," Mabel breathes.

Kora hesitates, and then she goes in for the kiss, tears tainting the taste.

Mabel doesn't mind, nor is she anything but receptive when Kora rolls on top of her.

Kora stirs from her slumber in Mabel's bed, her jutting leg flinging her girlfriend's discarded clothes off the sheets, nourished nightmares violating her vision. Her heart beats beneath her bare chest, the blanket a bastion over the both of them. Kora swallows, presses a hand against her heart, the thumping slowly dying down.

Crack, crack, crack, crack, crack, crack—

The nightmares would never go away now, that much was for certain.

Mabel clings to Kora even in sleep, fingers tracing down her sensitive side. Kora steels her breaths. *Only another dream. Only another dream.*

"I'm going to get some water," Kora whispers to her sleeping partner. Mabel stirs, mutters some unintelligible response. She's probably still out like a bulb. Kora slowly pulls away, Mabel's hand running longingly across the sheets in her absence.

Kora trudges across the carpet, not bothering to dress. She doesn't intend on leaving Mabel's side for long, her heart speeding up with the swift return of perpetual paranoia. The panic is omnipresent, the guilt overbearing, and she cannot hide from it. She can merely look away, pretend it isn't there.

She steps into the kitchen, flips a light on, yanking the fridge open with more force than intended. Kora swears under her breath as several sauce bottles tip and nearly shatter, retrieving the little pitcher of purified water.

It'll be okay, it'll be okay, it's over, you're done, no more, you're here with Mabel, you've got an actual girlfriend, an actual, beautiful, kind girlfriend, you're going to be—

Kora turns to the counter, breath stolen from the face she cannot escape. She drops the pitcher, water splashing all over the kitchen tile.

On the counter sits her bloodstained kabuki mask, her hunting axe and her crossbow. The mask lays propped up against the crossbow, staring her right in the eyes, almost amused by her attempt to evade it — to evade her destiny.

And she screams, the mask's static expression empty of all but sadistic glee.

CYCLE SEVEN

Another Nail in the Coffin

/// **The morning after, October 20th. Eleven days until Halloween.**

It's snowing.

Kora Lynch imprints it with the footprints of a worn-out corpse, running with more vigor than she had ever managed in life. She is given little relief from the cold in Mabel's old leather jacket, the one her Hyde had taken a liking to. She almost wants to detest the gift just for that, but she can't bring herself to resent such an innocent gesture.

And she doesn't want this, she doesn't want to be this, but there is nowhere to run, and she gave up hope for a nightmare sick and twisted—

She nearly trips as she reaches the street, a blanket of morning blue an inappropriate background for her call from the grave. Snow flutters down with a lazy, picturesque quality, one ill-fitting to her panicked heart. The mask is tasting the icy air, held within her bloodied hands, not caring if it's seen, not caring if *she's* seen—

And what will she tell them? That she isn't her beneath the mask? That she loses control, that she falls for the frenzy, tingles for the thrill, adores the adrenaline, longs for the feeling of karmic rivers running down her skin?

That the monster she can't help but separate from herself keeps coming back, keeps reminding her, keeps laughing, keeps jeering—

Because it *is* her, it is the lord of her world, and its curled claws are hooked parasites upon her neck—

She hobbles into the heart of Lake Leer, the town that knows naught of the evil it invokes. Kora leans against a wall to take a breather, tucking the mask behind her as a woman and her dog walk by. The shih tzu gives Kora a wary glance, giving her a wide berth. Kora can't blame it, even with her homicidal face hidden away.

It's funny, really, how she's running to a police station to confess it all, and she's still too ashamed to show the world what's within.

She kicks off the wall of the pharmacy, breaking into another sprint.

And she feels more sorry for Mabel than anything else — to imagine getting a girlfriend, only for her to run out your door after screaming her lungs off in your kitchen, ignoring your best efforts to comfort her. Then, not long after, the news breaks out that your girlfriend was a fucking serial killer, and you had had her in your *house,* in your bed, in your arms, inside—

And Kora can't imagine, and she is somehow sorrier for that than she is for the murders.

The police station is in sight, her aching legs running for their life — like she knows Ira will find her, like she knows the murderer in her mind will rebel, turn her around. It's like she has nothing left to lose, and Kora knows she doesn't.

She looks both ways, the street clear. Kora darts across the road, feet kicking up snow. She's sorry, so fucking sorry, so foolish, so far gone... and all she wanted was to forsake that forest, save herself. Now, all these things that she's done? The weight of them is settling in, the pigs are crowding around her door, and it—

And she's draped in light, she's longing for death, and Kora hears the horn, turns halfway across the road, there's a truck, and she has no idea how the truck got there, the massive goddamned delivery truck certainly wasn't there when she looked down the road, and yet it was just inches from—

Kora barely has time to think, her hands flung high, her brute strength her first instinct. All she can wonder is, where the hell did this thing *come* from—

And then it plows right into her, sending her tumbling across the street. She flops down the road like a ragdoll, the first blinding pain shooting up her arm as bones crack and rip through her skin. The next two clench across her back like stone hands, vertebrae vivisected as the subsequent snaps send her body into a convulsive fit.

Kora slumps onto her side in scrapyard suffering, the pain of her misaligned spinal cord so fierce she forgets to feel. She fails to even open her eyes, her hand overcome with feverish pinpricks as it searches the road, her sense of touch rapidly fading. Her ears ring away any other noise, her breaths a slowing sensation, her bone-pierced hand bent backwards... bent far more than it should be.

Fuck... me...

Kora blinks blearily, the world wearing the visual impression of a psychedelic rave. The truck turns sideways and spans the road's width, horn blaring, as if the driver's lost all control. It tips onto two wheels, one side aloft, snow flying up with it.

And Kora realizes far too late what is about to happen, the truck's shadow snuffing away sunlight.

What she anticipates to be her last thoughts are decidedly ironic ones — how karmic a punishment this is.

The truck lands atop Kora with a deafening crunch, and her consciousness fades without delay.

Hell has no fury like a woman scorned...

For every beat of the heartbeat monitor, there is a listful lyric.

She has no mournful mind, no memories to mollify...

Kora can feel every shattered bone, her body a scorched pyre.

Hell has no fury like a woman scorned...

She feels someone ruffling above her, *smells* them, cherry perfume, dangling hair...

Abolish the angel, ashes adorn the sky...

Kora's eyes snap open.

She takes in the hospital room with weary noncommitment, a twitch of her head proving to be a mistake. Her neck audibly pops with the motion, setting off several seizing pains down her spine, mangled nerves firing off erratically. Kora spasms in her bed, gasping, a nurse leaning directly over her eyes.

Well, a woman's chest isn't necessarily the worst thing to wake up to, especially when it's as ample as this one. Kora groans, signifying her survival. The nurse's beautiful hair cascades down onto her shoulder as she fiddles with the machine besides her patient, and Kora's heart remembers how to beat.

That blood red hair is far too striking to belong to anyone else.

Kora shrinks away, digging her nails into her sheets. The nurse pulls into view, an omnipresent smirk on her patron's face.

"Kora," Ira purrs, just as recognizable in these immodest scrubs as she is in her regal robes. That, and her smirk... her incorrigible smirk. "Good morning, my wicked little wrathchild."

Kora blinks, the action somehow more arduous than death itself. It would be faster to list the places where her body *doesn't* hurt than where it does, and her mind is a storm cloud threatening, murky and impenetrable.

She reaches out, trying not to puke at the sight of the bloody bandages that wrap around protruding bone, her arm bent beyond recognition. She barely manages to brush her freezing fingers across Ira's cheek, but the sensation is enough to send her body into another trembling fit. She lets her arm fall besides its pair, suffering a splint, watching Ira in disbelief.

"You're..." Kora chokes, panting for breath. "Here... How?"

Ira chuckles, the door behind her locked. "You think so little of a *god,* Kora... You mortals, endlessly amusing..."

Kora blinks again, exercising the mountainous weights her eyelids have become. "You're a..."

"What did you think I was?" Ira teases from the edge of the bed, resting one delicate palm on Kora's shattered leg. "A common fae? Some sort of jinn, perhaps? The devil?"

"I didn't really think about it," Kora admits, wishing she could drag away the nest of broken bone and spider-webbed skin her body has become. "What are you a god of, then?"

"Meaning?" Ira asks softly, watching Kora with eyes she cannot read. Sins she cannot decipher, a mind too alien, too far out of mortal comprehension for Kora to even begin.

"Well, you know," Kora begins, pausing to break into a coughing fit. "Like... like, you know, in myths and stuff, there's gods... gods of earth, and fire, and things. What are you a god of?"

Ira rolls her eyes. "Well, if you must simplify a multifaceted individual so crudely... I suppose you could call me a god of wrath."

"Wrath," Kora whispers, fighting her numb lips. "It fits."

"Hm," Ira purrs. "You, on the other hand... Look at you, still surviving, despite everything. Hell..." She pokes Kora's backwards wrist, pain shooting the killer's arm. "Your body is all misshapen, and you never even stopped breathing."

"I suppose I have you to thank for that," Kora growls through grit teeth. She does not wish to thank anyone, particularly, not for this sham of a second chance.

"Hm, mostly. Some of it comes down to willpower, I must admit. And you seem to have that in *spades*."

Her tone is almost... admiring. Kora shivers. "Why are you here?"

"You were terribly injured, Kora," Ira coos, leaning in. "How could I not be here?"

"I've had worse," Kora says, and she has. Once.

"And I was there when you died, when you had no one. When the world had disappointed, when you had nothing but your name... I was there, wasn't I?"

"Maybe I was better off that way."

She's not sure whether the tears on her cheeks are from her ravaged body or the turmoil within. It's not pretty, either way.

And for the first time since they've met, Ira looks... hurt. She frowns, but before Kora can really register it as real, the smirk has supplanted any deviation. "No, Kora. You have become something... *more.*"

"What, the law? Justice?" Kora snarls. "I'm a murderer, a deviant who talks to herself in the mirror. I'm a killer, I'm a monster, I've become something I can't... I can't look at myself without the mask on. It's a fucking drug, that's what it is, and you gave it to me, you came in and you *took* everything!"

And she doesn't know when she started yelling, but it's all free before she can cage it.

Ira's eyes flash, the nerves of her cornea deepening in color, and Kora shrinks back. Ira grabs hold of her collar, her leg pressuring Kora's shattered knee, black spots flooding her subject's vision.

"You best be grateful, child," Ira whispers, the threat an implication, disguised within pleasantries. "There is a time and a place to bite the hand that feeds... and this is not it."

Kora swallows, beads of sweat running down her immobilized neck. "I'm sorry."

Ira doesn't lessen the pressure, her free hand trailing up Kora's cheek. "We made a deal, Kora. You made me a promise... You bathed in my blood. You think of me as something horrifying... Well, you should see what comes when you forsake such an intimate oath, young one.”

Kora shakes her head, just enough to get the point across.

The fountain. Of course it was blood, of course it was *hers*...

“Then why the hesitation?” Ira sighs, her lips just flattering Kora’s ear, barely grazing the skin. “Why the fear? Why the pathetic little displays of emotion? You could be better. You are mine, I made you anew... Don’t you think you ought to display a little loyalty?”

“I...” Kora’s stricken, paranoid eyes meet Ira’s. “I’m... I don’t like feeling guilty. I... I lost control. The first guy, he deserved it, he... he was a monster, but... the other two... I don’t think I needed to kill them. I...”

“What’s done is done,” Ira soothes. “You have a gift. You have knowledge no one else does, strength no one else possesses. Use it. A weapon is only as dangerous as its wielder. You want to kill? Find the scum of the earth. Hunt them down, be their bane, make them rue the mask. The art of restraint is something well worth practicing, Kora... it will make the following hunts so much more satisfying.”

Kora wonders how much longer she has on this earth, but what scares her isn’t that. It’s the thought that she’s not hoping for a long run. Ira leans in further, pulling Kora closer, pulling her into a...

A hug.

And despite all that’s happened, despite the fact that this is a homicidal god dressed as a nurse, one that has forced her to kill, forced her to fear her own face, her own mind...

She so rarely gets a hug.

And so she leans in, broken bones crying, this mess of malformed skin and failing organs resting against Ira’s chest. Ira runs her hand over Kora’s back, spinning soothing circles. Kora breathes, tears running down in full force now, the sobs loud and messy.

Eerily enough, Ira does not seem to mind.

If her arms weren’t broken, Kora just might return the gesture.

“Do you miss your mother, little Karma?”

Kora stiffens painfully, her mother’s lullabies resurfacing in her mind, the stories by the fireplace, the painting they did together...

“Yes,” Kora murmurs. “Yes, I do. Very much.”

“I miss mine as well,” Ira says simply, but she knows it is enough for Kora to understand. And Kora does, with a heavy heart and a malignant mind.

“I’m sorry.”

“I do not wish that feeling on anyone,” Ira continues, a hand brushing Kora’s hair. “Not one more... Never again. The world is cruel... even to gods."

"I wanted to fix it all as a kid," Kora mutters, ashamed to remember she was ever so naive.

"I know. It's why I picked you."

Kora blinks, squirming in Ira's arms, this homemade haven.

"I am... bound to inaction, by circumstances outside my own control," Ira confesses, the words possessing a bitter edge. "But if I act indirectly... well, there's no rule against that."

"Loophole."

"Of course," Ira smirks. "For the gods, this sort of thinking is... customary."

"I don't want anyone else to end up like me," Kora sighs, her heart a steadying thump.

"Then don't let them," Ira implores.

Kora licks her lips, listens to her own trembling breaths. She finds the thud of her heart, her aching heart.

"I won't."

Ira smiles. "That's my girl."

Before she catches herself, Kora smiles in return. "I have one request," she ventures.

"Yes, my child?"

"The person who killed my..." Kora hesitates, knowing the meaning will get across. "I want to hunt them. I want to kill them."

"Then show me you're worthy of such a reward," Ira lilts. "And I will light the way."

Kora nods, without a second thought.

"For now," Ira continues, "we need to get you back into fighting shape. There is a girl who needs your help."

"I should be dead. I'm not so sure I can fight, or even walk..." Kora looks down to her shattered body. "Not unless you can do something about that."

"I can. Let me show you your query, little hunter..."

Ira's delicate fingers cup Kora's cheek, tearing away the fabric of her reality. And she trips, and she fades, falling, hurtling into a haze, overtaken in the ocean...

And they said it was only wine, they said it wouldn't get me all that drunk, Nick said, I thought I could trust him, he seemed so nice, and that's just what I need in this life, this shitty miserable lonely insufferable life, oh god I feel so good...

It's too hot, get these clothes off... and Nick wants to watch, and I can't tell him no, and his friend comes in, and it's too late, and they're feeling at me, and it should be nice, but something's off, my skin's prickling, I keep falling away, almost like I want it, maybe I should scream...

I can't, really, the headache's too loud, there's a hammer battering its way through my skull, and every flash of the camera doesn't help, and I wish I hadn't left my underwear lying around, but they like it, they're giggling, are they smelling it, what's happening, what's...

Karma gasps for air like she's been tugged out of the lake.

She blinks under her mask, Ira's lips upon her forehead, her arms up her revived sides.

"You put my face on," Karma breathes.

"And?"

"It's good to be back," Karma smirks. "I almost lost myself there. Uhh... are we on a first name basis?"

Ira ignores her question. "The girl is named Violet Vance."

"Billy's crew. Couldn't leave things well enough alone, could they?"

"No. Laurie and Olivia are with them."

Karma involuntarily growls like the predator she's become.

"Karma?"

"I'm fine," she replies.

Ira runs a hand down Karma's warm, throbbing arm... and Karma gives it a stretch, astonished to see that every inch of her body has been eased into recuperation. Every pile of dust reverted to bone, every cut and scratch faded into scars, every ache submerged.

Karma smirks, and forms a fist. "Oh, I am *more* than fine."

"Your weapons, they will come to you," Ira says, jumping off the bed and dusting off her scrubs. "Give them hell."

"They'll get it," Karma agrees, hopping off the bed herself. Ira waves her hand, a chunk of the wall simply vanishing. Nothing crumbles or falls, the building standing the same as it ever has. "I don't have time to go home and fetch some crossbow bolts. Mind delivering some with my favorite toys?"

"Not at all," Ira smirks. "Karma?"

Karma turns to face her, silhouette framed in the star-speckled square in the wall. "Yes, my lady?"

Ira widens her eyes, a confident grin forming on her lips. "Do take care of yourself. It breaks my heart to see you in such states of disrepair."

"Anything for a lady so lovely," Karma responds, vanishing into the lonely night.

"I'm just getting into the Halloween spirit, darling," Karma says softly. She adjusts her chin upon the smaller girl's shoulder, hand in hers, kabuki mask hoarding the heat of the convulsing crowd. The lights pulsate in pinks and purples, bittersweet color clinging to her — a fitting palette for her last day as something properly human.

Chelsea, if Karma remembers the girl's name right, sways with the masked killer. Her tempestuous body is in faultless tune with the throb of the beat, every swell of the song, every drop of the bass. Her body is lithe and nimble, curves accentuated with the tightness of her dress, swelling chest pressing against Karma's warm, starving body.

Karma licks her lips, watching the bathroom in the corner, waiting for her prey to vacate their nest.

And the song begins to play.

Bid your blood boil, mar and maim as I may...

"What are you supposed to be?" Chelsea responds, yelling over the thundering drum and bass.

Karma shrugs. "A serial killer."

I think you'll be some easy prey.

"That's..." Chelsea begins.

Karma rubs her second face against the girl's neck, taking in the sensual scent of her curled blonde hair. She could almost taste her from that alone.

"That's kind of hot," Chelsea giggles, the stench of alcohol escaping her mouth.

Karma smirks. "Oh, you know it... If I weren't here on business, well..."

She growls, dragging sharp nails down the girl's neck, letting them slip just down her back.

Chelsea sharply inhales. "What... what kind of business do you have here, of all places?"

"Oh... pest control," Karma smirks. "But don't tell anyone I said that, you know. Managers wouldn't want patrons to know about all the... rats, scurrying about..."

"I won't," Chelsea responds, almost moaning as Karma takes in her smell again, holding her close as they dance, two evils entangled.

"Speak of the devil," Karma mutters. Nick's head pokes out of the bathroom, a drunken, half-dressed Violet Vance nearly trampled by the dancers. Harrison shakes her awake, spitting out some undoubtedly educated words.

The two don't plan to stop with the roofie.

"The devil?" Chelsea asks. "Who's the devil?"

Date rape.

Karma's eyes brim over with rage, fury, tranquil hatred.

And for once, the guilt is gone.

"I am," Karma answers, taking the title with pride. She pulls away, drifting down her hand to slap Chelsea's ample rear. Chelsea blushes intensely, nails digging into Karma's leather.

"I'll be back for you later," Karma says softly. "After I deal with these rats. We'll have... fun. Lots of it. You got that?"

Chelsea nods. "Don't make me wait, Ms...."

"Call me Karma," she growls, letting Chelsea fade into the crowd.

Unforgotten. Unforgiven.

And as she slips towards Nick and Harrison, she ponders, plans her next perverse pleasures.

She looks back to Chelsea in the crowd, and she knows what she's done.

You killed a husband and wife out of envy, little blondie. And there's just too many damn sinners in this town...

It is good, then, Karma concludes, that all things come to change.

CYCLE EIGHT

Spite Alone Holds Me Aloft

/// **October 21ˢᵗ. Ten days until Halloween. Minutes after the school slaughter.**

Let's heed your hopes again, all those vices you hold so dear / I won't look quite the same next year / New name, new face, let's make this right / Still waiting for the ideal identity to blunt my bite...

It is a harrowing, twisted song, a trait slightly tempered when you consider the music artist goes by the name of Quackpot Hammerhead Deathducks.

Even so, it fits the scene.

Kora Lynch stumbles into an alleyway, the scourging storm around her relentless. The rain batters down her body, a blasphemous baptism. The shuddering buildings close in around her as she slithers out of sight, slipping onto her hands and knees. She gags as the weight of what she's done comes right up, tattering her throat, bile swimming off in puddles and streams.

The moon hangs high above her, foretelling her forsaken future.

"You didn't have to do it," Kora growls, the taste of her expelled dinner still tainting her tongue. "You didn't have to k... ki... God!" she sobs, another round of vomit emptied onto the pavement.

"How can you even say that, Lynch?" the killer asks, looming over Kora's helpless body. "That was the most fun I've had in a *century.* Gods, I'm just— I'm fucking exhilarated, Lynch, I really am. I haven't felt this good in ages. I could *fuck* the world right now."

"You could pretend to care," Kora hisses, curling up in dirty water. The rain nearly drowns out her words, a villainous vapor to shut the world away, leaving her to her fate. She raises her pounding head, facing down the murderer she's made. "You *get off* on this?"

And there Karma stands, an identical twin to her whimpering shadow, but... different. Confident, buzzing with energy, propelled by enthusiasm. And it's all wrong, it's all so horribly wrong, and she is so horrified it wears her face, and she is so glad it hides that stolen face under a mask of its own-

"Yes," Karma answers, unashamed. "Of *course* I get off on it. The thrill of the hunt, Lynch. You should know what that is. You used to go with your dad all the time. What, is this intolerable because our prey can plead?"

"That's one fucked up way to moralize this," Kora snaps. "That wasn't a hunt. That was a massacre!"

"Oh, but it *will* be a hunt," Karma says pointedly, pelting rain bouncing off her mask. "Oh, that Laurie... I can see why you were so fond of her, Lynch, she's good. She knows how to put up a fight. She knows how to run. I could have a long, slow dance with her, with that crafty little mind of hers... I'm breathless just *thinking* about it."

"What the hell are you?" Kora breathes.

Karma laughs, like the question beckons forth an obvious answer. "Oh, Lynch. I'm you. I've been you all along. I just know how to bite back."

"That what you call it?"

"No," Karma meets her paler self's eyes, purple fury simmering within the mask's slits. "I call it warranted wrath. Rightful retribution. How can there be anything wrong with me, Lynch, when nothing in this world is ever right?"

"You're a monster," Kora whispers, tears swept away with the rain.

"I am," Karma agrees, crouching beside her. "And right now, that's what this world needs. A necessary evil."

"I don't need you."

Karma tilts her head, an invisible smile forming on the mask's static lips. "What was that, Lynch?"

"I don't think I need you anymore," Kora stands, knees wobbling beneath her. "Get out of my head. Get out of my life. Find a new killer, one that wants the job."

"Oh, Lynch," Karma chuckles, somehow looming over her

progenitor as she rises in response. "You think anyone *wants* to end up like this?"

And to that, Kora has no reply.

Karma giggles, backing Kora towards the wall with an air of consummate condescension. The killer reaches out, gloved finger softly drifting down her cheekbone. "So much potential, Lynch... and it comes down to me to utilize it."

"No one asked you to," Kora growls, hand wrapping around a crossbow bolt, one of many beneath their — her — jacket. "And no one ever will."

And with her enunciated epitaph, Kora drives the tip of the bolt towards her captor's neck. The Karma Killer lazily grabs Kora's wrist, snapping it in one indifferent motion, the crack deafened with a clap of thunder. Kora tears up, falling to one knee, the bolt uselessly hitting the ground.

Karma chuckles, yanking Kora up by her limp, battered wrist, ignoring the girl's pronounced pain. "Finally, Kora, some fucking *guts!* It's a shame you didn't show those off earlier... or, you know, against literally anyone else."

"I'm you," Kora says faintly, barely able to spit out the words. "I can handle me. I can take it."

"Oh, humans," Karma replies, drawing a crossbow bolt of her own from her jacket. "You all think that. The naivety, it's... adorable."

Karma lashes out with a sudden roar, pinning Kora's arm to an alley wall with the quarrel. The bolt reprimands reality as it cracks stone, blood running down Kora's skin in a splintered web. She screams and tugs, feeling nerves twist and rip as she yanks, her arm locking up. Her struggle does her no good.

Karma watches the scene with a condescending click of her tongue and a shake of her head. "The strength lies with me, Kora. That's the thing. You've always been a coward, hiding behind your books, your headphones. You let people kick you and trample you, you let them do whatever they please, all because you can't handle the thought of ripping off that bandage. You can't run from your problems forever. You can't run from *me* forever."

The predator's eyes pulsate with a pearlescent purple, trapping Kora with no small amount of greed. Kora shudders as her sinister self speaks.

"I am Kora Lynda Lynch, the way the world wanted us."

The rain howls down, thunder tantalizing terror, as Karma draws two more crossbow bolts. Kora tries to kick at her, but Karma breaks both legs, crushing them between her boot and the wall, one after another. Kora screams, suffering met with cold indifference.

"Alone, broken, loathing, bitter, left behind..."

Karma twirls the other crossbow bolt, dragging it up Kora's helpless body. It slithers up her side, trails up her neck, leaves hesitation marks.

"Miserable, rejected pariah... mangled, afraid, sick of it all..."

The crossbow bolt traces Kora's jawline, Karma's mask leaning in close to enjoy the girl's palpitating breaths. Her fear. Her regret. Her abject despair.

Karma shares it with her.

"There is no light in the dark, no fire in this winter..."

She places her free hand upon Kora's left cheek, the bolt proving hesitant. Even she doesn't want to do this, not to someone so...

But that's life, isn't it? It crushes the best of us. It finds those with real good in them and buries it. Kora... she's already lost.

Yeah, that's life. Starting tonight, Karma's paying it back.

"I need only spite to survive, to carry on..."

Karma rests her forehead on Kora's, the girl stunned into silence. Already, Karma mourns.

"You need more, more I cannot give."

Karma pulls away, purple eyes kin to their kinder pair.

"I will take you with me, Kora. It's the best I can do."

Karma plunges the bolt into Kora's cheek, blood bubbling free, arrowhead seeking the space separating skin and skull.

Kora screams bloody murder, and Karma wrenches the bolt upwards, severing flesh from bone, any remains limply flapping into the storm. Karma works her way upwards, tears running down her face, rightfully hidden from the world. Kora's body spasms in her grip, unwillingly jarring the bolts that hold her to the wall. Karma squeezes her tight, reaching her forehead, one of Kora's eyes starting to droop forward.

"Just die!" Karma screams, tugging the bolt across her forehead with reckless abandon, the mutilated body drenching her in a crimson tide. Karma howls in anguish, a symphony with her victim's own pain. The peak of Kora's face comes loose, tearing loose like a wet bandage. The head falls forward, and Karma slams it back against the wall, Kora's left eye severed. It falls free and loses itself somewhere down her killer's shirt.

"Die, so they don't hurt you! Die, so I don't hurt you! Die, so you can be happy! Just..."

Karma rips the bolt out and slams it back in, detaching nerves as she cuts free Kora's right cheek, slicing open the skin with emotional brutality. More crimson cascades, Kora's remaining eye caught in the arc, split in half and spitting juices.

"Save!"

Karma roars in anguished anger, castigating flesh and muscle, shattering Kora's exposed skull against the wall. Kora's face tears free of her body, pulled from her corpse like paper. It spits its bloody last all over Karma's gloves, the body lifelessly slumping forward.

"Yourself!"

Karma screeches herself hoarse, splaying the remains against the wall and throwing herself away from the crime. She looks up at the moon, the mute, mocking moon, howling at the heavens like some sort of broken banshee.

"You did this to us! You did this, you hear me? You judgmental, heartless, *vindictive,* hopeless world! You wanted a killer? You got one! You fucking got one! I'll kill everyone here if I have to! Cut every last cancer out of this planet, I promise you that! I'll kill them all!"

The moon submits in somber silence.

Karma pads forward, weeping, cursing every last name she can conceive, bitter with every last word. She clutches her former face, the killer falling to her knees. She can do no more than weep, cry and curse, sob and swear out every imaginable vengeance.

Karma shudders, defiant in the cold. Her hands spread the face out, turning it over. She presses it against her mask with a sickening *squelch,* bits of shredded skin and severed vessels squelching against her mask. The blood trickles down her chin, chunks of flesh caught in the collar of her shirt.

And Karma is sorry, more sorry than she ever will be again, mourning innocence in exile. Her hands tremble and her teeth chatter, but she holds the former face to hers, knowing it is the last time she will ever bear it.

Survive. She will survive. On spite alone, she shall survive.

And when she has found them all, when she has saved every sullied soul, when she's paid back every vindictive villain, the lynchers at large will need more than thoughts and prayers to document the destruction.

Survive.

Kora is running on two hours of sleep, and somehow, that's not what's fueling her nagging lethargy.

She can see why her meek, innocent shadow had had so much trouble with this prison, the aimless activities, the lengthy lectures. She wouldn't even try the lunch, for the sake of her mental and physical health. The inside of her own mutilated face had looked more edible.

High school, Kora had decided, was a special kind of hell. It was the same conclusion she had landed on years before, but the methodology was different, her mind a brand new beast. It was funny, really, the ways in which she had changed and the ones she hadn't. She didn't wish to be here. She didn't need to be here, not unless they had a class on murder, and even *then...*

She is glad they don't, honestly. This ghastly institution was perhaps the only place that could find a way to make elaborate killings *boring.*

And for that matter, really, it's hard not to think about all the gruesome murders that had happened last night, within this school's very grounds. Normally you'd shut down this preparatory prison over this sort of thing, she thought, but no such thing had happened. It was a fact that she almost took as an insult, a very slander to her face that her art hadn't been good enough to be treated like any other mass killing. Everyone had just insisted on going back to normal, much to her chagrin, even as four students were absent... for good reason.

Should be, *will* be, five. Once she gets her hands on that little vixen...

Kora exits the classroom in bubbling anticipation, wrapping her fingers around her wrist like her other self used to. It was all too much. She missed the kabuki mask, she missed her face, she missed the thrill, she missed the hunt... This lass she wore was ugly, routine.

That girl she saved last night, Violet Vance, passes her on the way out, giving her a captivated glance. Kora remembers now that she spoke out loud in class, though she fails to find any misfortune in the matter. Violet knows Kora is the Karma Killer... so what? Kora saved the girl's life. She better be grateful.

Violet doesn't say a word. Kora winks as she passes, internally chuckling as the girl blushes bright and darts into the crowd. Cute.

Kora idly hums as she retrieves her headphones, the girl's former distraction one that the body's current owner happily adopts. She walks with the killer's trademark gait, a deliberate, looming pace down the hall, one no one notices. After all, no one acknowledged Kora Lynch in the first place, much less a subtle change in her behavior.

The school's PA intercom crackles with life. "Kora Lynch to the principal's office. Kora Lynch to the principal's office."

Kora lets out a long-suffering sigh. How many detentions had she accumulated over the semester again?

She pads off towards the principal's office, trying to remember his name. She really seemed to have trouble with remembering the bit players in her life. Moore... Moore? Yes.

It doesn't take her long to get to his office, the school sheltering little distance to cross.

Kora enters the office, her principal clearly overwhelmed and distraught, several police officers lined up around him. Her old friend, captain Lumis, stands with the principal, guns on every officer's hip.

So they did *notice my work. And here I thought I'd have to bring a gun next time.*

Kora has to resist smirking. If she didn't have an interest in keeping her cover, she'd really show them that they'd need more than those peashooters to deal with her. And it is tempting, so tempting, because just the *thought* of slaughtering these corrupt cowards really gets her going.

But Kora keeps her cool, mimics surprise, assuming false emotion with ease. "Uh... Captain Lumis... what is this? I don't suppose this is about the... the bar thing, because I don't think you'd have found any proof of my... intentionally being there..."

Gods, mimicking her former form's mild manner drives her up a fucking wall.

"Not one to stay out of trouble, are you, Ms. Lynch?" Lumis smiles, his men mere mannequins, waiting for his command. Pathetic. They really couldn't bear facing an unarmed teenage girl without outnumbering her twelve to one, could they?

Kora shrugs, projecting an air of innocence. "I can't say I have any idea what you mean."

"Let me get straight to the point," Lumis says, settling down in the principal's chair. Moore meekly steps aside, shrinking into the corner. No surprise there. "I'm sure you're aware of Lake Leer's recent string of murders."

Fuck it. Subtlety bores her.

"Vaguely," Kora shrugs. "I'm a high school student, Mr. Lumis. I spend my time doing my homework and watching horror movies, not searching the web for nasty murder scenes. I believe that's your line of work, if LLPD works at all."

"It is," Lumis replies tersely. "And my line of work has led me to a number of strange accounts, Ms. Lynch. Accounts I'd like to consult you about. Sit down?"

"I'll stand." She doesn't move.

"Very well," Lumis agrees as he unveils a couple photos, sliding them across the table. Blondie and Ginger, huddled up together, all grins and laughter. "Do you recognize these two women, Ms. Lynch?"

Hellfire, hellfire, gon' take my soul, lay me, slay me, soul ready to sow...

"Yeah. They were the two chicks that helped Billy implicate me. What about them?"

"They were found brutally murdered, Ms. Lynch."

Kora barely remembers to widen her eyes, put a shocked hand over her mouth. "Oh, God," she croaks out, faking a couple tears. "What... what happened?"

"Well, Ms. Lynch, they seem to have angered our suspect." Lumis slides another piece of paper across the desk, a handmade drawing. It is a sloppy recreation of her very own kabuki mask, her face, and for all its reliance on vague details, it *is* rather close. An eyewitness' description. She takes a peek through the window to his soul, just to make sure.

Yes, Laurie thought she could get away with snitching. Kora lingers a time longer, intrigued by what she finds in his mind.

"So, your murderer dresses like some sort of nutty 80s slasher," Kora says, pretending to gather herself. "Why are you telling me this? Why does it matter?"

"Last night, as I'm sure you're aware, this 'Karma Killer' murdered another four students. I'm sure you know them. Billy Grant, Nicholas Nelson, Harrison Krueger, and Olivia Kemp. Laurie Thompson was also attacked, but she survived."

Nothing Kora didn't already know. She glances at him numbly. "Okay." Her voice trembles, and she knows Lumis takes her barely-restrained rage as a display of rapt anxiety.

"Our eyewitness—"

"Laurie."

Lumis frowns.

Kora shrugs. "Who else could it be? You said everyone else was..." She swallows, sniffing. "You know."

"Our eyewitness. They drew us up this mask, pointed out silver hair. Informed us of some... grotesque crimes, on their part." Lumis settles back in his chair with an air of self-satisfied confidence. "Our eyewitness claims that the killer shared your voice. They believe you are the culprit."

"That's ridiculous, I—"

"And, Ms. Lynch, the victims are all people you have come into conflict with in the past. When our eyewitness made their claim, it was hard not to notice that this looks like a series of revenge killings."

"It wasn't me," Kora says, projecting weakness. "I'm telling you, it wasn't me."

"Ms. Lynch... I don't mean to cast your words into doubt, but the evidence is not favoring your argument in—"

"You know, it's funny," Kora snaps, shedding her last fabricated tear. "You haven't meant to doubt me twice now."

Lumis narrows his eyes.

"Captain," Kora says. "Have you ever heard of Jackie Winters?"

He shakes his head. "Ms. Lynch, if you can stay on topic—"

"Oh, I am," Kora asserts, plucking her phone from her pocket. "May I show you something?"

Lumis huffs, nods his head. Kora opens her phone's Internet browser, typing into her search bar. "The funny thing is, captain, I never had problems with Laurie. She had problems with me. And, if you had done a scant amount of research, you'd see I'm hardly the first person she's had this sort of pattern with."

"Lynch, what on earth are you claiming—"

Kora slides her phone over the desk, open to a headline. *Local high schooler Jackie Winters hospitalized after failed suicide attempt — another victim of America's chronic cyberbullying crisis.* "Scroll if you like."

He does, his poker face failing.

She suffers herself the slightest smirk, just out of sight. "Jackie Winters was an old acquaintance of mine. She used to date Billy Grant — I couldn't tell you why, maybe she didn't know what he was really like, but she did. Now, Laurie, our resident envious eyewitness in question, wanted Billy, and he wanted her, and they'd do things behind Jackie's back. But Laurie wasn't satisfied.

"So, Laurie spread it around her friends, on Discord, Instagram, in school, wherever she could, that Jackie here had herpes. She knew Billy would finally abandon ship once he heard that, and he did. That wasn't enough for her, though. With Laurie, it never is. So, Laurie started flaunting her new relationship with Jackie's former boyfriend. She goaded her friends into terrorizing Jackie, at school and out. And you know what happened?"

Kora points at one word. *Hospitalized.*

"I didn't know what Laurie was like until I got on her bad side. I asked her out. Turns out she *really* doesn't like the idea of being with another woman. The reason you found me black and blue that one night? It's because she had her boyfriend and his lackeys beat the shit out of me and dump me into that bar."

Lumis shifts uncomfortably.

"Now, even I'll admit her story isn't half bad. But I'm not a murderer. I'm not capable of it. Hell, *look* at me. I think Billy or his friends would've flattened me like they did the other night. I'm not even physically capable of it if I *wanted* to. And when you consider your particular witness' history... well, it sort of looks like she's using this to further her own agenda, doesn't it?"

"Ms. Lynch, be that as it may, that doesn't change the particular selection of the targets—"

"No," Kora shrugs, leaning onto the desk. "No, you're right, it doesn't. And I won't lie, I didn't like most of the people who died one bit. But that doesn't mean I wanted them dead. I just wished they'd leave me the hell alone. Kind of the same way I feel about you, captain."

Kora smirks wolfishly, her words a weapon. He has completely abandoned composure, taking in the threat. She almost hopes he'll order his boy toys to raise their guns.

Kora stretches out, looking around the room. "And I take it the school will actually close down for a bit after today, while you guys investigate? I'm guessing you just wanted to ambush your assumed killer when she didn't expect it?"

"Yes," Lumis admits.

"Well, I didn't expect it. I didn't expect to be your scapegoat a second time, captain. You got me there. Then again, I hear this sort of thing happens a lot with you."

Lumis glares at her, unable to rein back his rage. "And what is that supposed to mean, young lady?"

Kora smirks, his sins her sharpened spear. "Me and my dad, we have a family friend. Kevin Whitesell." The first sentence slips out an undiscovered lie, indistinguishable from her every truth.

Lumis stiffens, eyes widening. "What—"

"Well, I *should* say had. He's in jail now, you know that. Has been for a while. I know you have the press convinced that he used to deal drugs to high school students, but I knew him for years. I know he was just a little too fond of your wife, in a way that you forgot to provide, and just like Laurie, you got a little upset that she just... hm. Lost interest?"

Lumis' face curls hideously into an expression of astonished abhorrence. Kora smiles, unable to help herself. "Captain... I hate to say it, but it looks like *you've* also got a personal grudge. I am a goddamn twig, officer. I can barely get the cap off a jar of jam, and you're accusing me of *murder*? Cause you don't like my dad, right? He's told me all about all that."

He is silent, fuming, his past misdeeds her open book.

"So, Captain," Kora says, glancing at the officers around her. "Maybe once you find some credible evidence, you and me can chat again. But for now, I think we can agree that your witness' claims are... well, unfounded."

The air twitches behind her, and she notes the near-silent motion of a gun unclipping from its holster. She doesn't move.

Lumis motions at the man. He returns the gun. Kora smirks victoriously, breathing in slowly.

The police captain speaks, his voice betraying his vindictive acceptance. "I could bury you for talking to me like this, Lynch."

"Bury me like you buried an innocent man? Maybe you ought to do a better job attending to your wife and that won't be a problem."

She lets the words wage her war. He shakes in his seat.

"You may go. But keep those... anecdotes to yourself, Lynch. For your sake."

"The same to you," Kora shrugs, slinging her backpack over her shoulder, struggling not to burst into laughter as she catches Principal Moore's stupefied gaze. "People already hate me here well enough, Captain."

"Fine," Lumis growls low. "Get the hell out of here."

Kora barely has the time to even concoct a congratulatory strut before she spies Laurie Thompson.

Typical. The bane of her existence, pissing on every blasted victory.

Laurie, however, exceeds expectations. She ducks out of sight, a scowl on her face, and Kora smirks, stretching out her stiff arms. She takes longer than is strictly necessary, lets the girl take in the sight of her cuffless hands. Laurie clearly thinks Kora doesn't see her, trying to blend in with the crowd.

Sorry, lovely, Kora thinks. *I could pick up your scent anywhere.*

Laurie waits, just watching, and Kora experimentally spins on her heel. *Say, Laurie, don't suppose you're dumb enough to shadow a superhuman serial killer...?*

Laurie follows, ducking through crowds, around corners, a hood thrown over her head.

She *is* trying to shadow a superhuman serial killer. What's worse, she actually thinks it's working. Kora could laugh.

Kora throws the poor woman a bone, lets her leer. Instead, the bemused killer alters her path, heading for the bathrooms. She knows Laurie wants to ambush her, so she'll let her. After all, Kora is in no danger... and she could use a good laugh.

Within the crowd, she catches the chime of an unlocking phone, casts back one eye. Laurie ducks behind a taller student. Kora keeps walking, approaching the bathrooms.

Interesting little rabbit, Laurie was. Endlessly interesting.

Kora steps into the bathroom, letting her abnormal hearing act as her watch dog. She bends over the sink, washes her face over, waits for her query. She stares at herself in the mirror, purple eyes glittering in the glass, exhausted and soulless.

Twenty seconds pass. Thirty. She considers the *clack* of Laurie's overpriced shoes outside, surveys her shadow slipping by the crack of the door, smells her distinctive perfume wafting between its hinges. Kora cracks her neck.

Finally, she opens the door. Kora turns slowly, faking disinterest. Her face molds effortlessly to every lie.

"Leg Singular, huh?" Laurie asks, her voice quivering. "Cool band."

Kora looks down at the band shirt she's wearing, battered and fading. What is it with punk bands and their ridiculous names? "You've never heard them," Kora says dismissively, knowing the truth in her words.

Laurie tries to make her approach a brave one, even as her knees wobble. Kora can practically taste her fear, savoring the sensation. It's a good thing Laurie's such a coward, honestly. The sheer amusement she's getting out of this adorable little attempt at bravery is the only thing keeping the girl alive.

"Maybe not," Laurie admits, wringing her hands nervously. "I just didn't want to start the conversation with calling you a murderer and a lunatic."

Kora rolls her eyes. "What're you playing at, Thompson? You're not exactly a good shadow, nor are you the image of intimidation."

"I just want to hear you say it," Laurie growls, seemingly surprised by the kick in her own voice. "I want you to admit you killed all my friends. I know you won't hurt me here. Not in public."

"We are in a bathroom with no cameras."

"Admit it," Laurie says, breaths hitching. "Just admit it. You clearly don't care. You don't have a heart. Why can't you just say it?"

Kora lumbers forward, looming over Laurie, no emotion embracing her eyes. She presses one hand against the bathroom door, pinning it closed, the smaller girl barred between her and freedom. "If I really wanted to kill you, you'd have just put yourself in the perfect position for it. All I'd have to do is tear your throat out, climb out that tiny little window back there. No one would know. And even if they did? I'd just kill them too."

Laurie shrinks away from her. Kora's wrist leaps out, pinning her prey to the door by the throat. It shudders under Kora's force, but none of the passing students notice in the bustle of the crowd. Laurie whimpers, spit snared between her lips.

"Scream, Laurie. I dare you."

She pauses and thinks over her options. Stares. Shivers.

Kora leans in, tasting her horror. Quietly, she slips her hand into Laurie's back pocket. Laurie squeaks in fear as Kora pulls out the girl's phone, dangling it in her hands, a recorder app active. "Interesting."

Laurie freezes, guilty as sin.

Kora smiles and smashes the phone in her hand, the glass

cracking, sparkling shards frosting the floor. She grinds it in her palm, destroying whatever remains, pulverizing it until there is absolutely no hope of repair.

Laurie lets out a small sob. Kora giggles.

"Of course I killed them all, princess!" Kora cackles, her breaths sailing Laurie's lips, the two close enough to kiss. "Why the fuck wouldn't I? You kicked a sleeping bear, Laurie, and now you're going to pay for it. Life's full of consequences like that. It's just a shame you couldn't have learned your lesson earlier."

"Lesson?"

"Yeah. What, do you think I just go around, killing for kicks? I mean, I sort of do, but I don't just kill anybody. I kill bad people. People like you. People that get off on the misery of others, people that have no reason to live if they aren't taking someone else's. You know, monsters."

Laurie whimpers, as if she's the victim here.

"I've judged you, Laurie, and I find you wanting. Ripe for an execution." Kora smirks.

"No," Laurie breathes, eyes watering. "You've gone fucking mad."

"Yeah, I have," Kora hisses, her eyes occupying every iota of Laurie's vision. "And you? You *brought* me there!"

Her eyes flash a deeper, more violent shade as she draws blood from the side of her final girl's neck. "This is on you, Laurie," Kora intones, holding back a single tear. "You bastards... This world is just full of sickening people... you just push, and you push, and you fucking *push,* and when one of us bites back... well, then we're the monsters, aren't we?"

Laurie doesn't answer.

"Is it *altruistic,* then, to lay back and take it?" Kora growls. "Nah. I'd rather be a monster. I'd rather bite back."

"Good," Laurie chokes. "Because you are one."

"Good! That's good. I didn't expect that from you, whore. Some actual bravery."

"You better kill me now. If you don't, I'll make you wish you fucking did."

"What a cute little cheerleader you make," Kora shrugs, thoroughly unfazed. "I don't think I will, you see. It just isn't fun this way. This isn't a hunt, it'd be an execution. Too disappointing."

"And that's what you want? Fun?"

"Vengeance, pleasure, recognition... roughly in that order," Kora smirks.

She shoves Laurie away from the door. Laurie slams into the wall and collapses onto the floor, yelping out in pain.

Kora rests her hand on the door handle, leering at her favorite victim. "Consider yourself lucky, Thompson. Lucky that I find you to be such a fascinating dancing partner."

And with that, she leaves.

Laurie lies in loneliness and lessons learned.

Violet squirms in bed, one with her blanket, skin swimming with anxiety. Her teeth chatter, her sheets soaked in sweat. Bouncy, pulsing pop sings the silence away, the overwhelming, encompassing silence. She just lays there like she did the day before, the incident still fresh on her mind.

Innocent. Innocent. She is innocent. So why is she afraid?

They're not coming for her. They're not.

The Karma Killer found her innocent.

And she knows who they are. She knows. And with the way Kora winked at her, maybe she knows that she knows. Is she on the chopping block now? Did she make a mistake, figuring it out? If she just never spills the secret, maybe it'll all be okay.

But then, what is she at that point? An accomplice? A coward?

The next song starts playing, Violet's dilated eyes darting around her room.

There's a knock at the door downstairs, and she can't help but fear that karma has come calling, metaphorically or otherwise.

She clutches onto her precious, beaten teddy bear, waiting and rocking.

"Violet! You have a visitor!"

Violet closes her eyes, praying.

Praying to no one in particular, to anybody who is listening.

Praying for mercy in a world that knows not the meaning of the word.

CYCLE NINE

Forgiveness & Other Foolish Fantasies

/// October 21ˢᵗ. Ten days until Halloween.

"You owe me, Vance."

Violet glances at her childhood home with nostalgic longing, the windows hiding what's within behind drawn curtains. Kora Lynch starts the car's engine beside her, drumming her fingers against the steering wheel.

Violet squirms uncomfortably. "Because you got me the photos?"

She sounds more scared than she is, unbelievably, considering just how frightened she *really* is. She is somewhat convinced that she is not making it out of this car alive. She squirms, squeezing her winter jacket to her chest. Rain patters against the trunk and windshield with surprising force, a fine match to her driver's tempestuous inclinations.

"Ding ding ding, the little lady gets a prize," Kora smiles cockily, shooting Violet a raised eyebrow. "Oh, ease up, Vi. I told you already, you're innocent, and it looks like you've kept that up for the last... thirty-six hours or so. Might not seem like that long a time to stay out of sin, but humans really are pernicious creatures."

"You say that like you're not one."

Violet shrinks like a mouse as Kora locks eyes with her, devilish purple pulsing. "Who is these days? The human soul has become the rarest of commodities."

"You're different now."

"Oh, you noticed? Is it the hair? The hunting hobby?"

"Hunting, if that's what you want to call it."

"It certainly is hunting, is it not?" Kora chuckles, flashing her another winning grin. "Look, Vi, I'll spare you the details, your stomach looks like it's barely holding together as it is. I just need a little help with something."

"Not hunting?" Violet hesitates.

"No, no hunting. I don't think we're quite *that* close. No, I just... I have a recording here. Two girls confessing that I did not, in fact, intend on being in that bar where the police found me, about a week ago."

"That's your priority? Not all the... you know, big game?"

"Oh, they don't know it's me," Kora says, raising a finger to her lips. "It's a secret, see. Kora and Karma, different people, at least on paper. Keep it that way, and we'll be good friends."

"And you won't kill me?" Violet asks doubtfully.

"I really have no intent to kill you, Vi. Look, I get why you might... doubt that. I do have a few unsavory habits, but it's only the guilty, okay? They were going to... Vi, they were going to ruin you. Break you. I had to kill them."

"So... you only kill bad people?"

"Uh-huh," Kora nods. "Only bad guys. You know, since the police are about as useful as Platinum Dunes, somebody's got to do it. Just consider me Lake Leer's citizen of the year."

"Okay," Violet nods, rubbing her shivering hands together.

"See, I'm not so bad. A little twisted in the head, but aren't we all? Now, I promise, I'm not involving you in any of that. I just... need to send this little recording I got off to a certain police officer that might actually listen to it."

Violet blinks. "And you want to send it to them anonymously."

"Right. And this is really, *really* important to me, so I'd appreciate it if you could give me a hand with this. I know tech is your thing, computers are your thing. I got a feeling that you're my gal. So, help a little vision of vengeance out, and she'll be on her merry way."

Violet swallows, her head spinning. She leans against the smooth leather of her seat, watching her trembling chest rise and fall. Count them all. One, two, three... Breathe, breathe...

"Okay," she croaks.

Kora smiles, hitting the gas. "Right, then! Where should we go?"

"Um," Violet murmurs, thinking. "The library? Yeah."

"Library it is!" Kora consults her phone, the car's speakers sparking to life with some pulsing post-punk. Violet jumps, her heart a careening sledgehammer. The car spins out onto the street, engine roaring like a lion.

And I don't think I'll be just another meaningless memory / Think I'll eat my way out & absorb everything you put through me / And I don't think I'm just another head in the crowd / A raving lunatic, post-traumatic beneath this shroud...

"It's a nice car you got," Violet yells above the music.

"Huh?"

"Your car, it's nice! Looks real expensive!"

"Oh, this?" Kora cocks an eyebrow. "It's not mine!"

Violet has decided Kora drives just as dangerously as she hunts, and she does not like it.

They come to a stop in the parking lot of the library, headlights hindered in a sea of rainy fog. Kora turns to Violet, regarding her soaked clothes. Violet wonders with no small amount of deep-rooted fear and inexplicable excitement if she's about to get stabbed here and now, but she doesn't.

Kora loosens her black denim jacket, easing it off her shoulders. She gently scooches forward and throws it over Violet's trembling body, propping the hood up over her head. Violet gives her a glance of confusion.

"Cold doesn't bother me much, Vi," Kora shrugs, opening the driver's door. "I'm dead, after all."

She steps out into the rain, and a stupefied Violet follows.

The downpour drenches Kora, her hair and her T-shirt soaking against her skin. Violet stares at the shirt with admitted interest, the graphic gracing Kora with the image of a large tank sporting a rather... phallic cannon.

It advertised some band called Fuck Panzer, if the shameless logo had any say. Even Violet can't help but chuckle.

"What?" Kora asks blankly.

"Nothing," Violet blushes, gesturing towards to the library's doors. "Shall we?"

Kora shrugs, leading the way.

A bell chimes with their entry into a rather minuscule library. There is a measly twelve bookshelves – three dedicated to nonfiction, one to collections of short stories and poetry, and the rest to various genres of fiction. Three tables dot the center of the room, a few computer stations facing the far wall. Computers that look like they were pulled from Steve Jobs' childhood bedroom, Violet sadly muses.

"This isn't much," Kora dryly remarks, tilting her head towards the shorter girl.

"This is Lake Leer," Violet reminds her.

"Ah, right. Too many rednecks, not enough reading. You think they have a copy of *Perfume?*"

The elderly librarian coughs at them from behind the desk. She speaks, her brittle voice imitating crumbling parchment. "It's not much, but it's tidy. Young lady, I might ask that you accept a towel? You're dripping all over my carpet."

Kora glances down, her soaked T-shirt and skinny jeans clinging to her skin. "Ah." The librarian scurries off, disappearing into the back room.

"Sorry, she's kind of... devoted, to this place, I probably should've remembered before you got all..." Violet gestures to Kora's dripping clothes, the physique of her body made rather... obvious. She gesticulates helplessly, any meaning the motions once had quickly lost.

"Wet?"

"Yeah," Violet mutters, blushing as she reluctantly looks away.

The librarian rejoins them, handing Kora a towel over the counter. Violet waits for her companion to pull out an axe, declare some abrupt judgment, but no such thing comes. Kora just smiles and thanks her, patting herself dry without complaint.

"The things kids wear these days," the librarian muses, turning her eyes up at Fuck Panzer.

Kora shrugs smoothly. "It's okay, ma'am. They're a great band, really. It's all metaphorical. There's a lot of political nuance to their work, you know?"

The librarian raises an eyebrow.

"We'd just like to use a computer station, if that's okay," Violet interrupts, pointing to the corner.

The librarian lets out a long-suffering sigh and nods. Violet can't help but suspect that the machines are about the only reason this place gets any traffic these days. "Don't be too noisy, now."

"We won't," Violet chirps. "Thank you." She leads her unlikely companion to one computer and sits, avoiding the view of any windows. She logs in, biting at her fingernail as she gets to work. She's never done this sort of thing, but she knows how to pull it off.

In theory, anyway. She fears her muscular friend more than the police, at any rate.

"I'm going to need the recording," Violet says, hoping this much would be obvious.

Kora leans back in her own chair, kicking her feet up on the table. She tugs a smartphone and a beaten USB cable out of her pockets, unlocking the phone and handing over both. She points to a file in a list of them, labeled simply as *World's Greatest Private Investigator.wav.* "It's that one," she says.

"Odd name," Violet answers, plugging the phone into the machine.

"You know that librarian watches anime?" Kora asks, tilting her head back. "Last person I'd expect that from, honestly, but it seems to make her happy."

Violet pauses, raising an eyebrow. "How do you know that?"

"Huh? Oh, that?" Kora smirks. "Oh, *that.* Consider it my little gift. I just know things. It's real cool."

"Know things?"

"Uh-huh. You know, the details of people's lives and all that."

"You're making this up."

"Hmmm..." Kora stares into Violet's eyes, the purple in her irises burning brighter. "Raised by your mother alone, dad ran off when you were three, older brother died in the war. Lesbian and damn deep in the closet... all because you had a childhood best friend that ran off when you admitted you loved her. Lot of abandonment issues, huh?"

Violet could swear she is dead, for how little her heart beats.

"How?"

"I told you. I know things. That enough proof?"

Violet nods nervously. "So that's... that's how you decide who's guilty or not? You... read their minds?"

Kora shrugs. "Yeah. What, did you think it was arbitrary?"

Violet looks back at the computer screen in lieu of a response, nervously typing away.

"I'm, uh..." Violet clears her throat. "I'm going to need the name of the guy."

"The guy?"

"The guy. The one you're going to send the recording to."

"Oh, right." Kora stands, leaning over Violet's shoulder.

Violet turns to face her, quivering under the killer's alluring eyes. "So, do you think you could use your powers to like, cheat in Vegas, or —"

"I'm not supposed to use my powers for evil, Vi."

"Right, right."

"So, you're a friend of my daughter's, then?"

"Something like that." Kora leans against the dining table, a tiny little thing buried in a tiny little kitchen. Rain patters the window behind her, the moon a specter within the storm. She rests her cheek upon her fist, trying her best to feign interest, but even her "people powers" weren't designed with the intent of charming religious fundamentalists.

"I didn't even know. What was your name again? Carrie?"

"Kora," she answers, hoping her face doesn't illustrate just how badly she just wants to skin this person alive.

It's been too long since she's indulged herself. She's starting to shiver again. Kora sits up straight, resting her hands in her lap so she can squeeze her trembling wrist.

"Kora, of course, my apologies," the woman says, permanently perplexed under her comically large glasses, her mop of graying hair combating dandruff. She grips her tea like it might run away from her, gesturing to the cup she made Kora a few minutes ago. "It's going to get cold, dear."

"Right," Kora swallows, her throat dry with anticipation. She hesitantly takes a sip, the heat humble under her tongue. She turns up her nose, trying to hide her grimace behind the rim of the mug.

"Mmmmmm!" Kora gives her a thumbs up, hoping her acquaintance takes the noise as one of gratitude and not of absolute disgust. In truth, the tea makes her want to drink the wretched crone's blood. It'd taste like a pinot noir in comparison.

It seems to work well enough. The zealot shakes her head and takes another sip of her own tea. "You know, I mean no offense, dear, but I really thought Laurie spent time with a... *different* sort of crowd."

Kora had had the foresight to change out of her Fuck Panzer shirt, but the leather jacket and her other usual affections aren't doing her many more favors. She's not wearing the mask tonight, so she thought she'd give her little pet something she could recognize more immediately. Have some fun with it all.

"Dear, is that blood on your shirt?" her prey's mother belatedly asks, narrowing her eyes.

Kora smiles. "Yeah, cut myself cooking by accident, never got the blood out of it. I apologize. It's dark enough, it normally blends right in, you know..."

Truthfully, she just likes to keep people in line. And judging by the amount of questions Laurie's mother doesn't follow up with, she decides it's clearly working.

"I'm a little less girly than you expected, huh?" Kora says, fabricating sheepishness.

"I suppose you could put it that way. You said you met her at her church gathering?"

"That's right, ma'am. You don't go with her?"

"No, no," Laurie's mother posits, shaking her head. "I am satisfied with the scripture. Laurie is still questioning and uncertain. She needs her time alone with Him."

Kora scoffs, turning the motion into a cough. "Excuse me," she says, trying to come up with a legitimate reason not to ram this mug down the woman's throat.

The sound of a car buzzing down the road perks up Kora's ears, sparing her the depths of this woman's deranged devotion. "Well, it appears my daughter is back," Laurie's mother says, her reaction delayed by an astonishing full minute.

"Yeah," Kora says. "Thank you for the tea, it was wonderful. Do you mind if I have a second alone to ask her something? It's... personal stuff. I'll be right out of your hair afterwards, I promise. I know it's late."

"It *is* late."

"Well, you know, they closed down the school for a while now because of all the... incidents," Kora says, gesticulating ambiguously. "Bad things. Figured I could stay up a little bit."

"Maybe so, but not in my house, not for too long. Make it quick, please."

"You got it, ma'am," Kora says, flashing her winning smile.

Laurie's mother mutters something about irresponsible parents as she hobbles out of the room, the creak of the stairs drifting down into the dining room. Kora leans back in her chair, pushing the tea away from her with immense relief.

A key wrestles with the lock and the front door bursts open, dragging along the welcome mat like it always does. Laurie pads out of the rain, wet boots squeaking against tile, every sound as loud as thunder to Kora's well-attuned ears.

"Mom?" Laurie Thompson's voice calls out. "I'm home!"

She turns the corner, looking positively like a drenched Catholic schoolgirl, and Kora can't decide what's funnier – the more conservative clothing she clearly threw on in the car, the cross around her neck just topping it all off; or the look on her pale, white face, the fear in her eyes, the stolen breath as she sees her stalwart stalker.

"You know, Laurie, I thought you just hated gay people," Kora says, words cutting like a knife. "It's not you, is it? I can see it in your mind. You're not as bad as I thought – well, hold that thought, you're still a manipulative bitch. But you're not an actual bigot. You're just scared of mommy malicious and daddy dastardly, aren't you?"

Laurie finally remembers to breathe. Her chest draws in, scream forthcoming.

"Don't make a single *fucking* noise, Thompson," Kora growls, beads of starved sweat running down her temple. "Keep that pretty mouth shut, or I will kill *everyone* in this goddamn house, just like I killed all your friends."

Laurie's chest freezes. She nods slowly, bottom lip trembling.

"Better," Kora smirks, gleaning every bit of gossip she can from Laurie's tantalizing thoughts. "Much better. Come on, sit down." Kora pats her lap, drumming her fingers along the table.

Laurie shakes her head slowly, swallowing, her own sweat double that of Kora's.

"Fine then," Kora sighs. "Want to play it that way. Which one should I lop off first?"

"What?" Laurie chokes.

"Which one?" Kora points at Laurie's chest. "Left or right, pick one. I'm pretty sure it'll hurt like hell either way, especially if I take it chunk by chunk, but I don't know if you have some sort of odd preference—"

"I'll sit!" Laurie hisses.

Kora smiles, tilting her head. "Good... come then. Sit." She pats her lap again.

Laurie swallows, feet dragging along the ground, the cross around her neck no protection from the devil in her kitchen. She hesitates, cringing as she drops into Kora's lap.

Kora smiles, one strong arm wrapping around Laurie's neck, applying the lightest of pressure. Laurie yelps like a wounded dog, stiffening as she chokes.

"Sorry, beautiful," Kora says, no sympathy in her apology. "This is just about the only way I can get you to shut your stupid little mouth for longer than five seconds."

Laurie shuts up for longer than five seconds.

"Better. That's better," Kora smiles, whispering woe into Laurie's ear. "You know, it didn't have to be this way. And I'm not even talking about the whole crush thing, because high school is a fucking battle royale for that. That doesn't matter in the long run, really. But tormenting me and so many others, all for kicks? I now see you're just lashing out, because of your parents, but that's... that's no excuse."

"You're going to moralize with me?" Laurie sputters in disbelief. "You killed my friends!"

"Oh, quite gruesomely, yeah. But no one's going to miss three fuckboys with a penchant for date-rape and a dumb bitch of a cheerleader that would let a child die under her feet so long as she got to hold onto her social cred."

"And that makes it okay?"

"No," Kora admits. "No, I'll be frank with you, Laurie, it doesn't. But I don't think you understand the feeling just yet. I don't think you understand what it's like to be pushed so far over the edge, by everyone you meet, pushed and pushed until you snap, because you know that's all your life's ever going to be. If I didn't snap, I'd be living on that edge for the rest of my miserable years, or I'd be hanging in the more literal sense.

"And you brought me there, Laurie! You and a bunch of other animals in this twisted, shitty world. And I have to ask you, Laurie, what you really think I have to lose. You call me a monster, but as far as I'm concerned, I've been treated like one since the day I was born. Nothing's changed. Nothing at all, except I finally get to lash out for once."

Kora's breaths shake, oiled in anger. She tightens her grip around Laurie's neck, bruises blooming over the girl's soft skin, a tremoring tear rolling down her face.

"You don't get to do this. You don't get to just help take

someone's life out of their control and then bitch and whine when the same happens to you. Because right now, you stupid, intolerable, selfish, petty *bitch,* I have the power. I have the fucking power, and you're scared to see someone other than you getting off on it."

"You think this will change my mind?" Laurie coughs. "Care about what you say?"

"No, but even with the mask, nothing's changed. In the end, nobody's listening." She smirks. "Not unless I get them in a choke hold, of course."

"Are you going to kill me?"

"Yes," Kora giggles, feverish breaths lingering over Laurie's ear.

"When?"

"When I've had my fun. When you've felt what I've felt. When you know what it feels like to have the whole world hate you, what it feels like to have every manufactured sin weighing down on your shoulders. When you know what it feels like to be alone, when I tire of our little game."

Laurie squirms.

"Then I'll kill you," Kora murmurs. "I'll kill you, and I'll even kill anyone that tries to bury you."

Laurie sobs.

The tears snake down her skin, redirected with every restrained breath.

They drip upon Kora's arm, the leather jacket Laurie is so familiar with bothered not by their presence.

"I'm sorry," Laurie cries. "I'm... I'm really sorry."

Kora smiles wide. "You're so beautiful when you cry."

Kora releases her grip. Laurie breathes, like a fish cast back to sea.

Kora glances to the ceiling, vibrations rippling the floor above. She smiles, picking Laurie up and transferring her to sit upon the table. Laurie yelps, but doesn't struggle, taking her current lease at life with eager obedience.

"Kiss me," Kora whispers.

Laurie blinks. "Have you lost your—"

She realizes how stupid that sentence sounds.

"Kiss me, and I'll give you a week before I kill you," Kora coos. "I just want to see what could've been. Just the one. It won't hurt." She raises her unarmed hands, a gesture of goodwill. "Please."

Laurie narrows her eyes, heart trying to slam its way out of her chest like a howling inmate behind a sanitarium door.

And like that inmate, she is trapped at the whims of this woman's lust for control; a deranged madwoman she created, a call from the grave she conditioned.

Maybe she deserves this.

"Please," Kora repeats, purple eyes mesmerizing.

Laurie sniffles, not in any state for a good make-out session, but she doesn't say that. "One week? For just a kiss?"

Kora nods.

Laurie swallows, disgusted with herself, horrified with her cowardice, seething at her past and the pariah she made, frightened for the fate she's forged.

It is so hot in this room.

She brushes sweat from her face, dangling locks of hair stuck to her forehead, and leans in to kiss her predator before she can bow to rationality.

Kora purrs happily into Laurie's lips, tugging the blonde's body close. Laurie's punishment becomes passionate, the table scraping against the floor under Kora's strength. Laurie trails her hands up Kora's head because they have to go somewhere, fingers worming through silver hair, and she wonders if she could get the drop on her stalker, take advantage of this first and final kiss, get a good grip and *snap*—

Kora's lips taste of amorality alluring.

"Laurie!"

Laurie jumps, tearing her mouth away from Kora's, the stalker's lips contorting into an evil, satisfied smirk. Laurie meets her mother's eyes, hypnotized in horror, mouth gaping in devout disgust.

Laurie reaches and grabs for the cross on her neck. Not because she believes in Him, mind you. She simply needs something to hold.

"You—" her mother begins, looking like she might explode, vaguely resembling some sort of swelling balloon with the way her skin practically purples. Kora smirks in all her smug confidence, and Laurie comes to the cataclysmic conclusion that she had planned this all along.

Just one kiss. Just one. You insufferable, self-satisfied, clever bitch.

Kora effortlessly conjures up an impression of coy discomfort, a hand running through her scruffy silver hair. "Oh, I'm terribly sorry, I thought you knew I was dating your daughter—"

The hell did she just say?

"Get *out!*" Laurie's mother shrieks, the bare image of a banshee, bewildered by the blasphemy before her.

"I'm so sorry, Ms. Thompson—"

"Now!"

And Laurie can only sit in shock, her tongue refusing to work, failing to find the words — something like "hey mom, that's my murderous stalker" might work, but she can't find them.

And despite it all, despite what will happen to her next, Laurie still isn't sure if she wants her mother to make her way to the pearly gates of her imaginary Heaven just yet.

Luckily, Kora makes no such move. She just darts out of the house like a startled deer, a fabricated fear.

The door shuts behind her, the night cold and inviting, the rain washing over her sinner's skin.

And all is good.

Kora only hears five words through the door, her hearing enough to compensate for the thick walls of the home.

"Pack your bags, Laurie. *Now!*"

One week, Kora thinks. *One week, Thompson.*

Let the hunt begin.

"You're soaked, Violet!"

"Sorry, Mom," Violet grimaces, kicking off her soaked sneakers and hanging up her new jacket. "I'll be back in a sec."

She runs upstairs, digging up some dry clothes to slip into, warm ones. She runs her hands over her shivering arms as she darts back downstairs, her heart still beating far faster than it should. Her mother stands over the stove, attending to a boiling pot of spaghetti, and she knows dinner will be good. It always is.

She settles at the table with her current dog-eared novel, waiting for her mother to finish the meal, the light flickering over her pages. Violet's foot taps against the tile, fingers trembling in tension.

She was midway through a murder mystery. It suddenly felt a bit too close to home.

She dog-ears it again, relegates it to the side of the table.

Spaghetti is placed before her, looking as delicious as usual. "Grazie," Violet manages as she digs in, mind running wild.

"Who were you out with, cattivella?" Violet's mother inquires, attempting small talk.

Violet shrugs. "Just a girl."

"A girl, like... a friend, or—"

"Just a friend," Violet blushes, twirling noodles around her fork.

She shivers, body in resounding revolt to every soothing song in her mind.

Violet locks her gaze on her plate, a possible panic attack pulsing in her chest. She avoids her mother's gaze, unable to understand this irremovable shame that holds her hostage.

"Mom," Violet breathes. "Do you ever feel like... I don't know, you just want to go for a bit? Go somewhere, get out of this town for a little bit? I know that might sound weird, but I just... there's so much going on, and..."

Violet's eyes drift, her mother's arms much skinnier than usual.

She looks up and screams.

A tall woman with short, scruffy scarlet hair and matching eyes raises a finger to her mouth, a bloody red smirk gracing her perfect lips.

Violet doesn't find it in her to move.

"Run, little Violet?" Ira asks, eyes bubbling with brimstone. "My dear, this little game is just hitting its stride."

CYCLE TEN

Imagination Is the Only Weapon in the War with Reality

/// **October 25th. Seven days until Halloween.**

Laurie Thompson aches with regret under the overpass, roiling rain cascading around her. She drags herself up from her stiff side, the malicious moon watching her pitiful plight. She grimaces and wipes at the wet mud that clings to her cheek.

Laurie clings her jacket tight, caked in dirt and drenched in rain. The darkness swallows her up, the bridge above her shedding sediment beneath the weight of passing cars. Laurie bites down on her thumb to reignite reality, the grit in her fingernails grinding beneath her tongue.

Her neck prickles and throbs against her overflowing backpack, the boulder of clothes within exemplifying her ill-considered vanity. She should have brought more food.

For a moment, Laurie almost thinks her muddy thumb doesn't taste half bad.

Great gusts of wind tackle her with eager ecstasy wherever the rain cannot leave her cold. Her side is in shambles, begging for relief after four nights against cracked concrete. Her teeth tug at her nails, her shivering fingers making a mess of what remains. Her other pale hand lays buried between her thighs, desperate for warmth.

Her anger amplifies with the next roll of thunder.

"Fuck!" Laurie bellows into the storm, her body shaking with the unexpected exertion. "Fuck you, Kora Lynch! Fuck you, fuck you, fuck you, fuck—"

She jumps to her feet, kicking at the stream beside her. She nearly tumbles in, terrorizing tufts of dirt with her thoroughly tainted boot, roaring in frustration.

"God! How did I get here, how did this *happen?*" she babbles, slowly losing coherency, devolving into more screams. She lashes out in loathing, slamming her fist against the sloped brick of the overpass. Laurie punches, again and again, screaming as bones crack and skin rubs raw against the wall.

"It's not fair, it's not, it's not, *God!*"

She slumps against the brick, resting her forehead against the crook of it.

And, she reflects, these last few days have only shown to her what she was convinced of all along.

There is no God. He was some crackpot myth fantasized up by sniveling sycophants to help them cope with a life they couldn't handle, to bury the burdens they couldn't find a shovel for.

Well, Laurie Thompson was going to find a shovel, and then she just might beat her delusional parents and Kora Lynch to death with it.

She stares at the blood dripping between her shattered fingers with seething eyes, fist still quivering against the wall. She pulls it away, purpled and warm, skin cracked like dirt, joints bent out of position. It throbs and pulses in pain, fingers bent in ways they certainly shouldn't be.

"Fuck me," Laurie whimpers, cradling the remains of her rampage, tears running down her cheeks.

Laurie stumbles down the sidewalk, shattered hand shoved beneath her jacket, resenting the fact that it only took four nights alone to make her look like every other wretched hobo in Lake Leer. She leans against a barber shop for a breather, one passing car stirring a silent night.

Laurie breathes.

She surveys her surroundings, the nearby apartment complex intimately familiar — in fact, it's just about the only one you'll ever really find in Lake Leer. She recognizes it not for that, though, and more for how many times she was here as a kid, here to see...

Laurie forces herself to swallow, her lumpen throat protesting.

She eyes the various posters and pages pinned to the wall with lazy disinterest. The contents always change, but these posters are a permanent fixture amongst these apartments. Laurie always used to jokingly refer to this place as a maximum-security prison — a joke that looked a little harsher than she had ever intended once she had learned that this was the low-income housing people of color and impoverished backgrounds were often forced to retreat to.

She raises an eyebrow, regarding one soaked selection with languid curiosity.

MISSING: Violet Vance, aged 16. Please contact the phone number below with any details.

Laurie tilts her head, regarding the photo. The meek, raven-haired girl looks awful familiar, though she can't quite place her finger on it.

Whatever. A curiosity for another day. Laurie stumbles through the grass, heading to the apartments proper.

She stumbles around a corner, climbing up some rickety steel steps. She has to drag herself up with the rickety railing just to combat her knocking knees, teeth grit. Laurie desperately realizes she needs food in her, and she needs it soon. That's quite the task, given she isn't planning to go crawling back to her parents anytime soon.

No, she's doing something that most would find even more pathetic.

She approaches the apartment numbered 237, her broken hand instinctively moving to knock. This mere motion stirs up unbearable pain, and Laurie begins to wish that she could've been ambidextrous.

She grits her teeth and oafishly knocks with her left, vision wobbling.

After several seconds in suffering, Jackie Winters opens the door, her eyes widening and her mouth contorting into an instant scowl.

Laurie smiles awkwardly.

"What the *fuck* do you want?" Jackie asks, contempt contaminating her voice.

Laurie winces. "Look... I know I'm probably the last person you want to see right now—"

"Kind of, yeah," Jackie agrees, crossing her arms over her chest. Her dyed blue curls dangle before her round, soft face. Given the hour (and her clad pajamas), she had likely just gotten out of bed.

"Yeah, okay, I never apologized for the... the stuff that happened, but—"

"Oh, yeah, *that's* what I've been waiting for my whole life, Thompson. An apology from the queen bitch of Leer High herself. I'll have to thank your Lord for humbling such a loathsome bottom-feeder."

"I'm no stranger to sarcasm."

"And I'm no stranger to humiliation and isolation, thanks to you."

Laurie bites her lip, the world rocking around her. "Look, yeah, okay, I'm an asshole. I'm a massive asshole. But you know I don't hate your, uhh, your being a, uh, girl, thing—"

"Eloquent as always, Thompson."

"Okay, you never used to call me that. What happened to our first-name basis?"

"You started calling me a tranny," Jackie shrugs. "Things change."

"Well, I won't anymore, if that helps."

"What, so since you've suddenly decided you're not a bigot anymore, I'm supposed to let you in with welcome arms?"

"Well," Laurie begins, "that would honestly be quite nice—"

She notices the venom in Jackie's eyes and quickly changes tact.

"Look, I never hated your trans... ness, I never hated gay people either, or... or anything, okay? It's just hard, my parents did, and I just —"

"Oh, yeah, you wanted mommy and daddy's love," Jackie says with no semblance of sympathy. "Yeah, Laurie, that really was a relationship worth saving. I hope it was worth it."

"Well, they're kind of the reason I'm homeless right now, so..."

"Wow," Jackie monotones. "That didn't work out for you, did it?"

"Look, I'm sorry. But I've been sleeping on concrete for half a week now, and..."

"Sorry for what?" Jackie snaps, shutting Laurie up instantly. "You're sorry for outing me to the entire town? Sorry that all of the beatings and abuse I've gotten for it over the years have been your goddamn fault? Sorry about all the weird... *skeevy* shit you said I did so you could pretend I had an STD and steal my boyfriend? I mean, I found out later that he was kind of a horrible person, and then he died, but... do you know how fucking *hard* it is finding a guy in this town who would actually be with a black transgender woman?"

"I mean, you fit two popular Pornhub searches right there," Laurie responds, clouded head killing her common sense.

Jackie scoffs in baffled disbelief. She moves to slam the door.

Laurie's eyes widen. "Wait, wait, hold on, I'm sorry, that was insensitive!"

Jackie pauses, the rising sun casting rays over her tired eyes.

"Look," Laurie tries. "Look, I'm a massive bitch, I know that. And that's probably not all my family's fault, but... but I really want to be better, and... and I don't want to live on the streets, Jackie, and I'm scared, okay? I'm fucking scared! There's this crazy bitch that I... that I set off, and now she's ruining my life, and I don't know why I deserve all this, but—"

Jackie shrugs. "So exactly what you did to me?"

"I—" Laurie pauses, a rising sickness in her stomach. She could see how it sounded the same to the uninformed observer, but Kora was a fucking killer, and Laurie was just—

She was just a monster.

"Never come here again," Jackie says in finality, slamming the door shut.

"Wait—" Laurie sobs, collapsing on the steps. "I can't— I'm sorry! I can't handle this alone, I just can't, I never meant to— *fuck!*"

Her nails draw blood as she rakes them down the door, her broken hand throbbing as she helplessly pleads like a dog. Laurie Thompson hates this feeling, this new noose of desperate isolation, of hopeless despair.

And it begins to click, really. And she starts to see what they mean when they say everyone is the hero of their own story.

"I'm going to fucking kill you, Kora Lynch, so help me God..." Laurie pulls out her phone, fumbling around on the screen with her lesser hand. "Two can play this game, Lynch. I'll show you. I don't need superpowers, you'll see..."

She finds Sky in her contacts, calls him.

He answers quickly despite the hour, sounding like he has just jolted awake from a pile of untouched homework. It's an educated guess. "Laurie? You're up late. You're also calling me, which is equally weird. And a first. When did you even get my number?"

"Sky, I need to stay over at your place tonight. Shit is bad."

"Uh, I don't know, my parents are terrified of women. My mother breaks down crying whenever she sees a mirror."

"I'll sleep with you," Laurie says bluntly.

"You'll what?"

"This is important. Please."

"Um, okay, but I don't want you to think this is just because—"

"Yeah, yeah," Laurie says, rolling her eyes. She knows he only caved because of her offer, and she doesn't particularly care. In a situation like this, her body was about the only asset she had. She stands up, face scrunching up in silent suffering, the pain paralyzing. Slowly, she forces her expression into that of an old classic, the mischievous smirk, even if no one's there to marvel it. "Say, Sky, have you heard about the nasty shit Mabel's gotten into?"

Violet awakens with understanding and unease, cradling a knife of bone in her hands.

Her heart resuscitates as she squirms on the couch, groaning as her entire skeleton pops free of its rest. She forces one eye half-open, recognizing her living room. She must have escaped Ira's... Ira's...

Ira's home, whatever you would call it.

But no, she's here now, her heart is hammering in her chest, she's no longer made of those... weird, black ribbons, her hair is back, her skin is back, everything is back, and she can breathe—

And she *knows*. She knows what she has to do. There is no more longing, no more confusion, no more desperation... only purpose.

She studies the knife, a blade of serrated, alien bone, made to tear, the handle cold like steel. She flips it around, engraved veins of red running down the handle, pulsing with a life of their own.

"I will," she answers, unsure if Ira even hears her anymore.

"Violet?"

Violet glances over the couch with a start, finding her mother standing in the kitchen. Violet slips the knife behind her back, strings of hair ensnared between her parched lips. "Mom?"

"Violet, where... where did you go?" Her mother stumbles forward, pale as a ghost. "I thought we lost you— like Eddie, you just—"

"How long was I gone?" Violet asks, breathless.

"Four... four days," Mom says, tilting her head. "You don't

remember?"

"I just... I don't know what happened, I'm sorry. God, I'm really sorry, I just... I wandered, and got lost—"

"Oh, my God, come here, cattivella," Mom sobs, stumbling across the kitchen. Violet quickly tucks the knife into the denim jacket Karma lent her, forcing herself to cry along with her mother.

Mom tackles her, squeezing her tight, almost like she needs to convince herself Violet's real. Violet just tries to smile, truly tearing up a little as she sheepishly returns the hug.

"I'm sorry, Mom, I feel horrible," Violet admits. "I didn't... I won't do it again, I promise."

"I'm just glad you're here, Violet. I love you so much, I couldn't stand to, to—"

"I'm not going anywhere, I'm sorry," Violet reassures, shaking. "I'm sorry. I didn't mean to scare you."

Her mother shudders, reluctantly pulling away, as if her daughter might vanish the instant she lets go. "Are you hungry?"

Violet nods, her eyes radiating with gentle care. Her heart twinges with regret as she remembers her older brother Eddie, out the door one day to join the military. He had never found his way back. And now, to make her mother feel like that again...

Her mother gives her a shaky smile, trying to get a hold of herself.

She pauses, looking at Violet in wonder. Violet tilts her head inquisitively.

"Violet, your eyes are... they're purple."

Karma raps on Mabel's door, bouncing on tiptoe with anticipating breaths before a surge of panic reminds her that she's still in her work clothes.

She sheds her face, embracing Kora's mask, stuffing her bloodied identity in her backpack. She contemplates the stained axe in her hands, freshly dripping with the gore of a corrupt local banker.

Well, she supposed he wasn't really corrupt anymore. Death

worked wonders like that, and it had provided her a free few thousand dollars in cash. She'd surely find a use for that.

Kora sighs, hurling the axe behind her. It disappears in midair, waiting for her beck and call in some other realm. It's a power she doesn't understand in the slightest, but she doesn't really care how it works so long as it does. She straightens the leather jacket her sweetheart gave her, tucking it over a bloodstain on her shirt's side.

She is about to knock again when she hears footsteps, quiet but plain to the attuned ear. She pockets her hands, waiting with a whistle.

Mabel fumbles with the lock, hands trembling with the movement. Kora raises an eyebrow as her girlfriend opens the door, eyes widening when she sees the tears streaming down Mabel's face.

"God!" Mabel gags. "Kora, I—"

She wraps her arms around Kora, clearly needing the support, weeping against the taller girl's chest. Kora shifts uncomfortably, knowing this part of the job would be the *real* Kora's department, but, well... she was a little unavailable, engaged with her metaphorical afterlife.

"Uh, Mabel, you good?" Kora gives her girl her best hug, tears staining her shirt. "Hey, what happened? Bel?"

"I—" Mabel chokes, iron grip clenched around Kora's shirt. Kora rubs her back gently, trying not to show any impatience. She's pretty sure that's considered rude.

"You?" Kora inquires, mentally slapping herself. Manners. "Bel, you're—"

"She fucking... she made up all this *shit,* and... I'm dead, Kora! I'm fucking dead!"

Mabel completely loses composure, claiming the color of Kora's cheeks. She tugs her partner into the house, wide eyes red. Kora slams the door behind them, cringing with the unintended force of it. Mabel doesn't notice. She just paces, swallowing down choked sobs.

"Hey, calm down, you're stressing me out, sit down for a second," Kora pleads, sitting Mabel down, a twang of...

Was that *concern?* She shakes her head, disgusted by the influence her body's former owner left with it.

Mabel doesn't notice the motion, and Kora holds back her scowl. It's not the girl's fault. Well, maybe it is, but it's not something worth killing over.

"Laurie, she..."

Kora's fist curls into a ball, her eyes sparking with life. She pulls Mabel onto her lap, cradling her shaking body, kissing her hair.

Muscle memory. "What? What did that... what did she do?"

"She..." Mabel gags. "She made up all this shit about me fucking... you know, about... *being* with that batshit crazy killer going around, that Karma woman, she made this shit up about me being an accomplice and a sexu—" She leans over, clearly about to throw up.

"Whoa, whoa, whoa, hold on!" Kora darts into the kitchen, fetching a large mixing bowl. It's filled with the residue of tres leches cake ingredients and smells suspiciously of marijuana, but it'll do. She hands it off just in time for Mabel to vomit into it, her body tensing as she empties herself of her favorite dessert.

Kora sits there helplessly, patting Mabel's back as she gasps, cringing with every sickened sound. It's almost ironic, really — she can't actually accuse Laurie of lying, even if Mabel doesn't know that.

I gave you a week, Kora thinks. *A week to run free. And this is how you repay me.*

"I'm not doing that," Mabel shudders, face clouded over with snot and tears. "I'm not! I'm— even if she wasn't a deranged serial killer, you're my... my mariposa, Kora, I... *God!*"

"I know, I know," Kora reassures, restricting her words to bury her fury.

"God, why would she... why does this always happen?"

"What do you mean?"

"Just... this shit!" Mabel growls, wringing her hands. "This bullshit! Why do people throw other people under the bus for... for no goddamn reason at all? Why does it seem like only good people get hurt? It's not fair. I'm no egotist, but... I didn't do anything to her. Hell, I was her... well, not really her friend, but I was her plug!"

"Some people are just... some people are just bad," Kora tries.

"It doesn't make sense," Mabel cries, collapsing against Kora's chest. "It's just... the bad people, they never suffer a thing, do they? I tried to keep my nose down, and here I am, the next fucking Jackie Winters. Why do people have to get their lives ruined over nothing? Over shitty jokes and gossip?"

"Your life isn't ruined. Honey, you'll be okay—"

"I didn't do anything to her," Mabel whimpers, face buried beneath tangled hair. "God, Kora, it very well might be ruined. It's hard enough being brown in this hellhole, I already get enough shit with that. Now people think I'm some serial killer's *lover*. I'm going to get stoned to death, or shot, or—"

"Mabel, it's not your fault," Kora implores. "And you'll be fine. I'll protect you."

"Kora, they'll ruin you too, you can't just—"

"Mabel, you are *all* I have. They've already taken everything else. They won't get this."

Mabel's breaths shudder, trembling eyes locking onto Kora's purple.

"I promise," Kora growls. "The bad people... they're good at getting away with shit. They're good at shoving the best people over the edge, and they're good at finding happiness by leeching it from others. But not tonight."

Kora bristles as she meets Mabel's eyes, palpable terror and fading innocence imprinted in the irises.

"Not tonight," Kora promises, regretting every innocent victim she couldn't avenge.

She's never felt such funneled fury, such rampant rage, such delirious desire. Karma stalks the streets of Lake Leer, the moon looming above the town's rolling hills. The killer's boots crush tufts of grass with every steadfast step, a pant and a swing of her axe with every inch forward.

She fixes her true face back into its rightful place, her weapon in hand, spit worming its way through grit teeth. She comes to the hilltop, the street behind her sloping down unto the land of those less fortunate.

Karma surveys its counterpoint, its privileged oppressor, the lawns of Lake Leer's well and privileged. Sure, they aren't the sort of glittering mansions you see in California, but for houses in a small mountain town, they are needlessly extravagant. Two or three stories looming over empty driveways, three or four cars to each house. It makes her lust for blood even more than she typically does, and that's no easy thing.

Karma scoffs derisively, remembering several houses for later, the smell of sin smothering the evening dew like crumbling carrion. For now, though, she follows a much more interesting scent.

A scent she loves and hates with empirical equality, a scent still enticing. A scent now infuriating, a scent tainted.

A scent in need of erasure.

She follows it up another empty driveway, catching another whiff immediately. Skyler.

Her bunny's desperate.

Her scent trails upwards and Kora follows it. She leaps, fingers grabbing hold of a second-story window, heels safe against the wall. She confirms the streets are still empty before heaving herself upwards, flipping up the side of the house. Karma balances on the windowsill, white knuckles tight around the handle of her axe. Cautiously, the predator leans against the glass.

The curtains are drawn close, but that only presents her an advantage. She leans in, muffled moaning making voyeurs of the stars.

Oh, for God's sake. Hurry up, kids. It's your bedtime.

She grabs the window, forcing it open. The lock snaps, a motion most unsubtle, but the tangled couple doesn't notice, Laurie's pleasure rolling down the streets.

Karma raises an eyebrow, easing the window up, wondering if the two will even notice the draft. They should. It's not exactly easy to miss.

A kabuki mask peeks through the curtains, crying eye a peeping Tom.

She doesn't particularly mean to leer, but she also doesn't regret taking in the sight. Ignoring the fact that Laurie is having sex with Skyler Simmons, of all people — the foundation for a beautiful rumor if she had ever found one — that body was one Karma could appreciate, even in her roiling rage.

The nastiest people get the nicest skins, don't they?

Laurie's sweating thighs straddle Sky's waist, fingers tugging at the sheets as she flings sweat with every bounce, the man's hands trailing over her naked curves. Karma sighs and waits, lightly tapping her fingers against the window, strangely reluctant to murder them mid-coitus.

She *could* slaughter Laurie right now, easily — summon her crossbow and put a bolt through her naked chest. Hell, if she had a spear, she could recreate one of her favorite slasher kills. But, sadly, Laurie deserves more than that. She deserves far more punishment, and beyond even that, Karma cannot be satisfied if Laurie dies to an ambiguous assailant. The sinner has to see Kora's eyes when she finally leaves this wretched existence. She has to know wrath.

Even Karma has trouble taking her internal monologue seriously as Laurie moans and swoons with increasing intensity in the background. It's too exaggerated to be real, Karma tells herself.

"Come on," Karma murmurs under her breath, resting her cheek against the window frame. "Any day now."

They just go on and on and on, the bed obnoxiously creaking with every rock of her hips. Karma runs a hand over her mask, sighing in annoyance. Now she knows why the horror movie killers don't bother to wait. It's just not time-efficient, and this wasn't much to get off to anyway. When you decide to make a hobby of killing people, sex isn't all that stimulating. Maybe if Laurie was bleeding, maybe if those squeals turned to screams...

Finally, mercifully, after what feels like hours, they come to what Karma has to assume is a climax, the pleasure reaching its peak. Karma shakes herself awake, mentally slaughtering her thirty-eighth sheep. Her naked prey leans over Sky, panting. "God, Sky..." she sighs.

Karma rolls her eyes, preparing her dramatic entrance.

"You got a second round in you?" Laurie smirks, the cross around her neck dangling over his lips.

Karma freezes. *Oh, come on, it's Sky. Of course he doesn't.*

"Yeah," he stammers, kissing up her neck. "Yeah, keep going."

Karma's eye twitches. *No, no, no, no—*

The bed squeals in practiced protest, rekindling the agonizing wait. Karma could screech.

In this moment, she thinks she finally understands why Jason Voorhees was such an angry man around horny eighteen-year-olds.

"Oh, fuck this," she growls, chopping through the curtains with her trusty axe, her boots quaking the carpet.

Laurie and Sky scream, a symphony to her ears. If Laurie sounded like this while she entertained herself, Karma might still desire the woman.

Laurie jumps to her feet, Sky modestly hiding himself beneath the blankets — an odd gut reaction to an invincible killer invading your bedroom, but she supposes she's seen stranger things. Laurie backs against the wall, unconcerned with her dignity, clearly more concerned for her life.

"What the *fuck?*" Sky shrieks, panicking even more than his companion. "Who the hell are you? Why are you in my room? I—"

"Oh, I'm the crazy serial killer that's been making sliced delicacies out of all your classmates," Karma affably replies. "Call me Karma. Laurie! Long time, no see."

"How did you find me?" Laurie hisses, stricken by the sight of the devil itself.

Good, Karma thinks. *Taste what I tasted, girl.*

"I followed the noise," Karma chuckles, nodding at her naked body. "Don't make yourself a beacon next time. Us insane undead killers, you know... we're like bloodhounds for the indecent."

"Undead? I—" Sky begins.

"Shut up, princess," Karma growls, raising a finger. "Scream, call for help, and I'll throw you out that window."

He whimpers, a tear trailing down his cheek. Karma winces a little. "Sorry. You're not evil, just annoying. I'm on edge, so please stay quiet."

"Since when do you care?" Laurie snaps, backing up against the wardrobe.

"Since when—" Karma sighs in exasperation. "Really? Since when do I care? I saved Violet from your predator friends. I'm not just some heartless killer, you know. I have rules."

"Rules?"

"Rules, like he's innocent, and you're not," Karma snarls, pointing her axe at Laurie's chest. "I forge fates, you see, like the one where you're going to die tonight, far from home, a naked whore with nothing on her but the mark of a useless God."

Laurie sniffles, shaking her head, hands clasped tight together. "You gave me a week. You promised!"

"Yeah, I did."

"You really don't have a soul, do you?"

Karma scoffs, raising her leather jacket to properly expose the bloodied shirt beneath. "Really? It's the broken promise and not the trail of corpses that bothers you?"

"You gave me a week."

"You just ruined an innocent girl's life," Karma hisses. "You pay with yours."

"So this is about Mabel? Interesting. You do have a conscience."

"Never gonna make up your mind on that one, are you?" Karma growls, shaking with rage. "Let's find out, girl, because I'm about to cut every limb off of that slut body of yours and *make you eat them!*"

The handle of her axe splinters in her fitful grip. She looks down, chest heaving in fury.

"Never seen you this unhinged," Laurie whispers, the words slipping off her forked tongue, and Karma bristles at the sound. She hates that smugness, that... that egotistical *fucking* superiority she used to employ with every tease, every biting comment.

Maybe she is unhinged. Maybe she just doesn't give a shit anymore. Maybe those amount to the same thing in the end.

She prepares her axe, closing the distance. "I'm going to kill you, you *freak!*"

Laurie backs up into the wardrobe, a stack of DVDs tumbling onto the ground. She opens her mouth to scream, Karma's axe rising for an executing stroke—

Sky hurls himself between the two of them, thrusting himself before the descending blade. It freezes before him, Karma's swing sharply restrained. She glares at the smaller man, spit coating her unseen lips.

"Sky," she growls, her voice more demonic than she's ever known. "Get out of my way."

He shakes his head, raising his trembling hands. "I... Kora, I know that's you. The hair, and the voice, and... look, I don't know what you're doing, but this isn't you."

Is he really trying this cliché? "Sky," Karma repeats, slowly lowering her axe. "Kora Lynch is dead. She lived up to her name. I am avenging her, making her tormenters pay, and you? You're in my goddamn way."

"Kora, we were friends. I don't know who... who pushed you to this, but—"

"You are standing *right* in front of her!" Karma howls. "Get out of my way, *now!*"

"What?" Laurie snaps, keeping Sky between her and her hunter. "Conscience got ahold of you?"

"Shut *up!*" Karma screams, stomping the floor. "Sky, move. You are innocent, you are decent, if not quite *good,* and that's why you're standing here right now, because, frankly, this situation does not portray me at my best—"

"I wonder why," Laurie interrupts.

"Shut the *fuck* up!" Karma snaps. "Sky, I swear, she is evil, she is twisted, she is a manipulative... You need to get out of my way."

"Kora, I can't let you kill anyone else," Sky says, licking his lips nervously. "We can sit down, and talk about this, and—"

And he can hold Karma here while someone calls the police, and they can take care of her—

"Sky," Karma sighs. "You've always been a terrible liar."

He pales. "What?"

She grabs him by the shoulder, flinging him aside. He slams into his bedside table, his lamp tumbling onto his chest and casting Karma into shadow.

"I said I wouldn't kill you," she murmurs. "Never said I wouldn't hurt you."

Laurie backs into the corner, hand reaching behind a dresser.

Karma turns to face her, cracking her neck. "Now, lover, any last words?"

"Yeah," Laurie pants, eyes wide. "I should've let Mabel taste me when I had the chance."

Karma raises her axe. "Why, you cheeky little—"

Laurie yanks a steel baseball bat out from behind the dresser. Karma blinks, remembering too late that Sky used to play in middle school—

The bat connects with Karma's cheek, her axe thrown astray, the killing wound worthlessly splintering the dresser. Karma regains her footing just as the bat slams against her chin, her head jutting upwards. Karma staggers against the bed, stabilizing herself against the frame.

"Sky!" Laurie yells, narrowly dodging Karma's flailing hand.

"Give me that bat, you little *shit*—" Karma snarls, just as a blanket cuts off her breath. She changes tact, flailing backwards in blindness as Sky attempts some sort of choke hold with the sheets. She drops the axe, growling in frustration.

Sky has a shocking amount of strength for such a sedentary man. Karma's hands find a target, the boy's fragile arm, and she yanks him forward, flipping him over her head. He hits the floor with a squeal as she spins in a graceful circle, tearing the sheets in half and freeing herself. She scans the carpet desperately, looking for—

"Hey, freakshow! Drop something?"

Karma whips around, eyes resting on the naked woman with the axe.

In any other situation, this would be darkly comic and strangely titillating.

"Let me give it back to you!" Laurie snarls, plunging the axehead directly into Karma's chest. She stares down in disbelief, the blade drawing new designs in her chest with every ill-considered twitch.

"Well, this is embarrassing," Karma mutters. "Now, don't think that'll stop me from killing you—"

Laurie snatches up the baseball bat from the freshly unmade bed, cracking Karma's jaw with the next blow.

Ow.

Karma spins on a dime, slamming into the bedroom wall, catching one last sight of her assailant as she trips over the windowsill. The night sky embraces its demon as she flips, tumbling towards the yard below.

Laurie pants and drops the bat, head spinning with shock and fear and elation and so many other things, her heart working itself to death. Sky stumbles to his feet, groaning. "Did you just..."

Laurie sprints to the window, peeks out at the ground below. Karma lays there, blood seeping into the grass, her own axe firmly impaled between her breasts.

Laurie grabs her T-shirt and underwear out of their abandoned pile of clothes, tugging them on as she bursts out of Sky's room, hurtling down the stairs. She nearly slips twice, her feet shaking with panic and excitement.

Laurie bursts out the front door as Sky tears down the stairs behind her.

And on the grass, only patches of blood remain, no slasher in sight.

Sky comes to a stop behind her in his boxers, panting. "What the fuck? Laurie, what the hell was that? What—" He looks over her shoulder. "She's gone. Why is she gone? *God*, I am so glad I convinced my parents to go have their first date in fifteen years..."

"I got a lot of 'why' questions right now myself," Laurie mutters, struggling to keep the vomit inside her. She clutches onto her stomach, thinking she might be sick. Her words feel as if they come from a different person, her body a vindicated vessel below her.

She lived. She fought back. She survived. She can hold her own.

Laurie smiles. She can fight back.

"Laurie? Laurie, what the hell do we do? She'll kill me too, probably, now. I mean, what the *fuck* are we supposed to—"

"Sky," Laurie asks, ignorant of his panic. "Have you ever seen *Dream Warriors?*"

CYCLE ELEVEN

The Devil in Her Hands

/// **October 27th. Four days until Halloween. Lake Leer General Hospital, ER.**

One. *Thump.* Two. *Thump.* Three. *Thump.* Four. *Thump.*

Despite all odds, Kora Lynch's undead heart still beats.

She rests her eyes, lids too weary to consider opening. She doesn't fight her languid instincts, silently contemplating.

She got stabbed in the chest by a crazy, naked woman — with her own axe, no less. Fell out the window... landed on her arm with a nasty *snap,* and considering its current burning, throbbing state, she can conclude that it's likely broken in several places. She stumbled away, painting the lawns and hedges of the affluent with her vagrant blood, and somehow managed to make the long walk to her house.

She stowed the mask and leather jacket away... unwisely tore the axe out of her chest, hid that too. She stumbled downstairs, and...

Well, she doesn't actually remember reaching the bottom. Maybe that's when she passed out.

God, her head aches.

Her right hand, long clamped shut, slowly unfurls with her mental pleads. Her bones crack of disuse as she remembers how to breathe again. With every movement of her bloodstained chest, she feels tissue shift and bones dig into flesh, the pain drawing forth intermittent spasms. That axe must have went in pretty deep.

And just when Kora thought Laurie could impress her no further.

"Kora Lynch?" a woman's voice murmurs. "Are you awake, sweetie?"

Kora weakly groans in assertion, forcing her eyes open. She re-familiarizes herself with the same hospital room she had occupied not so long ago, a rather motherly nurse smiling down at her — an *actual* nurse this time. "Ms. Lynch? Can you speak?"

"In theory," Kora croaks, a blink of her eyes nearly returning her to her stupor.

The nurse breathes in relief, idly observing the little computer monitor they have hooked up to her. Kora pokes at the IV hooked to her arm, apathetically observing the large, bloodied bandages wrapped tight around her chest and the tubes that run out from under it. She squirms, one arm in a sling, more bandages wrapped tight around her forehead.

Christ. She was never going to get out of here. Her fingers jolt erratically, cold, and she swears she can feel something crawling up her throat.

God, Kora mentally screams, *I need to move, I need to hunt, I need something, I am going to fucking die—*

She breathes, the coping mechanism a little less relieving this time around. It just reminds her of the gaping crater that bitch Thompson has made of her chest.

"Ms. Lynch, I'm afraid there's a lot to discuss. The doctor will be in shortly, but—"

"For God's sake," Kora slurs. "I know what the problem is. I got stabbed in the chest, I fell really far, broke my arm, I don't need a whole scene—"

"More than that, hun. You have a concussion, you're covered in bruises—"

"A concussion," Kora groans, feeling her head with her undamaged hand. The lights in the hall blind her eyes with every errant glance, as if to confirm this diagnosis. "Brilliant."

"You'll be okay, sweetie," the nurse reassures. "Your father found you at the foot of the stairs when he got home, not too long after the accident. It's—"

"A miracle I'm still alive? Yeah, I'm sure."

"He's outside in the waiting room. Would you like to—"

"Who?"

"Your father, hun."

Kora rubs her throbbing head. "Oh. Right."

"Would you like him to come in and visit, or—"

"No, just..." Kora sighs, really not up to that right now. "Just tell him I'm sound asleep or something, honestly."

The nurse purses her lips, but nods. "Try to stay calm. A doctor will be in shortly."

"I'm very calm. I've had worse."

The nurse raises an eyebrow. "Oh... a very sweet girl called while you were unconscious, asked you to call her when you woke up. She left her number, I wrote it down for you. It's besides your phone on the bedstand."

Kora nods, wondering why Ira didn't bother to just take another nurse's body this time around. A mystery she'd never unravel, that woman.

"Thanks," Kora grunts. The nurse leaves the room, closing the door behind her.

Kora juggles her phone and the slip of paper one-handed, nearly dropping both as her chest flares with ebbing pain. She sluggishly dials the number, wincing as she holds the phone to her ear, waiting for her favorite voice.

For what it's worth, the voice is familiar, if not at all what Kora expected. "Oh, thank God, you're awake."

Kora squints, convinced she's hallucinating. "Violet? The hell are you—"

"Look, we don't have a lot of time, Karma," Violet brusquely replies. "Where did you leave your axe and your mask?"

Kora's heart prickles with excitement at the sound of her real name. "Violet, I'm not that dumb."

"You're not the brains of this operation, Karma, not anymore. I've met Ira, okay? Quit arguing and trust me."

"You've met—" Kora's head whirls, and she doesn't think it's the concussion this time. "Fuck me, *what?*"

"She told me to help you, so I'm helping, but I need you to work with me here. I'll explain more later, but right now, there's going to be a lot of people searching everywhere that has to do with you — a lot of people that are still convinced you're the Karma Killer. Laurie knows, the police only need a clue or two more to have acceptable evidence of that, and the only thing stopping them is your father. He's making them get a search warrant, I think."

"Are you calling me sloppy?"

"I'm not calling you anything. I just want to help."

"For God's sake," Kora replies. "Fine. They're in my closet. My mask, my axe, my crossbow, my jacket, all of it. Don't forget the jacket, please, it's—"

She hesitates at the word *sentimental.*

Oh, *fuck* — Mabel's probably freaked.

"Is there like..." Violet pauses. "Like, some sort of secret door, or a board in the floor you have to lift, or—"

"What? No, no, just look in my closet, man. They're right there."

"And you... you..." Violet stutters, sighing. "You *didn't* think that maybe you shouldn't hide incriminating evidence in the *first* place that everyone would check?"

"Well, now I am," Kora admits. "It's fine, though, isn't it? Is anybody even—"

"*Yes!* The whole town knows you're in the hospital. Do you know how few people live here? Someone could stub a toe and it'd circulate in seconds."

"Shit," Kora says. "Yeah, okay, put like that, that's not great."

"It's fine," Violet responds, assuming a gentler tone. "I got it handled. I'll be by to pick you up in a couple hours, with your stuff. We'll go hide out somewhere a little more... uh, subtle."

"Violet, I feel as if I'm being held together by fruit roll-ups right now," Kora protests. "My healing factor doesn't seem to be doing me much good at the moment."

"How long has it been since you killed somebody?"

"What?"

"How long?"

"I don't know," Kora stammers. "How long have I been out?"

"Two days."

"Then..." Kora thinks, remembering that banker. "About that long. A little longer."

"That's why. Your healing factor slows down the longer you go without killing somebody. You need another hit."

"What? How do you even *know* that?"

"Ira told me," Violet says, as if this were all obvious. "Haven't you noticed how you get real shaky when you haven't killed in a while? You get feverish, and you don't exactly think as cleverly as usual, and pain is a little clearer?"

Kora remembers why she found and killed the banker in the first place, remembers how hard she had tried to let Blondie and Ginger live, remembers how *relieving* it was to chop them up and burn the bodies — like some sort of climax after hours of edging herself, some freedom after being locked up and left to rot for so long.

"Yeah," Kora admits. "Yeah, I guess that makes sense. You'd think she could've told me that, though."

"She probably wanted to see how you fared without any guidance. Test drive."

"She tell you that too?"

"No," Violet says smoothly. "Guesswork. Or maybe she just found it funny. I have no idea. I don't know an actual thing about her, okay? I'm just going with what she told me. I really need to go and get your stuff now, before someone else finds it."

"Right. Okay."

"The police are probably going to come and interrogate you. They'd be stupid not to, your case fits the M.O. they have for... well, you. Karma. Axe wound and all that. Just tell them Karma tried to kill you, it'll get them off your back. Hopefully. At least for a while."

"Yeah. Okay. That sounds like a good plan."

"And say you didn't recognize anything in regards to the killer. Just identify her with facts the cops already know. The less clues they have, the better. Oh, and smash your damn phone."

"Okay," Kora repeats. "You got all this in the bag, right?"

Violet hangs up.

If you fall, you fall together.

Violet twirls the blade of sacrifice in her palms, contemplating the devil in her hands.

She is a force of nature, a weapon waging war, wrath incarnate.

Violet shivers, the heater doing little to dissuade the freezing rain that batters the windshield of her mother's car. It hums idly as it sits, headlights off. She hugs Eddie's abandoned green army jacket close to her skin, the one keepsake of her brother she has left. She barely remembers him, really. She had been so young.

You're so lonely, aren't you? You need something to define you, don't you? Someone?

Nonetheless, his specter had always lingered over her as a strange comfort, and his keen sense of justice and protective nature had become fixtures in her mind. She can't help but wonder if her hesitant attraction and need to care for her new charge had some tie to that, some tie to the personality traits these two just happened to share.

Tell me, Violet, what is a weapon without a wielder? What is nature without a guide? What is wrath without direction?

She runs the blade of bone over her skin, feeling the serrated grooves teasingly nip at her flesh. The crimson veins snaking down the handle are dark and cold, devoid of color. Lifeless.

Purposeless.

A drop of blood stains the driver's seat, dripping between her shivering thighs. Violet blinks and recalls reality. She puts the knife away, not so desperate as to attempt self-sacrifice just yet.

I'm sure you can sympathize with her plight, Violet.

She stares out the windshield, wipers waging a losing battle against the deafening deluge. Kora Lynch's house sits not a couple feet away, lights all out. Her father must still be at the hospital.

After all, purposeless, on your own... isn't that where I found you, Violet?

And she longs for the emptiness to find its way to her again.

You are to protect my Vision of Vengeance, Violet. You are to be her guardian.

Protect... protect *her,* the superpowered serial killer chopping up teenagers with ease. Embody the accomplice, cast away your innocence...

She protected you, Violet, when you needed it most. Now she needs rationality behind her retribution.

It's not even a question of if, and yet it is. It's like shoddy memory, really — every so often, Violet will remember that this is absolutely insane, that *she* has completely lost her mind. She will remember she is aiding a serial killer, she will remember she very well might have to harm or kill as well, and she will remember that just covering up the crime scene might as well leave her responsible for the stabbings.

Kora is a soldier. She is no tactician. That role belongs to you, my cunning Violet.

And it matters not when the haze settles over her again, the blind fog finding its form. Violet remembers her purpose, and there are no more questions. She leaves that discomfort to other devils, and she pities the grateful good, home in restful slumber.

The blood in your blade belongs to our little Karma Killer. Kill, stab, rend — she will recover.

For perhaps a life of sin and glory is better than a life of righteousness and empty dreams.

If Kora Lynch dies, you die with her. If my vision fades away, I promise you...

Violet spontaneously slams her arms against the dashboard like a thrashing ghoul, head colliding with the steering wheel. "Crap," she mutters. "Damn it!"

If Kora Lynch fades away? I will show you even less pity than Iraq showed your brother.

Violet Vance has never been a blasphemous woman, but it's becoming clear that God has long overlooked this blasted lake. "Goddamnit! God, just fucking let me *go!*" She kicks the gas pedal in one last outbreak of teenage rebellion, startling her out of spite and disrepair.

You can't save everyone, Violet. But you can save her damned soul.

"I want to go home," Violet murmurs, the tears rolling down and clinging to her jacket. She clutches the wheel with an iron grip, sickly sobbing over it. "I want to go home. I want my mom. I want stupid video games, I want dumb romantic comedies, I want to keep studying. I want to go to college. I want to be an architect..."

She slumps, giving the dashboard one final, half-hearted slap.

Is this just how it works? Fate rolls a die, you get a 1, congratulations, you're now the puppet of some gothic Lovecraftian monstrosity? Who rolls the die? Who decides? Why do they decide? Why does she finally have so many questions she can't answer?

Why does she have what feels like a hundred guns pointed at her head, and why is she the most frightened of her own?

Violet knows of the forest. She was tantalized with a taste. She will never take it again.

And what will you sacrifice of your stolen soul to guarantee that, Vance? What will you give of yourself?

She's read a certain sentiment before, one common turn of phrase.

There isn't anything more dangerous than somebody with nothing to lose.

Violet reluctantly reaches for the door handle, proving true that ancient adage.

"Kora, I don't know if I can trust you."

Mabel says the words like she's choking on them, her face shrouded in shadow. She is too far away in her crappy plastic chair, and Kora frowns uneasily, wishing she could hold her hand. "Mabel? What do you—" She coughs a little, blood seasoning her lips. "Shit..."

Mabel turns towards the window, crossing her legs with a defeated slump of her shoulders.

"Why are you hiding your face?" Kora says. "I told you, I'm okay —"

"I know. Twice now, you've been okay."

Kora blinks.

Mabel fixes her eyes on the raging storm outside. "Kora, I can't... I've been trying to delude myself, and like..."

Kora's heart skips a beat. "Don't tell me."

"I'm not telling. I'm asking."

Kora shifts uncomfortably, feeling the fabric against her fragile fingers.

"You've been to the hospital twice, in about as many weeks. Both wounds... they *happened* around some strange circumstances, to say the least—"

"I was attacked," Kora croaks. "By the killer. I told you."

"Told the police, too."

Kora swallows nervously, her dry throat preparing to expire.

Mabel's voice shudders with every statement. "You never explained to me why you just ran off that morning we... I just hear you screaming, stumble out, and you're... you're running out my door, shoving something under your jacket? I—"

"Nightmares," Kora mumbles. "I had nightmares."

"Yeah, and I'm having nightmares now too!"

Kora flinches, squeezing the sheets.

Mabel's heel bounces against the floor, the sole soaked through from stomping through the evening's rain. "Sky's saying he recognized the voice, Kora. He told me... his version of the weekend's events. I—"

"Sky is out of his mind," Kora says desperately, trying to sit up.

"Shit, ow... I... are you saying you think I'm some serial killer? You really think—"

"Why would everyone say so, Kora? Why would the cops be sniffing around so much if they didn't have sufficient reason to do so? Why would you end up in two hospitals with concussions and impossible wounds?"

Kora feels a tear run down the bridge down of her nose, shakes it off.

The woman is a weakness. She knows this.

It's still a shame to see her go.

"It's not true," Kora says softly.

Mabel stands, hesitantly approaching the bed. Kora considers her next move.

Don't make me.

She comes into view, the running tears beaten by her beauty.

Traitor. Traitor. Killer. Judas.

Kora squeezes the sheets tighter, tearing at it, ripping anything but her skin.

Killer. It's what you are. It's what you are. Accept.

"I don't know if I can trust you," Mabel repeats, unable to believe herself as she hides her face away.

Kora reaches out, gesture met with a violent recoil. Kora stiffens up in shame, knees scraping against each other as she vainly tries to pull herself up.

"Mabel!" Kora says, unable to hold back desperation. "Please, you have to—"

Mabel visibly shudders, turning away. "Clear your name, and I'll believe you. Or tell me the truth."

"Mabel..." Kora says, the IV ripping free of her arm with the smallest of stings as she tears loose the tubes that bind her. "Mabel, come on, please. Please. Trust me. Just... please."

Mabel looks over her shoulder, breaths shallow. "You're crying."

And so she is. Kora wrenches free of the bed, hitting the ground with enough force to daze her, jaw cracking against tile. She groans and rolls onto her broken arm, pleadingly looking up at Mabel.

Mabel matches her gaze, eyes glassy and horrified.

"Mabel," Kora begs. "I need you."

Mabel considers the distance between them, her eyes torn apart by the one she called her own. Her former stalwart serenity.

"I needed you too," Mabel whispers, yanking the door open.

"Mabel!" Kora shrieks, tearing herself to her aching feet. Mabel disappears into the hospital hallway as Kora staggers out the door of her room, stumbling within the sea of fluorescence.

"Hey, where's that patient going—"

"Who's shrieking—"

"Yeah, that's the one, the police were just here for—"

Shut up, Kora wants to plead, to scream. *Shut up, shut up, shut up, shut up!*

Damn this concussion, damn her carelessness, damn Laurie's craftiness, damn her blabbering fucking mouth, damn it all, why couldn't she have just died properly, why does it always come back to this rotten old misery—

"Mabel!" Kora screeches again, shambling through the light, tripping over a chair leg. She tumbles, kicking the chair across the hallway as her head smashes into the tile.

"Miss, miss, settle down, settle *down!*"

Several orderlies and nurses grab hold of her arms, raising her up. Kora summons what little strength remains, flinging one nurse across the hallway in blind panic. She hears him slam into a vending machine, the lights giving her a blinding migraine.

"Miss, calm down, *calm down!*"

They grab hold of her, all trying to pin her down, and if she wasn't weakened and woeful, she'd stand a chance, more than a chance, she'd slaughter them all, she'd crush them all, anything to take back the one thing she has left—

She hears Mabel's panicked footfall grow distant, and it is like hearing the sound of your last little innocence fleeing the asylum it used to call home.

"Mabel, please!" Kora sobs as a syringe punctures her skin, injections dulling her head.

They slow her mind, but that's okay, because it lets her focus on the face. The face she needs to save, the face she could recover, the face she could reassure and promise, it was an accident, she could protect...

Damn this life, damn everything it's taken, and damn the devil she demanded—

She collapses against the floor, foggy with fate and reminiscence.

"Please," Kora murmurs. "Don't leave me alone again..."

She thinks of Mabel's embrace, the bright lights fading away, welcoming her last stolen security back to heaven.

"Anything but that..."

And then Kora remembers her heart in hell, and all is black.

Violet wrestles with Kora's sliding closet door, the decrepit piece of shit getting stuck a thousand times. She gives it a good heave, splintering the wood as she wrenches it open. She frowns and stretches her arm, feeling a whole lot stronger than she ever has.

Maybe Kora wasn't the only bearer of gifts.

Violet decides not to think about Ira again. That'd be far too distracting, especially when she was already on the verge of a complete mental breakdown and she needed to focus, lest Karma go down and she hang in the—

Breathe, Violet, breathe.

She catches her breath and sorts through Kora's clothes, feeling a little bad for intruding on the woman's privacy, of all things. She finds the axe when she nearly cuts her palm open with it. Violet flinches and carefully throws clothes aside, unearthing the bloody axe.

Wow, Kora really didn't hide her stuff well at all.

It only takes a couple minutes to find the rest. She digs a forgotten duffel bag out of one corner, shoving various items of interest into it — the axe goes in first, a tight fit. She gently nestles the crossbow in on top of it, gathering up every last bolt she can find and slotting them wherever there is free space. She hums as she works, not out of some cartoonish, villainous apathy; more out of anxiety and a need for distraction.

Ashes, ashes, we all fall down...

She throws the weathered leather jacket over all the weaponry, using it as a cover — a precaution that would likely prove unnecessary, considering Lake Leer's evening inactivity, but one that reassures her nonetheless. She takes the mask last, overtaken by the beautiful eyes that almost match its bearer, eons of strife and sin worn into every groove.

She shakes herself out of her stupor and tosses it into the bag, hurling it over her shoulder with a grunt. She sways as she stands and takes off for the stairs, stumbling down every creaking step.

Violet's halfway down the stairs when she notices the headlights shining through the window.

She gasps and hits the ground floor. The car's engine hums to a stop, headlights disappearing in a moment's notice.

Violet crawls across the kitchen tile, taking cover behind the island. She leaves the duffel bag beside her, peeking over the counter.

Who the hell is here? Why now? Why now, only after she had taken all of Karma's incriminating belongings into the one place *more* obvious than the closet? Fate has one twisted sense of humor.

Words outside pierce the cracked window, a souvenir of Violet's little home invasion. A male's voice. "Hey, there's another car here."

She recognizes the second voice instantly, Laurie Thompson's. Violet grits her teeth at the sound. "Just be careful going in. Lights are all out, I don't think anyone's here."

Another male's voice — Sky, she remembers, Skyler Simmons. "Her folks might have two. Let's just hurry this up, please? Breaking and entering isn't exactly my scene."

"Pussy," Laurie quips. She bashes the door handle with something, the whole thing shuddering under the blow.

Violet dives back behind the island, throwing a hand over her mouth. Quiet. Quiet. Just sit back and think of a beach or something.

After a few more blows, the door gives in, tilting ajar with a creak. "Could you have been any louder?" Sky asks. "Tony, hand me that flashlight."

There's some rummaging as a flashlight splays over the ground floor, shining right over the island for a moment. She just holds still, hoping the duffel bag isn't visible from their position.

Luckily, it doesn't seem to be, and the light jerks back towards the stairs. Her sweat sticks to her hand, coalescing on her lips. Why do you always seem to get itchy exactly when you can't risk moving?

"You said we got one more stop after this?" Tony asks as the three search the kitchen.

"Yeah," Laurie brusquely replies. "We got to get some guns after this. That old hunting store's probably still got some, just gotta step over the police tape."

"Guns?" Sky squeaks.

"Yeah, guns. Sky, we're taking on someone who has survived stabbings, long falls, axes to the chest, and God knows what else. Why wouldn't we use guns?"

"It's sound logic," Tony agrees.

"I thought you said this was like *Dream Warriors,*" Sky protests.

"Yeah, except without the whole 'dying at the end' part," Laurie says, upturning a couch cushion. "And they all died because they tried to murder Freddy Krueger without guns. Ooh, penny."

Guns? That's cheating, Violet sorely thinks.

"I guess," Sky says, defeated. "But if we find evidence here like we hope? Will we even need to take her on at all?"

"Hopefully not, but the police here are about as useful as an infertile sperm donor."

"Better safe than sorry," Tony agrees. "Especially if she's as bad as you two say. I, for one, think the plan of 'shoot her twenty-five times in the face' is way smarter than any horror movie shenanigans. You think they have any Cheetos?"

"Are you going to steal their *food?*" Sky stammers.

"Tony," Laurie interrupts. "Speaking of that plan, did you contact the art club?"

"Yeah," Tony says. "Yeah, and between them and all your friends, we'll have ourselves a little army. Should work out fine. Hopefully."

"This is insane," Sky breathes. "I think I hate *Dream Warriors.*"

Violet has decided she also hates *Dream Warriors.*

"Sky," Laurie interrupts. "I doubt there's anything down here. Let's go check around upstairs before anyone comes home. I don't know how long they'll be at the hospital."

"I'll do a double check down here," Tony says.

"Whatever," Laurie says, two sets of feet stomping up the creaking stairs. Tony starts rifling through cabinets, no subtlety in his step.

Violet swallows nervously, giving the duffel bag a side glance.

Bad things. Bad things.

She pulls out her dagger, veins black as pitch.

Bad things are upon them. Karma might die. Karma needs blood. They're going to get guns, and they're going to kill her. If Karma dies, Violet dies. If they die, they hang in a forest of revelatory rot and declaiming decay.

Kill or be killed. Murder to survive. It's just the food chain. It's nothing personal. It's not evil. It's necessary. It's survival. It's *survival.*

Her body and her soul are at odds, her panicked mind pissing right off to greener pastures. Violet cradles the dagger, weighing her options. No, option singular.

She doesn't know how many crazy kids with guns Karma can handle, and she knows she can thin the herd here. It won't do much, but it's better than nothing at all, and without leadership, they might scatter and dissipate. Cut off the head of the dragon and hope it's not a hydra.

Violet ponders the duffel bag as Tony tears open a bag of chips on the other side of the island. Her heavy breaths ripple against her sweating palm.

There's nothing more dangerous than someone with nothing to lose.

Violet retrieves Karma's mask as quietly as she manage. It has no straps or anything, but when she presses it against her face, it clings like it belongs there, a warming wave of reassurance running down her spine. She squeezes the dagger with both hands, counting her breaths, a proven elixir for anxiety.

She is no villain. She merely needs to survive. She must sacrifice to live, leave her offerings for the serial killer that has become her charge. It is purely pragmatic, no malice, no spite, no failure of character.

Violet Vance is prepared to sacrifice a lot. She isn't prepared to sentence herself to an eternity of failure.

Let's go with the next best thing, she decides, a hidden tear running down her anonymous face.

Do it fast, regret it later.

I'm sorry, Mom.

The fridge opens and floods the room with white light. Tony hums some shitty pop song she's heard on the radio. Violet bites her lip, hands shaking so badly that the dagger trembles with her.

She forces herself to move, staying low as she creeps around the island. She pokes her masked face out into view. Tony doesn't turn, attention occupied with refrigerated treats.

Do it fast—

She darts across the kitchen—

No time to hesitate—

No, no, no, no, turn around, turn around—

No time for regret—

Violet, no, no, no, no!

Now—

She takes her first breath as her fist seizes a clump of his hair. He jumps before he thinks to scream, and she jams the dagger down his throat before he gets the chance. His hands spasm as he sputters into the blade. He stumbles back, nearly knocks her flat over, but she stands her ground.

She takes her second breath, her body moving on instinct, a

different animal entirely. She shoves the knife deeper, cross-guard bashing his teeth inward, some of them tumbling down his drowning gullet.

His thrashing hands knock hers aside and she loses grip of her weapon. He kicks at her legs even as the pain overtakes him, trying to scream. She stumbles back, acting before she can think twice.

Violet throws him against the counter, crunching in his knee with the sole of her shoe, the boy thrashing under her supernatural strength. She seizes the open fridge door and slams it against his head, wincing with the first *crack.*

His struggles intensify as his nails tear furrows into her hand, blood showering milk and butter. She opens it wide and slams it again, *crack,* and again, *crack,* and again, *crack,* and again, *crack—*

Scarlet smothers the eggs, then the cheese, then it's running down the fridge's walls, then it's painting fruit, then it's dripping down onto the floor, then it's overtaken the color of his shirt, then it's—

Tony's body, overtly deceased, crumples against the floor.

His body stills against the wet tile, head sodden in sanguine, eyes bulging out of their sockets like some cartoon from Hell. Violet grabs her stomach and doubles over, barely managing to hold back her bile, free hand clinging onto the island for support.

Shit. Shit. Fuck. She's a killer. She's a murderer. She just killed a man, and she wants to cry, and she wants to laugh, and she wants to scream, and she wants to dance, to jump, it's too much, too much energy, too much confusion, too much fear, too much—

"Tony? Did you knock something over?" Laurie calls from upstairs.

Violet's eyes dart towards the steps as she hurls herself back behind the island.

She cradles the dagger in her hands, examining the handle. Its veins glow and pulse a bright crimson, pleased and satisfied.

Heal, Karma, please. Heal. Don't ever make me do that again.

"Oh, my God, oh—" Sky begins, his words trailing into the sound of vomit hitting the floor.

"Sky, Sky—" Laurie snaps.

"Tony's *dead,* oh my God, there's someone in here with us, oh fuck, we need to—"

"Sky!" Laurie shouts. "Run for the car, *now!* Do *not* fuck around, just run, you can panic later! Let's go!"

"But we need to—"

"We'll kill her later, when we can, let's *go!*"

Laurie grabs Sky's arm, and they start to run.

Violet lunges for the duffel bag, snatching the axe for herself, taking the opportunity before she can convince herself otherwise. Sky makes it out first, but Laurie turns back just in time to see Violet raising the axe above her head.

"Oh, fucking *hell!*" Laurie screeches, ducking instantly. Violet stabs through the front door, splintering wood. Sky sprints as fast he is able across the lawn, thunder cracking over him with all the menace a proper horror story deserves.

Violet, unfortunately, is not a proper horror movie villain, or else she would've nailed Laurie with that swing. She kicks the crawling girl back into the kitchen, knocking Laurie onto her back. Violet wrenches the axe free from the door, her muscles aching as she faces her prone enemy.

Laurie, thoroughly unintimidating in her raincoat, gets to her feet, standing opposite the pale shadow of her rival. "You're not the Karma Killer," Laurie says coldly. "You're too short."

Violet remembers how Kora got caught in the first place, and accordingly keeps her mouth shut.

"You're also not as funny," Laurie snarls, lunging forward.

Violet, admittedly, did not expect the fight reaction. She tries to catch her with the axe, but finds herself just a second too late. Laurie tackles her through the front door, sending them stumbling.

They both sprawl onto the lawn in a heap. Violet barely keeps hold of Karma's preferred weapon, determined not to get stabbed in the chest like the woman she mimics. The rain thrashes their intertwined bodies as they struggle, the copycat killer deterred by Laurie's aggressive kicks.

Violet gets to her feet, swaying uneasily as she rears back the axe. Laurie hurls herself away as the head of it obliterates dirt, a guaranteed kill had it landed a moment earlier.

Laurie darts towards the car, diving into the passenger seat. She tugs the door closed just as Violet slams into it, shattering glass. Sky screams and hits the gas, the car launching forward. Violet holds onto the side of the busted window with a growl, trying to hang on.

"Hey, wannabe!" Laurie shouts.

Violet prepares a killing blow as the car starts to pull her away.

"Leave a message for the real deal, would you? I miss her!"

Laurie blasts Violet in the face with a can of pepper spray. Violet loses her grip, collapsing against the gravel as she bats at her eyes. The car tears away into the rain, swerving up a hill as Violet sputters and screams.

She rolls onto her front, tearing off the mask, rubbing at her watering eyes. "Ow! Ow! Christ!"

When she can finally see again, she watches the car's taillights disappear into the town proper, throwing the axe aside in frustration.

No wonder Karma got a kick out of hunting that one.

In the car, the heater billows over them, deafening Sky's tears. He slams on the wheel in frustration. "Fuck! He was my best friend, Laurie, my best... Do you even *care?!*"

"I'm coping!" Laurie snaps, the wind buffeting through the broken window. "Someone had to get us out of there, okay? I'm sorry!"

"Fuck..." He shakes his head, opening his own window. "You were right. Let's go get some guns... Let's make her pay."

Laurie's phone starts vibrating on the dashboard. She stills her hammering heart, the cool night air running over her face. She picks up the phone, checking the caller ID.

Mabel Alexander.

Laurie smirks. "Yeah, let's bag us a slasher."

CYCLE TWELVE
Tango Till They're Sore

/// October 29th. Two days until Halloween.

The bolt bullseyes the hay bale as Kora Lynch appraises her aim. She purrs approvingly, resting the crossbow atop the grass and preparing another quarrel.

Kora's old leather jacket lies in the dirt somewhere, food for the worms. Right now, it just feels like a reminder, a tragic parting gift, something she can't look at without conjuring up uncomfortable thoughts and shamefully emotional memories. Thus, it lays in the grass like she'd leave a butchered corpse... like the butchered corpses she *will* leave, for what the world's done to her.

The wind tackles her thinning stature, ominous clouds darkening the sky, threatening those below with more rain. Birds scatter into the sky, trees shake and hum in the wind, leaves dance as they descend. Far along the forest trail and down the exposed hills, the waves of Lake Leer crash against the shore, proving particularly tempestuous today.

Kora pays the lake no heed, for she is something fiercer. She looses her second shot, nearly splitting her initial bolt in two.

"Maybe for dinner I'll go hunt a bunny or something," Kora suggests, her sullen tone breaking the silence of the wilds. "I could use the exercise. And practice."

There is no reply. Kora turns her head, crossbow dangling against her thigh. Violet sits in a rickety lawn chair before their stolen log cabin, her hair blowing into her face with every gust of wind. The home lays nestled on the peak of a rather impressive hill, sprawling forests surrounding them in every direction. Violet's mother's car sits in silence, wheels caked in dirt and grass.

Kora tilts her head. "Vi?"

Violet looks up from her laptop, jury-rigged with an imposing mess of cables that have somehow bestowed upon it the feeblest incarnation of an Internet connection. "Yeah?"

"Rabbit. For dinner." Kora shrugs. "Tonight. I'm bored, wanted to go hunt something."

"Thought you moved on to people."

"You said to hold off. I'm letting you call the shots. Also, I don't *eat* people. I'm not a savage."

"Right," Violet says, turning her attention back to her laptop.

Kora takes a peek at the screen, gingerly resting her crossbow against the cabin. "What are you up to?"

Violet shrugs noncommittally. "You."

Kora raises an eyebrow, strands of silver hair blowing in the wind.

Violet blushes deeply, glancing down at her lap. "Not like... okay. Your mask."

Kora shrugs. "What about it?"

"You're not the first person to wear it."

Kora crouches down beside her, resting her elbow on Violet's thigh. "Hm?"

Violet tabs over to an Imgur collection, pictures presumably collected from across the Internet. "Look. Okay, like, so what you've got is a kabuki mask, right? It's for traditional Japanese theater. The word means the 'art of singing and dancing', roughly, uh... a lot of focus on emotion and character, like... they'd have these masks that represented different feelings and characteristics, and... so, it started during the Edo period—"

Kora pleads with her eyes.

Violet sighs in disappointment. "Right. Bored. Okay, so, look, this mask... *your* mask, not just one of the same type, look... can I see it?"

Kora frowns, summoning her face out of thin air and reluctantly handing it over. Violet runs her thumb over the deep wound on the left cheek — some scar from an unknown skirmish, as far as Kora could gather. "This. There's this, uh, scar, for lack of a better word. One teardrop under one eye. Besides all the damage, the eyes and the tear, this thing's pretty much blank. That is pretty unusual. They usually have much more elaborate designs."

"Yeah, so?" Kora asks. "I got it from a battle-horny Lady in the Lake. I didn't think it would be all that typical."

"You'll see in a second," Violet rebuts, scrolling up her document. "Look."

Kora tilts her head. The screen shares a scan of some old scroll or parchment, covered in Japanese kana that Kora has no hope of understanding. What catches her eye, really, is the drawing of a haunting kabuki mask. A long, jagged scar runs down the left cheek, a tear drawn under one eye.

She's not sure if the goosebumps that follow originate from the picture or the wind.

"It's from the early 1700s," Violet explains. "I can't read Japanese, but the article I got this from says this mask belongs to some vengeful spirit of folklore. Her name was Oiwa."

"Folklore?"

"Yeah. It was... she originated as a story about a woman dying and haunting her... vile husband until he snapped, but then it got added onto millions of times over the years. She'd supposedly enter the homes of those who had committed grievous misdeeds. Sometimes she was called upon, sometimes she'd show up on her own, but the end results were always the same. She'd torture and slaughter the aggressors, no matter where they lived, no matter who they were. Rich or poor, good or evil, no one was safe. They treated her as a sort of onryo, which is like... a wronged ghost or spirit, usually a woman, that come back from the dead in search of vengeance for the ills that plagued their lives.

"It's largely treated as fact, too — at least it was at the time, not just some bedtime story to scare kids off, but I think that's pretty typical in Japan. The biggest actual story I found, was this description of a bloodbath onstage. For one of these kabuki shows, I mean. Apparently, our winter wrath here performed like normal, until she just..."

Violet hesitates. "Well, a lot of people died. Let's leave it at that."

"So..." Kora murmurs. "This is an old mask."

"Bloody history, too. Look, I've found so many pictures."

Violet starts scrolling. "Look, the Great Depression here. Kids in a steel factory. Look in the back left corner. There's a girl back there, ten years old or so, nearly obscured by machinery, but you can see the mask on them."

Kora squints. It's all true. Blurred and barely visible, but she's there, haunted eyes meeting Kora's own. Violet scrolls down again.

"World War II, North African campaign, I think. There's a big group of soldiers here. Normal picture, really, but look inside the plane behind them."

Kora finds someone sitting in the cockpit, wearing a rather familiar kabuki mask. The other soldiers in the picture are completely unaware of their stalker, by all appearances.

"Hell, not even the first time the mask's been to Lake Leer."

"What?" Kora asks.

"Yeah, look," Violet points. "Rather famous killer, even by our standards, from a couple decades back. Fourteen, fifteen years ago. Police just called him the Bleeding Bear, never found a real name."

"Yeah, I've read about him," Kora grunts, slinging her crossbow strap over her shoulder. "I'm getting hungry. No one's going to find us here, right? I don't want you getting into any trouble while I'm gone."

Violet shakes her head. "It's my, uh... my brother's cabin. He used to come here when he needed a break. He built it himself, I'm not sure anyone even really knows it's here. No one owns this land."

Kora raises an eyebrow. "What happened to your brother?"

Violet licks her lips uncomfortably.

"Right. I'll be back. Laurie and her goons still meeting as planned tonight?"

"As far as I know. She thinks I want in on her 'Dream Warriors' plan, so..."

Kora gathers several bolts. "Good. Deer doesn't make captivating game."

Violet feels her skin crawl, closing the laptop. "Hold on. Aren't you cold?"

"No," Kora mutters, but Violet vanishes into the cabin anyway, the door swaying in the wind. Like some sort of cartoon, she tosses a gluttony of random items out the open doorway, her overflowing stash of shit seemingly bottomless. Books with dreams of high art, kitchen utensils, sticky stacks of homework, a weird puzzle box in the shape of a cube, DVDs, clothes...

With a vocalized "a-ha", Violet emerges into the bitter air, presenting a large, green army jacket – too big for her, but probably the perfect size for Kora. It bolsters a number of pockets, spacious and insulating. The sleeves cuff at the wrists, a furred hood dangling down the back.

Kora tilts her head. "Yes?"

"I've noticed you kind of..." Violet tilts her head at the rejected leather jacket, dead in the dirt. "Moved on. I thought you might like something to move on to."

"It's for me?"

Violet nods, passing the jacket to her partner in crime.

Kora examines it curiously and pulls it on. Violet blinks, and Kora is gone, the masked Karma Killer taking her place, developing pride in her new aesthetic. Karma fiddles with the jacket, one that easily makes her lean body look twice as large.

"How do I look?" asks Lake Leer's resident slasher.

"Like Jason Voorhees, but, uh, se... scarier," Violet stammers.

She can't see a thing behind Karma's expressionless mask, but she swears she can sense a smile.

"It'll do," Karma deadpans, trudging off towards the forest.

The high school is somehow less suffocating in the dead of night.

Violet fixates on the hyperpop emanating from the earbud she's tucked beneath her hair, her foot bouncing in time with the beat of the bass drum.

Tonight, we're going to make a killing / No value in a life without a need so thrilling / And if you're my only sympathetic savior, well / Cross my heart, hope to die, love you in hell.

She mumbles every lyric, every wretched word, every damning oath.

Because if she doesn't hyperfixate, she'll scream, and she'll condemn them to the forest. And the *only* thing that scares her more than the forest is what Karma will do to her under those forlorn canopies.

So she bites her tongue and sits, this sinner's anticipation soundtracked with The 20yo Trash Goblins.

Life, Violet thinks, *sometimes feels like a fever dream.*

"Violet, you with us?" Laurie asks.

Violet mumbles in assent, raising her head. She overlooks the conspirators with unease. Laurie stands at the front of the class, diagrams and instructions drawn onto the whiteboard. How to reload a gun, how to effectively fire, ideal target points, illustrations of homemade traps — all in Laurie's trademark, sloppy handwriting.

Violet looks over the amateur illustrations, truthfully taken aback at the accuracy of her information. Apparently Thompson *can* do her homework, given the pressure of certain death.

She has to hold back a chuckle at the sheer absurdity of all of this.

Around her sit a couple dozen of her classmates, at least — the assembled art club is here, sans Olivia and Tony (thanks to a small case of the deceased); every cheerleader in the school; a number of the jocks, and a couple other wannabe heroes. They had numbers, that much was certain.

Shame it wouldn't be enough. Guns were one thing. Using them effectively with two days' theoretical training and no stress control was another.

She gives Mabel a wary glance, who is currently working with Laurie on demonstrating the proper ejection and handling of an emptied magazine. Laurie painstakingly details the differences between the usage of an actual gun and that of one in a first-person shooter — of which there are many — and demonstrates proper reloading technique, as if anyone will be level-headed enough to remember it with an axe murderer before their damned faces.

Violet checks her phone texts, bouncing her heel.

Six minutes ago, she had messaged Kora and told her Mabel, of all people, had shown up to this meeting. It wasn't part of the plan. She knew Kora would want to know.

Kora hadn't answered. Kora, Violet presumed, was lending her body to a darker ego right now.

"We still haven't decided when we're going to lure our slasher in," Laurie drones, the words barely in Violet's periphery. "Everyone's going to carry some sort of melee weapon with them as well, just in case. A switchblade, we got plenty, whatever you want. We raided that old hunting store, got plenty of goodies. Looks like Karma did us a favor in the end."

"How exactly are you going to lure her in?" Violet interrupts.

"Me. I'm the bait. She's got a fixation, you know. She thinks I'm her 'Final Girl', and I intend on proving her right. We're going to prepare ahead of time, we'll set traps, we'll be armed, plus we're calling the cops as soon as anything goes wrong. She's tough, but she can't take on all of us."

"What if she can?" Violet presses. "What if we're all just going to get ourselves killed?"

"Then why are you here?" Laurie asks, narrowing her eyes.

"Just hope you know what you're doing. We got anybody on guard?"

"Yeah," Laurie says. "Several people. You don't need to be paranoid."

You're right, Violet thinks, leaning back. *I picked the winning side.*

Carl Helsley washes his hands. The lights of the school bathroom flicker like a horror set, as they tend to do in such an underfunded school. He hums the tune of some old Bint Finny song while he does, his assigned handgun lying on the nasty countertop. He wished the school would clean... well, anything, every surface looking like some sort of breeding ground for cockroaches and other assorted nasties.

He runs a hand through his dirty blonde hair, examining himself in the mirror as his phone rings again in his pocket. He ignores it, not wanting to explain to Amber where he is right now. Laurie's an old friend, and she needs help, and who *knows* who would be next if this Karma woman got her. If his girlfriend finds out he's possibly about to tango with a crazy killer, well...

He shrugs. He'll be fine, he knows, closing his eyes as he runs water over his face.

He opens his eyes. The Karma Killer stands reflected in the mirror behind him, sporting a new jacket and killer intent.

"Guilty," whispers the woman of Wrath.

He doesn't even think fast enough to scream. He turns as she lunges, slamming the back of his head against the bathroom mirror, his spine crumpling as it splinters against the sink, the mirror shattering. Karma inconceivably snatches one propelled shard of glass out of the air.

Thick and jagged, the shard becomes Karma's weapon, slashing a jagged line across both of Chris' eyes. He screams as blood spurts between Karma's fingers, irises draining themselves of life, coating the killer's mask in a fresh layer of scarlet. She carries on without concern, yanking his head forward and then slamming it back into the mirror.

His skull cracks with the wall, body spasming in its final death throes. It slumps free of suffering, head firmly interred in the shattered mirror, pieces of dirtied glass decorating the crime scene.

Karma clears her throat, approaching the sink beside him and washing her hands. The blood circles the drain, meditating, reassuring. She examines her maroon mask in the mirror, feeling energy dance up her veins, run through her blood, kickstart her heart.

If this is what it feels like to be bad, Webster ought to rewrite the dictionary.

"Thanks, you've been a real sport," Karma says, pulling her gloves back on to cheerfully pat the corpse's shoulder. She relieves him of his unneeded handgun, stepping out of the bathroom.

As Karma stalks the darkened school hallway, she lets the gun fade away, stored wherever all of her shit ends up. The logical next step of a slasher movie would be to cut the power, but that plan falls apart with a second's thought. They all have smartphones, after all, so the rudimentary parlor tricks of the eighties just wouldn't cut it anymore.

Karma clicks her tongue in disappointment. Best not to cut the power, anyways. They won't expect her that way, not yet.

She smells her next bunny around the hallway's corner, eyeing the nearby fire extinguisher. Karma flattens herself against the wall, ceasing to breathe. The petite cheerleader comes around the corner and Karma seizes her throat.

The girl sputters where she wishes to scream, raising her gun. Karma bats away the offending hand, snapping her wrist and throwing the pistol across the room. She pins the girl to the wall, sniffing her hair.

"Is my final girl here, beautiful?" Karma purrs. "I smell her on you, pretty thing."

"Y-yes!" the girl squeaks, red curls bouncing as she desperately nods her head. "I'll take you!"

Karma scoffs, pulling away. "Oh, I'm sorry to mislead. I know how to find her, I just like the whole interrogation thing. I hear it's a hit with this depraved generation."

The girl's eyes widen in a mix of utter terror and disbelief.

"No? Not a fan?" Karma shrugs. "Shit. Honest mistake." Karma wrenches the fire extinguisher free of its mounting, releasing the girl just long enough to splatter her head against the wall. The cheerleader doesn't scream long enough to matter, blood redecorating the wall as Karma batters her skull to shreds with her improvised club. The *thumps* echo down the halls, and Karma reckons the first 911 calls will be made within the next four or five seconds.

The body slumps down the wall and Karma throws aside the fire extinguisher. It hits the floor with a *clang*, rolling off with a guilty conscience. "I'll call you!" Karma chirps, walking away.

She smells him before she hears the clatter of footsteps, another student barreling into the hallway just in time to witness her little fling. "Innocent," Karma monotones, snatching him mid-run and throwing him against the wall. He hits the floor, unconscious.

"Terry?" a student calls from inside the biology classroom. Karma sniffs, the squalid stench of two unkempt teenage boys startled into movement. Laurie's trail wafts further down the hallway, luring her longing heart towards the stairs across the school.

"Just one moment, sweetheart," Karma purrs, one of her two hormone-riddled victims-to-be charging into the hallway, attempting some heroics. She lunges forward as he raises his gun, his first two shots sailing past her head. One of her ears goes deaf with the pressure, the noise blinding, but she keeps her grip.

"You know, kiddo, here in America, we frown upon gun violence," Karma chides, cracking his hand like an eggshell, bones grinding into soup. He screams for help as friend scrambles through the bio lab — jumping over a table, it sounds like.

Karma turns, her helpless victim held as a meat shield, one she happily uses to block the classroom door. The other student stops in his tracks, his raised gun trembling.

Karma clicks her tongue. "Boy, with hands like that, you ain't gonna shoot shit."

"P-put him down!" he insists nonetheless, his friend whimpering in Karma's hands. She squeezes the blackened blue sack that remains of his hand, making him squeal like a pig.

Footsteps congregate upstairs. The gunshots were heard. From her one working ear, she can hear the sound of sirens in the distance.

It won't matter. It'll just make this a hell of a lot more fun. Karma licks her lips in anticipation, an arousing, ecstatic high crawling up her spine.

"Listen," Karma says. "I've got your—" She leans down, sniffing her hostage's neck. "Hm. Brothers, huh?"

The standing boy hesitantly nods, their mutual traits obvious if you knew to look for them. Karma tilts her head, more predator than woman. "Please," he whimpers, gun held high.

"Lower the goddamn gun," Karma orders.

He shakes his head.

Karma takes one imposing step forward. He backs up two, jostling a table, his hand grazing against a microscope. His finger inches closer to the trigger.

"Fine, have it your way," Karma concedes, lunging forward.

He pulls the trigger and she makes ample use of his brother. The bullets carve up his own kin, bullets crafting craters in his skin. The shooter's eyes widen in instant regret, his executioner closing the distance in the time he wastes with remorse.

Karma's fist slams right through her hostage's head, so strengthened that it simply *explodes* into meaty chunks, showering the living brother in gore. Karma's fingers find their way to the survivor's jaw, digging furrows into his chin. He tries to struggle, of course, but he's pinned between a headless corpse and a table.

Of course, his resistance is of little use.

His jaw splits free, skin tearing like lettuce, jaw popping off and hanging on by the barest sinews. She throws him back, his hands reaching up to caress the mess she's made of his lower face. He looks like some sort of deranged ventriloquist's puppet, eyes trapped wide, a broken scream escaping his mangled mouth.

"Class dismissed," Karma growls, dropping his headless brother and snatching up the microscope.

She caves in the side of the survivor's head, the blood on her clothes doubling as she beats him down against the floor. His feet writhe and shudder, caking it in viscera as Karma bashes in his skull with all the efficiency of someone hammering in a nail.

Only when the floor looks like a slaughterhouse does she stand, leaving the microscope with one of the bodies. Her heart thumps faster and faster, whispering sweet, syrupy sentiments with every sacrifice.

She takes one moment to relish the feeling, but no more — two pairs of footsteps drag objects around upstairs, sirens drawing closer and closer. Karma tilts her head. Scraping furniture. They're making impromptu barricades, or something. Perhaps pieces of cover? That would make some sense in such a large hallway.

Karma chuckles, marveling at their creativity in the face of certain death. It was cute, really. The way they behave under stress, the last promises and confessions they make to one another, the things they'll do when they think they won't be around to see the consequences of their actions.

It's all fascinating, really, and when she's done murdering just about every blasted sinner in this loathsome town, maybe she ought to go into the field of psychology.

Karma summons and loads her crossbow, throwing it over her shoulder. She strides back into the hallway, her favorite axe called to both hands.

"Come on," she growls, taunting two sets of footsteps at the top of the stairs. She twirls the axe in her palms, breaking out into a startling sprint across the hallway.

A jock turns the corner, the stairs behind him leading to the deplorable rabble she came here for. He squeals like a baby when he sees her, dropping his gun as he trips down the steps.

What, did he expect her to slowly shamble over to him? Idiot.

She gleefully swings her axe, putting all her strength into the swing. It cleaves clean through his torso, halving spine, splitting guts. His top half flies over the railing and lands in some janitor's supplies, smashing headfirst into a mop bucket.

She kicks aside his severed legs, limbs wrenching free of his hips as every appendage collapses in a hemorrhaged heap. Karma spins on her heel at the landing, finding herself face to face with a rather terrified brunette.

The brunette backs up, all the color drained from her face, unable to even raise the gun in her hands.

"Innocent," Karma declares, flipping the axe around and smacking the girl in the forehead with the butt of it. She falls and hits the landing, unconscious.

Karma reaches the top of the stairs, panting, looking down the long hall that will become her battleground.

Nowhere to run, Thompson, nowhere to hide. Your time has come.

Several safeties click off, dozens of guns propped up on overturned desks and makeshift barricades — every single one pointed at her. She eyes Violet behind one, giving her accomplice the slightest nod. Violet ducks into a classroom, unseen.

Laurie stands at the end of the hall, angelic in the moonlight. The rain lashes against the window behind her, thunder roaring over the sirens outside. Laurie flicks off the safety on her handgun, stormy eyes set in their course.

Karma looks her over, taking in her latest makeover — a leather jacket, combat boots, dirtied jeans, one hand wrapped in a bloody, homemade splint. *Well, well, Laurie, aren't you getting a little familiar?*

Karma raises her hands, axe vanishing. "Laurie! Didn't I tell you to stop greeting girls at gunpoint?"

"Thought I'd experiment a little," Laurie snaps. "We've called 911, Kora. The police are here already. Any moment now, and they'll be storming in."

Karma tilts her head. "You don't keep up with the news, do you? I'd say I have about seventy-eight minutes before they dig up a pair of balls and actually knock down that door."

"You're not getting out of this, not again. You've killed enough people tonight."

Karma claps her hands, giggling. "Oh, you have *no* idea! Let's see..." She raises fingers, counting them off. "One... two, three... four... five... all in one night! Well, that's a new record."

"Is this a game to you?" Laurie exclaims. "Just going for a high score? What the *fuck* happened to you, Kora? You used to just be a quiet, sensitive kid, and now you're *mad!*"

"Yeah, keep pretending you don't know. Easier that way. Tear apart your undesirables and sweep them under the rug, right? It's happened to a million people since the dawn of time, it's what happened to me. No, my life isn't a game, Laurie, it's a tragedy. You ever read a tragedy? They don't have happy endings."

"I'm sorry for what happened to you, Kora, but that doesn't-"

"You're *sorry?*" Karma scoffs, breaking into an incredulous laugh. "Are you... are you fucking serious? Yeah, I'm sure you're sorry. People are only ever sorry when it's their hide that's about to be skinned raw. Yeah, Laurie, I don't give a damn if you're sorry. I'm not. I love you, I love this little game we play, I love this little dance, but all things come to an end. And, frankly..."

Karma draws the crossbow. "I am tired, and I simply cannot bring myself to care anymore. I've lost everything, lost everyone, lost my hope. You're scared, Laurie, you and your little Dream Warriors, because you have so, so much to lose. Me?"

She feels a single tear crawling down her cheek, hidden away behind her forged identity. "I got nothing, Laurie. Nothing but you to chase. I got fucking nothing."

Laurie chuckles, aiming her gun at Karma's head. "I take it back. You deserve everything you got."

For the first time since she's found her new face, Karma freezes, and for a moment it's all there again, all brought howling back — the meek little nerd in the back of the class, the little kicking post for all the hyenas and all the vultures to spit on and haze, the useless little fag that never-

And she had found hope, she thought she had earned good, and then she wasn't lonely, and now she's lost the good in her, she's lost her Mabel, and now she can't even live with the naive innocence of a paradise after this miserable life to cap it all off. No, she's earned nothing but a godforsaken forest, one still hanging over her shoulders.

The moment passes.

"I'm going to kill you," Karma hisses, her eyes violently flaring, and there is no longer anything human in her voice.

Laurie swallows, the smell of sweat and fear pervading the air. Her Dream Warriors raise their own guns, all shakily aiming for the bullseye — Karma's masked forehead.

And yet, she's more comfortable than she's ever been. This is her spotlight, her story, her staged suicide in the sun. After all, she's spent her whole life with a metaphorical gun to her head.

It's about time she took this whole blasted world with her, because there is no way in Hell that Kora Lynch is dying alone.

"Alright, here's the deal," Karma says, nodding to all the non-Laurie's in the audience. "Normally, I have a really big justice thing going on, you know? Make a big deal about that. Well, I'll be honest, the bitch that's connived you into protecting her — the one in the back, you know her well — she's rotten to the core, and I kind of have to kill her.

"So, to that end, anyone who gets between me and her is guilty, end of story. I don't care how much of a saint you've been, I'm dropping my code until that whore is dead. So, you step up, you try to play the hero, and you're getting slashed, you hear me? You're a stain on the ground."

No one speaks, no one runs, but the fear propagates, a miasma in the hall. When she wades in, when she starts executing, she's sure the majority will run. There aren't enough heroes in this world for anything else to happen, after all.

The police still don't bash down the door, as Karma expected, and she can see sweat trail down Laurie's skin. The one crippling failure of any half-baked plan was to rely on the government to cover your back when they were far too busy watching their own.

Laurie speaks — as per usual, the sole guiding voice for her adolescent hive mind. "I always knew your moral code was flexible."

"Isn't everyone's?" Karma asks.

She's killed a lot of people. She wonders how her healing factor's holding up.

"Do any of you believe in God?" Karma asks.

She raises her crossbow in her left hand, stolen handgun appearing in her right. The bolt fires first, whistling through the air and impaling one student's neck, the unwanted tracheotomy dropping the girl without a sound.

Her fellow students barely have time to react as Karma makes good use of her actual firearm experience. The first bullet flies, nailing one boy right between the eyes, his head jolting back.

"Best start praying," Karma growls.

She dives down as their reaction time catches up to her unnatural speed. The bullets shatter the air, dozens of them. Almost every single shot misses their mark, two catching her in the shoulder. She hides behind their own improvised cover, feeling her ebbing wound.

It throbs, but that's about it. Her skull throbs and pounds under the cacophony, the noise too much for her tuned senses. The pain is negligible, the sensation nothing more than a humming encouragement. Kill, kill, kill, the blood will heal, the slaughter will soothe, the vengeance will make her whole again.

Footsteps shuffle as one brave student dives over the desk, kicking her across the face. She hits the floor, reactions slowed by all the noise, and the boy crawls on top of her and aims his gun—

He is not fast enough. She whips up her own, firing point-blank into his chin, using up her last bullet as the blood drenches her chosen face. She throws the lifeless body aside, jumping to her feet with a scornful roar. She can't even hear it with the way her ears ring.

She embraces the animal and leaps into the air, summoning her axe to her eager hands. She pounces upon a retreating student, his legs snapping under her weight and crumpling against his chest. The crazed killer makes her execution, axe bisecting his head like a pumpkin.

As she predicted, several students dart for the stairs. Two more jump in front of her, one helplessly tugging the trigger of an empty gun, clearly too panicked to remember anything Laurie might've told him. The other brandishes a wooden baseball bat, his fight-or-flight complex throwing away his life. He charges.

Karma smiles wide, her mask bathed in purple.

She throws aside her axe, the weapon disappearing as it skids across the floor. She stands and raises her hands, roaring out her next words. "Come on, then! Give me a good fight! I'm fucking *starved!*"

The boy bellows out some horrified war cry, bringing the baseball bat against the side of her head. She doesn't even flinch as it shatters against her cheek, splinters raining over the floor, leaving Laurie's next sacrifice with a useless stump of a weapon.

He whimpers. Karma meets his eyes, licking her lips. "Cute."

Laurie screams from the back, clearly trying to get a shot in. "Andrew, move out of the—"

Karma grabs hold of the boy and lifts him horizontal, fingers digging into his skin. He screams and writhes, but of course, his struggles are no good. She slams him down against one of their makeshift barricades, the crack of his spine echoing down the hall. He hits the ground and twitches, completely paralyzed, tears running down his cheeks. "Hel—"

Karma's boot comes down on his head, leaving nothing but a dark stain.

She recognizes Dennis from Art Club, a boy thin enough to be a coke fiend. Karma rolls her eyes.

Dennis drops the empty gun, freezing up like so many do in the face of certain death.

"Dennis, *move!*" Laurie screeches.

He tries to back up, but Karma grabs hold of his sleeve, greedy for more blood.

"You really do look like a weasel," Karma muses. Her fingers plunge into his flesh, puncturing muscle. He screams and tries to pull away, Laurie's gun wavering as she tries to take proper aim.

Karma makes it easy. Her fingers find bone, find a secure grip, and she tears the boy in half, bones splintering as the two pieces of his body flatten against the hallway walls. The blood showers her, dulling her pain, sating her thirst, giving her life.

She strides through the valley of her dead classmates, boots crunching against bone and brain matter. For her credit, Laurie doesn't hesitate, tearfully emptying her magazine.

Even more impressively, most every shot hits. Karma barely flinches as the bullets penetrate her shoulders, arms, one piercing her side. Laurie's trigger clicks helplessly after her last round, and Karma doesn't drop, the axe appearing in her shuddering hands.

"Fuck my life," Laurie breathes, hurling the empty gun at the oncoming slasher's face. Naturally, it does nothing, but Laurie takes full advantage of the momentary distraction and Karma's dulled reflexes to run.

Karma flips the axe around, hitting Laurie across the head with the blunt end. Laurie twirls like a ballerina, slamming into the hallway wall with a gasp. Karma is with her in an instant. The axe head impales itself in the wall, the handle holding Laurie's throat to the wall.

Karma sniffs her hair, blood soaking through both their clothes. Her mask trails down the side of Laurie's shivering neck, taking in the scent, the axe handle leaving bruises on her final girl's throat.

"Game over, lovely," Karma whispers, her voice drenched in a mix of adoration and mirth. "Game over."

"Why?" Laurie whispers, letting herself cry this one time. After all, she's clearly beginning to doubt she'll get another chance to.

Karma shrugs. "Why not?"

"Why?" Laurie screams, spiteful spit slathering Karma's scarlet mask. "You couldn't just leave it well enough alone, could you? Couldn't just let this go. Don't you see what you've done? You've got nothing now. No future, no home, soon you'll be in a... a goddamn prison cell, if not executed!"

Karma tilts her head. "No future? My dear, I didn't have one anyways. You and everyone else in this fucking town made sure of that."

"Yeah?" Laurie screams, ineffectually kicking at Karma's knees. "Like you're trapped by circumstance, right? Sure, I'll admit it, fine, is that what you want? I was an asshole! I was! I was a terrible, nasty, rotten person!"

Karma shrugs and nods. "Yeah, that pretty much sums it up."

"You let that *define* you, Kora."

Karma narrows her eyes.

"God, I... you saw the environment I grew up in, Kora! You saw it! I-I've gotten nothing but shit my whole life, and I used that as an excuse to spit on other people, but... look, Kora, you've suffered. I've suffered. We've all suffered. But you know what? You *had* a future. Everyone does. Everyone fucking does! You had one, you could've survived, you could've endured—"

"What does it look like I'm doing?" Karma growls, more animal than human.

"It looks like you're *giving up!*" Laurie screams, thrashing against the axe handle. "It looks like you're giving up and dragging this damn world down with you! You gave up, decided there was nothing left, decided that before you even got a chance to really live... you're sixteen, for God's sake, and now you really have thrown it all away!"

Karma blinks.

"They're all dead, Kora!" Laurie spits. "Everyone you could've had a life with, everyone you could've proved wrong. They're all fucking dead, you've killed them all, and I'm sure that felt good in the moment, but one of these days it's going to catch up to you. At the end of it all, you're going to be alone again, everyone's gonna hate you, everyone who doesn't is going to be six feet under the ground, and this isn't like before, because before, you had a fucking *chance*, you goddamned idiot!"

Karma sniffs wetly, eyes fixated on her helpless prisoner.

"Just look at all the lives you've ruined," Laurie whispers, taking her last spiteful victory. "What are you going to do alone, Kora Lynch? 'Cause now there's no other future waiting for you."

"Well, everyone you know is dead too," Karma croaks. "I guess we'll have to be alone together."

Laurie spits on the kabuki mask, and Karma flinches.

"I'd rather die than spend another minute with you," Laurie declares. "Get it over with."

A lone crossbow bolt appears in Karma's dangling hand.

"I hope you live through all this," Laurie says. "I hope you suffer long enough to redefine the word."

"Fuck you," Karma growls. "Fuck you, for pushing me this far."

Karma prepares the killing blow, lining up the bolt with Laurie's forehead.

"Kora, wait!"

The killer recognizes the voice instantly, her dead heart stopping.

The bolt disappears, Karma's head hung low. She sighs in shame, turning to face Mabel Alexander.

Her ex-girlfriend stands shaking, hands practically glued to a hunting shotgun.

Karma blinks in disbelief. "Mabel, I... do you even know how to use that?"

"Kora, please," Mabel pleads, tears streaming down her cheeks. "Please, just talk to me."

She's lying, she wants to kill you—

Karma silences her inner sight, not ready for the truth tonight.

"Mabel, I—" Karma sniffs, irritant tears plentiful. "Mabel, it's not what it looks like."

Mabel raises an eyebrow, the shotgun pointed at Karma's chest. "Kora, I'm not mad, let's... I just want to talk. You don't need to kill any more people, okay?"

More sirens are loitering on the lot. Karma wonders how many minutes it's been.

"I haven't... I only killed a few," Karma chuckles nervously, cursing the old habit.

"You can let it go, Kora," Mabel whispers. "Please, Kora."

"Mabel, I—I didn't want you to see me like this, I... they hurt me, Mabel. I'm sorry, they... they just kept hurting me."

"I know, baby. I know. Just let go of her. It's not too late. It's not. I promise."

"Mabel, I'll..." Kora swallows, bloody tears trailing down her mask. "They'll put me away. After this, they'll... they don't understand. They pushed me to it. I couldn't... I just couldn't take it anymore. I—"

"I know," Mabel soothes, taking two cautious steps forward. "I know."

"Mabel, please, put down the gun, I—"

"I won't shoot you. It's a precaution. Please. I want to trust you. Show me I can trust you."

"I love you, Mabel," Karma desperately confesses. "Please. Please don't leave me."

"Never," Mabel promises. "I never will. You said you'd always protect me. Let me protect you."

Karma nods, smelling someone scurrying in the health classroom. Violet.

"Kora," Mabel whispers. "It's okay. We're okay."

Forget the pain, smell the flowers, taste the dream, just drop the—

Karma lets go of the axe, leaving Laurie still as a statue.

"No weapons, right?" Mabel asks gently.

Karma shakes her head, raising her empty hands, a display of peace. "Please, Mabel. Just... I just need everything to be okay for once. I just need... somebody..."

Her eyes well up again at the thought, her feet taking a couple tentative steps.

"I..." Karma croaks, raising her world-wearied eyes. "I'm so sorry, Mabel."

"Me, too," Mabel says mournfully. "I am. You were right... this world is too cruel."

Karma takes in the beauty of her only treasure, the only unambiguous good she's ever known.

"I'd die for you, Mabel," Karma sobs. "You know that, right?"

Mabel pauses, a fresh wave of tears running down her cheeks.

"I know you will," Mabel whispers.

Mabel takes her shot.

Karma stumbles as her world shatters to pieces, hands brushing the mess of gore that her side has become. She feels the cold, wet blood seeping through her pale fingers, every breath as loud as a storm. Her eyes meet Mabel's, her last hope ripped away with a deafening shotgun blast.

Karma looks down. Bone pokes out of decimated skin, her shirt soaked in scarlet, chunks of flesh splatting onto the floor.

Ever the dogged devil, Karma doesn't fall. She looks up from the crater in her gut, the fatal wound unable to put her down. Karma's broken lips crack open, buried beneath the weight of the world.

"Mabel?" she croaks, her last hope escaping her lips.

"Gotcha," Laurie chirps from behind her, pulling free of the axe handle's prison. Mabel prepares another shot, taking aim.

That's when a small girl in a black denim jacket leaps out into the hall, a cheap Halloween skull mask hiding her face. Karma recognizes Violet's scent in a second.

She told Violet to get a disguise, and that was her choice?

Violet seizes Mabel, knocking the shotgun out of her hands. The skull-faced accomplice pins her against the floor, struggling against Mabel's writhing body. Mabel, by all appearances, is much stronger than she looks, actually putting up a decent fight.

Violet grabs hold of the shotgun, punching Mabel across the face to deter her physical protest. Violet gives Karma a faceless glance, expression hidden behind the reaper that disguises her. She refuses to speak, but Karma immediately catches her meaning.

Go.

Laurie darts past the two entangled girls, taking an exasperated "useless fucking cops!" with her.

Karma runs her fingers over her side again, her healing process already grinding to life, new muscle and flesh splaying between her bones. So many kills tonight, and they've made her invincible. The flesh recuperates, leaving a prominent scar but saving her from mortal danger.

Her mental anguish makes the shotgun wound look like a bruise.

Karma no longer cares. She can't afford to.

Violet wrestles the shotgun free of Mabel's grip, and Karma sprints.

She runs faster than she ever has, barreling down the hallway as her prey makes for the stairway. *"Laurie!"* Karma bellows, the axe appearing in her hands. "For the last *goddamn* time—"

Laurie looks back and screeches, hopping onto the first flight of stairs.

"Call me Karma!" the Vision of Vengeance howls.

Laurie throws herself down the second flight of stairs, stumbling as she lands on the ground floor. She darts down the hall as Karma hurls herself over the railing.

The maddened killer shatters tile beneath her feet, overcome with rage. Laurie looks behind her, running like a woman possessed.

Karma takes off after her, double her victim's speed. The sirens sing outside, the school's front doors finally shuddering under police attack. Laurie turns to her left, leading Karma to slam right into a wall. She launches herself off it with ease, keeping her pace.

"You can run, little rabbit," Karma pants, slamming her axe into the wall beside her. She carves ravines into the plaster as she tears after her prey, her bloodied weapon leaving a crimson trail. "I'm always gonna find you! I'm always gonna hunt you! And, one of these days..."

Laurie squeals as the killer approaches, no appreciation for a slow burn, no care for a lumbering stride. Laurie desperately kicks at the abandoned fire extinguisher, catching Karma by surprise. She steps on it, heels sent flying.

Laurie dashes into the school library, slamming the double doors closed.

The axe clatters against the floor as Karma catches herself at the last moment, rolling across the tile and snatching her weapon of choice off the ground. Her nostrils twitch below her mask, the smell of a lighter pervading the air.

"What the hell do you think you're doing?" Karma growls, hurling the axe forward and piercing the double doors. Chunks of wood explode and expose the library, stacks of books scattered on the floor. Karma wrenches the axe back from the door, scattering splinters, preparing it for another blow.

She then remembers Jack Torrance really was an inefficient bastard, and decides not to follow his example.

Karma forces her hand through the gash in the door, fingers finding the lock. The room is unnaturally warm, the scent of fire wafting out into the hall. "Didn't know you were into fire, Thompson," she snarls, the lock snapping as she shoves the door open.

Blood patters against the carpet as she enters the library, panting for breath. Stacks of books lie scattered all across the carpet, dozens upon dozens of them. Laurie backs into a corner, throwing the lighter into the parapet of literature.

Karma's eyes widen, the killer realizing her dread mistake.

"I'm into survival," Laurie smirks.

Bitch remembered the car alarm.

Karma charges just as every fire alarm in the school starts to howl.

Karma instantly drops, the piercing screech overwhelming her every sense. She hits the floor, trying to cover her ears, skull feeling as if it might explode under the pressure. The world gets dizzier, the axe disappearing as it hits the floor.

Karma roars in pain, raising her pounding head just in time to meet Laurie's boot. The killer lands on her back as her prey sprints out of the library. Karma groans and tries to crawl, knees buckling. Her nails dig into the carpet, trying to pull her away from the fire, but the alarms pin her down. Like chains, the screeching holds her back, drilling holes into her cranium.

She collapses, struggles to breathe. She sputters, the smell of fire crawling down her lungs, *itching* at them.

She lays there and stares at her bleeding fingers for what feels like hours, the world swaying around her, Hell renewing its claim to Karma's soul.

She blinks, realizes someone's grabbing her shoulder, and Karma isn't sure what she's expecting – a cenobite, a devil out of hell – but it's a familiar reaper.

Violet throws one of Karma's arms over her shoulder. She groans and coughs as she tries to lift the damned killer up, clearly not possessing the required strength. Karma forces herself awake and remembers to help. With Violet's aid, she rises to her knees, panting and leaning against the wall.

"Where is she?!" Karma spits, struggling to make herself heard over the alarm.

"Not now, Karma!" Violet responds, stolen shotgun slung over one shoulder. "The cops are in the building, we need to *go!*"

"Like I couldn't kill a few pigs," Karma grumbles, as Violet helps her stand. "God, I can't hear *shit!*"

"Come on!" Violet snatches one of the books that has yet to join the raging fire, shelves collapsing behind them. She and Karma stumble behind tumbling shelves, nearly tripping over blazing wood.

"Watch it!" Violet says, throwing the book. It smashes through a glass window, armed police entering the room behind them.

Karma looks back, the two killers barely out of sight. "Hey, bad things!" Karma hisses. "Let me at them!"

"You can't even summon your axe right now," Violet grumbles, pushing Karma out the window. She trips and lands in the bushes, Violet right behind her. "Sorry."

"I bet Candyman doesn't have to deal with this bullshit," Karma groans, the sound quieter in the night air. Violet helps her up again, the two of them keeping their heads down as they trudge through grass. The police kick over shelves and search the fumes in the library, safely behind them.

"Who?"

"Never mind," Karma sighs, feeling at her wounded side. Her half-healed bones creak with every step, her gut feeling frightfully void. Karma grimaces at the sensation.

Unbelievably, they make it to Violet's car without being seen. She throws open both doors as silently as she can, keeping an anxious eye on the stationary sirens in the distance, counting at least a dozen. *So,* Karma wryly thinks, *the entire goddamned LLPD.*

They shut the doors, and Violet takes the driver's seat. They peel off the curb and tear away, deciding to make it quick. Karma keeps an eye on the parked police cars, making sure none veer off to follow.

"Change, quick, just in case somebody passes by," Violet hisses, driving with one hand as she tugs off her mask, throwing it in the back seat with Mabel's shotgun.

Karma obliges, taking off her own mask and stowing it in the glove compartment. She pulls off her jacket, wincing at the pain in her gut. "Fuck. Fuck! I almost had her! I *almost—*"

"You know, she's proving to be a pain in the ass," Violet pants, constantly checking the rear-view mirror. "I don't suppose she also has superpowers or something?"

"No," Kora growls, annoyed. "No, she doesn't." She tugs off her bloody shirt, digging around in the backpack she left under the passenger seat.

Violet nods, tapping her fingers on the wheel, humming nervously.

"Eyes on the road, Vance," Kora says, fiddling with her jeans.

"Sorry, sorry."

Kora tugs on the fresh shirt, staring back at the school, crumbling to the blaze that burns within. "Fuck!" she hisses, slamming her fist onto the dashboard.

Violet gives her a worried glance, her bloodied accomplice dreaming of gore in the passenger seat.

CYCLE THIRTEEN

I Let It In and It Took Everything

/// **October 30th. Seven hours until Halloween.**

Eleven killed, three injured in appalling high school massacre.

"Looks like they're coming for me."

President comments on Leer High murders — "Our thoughts and prayers are with those affected, and those responsible will be brought to justice".

"Isn't that funny? Before, I didn't warrant a quarter page on the school newspaper."

Breaking news: US army and Colorado state police mobilizing in reaction to the Karma killings — suspect still at large.

"I didn't want anyone to be afraid of me, but... maybe that's better than being forgotten."

Lake Leer Mayor Colón condemns Kora Lynch, the Karma Killer — expresses his sorrow and resolve to put an end to these murders, describing the killings as "sickening beyond words".

"Maybe I do regret it. But maybe they should look at themselves, you know? They pushed me. They just kept fucking pushing me, and look what happened."

Military support expected approximately 2:00 hours, November 1st. State police already mobilizing in Lake Leer.

"Yeah," Karma nods, shadows shrouding her kabuki face. "They shouldn't have pushed me. Right, Chelsea?"

She tilts her head towards her naked dance partner, Karma's own body at least covered with underwear. Chelsea, the girl she met in the nightclub so long ago, the one she promised to give the time of her life...

Well, she had. Scarlet stains decorate Karma's arm, Chelsea's lifeless eyes trapped on her killer. A bloodied kitchen knife protrudes from her neck, the improvised implement buried to the bone. The corpse curls against Karma's side, her latest work of art.

"Right," Karma remarks dryly. "I forgot you pushed me too."

Chelsea doesn't respond, a purple bruise lingering on her lifeless cheek.

Karma finds her heartbeat, sweat painting her chest. It pounds all too fast, her throat locked up with anxiety. She swallows, wiping her brow as she raises the volume of Chelsea's television.

For once, the newscaster doesn't sound bored out of her mind. "Lake Leer and Colorado police are securing every civilian they can find... if you are home and have yet to receive an armed escort, lock up your doors, barricade them with furniture, do *not* let in any strangers. Lynch reportedly employs accomplices. Keep your family and friends close, and wait for an officer escort. I repeat, do *not* leave your homes without an escort."

"Like I'd kill a child," Karma snarls.

She sighs, finding the same newscast on every goddamned channel.

"Like I'd ever..."

Karma stands, slapping a lamp aside in a random fit of anger. It flies across the room, shattering against the wall. Her chest rises and falls with every furious breath, eyes locked on the window's drawn blinds.

The sound of the sirens have surrounded her for hours.

"They made me do it," she whimpers, allowing herself one moment of meekness.

What are you going to do alone, Kora Lynch? 'Cause now there's no other future waiting for you.

"I won't be alone," Karma sobs, pressing her head against the wall. "Not again."

I'd rather die than spend another minute with you.

"I only loved you, and you had to give me to the lake!" Karma roars.

She blinks, cold wet trails running between her fingers. She finds her trembling fist within the wall, blood leaking from her knuckles.

Survive.

She will survive.

Survive.

Not out of want, not out of desire.

Survive.

Not out of hope, not out of right.

Survive.

She will survive, to spit in the repulsive faces of everyone who convinced her that she deserved a far fouler fate.

You earned this tombstone, Lake Leer. Damn you all.

The phone rings, freeing Karma of her internal monologue.

"Least you could do is get the damn phone, Chelsea," Karma groans, shoulders aching as she sits. She picks up her burner — a measure Violet had insisted on shortly after their escape, promptly before throwing their smartphones into the lake.

Karma still missed her old phone, but according to Violet, no one was going to track this clunky piece of shit. Karma believes it, too. It barely functions if you try to do legal things with it.

She answers. "Vi?"

"Yeah, it's me," Violet confirms. "You're still in hiding, right? You didn't go and kill anyone?"

Karma looks at Chelsea's naked corpse, raising an eyebrow. "I, uh... yeah, I'm still in hiding."

"Okay. Kora, look, things are... they're not good right now, okay? I don't—"

"I've seen the news. I know what you're about to suggest."

"Kora," Violet sighs. "We need to leave. We need to just pack up and—"

"I'm not leaving," Karma growls. "Not yet. Not without Laurie."

"Kora..." Violet groans, audibly frustrated. "Kora, the cops figured out pretty fast that she's your main target. They buy her story now, and she knows too much. We need to *leave*. We need to get the hell out of here, while we still can."

"What, you *don't* want to kill a few pigs?" Karma chuckles. "Whatever. Nothing we can't handle. I'm not running."

"It's not running, Kora! It's common *fucking* sense, and—"

"It's retreat, and it's not happening. Not until I handle Laurie."

"This grudge is going to get you killed, Kora. Gonna get both of us killed, okay? So get over it and—"

"This isn't a grudge, Violet!" Karma roars, leaping to her feet. "This is a goddamn *war*, you got that? We're not leaving until it's done!"

Violet falls silent.

"Is that *clear,* Vi?" Karma asks.

She presses her palm against the wall, blood trickling between her fingers.

"Fine," Violet growls. "Fine, but you're unbelievably stupid, you know that?"

"I'll allow you that this once."

Violet huffs. "Fine. Great. You know the police are almost certainly watching her, right? In large numbers, at that?"

"Yeah," Karma says, undeterred. "I guessed as much."

"Right. So we have a crossbow, an axe, a lighter, a car, and a shotgun with like, three or four rounds at our disposal. That pathetic little arsenal, and we're going to take on a police force with it."

"My axe will be enough," Karma shrugs.

"Great. We're gonna die."

"We're not gonna die."

"I hope you like that forest, Kora, 'cause—"

"We are *not* gonna die!" Karma snaps, pressing her forehead against the wall. "We'll figure something out, okay?"

"This isn't a matter of us... of us poorly planning, or... or us needing to come up with something, okay? This is a case of us being *severely* outmatched and outgunned. Not to mention, if we don't do this fast enough, the whole military is gonna come down here, and that's—"

"We'll be gone before then. We'll go tonight."

"Halloween. How fitting," Violet replies dryly. "We're still screwed."

"No. Not yet. I'm gonna get us some bigger guns. Meet me at the cemetery, at midnight."

"Kora—"

Karma hangs up.

"Alright, Chief Lumis—" Laurie begins, eyes pointed daggers.

"Captain," Lumis patiently corrects, wearily wiping at his eyes. "I'm only a captain."

"*Captain* Lumis," Laurie says in a huff, huddled up in a blanket. The police station buzzes with activity around them, citizens shuttled around like cattle. Funny enough, the cattle seemed better off in this situation. "You have a lot to answer for."

He raises an eyebrow. "Do I?"

Laurie's face cannot find a fiercer expression of distaste. "You left us all to die in that school, Captain. What were you *doing?*"

"Waiting for backup," Lumis sighs. "I had no choice."

"Waiting for... she was butchering us! Butchering *children!*"

"I am not proud of what happened," Lumis says slowly. "But you must understand, procedure is procedure. Now, I hear you requested this conversation with claims of information, so I'd prefer if you provided that instead of getting in my way."

Laurie weighs her options, licking her lips. As much as she wants to bury this cowardly little prick of a man into the ground, she knows she needs him, at least for now.

She buys time, starts bargaining. "Listen, I know you think I'm just a teenage girl, that I'm just... I know you think I don't know anything, but I've seen her, like, three times. I've survived her just as many times. No one else you're going to find can say as much, and... look, I know this is gonna sound crazy, but if we're actually going to take her out this time, we can't do it like you would anybody else. We blasted her with a fucking *shotgun*, point blank, and she just—"

"Got better?" Lumis raises an eyebrow, pushing aside a folder of the paperwork that weighs down his desk. "Yes, I'm aware."

Laurie pauses, her entire argument forgotten. "Pardon?"

Lumis sighs. "Do you know how I got to be captain of this... *fine* town's police force, Laurie Thompson?"

Laurie slowly shakes her head.

"Well, the man before me got eaten," Lumis says matter-of-factly.

Laurie coughs. "I... *what?*"

"Ever heard of the Bleeding Bear?"

Laurie shakes her head slowly, wondering if this is going anywhere.

Lumis shuffles through his paperwork, digging out a folder. "The Bleeding Bear... a rather nasty serial killer, operating from 1986 to 1989 before disappearing entirely. I say the captain before me was eaten because the Bear earned his name."

Laurie shivers, huddling the blanket closer.

"Now, he was similarly resilient. Survived several explosions, stabbings, gunshot wounds, and at least one electrocution with little damage. Not that anyone will tell you that part. Uncanny senses, beyond human. He may have worn the skin of a man, miss Thompson — but there is no one in this world that can convince me he was one. That Bear was... something else entirely."

Laurie catches her breath, watching his eyes.

Lumis slides her a composite witness sketch. "Anything catch your eye, miss Thompson?"

Depicted therein is a tall, wiry man, clad in a hunting jacket. His face is obscured beneath a ravaged kabuki mask, one teardrop trailing under the right eye. "That's..."

"Kora Lynch is *not* the first Karma Killer that's terrorized this town, miss Thompson," Lumis says. "If I could've taken her down before, I would've, for I saw firsthand what the Bear was capable of. Somehow, I survived it. Now, do you see why I hesitated last night?"

"Because you're a coward?" Laurie asks.

"Maybe I am, but the last time I saw someone wearing this mask, I watched them eat one of my longest friends alive in front of me."

"That's no excuse. It's your *job* to risk your lives. You're police. Does the phrase 'protect and serve' mean nothing to you?"

Lumis shakes his head, clutching his temple. "Laurie... I know you're young, but you have to understand that such blind idealism is rarely practical in the real world—"

"It's not idealism, it's your *fucking* job description!" Laurie exclaims. "Are you *insane*? We *died* so you and your precious men wouldn't have to!"

"Then help me catch her this time," Lumis growls. "*Help* me, if you know so much. I am eager to have it."

Laurie scoffs. "Why didn't you just... arrest her way earlier, before she could get this far?"

"Believe me, I tried. Until recently, my superiors were... not so convinced that it was a supernatural bogeyman dispatching teenagers.

Not many met the Bear like I did. Not many...”

He trails off.

“That, and I’m no good to anyone torn limb from limb, so I was never able to get her into a vulnerable position. In fact, miss Thompson...”

Laurie raises her head, inquisitive and infuriated.

“Given your... proven resilience, thus far, I was prepared to ask your aid with that.” He smiles. “Off the books, of course. But I know, like you do... I know we can’t treat her like a mere mortal. I know we can’t can’t meet her on her own terms. We have to adapt.”

Laurie breaks into abrupt laughter, clutching her sore sides.

Lumis narrows his eyes. “Miss...?”

“Oh, I’m fine,” Laurie giggles. “I’m fine, sorry, I’m just — I didn’t think you would just *ask* one of your meat shields for assistance.”

Lumis narrows his eyes. “Laurie, will you help me trap her or not?”

“I will, no matter how much I hate you,” Laurie says, amusement subsiding. “She’s after me. I’m her primary target. Wherever I am, she’ll follow.”

“That would explain all your encounters,” Lumis nods. “What on *earth* did you do to aggravate her?”

Laurie shrugs, biting her nail. “Well, I’m her final girl. That’s what she says.”

“Like... a horror movie?”

“Something like that,” Laurie agrees.

“So she’s attached, in her own peculiar way.”

“In love, it feels like,” Laurie admits, shifting uncomfortably. “You know, the form of love that involves hunting you down with an axe and killing all your friends.”

Lumis runs his hands over his face, evidently lost for words.

Laurie changes the subject. “Why are you guys gathering up the whole town?”

Lumis licks his lips. “The intention is to starve Karma of victims.”

“You... you’re using them as *bait?*”

“Please do not start another tirade,” Lumis says with a heavy sigh. “Chief’s idea, not mine. And I believe the intent is to protect, keep them under oversight, as we have no idea how destructive this fight will get. Once the military arrives, we plan on temporarily evacuating the town with their help. We’re not just locking these people in a building until we catch Karma, you know.”

“I don’t care what he told you,” Laurie frowns. “You’re using us as bait. All of us."

"Would you rather she be able to run around and slaughter people in the dead of night? This way, she'll have to fight through an army of trained gunmen."

Laurie purses her lips. "The police station big enough for everyone?"

"Nowhere close," Lumis admits. "We've been considering somewhere to barricade, overlook, set up an ambush. I'm in charge of that, so I'll actually have some flexibility—"

"Make it somewhere with a good sound system," Laurie interrupts. "Good speakers."

Lumis blinks. "Pardon?"

"Sound. Loud sound. You said it yourself, her senses are strong, *too* strong. I've gotten away from her before with a car alarm, then with a fire alarm. Gunshots seem to dull her reflexes too. It doesn't stop her, mind you, but it slows her down."

"That's a start."

"It should give people time to get away whenever she shows up. Find the time to set up a bunker or something, that's my advice. Oh, and one more thing."

Lumis raises an eyebrow.

"I know this is probably unusual and illegal, but I'd like a gun," Laurie smirks. "Something big, something with some kick to it."

Lumis tilts his head. "Oh, don't worry. America's firearm laws aren't *that* strict."

Karma's never tried this before.

That's not to ignore all the conversations she and Ira have had in the past – she's met the goddess a few times, more than anyone else, Karma imagines. No, the novelty here arises from the fact that Ira has always come to her. She's always appeared in the nick of time, lurking in wait with some revelation or sardonic observations, blood-red lips moving with malice.

Now, though, she's nowhere to be seen. Karma kicks off her boots, wiggling her toes in the sand. Ira's not here, right when Karma needs her most. She's not the type to admit it out loud, but the chips are down, the end is extremely fucking nigh, all that. The odds are against her, and loathe as she is to admit it, Violet's right.

She's gonna need more than an axe and misanthropic malice.

The sirens blare in the town proper, the sound today's ambience. She abandons her jacket, looking down at her bloodied T-shirt and jeans. Just a couple weeks, and it looked like she'd been through a bloody war.

What a wild afterlife she was about to lead.

Karma breathes, every nervous inhalation eliciting goosebumps from her pale, undead skin.

Mabel's gone. Hell, Mabel tried to *kill* her. Sky, predictably, is fully within the "hunt the slasher" camp. The police and military are coming for her, the scale of her rebellion extending far beyond just this tiny little town. Her father's gone. He must've up and left shortly after her name broke to the press, because when she stopped by home, him and all his stuff was gone.

She wades down the shore, cold shivers working their way up to her shoulders. Karma breathes.

But Karma has Violet.

She wades in deeper, the lake laughing, the waves whispering woe.

Karma has spite, more spite than anyone can possibly wish away.

The waves lap over her ankles, chanting lullabies.

Karma has the memories of her mother, the fire of countless injustices abandoned and forgotten. Unsolved, left behind, forgotten in file cabinets.

No more.

Karma breathes, the lake swallowing her knees, rippling against her skin.

And Karma has Ira, for all her ambiguity, all of her oblique ways. She still has her.

The moon sinks so low tonight.

She tips and she tumbles, skin meeting autumn waves.

Karma sinks, the lake wrapping tight around her, the dark embracing. She watches the fish drift by, jagged teeth, hopeless empty eyes—

Come, my Vision of Vengeance—

She feels the fingers wrapping tight around her throat, her lungs burning from within, ballooning, swelling—

Show me what little you've wrought!

Karma chokes, overcome with panic, the face of Ira bursting from the lake bed.

The god's eyes come into form in a matter of seconds, her rippling rage burning into Karma's eye sockets. Karma shakes, body bending backwards, crumpling like cardboard, the fish circling in ritual, brown murk and green waves a whirlwind around—

"You come with so little to show for yourself," Ira snarls. Karma gasps for breath, hitting the floor.

She stumbles as she stands, the black, shredded coils that make up her being marking the change of venue. They slither and snake to form her body, the sky bleeding purple and red and pink, dozens of black suns peeking through a canopy of crimson clouds.

Karma tilts sideways, her heart thumping, her feet fixed upon a spinning black tube. It slowly rotates beneath her feet like a drill bit, snaking its way through Ira's cosmos. Chunks of stone and glistening globules of blood float around her, horrific screams breaking through the enveloping clouds. Many-teethed creatures peek over the edges of these disembodied landmarks, winged monstrosities beyond description.

"Oh, my god..." Karma shudders, roiling with the platform's endless rotation.

"I *am* your god," Ira rumbles, her voice resonating throughout the infinite void around them. "Now, *kneel!*"

Karma obeys without a thought, dropping to one knee. Flecks of crimson flake off the spinning pipe, blowing through the black coils of her body.

"What the *fuck?*" is all Karma can manage.

And Ira rises, her form all the more breathtaking and powerful, easily double her previous height. A long, crimson cloak trails the ground, Ira's usual dress plated with blackened steel armour and regalia from the world over.

Tonight, the Crimson Queen wears Karma's kabuki mask, marked with its lonesome tear and its every jagged scar.

For the first time she can remember, Karma's voice trembles. "What... what the *hell* are you?"

And Ira speaks, her every word beating Karma into submission. "You want to know what I am, little girl?"

Ira's eyes glow bloody, setting hooks into Karma's soul. "I *am* Wrath, child — the very embodiment of it. The Voice of Vengeance, the Crimson Caller, the Invocation of Ire..."

Her eyes meet Karma's, void of all but spite. "I am Wrath, I am Vengeance, I am Karma, I am Retribution, I am Justice, I am Onryo, I am Báthory, I am Ira. I possess so many more names than you can possibly comprehend, nor can you even *begin* to understand an iota of what I am, so let this pathetic sample satiate your curiosity."

Karma whimpers, bowing her head, the screams of suffering sinners slithering down her swirling spine.

"I believe I chose you to carry out a specific task, Kora Lynch," Ira hisses. "I don't believe that task had anything to do with chasing one measly cheerleader around town, forsaking your vow in the interest of said pursuit, and proving unable to even *kill* the girl at the end of it all!"

"Ira, please—"

"That's *lord* to you."

"My Lord," Karma corrects herself, the tip of her tongue trembling. "I'll admit, I didn't think about how... frustrating I might have been until just now-"

"So, you're also helplessly daft," Ira hums. "Is that supposed to be a defense?"

Karma winces. "My Lord... I can win. I can beat... Like you said, she's just a cheerleader. I've merely had a run of shitty luck."

"And that run of 'shitty luck' should be easily conquered by someone as gifted as yourself, I should think," Ira responds. "You have proven... unsatisfying."

"I'll handle her, I—"

"I do *not* wish you to obsess over one girl, hunter!" Ira erupts, her anger drawing palpable pain out of Karma's limbs. "You are meant to be my Vision of Vengeance, a protector of innocence! You are *not* meant to chase down old rivals and carve bloody *obvious* trails in your wake!"

"She's a terrible person."

"That's not the point. You've made it far too personal. It has cost you your reason."

"I have a plan, my lord."

"Oh, was this whole mess *planned?*" Ira laughs. "Forgive me, that wasn't clear."

"No, I didn't have a plan then. I have a plan *now.*"

"It took you this long to take up forethought?"

Karma ignores the biting retort. "I can handle this. All I'm asking for is tonight. If I don't get her this Halloween, I'll leave. I'll be gone before the military gets here, I'll start over somewhere else, with more subtlety, more care. I just need this one night."

Ira raises an eyebrow.

"Please," Karma pleads. "And I'm not gonna just kill her, okay? I'm gonna make her suffer. I'm gonna make her pay penance for her sins, just like you taught me. I just need this one night, okay? I'm just asking for... no, I'm *begging.* I beg you, just this one night."

Ira stares at her, no sense of compassion in those crimson eyes.

"I'm begging you," Karma whimpers. "Please. I just... I need to do this."

"You are asking me to take much on faith here, child," Ira whispers.

"I suspect you appreciate a good gamble."

Ira looms above her, lost in thought.

"I'll bring her here," Karma says. "Laurie, I mean. I'll bring her here. I have a plan. I'm sure you can guess. Or read my mind, I suppose. But I'll leave Lake Leer tonight, I promise. No bullshit."

Ira turns, her cloak billowing in scarlet skies. She starts to walk away, circling the coil they stand on, gravity apparently on holiday. "I hope you know what you're doing, then. Tonight is Samhain. Wait until 3 AM — I believe that is what you mortals call the witching hour. You'll be at your strongest."

"Uh, thanks?" Karma asks. "Do I get special strength on Friday the 13th too?"

"Absolutely not," Ira deadpans, becoming one with her void.

"Valentine's Day?" Karma calls out. "I could even get a pickaxe and mining gear, and—"

The void doesn't respond.

"Yeah, I guess you don't get Shudder here," Karma sighs, getting to her feet.

She straightens, and delayed vertigo sends her head over heels. She falls, and before she can even grow accustomed to the walls of blackened brick that replace scarlet skies, Karma lands on her feet. The world flips around as she finds her footing in the dark chamber.

One of Ira's favored ornate fountains adorns the center of this dark hall. It trickles blood, a shallow pool reflecting red torchlight.

Instead of guarding a mask, though, this fountain holds an arsenal.

Two hand axes sleep in submerged presentation, razor sharp, the blades curved like crescent moons. Beside them sits a dark compound bow, slender and stiff, the string taut and daringly durable beyond possibility.

And upon each, she sees ancient symbols, ones she cannot recognize. Nonetheless, their meanings are clear as day to her.

The axes are *Judge* and *Jury.* The bow carries the moniker of *Executioner.*

Karma smiles, reaching into the pool of blood. It rises to envelop her arms, swirling limbs bubbling out of the fountain as her fingers wrap around the axe handles. Karma giggles, the churning blood flooding into the room, the walls rumbling inwards.

She smiles, laughing mad, as the Karma Killer sinks beneath sanguine.

And she drowns, cradling her newest gifts. Crimson shifts to a deep blue, the moon watching her from above.

Karma's hand spits free of the lake. Judge impales itself in the shore, her dreaded mask emerging to haunt Lake Leer once more.

Retrograde amnesia.

The words ricochet in Violet's forsaken skull, rattling around like hollow dice.

Retrograde amnesia.

She shambles to the hospital room, feet dragging across tile, the world a shifting kaleidoscope.

Retrograde—

"Friend, family...?" A nurse chirps at her, and Violet realizes she's reached her query. She gazes over, unable to hide her shock, shoulders bearing the weight of the world.

"Friend," Violet says, the word hollow.

The nurse nods. "Have you seen the news, miss? You need to go home immediately."

"I really need to see her," Violet croaks. "Please. Look, it's a hospital, and I've seen the extra security coming in. I'll be safe."

The nurse swallows doubtfully, tucking her hair behind her ear.

"Please," Violet presses.

The nurse sighs, gesturing towards the door. "Don't be long. The police will be arriving soon to transport the wounded."

Violet nods, shouldering open the door. She shambles into the room, closing it behind her.

Her guilty eyes find Mabel Alexander, bruised and beaten purple. She seems to sleep well, if nothing else, no disturbances beneath her eyelids.

Violet clears her throat, cursing what she's done. She pulls up a chair, resting her arms on the hospital bed's rail.

"I'm sorry," Violet mumbles, scoffing at her own admission.

You're sorry, Violet Vance? For what? Beating this girl into bloody batter, taking her memories with you?

Mabel doesn't say the words, but Violet wishes she could.

Violet stirs uneasily, damnation on her conscience — not of Hell, not of Ira's realm beyond, but of her own morality, her dreams of being something decent, maybe even *good*, ones that swiftly swept away with gods and grudges.

She's heard that survival, at some point, does away with life, and she feels she is well beyond that point.

"I'm sorry," Violet confesses, burying her face in her arms. "I'm just too scared to die. I'm just—"

She sniffs, wiping tears against her sleeve.

"I can't justify this anymore," she mumbles, words fit to be forgotten. "I can't... I can't keep telling myself there's a reason. That I'm okay, that I'm a good person forced to do bad things, I—"

She chokes on tears, swallowing roughly. "Maybe this world is just so full of bad people, and we can't afford to be picky and look for the good ones. And maybe that's where I come in."

Mabel sleeps like an angel, black eye besieging her beauty.

"And maybe I never knew you, or anybody, but you were Kora's only one," Violet continues, unable to seal up the dam. "Something like that. And we've been robbed, because this world's so fond of its shit hands. But I can't keep justifying this. I can't say we made the best of a bad hand. We threw it away."

Violet checks the clock on the wall, counting the hours. Three until midnight.

"You know," she whispers, words wrapped around the tip of her tongue. "The smart thing to do would be to kill you, here and now."

The silence leaves no indictments, but it spectates nonetheless.

"We need all the strength we can get," Violet continues, her voice as low as she can manage. "I make Kora stronger, the more people I kill, and maybe she needs a boost."

She draws her humming dagger, the veins ebbing in their eagerness. Not bright enough.

Violet lowers the blade, almost grazing the skin of Mabel's cheek. "And you know so much... so much about Kora. You're a... fuck, you might be the biggest threat that isn't Laurie on the board. Not to mention the fact that I rely on my Karma to live, and you're her emotional Kryptonite."

The blade shakes with Violet's hand, the apprehension arresting.

"I could suffocate you right now... make it look natural. Just... solve so many problems in one go, save Kora no end of trouble."

Her eyes linger to the pillow Mabel lies upon.

"It's different like this," Violet sobs, wiping at her face with her free hand. "It's different. I've had to kill people before, but there was... there was adrenaline, there was need..."

She looks at Mabel's slumbering eyes. The tears keep coming, no matter how many she wipes away.

"But they had a chance to fight back. You're defenseless. You don't even remember your goddamn life. Maybe you won't get in the way. Maybe I can't justify myself if I really do this."

Violet pities herself, hanging her head low.

"Or maybe I'm a coward. Too scared to kill you, even if it's the smarter choice in the long run. Too scared to let myself die instead of aiding mass murder, even if it's the smartest choice in the long run."

She sighs and sheathes the dagger.

"Maybe I'm too scared to be the good guy here," Violet admits, pulling herself to her feet. "Maybe I know you're the only *real* good guy here. So, take this chance. Don't blow it. Do something good with your life. Win. Do what me and Kora could never do."

Violet wipes away her last tear, sealing the dam. "Maybe one of us can make it out of all this a hero."

She opens the door, shouldering her backpack.

Violet hears a yawn behind her, freezing in her tracks.

"Oh, God," Mabel mutters. "I just had the most awful dream."

Violet turns her head, the girl's groggy eyes gaining consciousness. "I'm sorry," she says, having a good idea of what that dream entailed.

"I'm..." Mabel blinks. "I'm sorry, I don't remember you. Are we friends?"

Violet sniffs, sorely realizing how red her eyes probably are. "Well, we could've been, maybe."

Mabel looks at her in innocent confusion, an expression that stomps Violet's heart into shreds. "Oh... will I be seeing you again? I...

I don't know who I called family, and..."

"You won't," Violet interrupts, straining to hold herself together. "You're too good for me."

Mabel blinks. "I... I'm sorry. I just don't want to be alone here."

"Then I hope you won't be," Violet says, voice cracking as she disappears.

When Lumis said he had a place in mind, Laurie had never expected he'd pick Lake Leer's one (and only) tourist attraction: their winter mountain resort.

True to its name, it was about as high as you could get, tucked away in the mountains, surrounded by forest and sprawling hills. It was perfect, really — the trees provided good overwatch and ambush opportunities; the building was big enough to accommodate hiding everyone *and* setting up traps and killing floors; and best of all, it had one hell of a sound system.

Oh, and a swimming pool. If she got to kill Karma tonight, she'd definitely be taking a celebratory dip.

Laurie strides into the resort's lobby, dozens of tables set up around the room. Civilians shuffle through the front door in an endless queue, providing names and information to the police, doggedly trying to track down every last inhabitant of the town. It is a slow process, but for once, it's actually going somewhere.

Up several floors, Laurie knew several police were preparing the massive VIP rooms and turning them into temporary bunkers to be guarded at all times. Other cops were checking on the speakers, making sure they were tuned and ready. As soon as they were, they'd be turned right up to eleven. The cops had wanted to wait until they had visuals, but Laurie had a sneaking suspicion that Karma would close in on them before they saw a thing.

Hopefully it didn't go that way. She was good, but she was angry, and nothing stifles skill and talent like a raging bloodlust.

Of course, such an overwhelming amount of good news cannot come without unfortunate pushback. So, naturally, Laurie had forgotten her parents would show up.

Personally, Laurie thought they should be sacrificed to the crazy axe murderer. Make a show out of it.

Laurie sighs, taking one last sip of the wine she had snuck out of the resort's rations, but now she wished she had grabbed something heavier. Her mother dawdles at the front desk, preaching at Lumis and a number of his officers as they sign her in. Her father must be collecting luggage.

Laurie walks up to the desk with as much smug confidence as she can muster.

"Margaret Thompson, you said?" the cop behind the counter confirms, the long list of names trailing off the counter.

"That's right," the old lady says, narrowing her eyes. "I don't suppose you found my daughter?"

The officer looks behind her as Laurie hovers silently over her mother's shoulder.

"Well," the officer stutters. "Yes, actually, we have, and—"

"She's not on any drugs, right?" Her mother leans in, pressing her hands together, like she's parting with sacred family secrets. "She hasn't been running around with that filthy *girlfriend* of hers?"

The officer looks genuinely bewildered. "Not to my—"

"Oh yeah," Laurie interrupts, smirking wide. "I've been having tons of hot, lesbian orgies, dancing around pyres in the woods and summoning succubi so that they can violate my virgin body. Yeah, been having a *hell* of a time."

Margaret whirls around with an expression of exaggerated comic disbelief, and Laurie cannot help but snicker. She tears her cross free of her neck and tosses it at her mother's gaping face.

"You were right to kick me out, Mom, don't worry," Laurie reassures her. "The devil really does have it out for me, and she's coming here tonight. I can only hope she doesn't take your Christian purity from you too."

"Laurie, what on—" her mother begins, prepared to launch into another speech that Laurie will no longer spend weeks crying over.

"I'm not coming back home, don't worry. I know you wouldn't want that. I just wanted to give you back your precious cross... oh, and this."

Before she thinks about what she's doing, Laurie curls her hand into a fist and decks her mother across the jaw, eighteen years of repression packed into the punch. Her mother hits the floor, wailing and writhing like an upended turtle.

The officer at the desk reaches for her shoulder, but Lumis grabs his. He looks at this captain in bewilderment, Lumis' eyes meeting Laurie's.

Laurie shrugs. "I just needed the one."

Lumis sighs and nods. "Get out of here, and get ready."

"I get that one?" Laurie asks.

"One what? We didn't see a thing."

Laurie smirks, hopping over her mother's kicking body. "I can't get up on my own!" the hag howls, cradling her cheek with (for perhaps the first time) evident disgust at the helpless authority before her. "My cheek, it's *throbbing!*"

Cross that off the bucket list, Laurie thinks as she runs down the hallway, heading towards the bedrooms. No better time to do it, really.

After all, she stands a pretty good chance of dying tonight.

Her heart doesn't stop with the thought; inexplicably, it speeds up instead. Her breaths hitch and her lungs constrict, but the adrenaline surges in her chest, a warm, warmongering drug.

The energy encapsulates her as she nears her room. She eyes the next one over, the one Sky has chosen for tonight's horror show.

Laurie had told him to screw off to the bunker with everyone else that couldn't or wouldn't pick up a gun, but he had said he'd pick up a gun. Blasted idiot, he always was, especially when he clearly had a crush.

For now, Laurie doesn't mind. She steps into his room, closing the door behind her.

Sky, for his part, does not seem to be taking his existential crises in stride. He paces around his room, hands running through his fluffy hair, breathing through his teeth.

"Sky," Laurie says slowly, not sure what she was expecting. "Sky, are you sure you don't want to stay in the bunker?"

He jumps, noticing her for the first time. "I..." he shakes his head. "Look, I'm just getting it all out now."

"Getting what out, whatever the hell it is you put in your hair?"

"I don't..." He shakes his head. "My *stress!* I'm getting the anxiety out."

"We're not gonna die," Laurie says confidently, though she knows they very well might. Some truths are better left unspoken.

"We very well might," Sky protests. "How the fuck are we supposed to kill her? Harsh language?"

"Well, we have a lot of guns."

"We tried that!"

"Right, but no one knew how to *use* them, did they?" Laurie says, exasperated. "The police are actually trained, *and* there's more of them. Besides, Mabel almost got her. We know she's not invincible, alright?"

"I just..." Sky runs his hands over his face. "I guess I just don't know how to be okay, after that. It's hard, just sitting around and waiting. If she could just be here already, and we could end it, it'd... but she's not. We have to sit and wait, with our mortalities hanging over our heads, and—"

"Don't get too philosophical on me now," Laurie says. "You're my favorite art club member because you *don't* do that."

"The others are all dead," Sky deadpans, apathy hiding sorrow.

"Right. But you... were... look, that's not the point."

"I just need a distraction. Just until we start shooting. Just— just *something.*"

"Yeah, that's why I came in here," Laurie admits. "Getting to be a bit much, and, well — just got too much energy. Can't focus."

Sky raises an eyebrow. "You have a weird panic response, you know that? How you gonna deal with that? A game of pool?"

Laurie slides off her shirt as a response, dropping her bra.

Sky stares at her, open-mouthed. "Wait. You want to—"

Laurie nods, gesturing to herself.

"Right now? You *really*—"

Laurie sighs and grabs him by the shirt, tugging him into a kiss. She teases her tongue between his lips, deeply aware that she might not get another chance.

She pulls away, breaths shaking. "I just need this one night to be okay. At least until things go tits up."

And even if you got no one to love, maybe the superficial sort will do.

"Looks like they already have," Sky jokes, gently running his palms along her chest.

Laurie scowls at the pun. "God's sake," she says, grabbing him by the hair and pushing him to his knees. She directs his mouth where it does its best work as she hears shouts outside the room, crackling over the intercom.

He shimmies her pants and underwear down her legs, and the first waves of pleasure disappear in a storm of sound, the building's speakers exploding with music. An open invitation.

'Cause whatever you want, wherever you are / This ends tonight, one last dance, my lost and lonely star...

CYCLE FOURTEEN
Waves Whispering Woe

/// Halloween night.

"You said you were gonna get bigger guns," Violet mutters, her forehead drooped against the steering wheel.

"I did!" Karma protests, gesturing to the pile of weapons in the backseat. Violet glances at the heap of implements — two axes, the compound bow, the stolen shotgun, Violet's dagger, and the lighter Karma gave her some time ago. At least, it *felt* like a long time.

"I was hoping for, like, actual guns, and on top of that, they look like a downgrade. Those axes are smaller than your old one."

Karma plays with her mask, thinking. "Yeah, okay, but there's two of them, and they're really fancy."

"That's the entire reason you're using them? And why the bow? Doesn't the crossbow have more power to it?"

"Yeah, it does," Karma admits. "However, *you* try loading one of those things in the middle of a murder spree. I don't ever have the time to reload in the middle of combat. I prefer the bow."

"Still, isn't one big axe better than two small ones?"

"One slows me down. Also, Ira gave me this new shit, I'm sure she'd have a reason for that."

"Oh, good, here we go again," Violet rolls her eyes.

"What?"

"Nothing."

"Sounded like—"

"Nothing," Violet insists, squeezing the wheel with a degree of force that isn't typically necessary while your car is parked. "Look, just... I'm not sure if we're gonna make it, okay?"

"We'll make it," Karma says confidently.

"Yeah, isn't your entire philosophy based on old horror movies, though?" Violet asks, biting her lip. "Doesn't the killer always die at the end?"

"Well, not usually. I mean, the studio always resurrects them for another sequel anyways. Friday the 13th ended like, three times."

"Seriously?"

"Never mind. Point is, we'll be fine."

Violet sighs in defeat. Karma examines their objective, struggling to make it out through the fog and the rain. At the peak of this densely wooded mountain, they can pick out the lights of Lake Leer's one and only mountain resort, the sound of music faintly wafting down the hills.

"This feels like a trap," Violet mutters. "It's too obvious."

"What do you mean? I followed her smell."

"Yeah, maybe she's counting on that. And I know you've been in a lake all night, but the police have put pretty much everyone in town here. It just feels fishy."

Karma raises an eyebrow. "What, gathered everybody up, all into one place? That seems pretty damn stupid, if they think I'm gonna be killing everyone."

"Yeah, so maybe they don't think that. Maybe they caught on, and they know you're after Laurie. They probably have her separated from the others. Besides, Lake Leer's police force is historically pretty tiny. I'd wager they find it easier to keep track of everyone at once instead of spreading thin across town and hoping a couple lone officers could potentially take out a rampaging superhuman. That, or they're trying to deprive you of victims so that you'll come to them."

"You been thinking on that one for how long?" Karma asks.

"Haven't been," Violet shrugs. "It just occurred to me now."

Karma watches the clock, heat rising in her chest.

"You know, they're probably hoping to knock you out with the music," Violet muses. "After the library thing."

"Yeah," Karma agrees, rummaging around in the glove compartment. "Good thing we brought these this time." She holds up two earplugs in their little case. They were made for concerts, but they'll serve just as well here.

"Just wear your hood up so they don't notice. Good for scare factor."

"Great. I assume you don't plan on just sitting around in the car?"

"No. I'm gonna poke around, see if I can't find a way to shut off the power. Might be a shed or something around here. You have night vision, right?"

"Something along those lines. Take the gun."

Violet raises an eyebrow. "Shouldn't you take the gun?"

"I'll have my axes and bow, Violet. You need more than a little knife to defend yourself, just in case. Besides, guns aren't my style."

"This another slasher villain rule?" Violet sighs, the clock hitting 3 AM.

"No," Karma says, kicking open the passenger door. "They're just too loud."

"We're doing this now?"

"Yeah, it's the witching hour," Karma replies, her weapons vanishing. Violet watches her put in her earplugs and throw up her hood, disappearing into the storm.

"Right," Violet says to herself, heart hammering in her chest. "Fuse box. Find a fuse box. Shouldn't be a problem."

Before she can contemplate the luxury of thoughts or second guesses, she kicks open the door of the car, darting out into the dark.

Sky awakens to frantic rustling beside him, greeted by Nosferatu's beautiful mug on the shoddy television across him. He turns his head, finding Laurie on her feet. She's chosen to wear her usual outfit, but she's traded the leather jacket in for what looks like some sort of stab vest.

"Laurie...?" he asks, holding his head. "Where on Earth did you get that?"

She turns with a brief start. "The police gave it to me. I was hoping you'd sleep through this."

"What, through a final battle between good and evil?" Sky says, trying to offer up one of his trademark, sly grins. "Couldn't miss it."

"That's not what this is," Laurie says grimly. "For God's sake, Sky, just stay here."

"I told you, I'm—"

"You're pissing your pants, Sky," Laurie interrupts, straightening her vest and rolling her shoulders. She seems to be trying to find some comfort in the thing. "This isn't your problem, you know? You're just a stupid kid."

"And you aren't?"

Laurie scowls.

Sky sits up, running his hand through his hair. "Look," he says, gritting his teeth, if only to stop them from chattering. "I know you might have a vendetta here. But when you think about it... this is all my fault, really. I got her to go ask you out in the first place—"

"It's my fault for reacting the way I did. You made a genuine mistake. I acted out of malice."

Sky tilts his head. "You've changed a lot."

"Well, I'm gonna graduate high school in a few months," Laurie chuckles, tugging open a drawer. "I gotta grow up one of these days, don't I?"

"She's got, like, super powers, Laurie. What the hell are you gonna do alone? What have you got on your side, huh?"

Laurie pulls an assault rifle out from the dresser, smirking and propping it against her shoulder. "Well, I got this little beauty that the police loaned me, the LLPD, the Colorado state police. I got plenty of help."

"Yeah. That, plus me."

Laurie shakes her head, annoyed.

"I'm not just standing to the side while people I give a shit about keep dying around me," he insists. "I've done enough of that, haven't I?"

"Sky, you haven't..."

"Laurie, all my friends are dead."

Laurie stops in her tracks, biting her lip.

"I couldn't save them. Let me help avenge them," Sky pleads. "Please."

Laurie hangs her head, solemn and painted with regret.

She sighs. "Get dressed, go find a cop, get a gun. They'll put you somewhere."

"Is she here?" Sky asks.

Laurie shrugs, opening the door. "I dunno. But I don't feel safe without a gun anymore."

He nods wearily. "You know, it's really hard to have a serious conversation with this fucking porno techno blaring—"

And Laurie's gone, off to sleepless wanderings.

"Right," Sky sighs, searching the room for his discarded boxers.

Violet yanks her belt loop free of another twig, swearing under her breath as she trudges through nature's bounty.

She could do without being pinpricked every five seconds, she thinks, but creeping through the trees is probably the smartest possible thing to do here. Besides just up and leaving, anyways – but she's already thought up and shot down every possible excuse that ends with retreat.

She's already determined she's a coward at heart, a rotten creature beneath the skull she wears. Even now, she has to remind herself that this is all real, not just...

Violet sighs, clambering to the top of the hill. She peeks through the trees, rain pattering against her mask. She shakes her wet hair like a dog, surveying the parking lot of the resort.

Her first observation just loosens another string of dissatisfied swears. Her eyes follow a line of police cars that blockade the main road, not an inch to squeeze through. At least half a dozen officers sit in or against the vehicles, chattering amongst themselves, watching the road and the grassy knolls around them.

Violet is very glad she decided to tolerate the inherent irritation of the forest.

Staying low, she licks her lips, thinking. They're all armed, and while she has a cumbersome shotgun slung over her back, she's thinking it won't matter against numbers — especially when said numbers are supposedly aware of how to properly use a firearm. Violet's been making it up as she goes along, and she only has half a dozen rounds.

So keep making it up, birdbrain. You're supposed to be smart, right?

Distraction. Karma just needed a distraction, and then Violet could run along and find the fuse box.

But how do you distract a bunch of bored, eagle-eyed police officers in the dead of night, short of finding a box of donuts or an unarmed minority?

She looks to the closest car, a tree branch dangling over its hood. Violet smirks, stumbling down the slope, taking care to avoid every twig and fallen leaf she can. Hollywood has taught her a lot about that.

She comes to a sliding stop halfway down the hill, nearly tripping over a half-buried log and faceplanting right into the dirt. Thankfully, she manages to avoid such a fate, catching herself with the trunk of an unusually large tree.

Thankfully, no one's in this car she stands beside, and no one seems to have eyes on her current location. Violet intends on keeping it that way.

The side door of a nearby car hangs open, left idle by one of more incompetent cops outside. Violet tilts her head, thinking. He didn't leave the keys in the car, which would've been convenient (and astonishingly stupid on his part), but another idea comes to mind.

Violet takes her keepsake lighter out of her pocket, sweating profusely.

A car on fire, that'll suffice. Give her a chance to sneak around while everyone takes in the smoky spectacle... or, alternatively, have them waste their time searching for whoever just set their property on fire, but maybe they'd take Karma as a little more supernatural than she actually is. They have no way of knowing, do they?

Violet bites her lip, heart hammering in resistance.

You picked your side, kid.

Violet throws the flickering flame at the car. Thankfully, she doesn't miss. The lighter lands directly into the passenger seat, licking leather.

She backs into the brush, waiting for the flame to spread. Her eyes anxiously follow the group of cops, thorns of fear piercing her chest without restraint.

She blinks as one cop turns and *winks* at her, zeroing in on her with ease. The officer brushes away her blood red hair, a crimson lollipop between her lips.

Violet spends her two free seconds of shock getting sidetracked by how nice Ira's chest looks in that uniform. Then wrath's envoy snaps her fingers, flickering out of reality.

Violet frowns, having expected something dramatic to follow. I mean, that's what always—

Then the car explodes, blooming flames propelling it sky-high.

Violet launches back, colliding with a fallen trunk. The second car in line follows the first, a violent explosion as crimson as its maker, taking another vehicle, and another, and another, creating an inferno of dominoes.

Several police officers rocket into the air with the first explosions, others screaming as they try to get away. One successfully escapes the initial blast, only for a jettisoned passenger door to slam through his head, nearly slicing it in half.

She pulls herself to her dazed feet, the smoke practically cupping the moon.

"Well..." Violet mutters, cradling her ringing shoulder. "That'll do."

She picks up her shotgun and darts out of the trees, the field of blazing pigs providing ample cover.

Karma is halfway up the resort wall when sound of the explosion nearly knocks her right off. She clings to the windowsill, the deafening inferno startling her like a deer.

Vengeful balls of fire paint trails in the sky, rocketing high enough to be seen over the roof. She cranes her head back, catching a bewildered breath.

"Well," she mutters, floored. "Well done, Vi."

She waits for her ears to stop ringing and jumps. She catches hold of loose brick, not exactly catlike in her movements, but managing well enough. Her feet ease up exposed footholds, fingers finding grooves to cling to. She glances up, hidden beneath the shadow of a balcony, one she surmises to be a good entry point.

She hopes it isn't safe, though. That would spoil the fun.

Karma sniffs with sudden certainty, the night's breeze delivering her the scent of a man. Sweat... fear. She smirks, grabbing hold of the balcony's railing from beneath.

She keeps to the side, expecting the man to be facing the explosion. She peers between the railing and proves herself correct, purple eyes trembling with passion. The police officer pulls out his walkie-talkie and tries to get ahold of the officers in the front lawn, a sniper rifle of some sort slung over his shoulder.

Not intending to give him any reaction time, Karma leaps with stunning speed and grabs hold of the railing.

He turns and screams, but he doesn't have time to draw his gun. She grabs hold of his shirt, hurling him over the edge. As he flips over the railing, she kicks him square in the side of the jaw, his head slamming into the side of the building with a crack. His body plummets like a busted Barbie, smashing into the bushes below to join two of his fallen comrades.

Karma flips onto the balcony, rubbing the blood off her boots. She peeks over the edge, counting the first three of tonight's spoils. "Should've had more guys guard the back," Karma murmurs as Judge and Jury appear in each hand. "But I guess you really don't have enough men to handle me, do you?"

She smirks, knowing she'll fill an open grave tonight.

Karma creeps up to the double doors that lead inside, listening with care. She barely catches hurried movement in the room. It is of such submerged volume that she can just make it out over their pulsing soundtrack, a song that manages to burrow into her head and lodge deep its hooks.

"Useless fucking earplugs," Karma growls, kicking the doors open with no hint of hesitance.

Gravitas, luckily, proves to be on Karma's side. With her entry, the power goes out, taking the music with it. Beautiful little whimpers emerge from the dark.

Karma purrs, her inhuman vision overcoming any loss of sight that should arise. She cackles with glee as she scans the **VIP** suite, discovering dozens of Lake Leer's citizenship crowded into the room. They huddle together in fear, startled into a sea of screams, their resident bogeyman taking in her latest twist of fate.

"Well, well," she chuckles, shaking her head. "Like lambs to a slaughter."

Several begin to cry, the devil herself towering over her cowering subjects.

"Oh, don't be so childish," Karma sighs, taking a couple plodding steps forward. The closest families back away, cradled babies wailing in the empty silence. Their cries almost mask the sound of someone loading a gun.

Karma lunges out without warning, snatching a nearby woman and wrenching her free of her crowd. She shrieks, her family's hands entangled with her own, outmatched by Karma's strength. The killer pins the trembling girl to her chest, arm squeezing her neck.

"Please... please... not in front of them, please..." the woman tearfully begs, her family's continued resistance trampled with the kick of Karma's boot. "Don't... please... my—"

"Yeah, yeah, your daughter's watching," Karma sighs, rolling her eyes. "Shut the fuck up."

The woman obeys, her young daughter in the crowd unable to follow the same command. The woman's husband clutches his hand, fingers broken and bleeding. "Let her go," he sobs, cradling his thrashing daughter. "She didn't do anything to you!"

Karma prepares to air out a very explicit and graphic threat when two police kick open the doors of the room — right when she was beginning to wonder if they left all these people unguarded, too. They take in the scene with visible horror, raising their guns. Karma raises Jury to the woman's throat in turn.

They hesitate, one of them swearing under his breath. Karma smirks, digging the axehead into the woman's throat, teasing them with blood and wringing fresh screams from the woman's daughter. "Hey, boys. Call for backup, and I make an orphan, you got that?"

The child lets out a broken sob, her father clearly torn between action and passivity. "I swear to God, if you hurt her—" he begins, his voice choked.

"Oh, don't bother," Karma growls, shooting him one paralyzing glance. "Your God isn't listening."

He helplessly turns his attention to the two officers, their implied authority worth little here. Karma tilts her head. "You two best have an ace up your sleeve, cause you're about as helpful as an anorexic restaurant critic right now."

"They do," Skyler Simmons interrupts, stepping into sight. He raises his own handgun halfway, sweating as he meets Karma's eyes.

Karma smiles. "Sky! We have really got to stop meeting like this."

"I agree," Sky mutters, putting himself between her and the officers.

"We'll handle—" one officer begins.

"No, no," Karma interrupts, amused. "I'd like to hear this. You gonna try to save my soul, Sky? You gonna preach to me the benefits of self-reflection and forgiveness? You gonna lie to me about being my friend when you're fucking the girl that ruined my life?"

"Well, you're killing people," Sky shrugs. "Not the highest moral ground there. Look, I'm not gonna pretend I was there when you needed it-"

"You weren't."

"And, really, this whole thing is my fault when I think about it. I mean, I told you to... yeah, and I didn't think... I couldn't *possibly* think it'd lead to all this, but maybe I feel guilty all the same."

"Huh. You're right. This really is all your fault. And that guilt, Simmons? Gonna get you killed. Better off just getting rid of it, like I did."

"Kora, this isn't you."

"I keep telling you people that Kora's dead," Karma snaps, the girl she chokes gasping in her strengthening grip. "Call me Karma."

"You're not going to get through to her," the skinnier officer insists. "Listen, *Karma,* let go of the girl, and make it gentle."

"Why? So you can put me in the chair? News flash, my friend — I don't think I'm that vulnerable these days."

"Anything can die," the officer responds tensely.

"You're right," Karma says, second axe leaving lacerations in her captive's thigh. The blood runs out her jeans, the woman dangling limp through the pain. Karma holds her up, her daughter on the edge of fainting. "Call for help. Shoot me. Order me around. See what happens."

The other officer, clearly gifted with more common sense, raises his hands amicably. "Listen, listen. Just calm down. Whatever you want, we can work it out. Just... please, let go of the woman."

"Not giving up my leverage. Don't treat me like I'm stupid, either. You want a deal? I'll give you a deal."

"Name it."

"Great. I want to play a game. My friend Sky here? Shoot him. Shoot him dead for me, and I won't kill a single person in this room. You have my word."

Sky's eyes widen. "What? What? Kora, look, we were... come on, just let go of the girl, let's talk this out."

"I am talking," Karma says. "They're killing, ideally."

"I can't just shoot him!" the officer says. "That's—"

"Inhumane, yeah. Truly, no one in uniform would ever stoop to such lows," Karma rolls her eyes. "Two minutes. One hundred and twenty seconds. Either one of you kill Sky here, or I start slashing, and *believe* me, when I get the ball rolling—"

"Kora, come on," Sky pleads, raising his gun. "Please, just... it's me, remember? I was always nice to you... or, at least I tried to be."

"Someone *please* shoot him," Karma emphasizes. "He's insufferable."

"Drop the hostage," an officer barks.

Karma tilts her head, a good grip on the woman's trembling jaw. "I see you two thinking. Better hope you're a good shot. Smarter yet, just take the deal. I really am a woman of honor, you know. I'm not that far gone."

"Drop the hostage!" the officer yells. *"Drop her!"*

"Then shoot him!" Karma screams. "Come on! One life for the greater good, come *on!"*

Sky clicks off the safety, taking aim—

The skinnier officer diverts his gun at the last moment, grimacing as he pulls the trigger. The bullet tunnels a bloody trail in Sky's forehead, splattering skin with a startling roar. Sky stumbles forward, blood trailing between his eyes.

Karma laughs, as surprised as her former classmate is.

He shambles forward, his gun hitting the floor. With a groaning lurch, he falls, his traitorous corpse crumpling.

"No!" an older woman screams hoarsely from the crowd, tears streaming from her eyes. She tries to stand, but those around her hold her back, saving her life.

Members of the crowd squirm and whimper, hands pressed over their ears. Parents hide their children's eyes, hugging them close. The woman sobs in Karma's grip, her terror seasoning the moment.

The other officer glares at his impulsive companion, panting in shock. "What did you just...?"

The thin cop ignores him, praying for the sanctity of his deal with the devil. "You said you won't kill anybody. Hold up your end of the bargain."

Karma chuckles, peeking out from behind her captive. "You. I like you. One thing, though."

Both cops' eyes widen in panic.

"I said I wouldn't kill any *people* in this room," Karma gloats. "I didn't say I'd spare any pigs."

Karma leaps, throwing the woman out of her way. She balls up in the air just as the two officers raise their guns. One of them manages a shot, but it sails by her hair, scarring her hood. She throws both her axes forward, each blade impaling the forehead of an officer. Both victims snap back in whiplash as Karma lands on one knee.

The bodies collapse, joining Sky's empty-eyed corpse.

Karma drops her hood, runs her hands through her hair, seeks serenity in the scent of slaughter. She wrenches her axes loose of two dead pigs with a gruesome squelch. She glances around the room, giving the crowd a curt, departing nod.

"I did say I'd spare you," Karma says, giving Sky's corpse one last kick to the cheek. "Happy Halloween, freaks."

She plods out into the hallway, trailing blood staining polished wood. She hears the oncoming officers immediately, turning towards the stairs that end the hall. They all raise their guns, flashlights beaming in the dark, Laurie taking the center. Karma winces as she splays a hand over her face, the light giving her a migraine.

Karma squints through her fingers, Laurie's hourglass figure easy to pick out from the crowd. She chuckles, raising one axe to trail along the wall. "Working with pigs, Laurie? I really don't know what I ever saw in you."

Laurie doesn't respond. Karma's eyes finally come into focus just in time to see the rifle in her hands.

"Ah," she grins. *Now I remember.*

Laurie and the police open fire. The officers' handguns discharge out of sync with Laurie, who doesn't take her finger off the trigger. It's bad form on her part, but several bullets still hit their mark and send Karma reeling, crimson craters blooming upon her shirt. Her body seizes up in some implausible combination of agonizing pain and shock.

"Son of a—" Karma finds a door to smash through, evading another flood of hot lead. She slams the door shut as she spits blood, slumping against it and feeling at her wounds.

"Lollipop Chainsaw ain't fucking around, is she?" Karma grunts, blood streaming between her fingers. She hisses through her teeth, the healing factor already begin to kick in. Even so, it's the first time she's really felt endangered since she got these powers. Her teeth chatter under the noise and her body shakes with a volatility she has not known since she was a meek little mortal.

More kills. Get more kills.

Footsteps storm towards the door, eager to finish her off. She can't blame them, but she has no intent on going down so easy.

She hastily locks it, lurking in wait. She focuses on the feeling of dripping blood, lets it fuel her, lets the hate drive her.

One, two, three...

Karma counts the footsteps, tracks their proximity. The door handle twists in a sudden fit, jerking about.

Without warning, the killer bites back, elbowing through the door. Wood shatters with the blow, her elbow connecting with an officer's face. Guns raise, silence marking their hesitance. Just as the officer begins to recover, she welcomes him with Jury, the axe lodging itself in the man's head.

They shout, out of fear or anger or maybe both, guns risen towards the remains of the door and taking shots. They're a second too late. Karma darts to the side and wastes no time in preparing her next attack.

She listens for footsteps within the cacophony, plunging her fist through the wall. Her fingers find another officer's neck, that one screaming her last as Karma yanks her back with her full strength. The officer's neck snaps back, bones obliterated under the killer's force. The bones of the officer's throat pierce the skin as Karma's fingers find the vacuum that delineate blood vessels.

The police whirl around, beholding their bogeyman. She strides through the wall, debris rolling down her bloody jacket. The dead officer hits the floor, her crumpled neck sagging against the floor.

Karma smiles, licking her lips. "Do I even need to say 'guilty'?"

They hesitate, too scared to disperse. The bravest of the lot pops off a couple shots, catching her gut, but Karma lumbers on without pain. She grabs hold of the firing officer, his screams awakening depraved desire in her chest. She snaps his neck in one clean motion, his head spinning one hundred and eighty degrees.

Laurie tries to shoulder through the cops, dissuaded when Karma kicks ahead her newest corpse and sweeps Laurie's legs out from under her. The blonde lands facefirst in blood, sending her rifle sliding across the ground.

One officer remains, too terrified to threaten. Karma laughs as she slaps aside his gun, seizing his head with both gloves.

"Scream," Karma growls. "No one can save you."

He kicks at her regenerating bullet wounds. The flaring pain only foists upon her further motivation, further pleasure. She growls and slams him into the ground, straddling his chest. She holds his writhing body down, ignoring his pleas, no, *relishing* them, tasting every tainted word on the tip of her tongue—

Karma laughs, no hope of redemption in her ecstatic, murderous mind.

She digs her thumbs into his eyes, abusing her superhuman strength, making a game of seeing just how loud she can force him to scream. She feels the slime coat her thumbs, wriggling them into the narrow cavities of his eye sockets. The violence of his thrashing body, the screams that hew hoarser and hoarser, the blood that runs and pours and just doesn't stop—

She finally spares him the mercy of death, slamming his head into the ground over and over, listening to the bones crack and watching the body bleed as she batters his measly life away.

Reality floods her senses again, Laurie's horrified screams music to her ears. Then again, Karma supposed, her final girl was the only one left standing. She found herself in that position far too often.

She leans in, aware of her place in the food chain, smelling the desecration she's wrought. She shudders at the stench, tingling with ecstasy as she nuzzles the remains of the man's face.

Laurie stands up, scrambles for the rifle. Karma immediately summons Judge, tripping her prey with the handle. Without a word, the stalker rises and smashes the barrel of the gun flat, bashing it beneath her bloody boot, rendering it well beyond unusable.

She looks down to her chosen final girl, bloodstained mask radiating perverse pleasure. "There... I like it better when we're alone, don't you agree?"

Laurie coughs up phlegm. "You're not even pretending to be the good guy anymore, are you?"

"I don't believe I ever did," Karma shrugs, lunging down to seize her prize.

"No!" Laurie screams, kicking at Karma's face. For all the accumulation of her supposedly mortal wounds, the killer slows for only a moment. It's all Laurie needs. She produces a handheld taser from her back pocket and jabs it into Karma's gut, the killer seizing up in startled shock.

Oh, for—

Karma struggles through sparks, stiffly slamming into the wall. Laurie dodges the brutish reaction, abandoning the taser. Karma gasps as Laurie springs to her feet and runs, the taser's dancing darts urging her muscles into an erratic dance. Karma's flopping hands finally find their way to the electrodes, tearing them off her body and throwing them away with piercing prickles of pain.

"Oh, you little *fucking—*" Karma roars, overcome with rage. Laurie is halfway down the hallway when Executioner obediently finds its way to its owner's hands. She pockets the fallen taser, tailing her target with visible venom.

Laurie raises a walkie-talkie to her lips, screaming into it in unfiltered panic. "The cars were a diversion, she didn't blow them up, Karma's in the building, she's in the *fucking building!*"

Karma raises the compound bow, an arrow appearing for her. She draws back the string, stabilizing her shaky grip.

Laurie makes it to the end of the hallway, eyes fixed on the staircase that turns downward, down to reinforcements—

Karma looses the arrow, and it plunges into Laurie's thigh. She cries out and tumbles, slipping at the landing and slamming right through the window to the woods.

Laurie doesn't even have time to curse before she flips right out of the building, hitting the grass outside with a *thump*.

Karma blinks in astonishment, more footsteps rushing up the stairs.

She ignores the ascending boots, heart thumping as she rushes over to the window. The lawn laughs at her below, the killer bearing a strange, traitorous heartache as she looks for any sign of her final girl.

She sees Laurie in the grass — sprawled out and bruised, groaning, but still alive. They were only on the second floor, Karma reminds herself, watching the resilient little thing try to get to her hands and knees.

Kora smiles, almost proud of her plaything. She grunts and presses one foot against the windowsill, preparing to jump right out after her.

Naturally, a police officer chooses right then to grab hold of her shoulders. Karma barely has the time to sigh in exasperation, Laurie's endless escapes almost comical. "Oh, for the love of—"

The cop tries to tug her back. His strength proves nothing to Karma's, so she gives him a hand. She lets go of her weight, sending them both rolling down the stairs.

"What the—" the cop manages. He stops there, crushed between Karma and one particularly unkind step, blood coating his lips as he bites off his tongue. She rotates in their descent, hand reaching out in inspired improvisation. She grabs hold of the banister, tearing loose one rail as they near the bottom.

They hit the ground floor and both of Karma's hands wrap around the broken rail, using all of her strength and momentum to stake it into his chest. She doesn't give him any chance to get back up, raising her fist and beating it into his nose, feeling skin and bone shatter under her third, fourth, fifth blow, murder making itself mundane.

She raises her weary head, body wreathed in pain, but she doesn't feel any more danger. The bullet wounds seal shut under her shirt, skin rapidly crawling over every exposed injury. Karma runs her hands through her hair again, panting, crumbs of crimson in a sea of sweaty silver.

Karma remembers her mission, and she lingers no longer. She gets to her feet, accidentally crushing her victim's unrecognizable face under her boot. She plucks a spare taser cartridge from his belt, reloading the handheld weapon Laurie had been so kind to lend her.

She sways as she rises, lurching into a wall. Karma kicks off it, following Laurie's scent. She stomps down the resort's endless luxurious hallways, the trail leading her to a pair of double doors and a sign.

Swimming Pool, Deck, Grill, Bar.

Yeah, she warrants she'll need a drink after this.

She pushes the doors open, the evening chill refreshing her war-wearied skin.

The power starts back up with a vibrant hum, the wandering wrath raising a curious eyebrow. The bar and the pool re-activate, lights beneath the water coloring it neon blue. Laurie's horrendous Top 100 pop returns to life, giving Karma a creeping headache.

What the hell are you doing, Violet?

Karma cracks her neck as she steps onto the wooden deck. A swimming pool sprawls before her, more expansive than she'd expect for such a little town. The water looks illustrious and inviting, but Karma has no time for such a thing, eyes darting between the abandoned bar and the grill beside it. A large pair of unused speakers sit atop the counter, the cord to their power supply trailing off somewhere behind the bar.

Karma considers the swimming pool, innocent amidst blood and death. She watches the water, catching her breath.

She curses that Laurie isn't here right now, a thousand substandard jokes about wet bikinis running through her head.

This small peace fades away with a distant shotgun blast. Karma wakes up, remembering what she's here to do in the first place, how little time she has, how much of this revolves on luck and dogged detachment.

Before she can move, a second shotgun blast rings out, somewhere in the forest. She catches footsteps behind her, the smell of three men.

She turns to meet Lumis and two of his men, all raising their firearms.

"Now, now," Karma chides. "I don't actually have time for this."

"Then make time, Lynch," Lumis responds, clicking off the safety of his gun. "I guess it really was you, huh?"

"Look at you," Karma hums. "So confident and brave, all because you didn't die when you ran away from a cannibal killer a couple decades ago."

Lumis narrows his eyes, finger hovering over the trigger. "Why do you think I'm not running? You're just a pale imitation."

Karma tilts her head. "Aw, someone's still sore. Gonna take me to a prison cell, officer? Gonna stake me like Salem, preserve the decent folk?"

"No," Lumis says. "I'm just going to put you down."

She ducks as he and his friends take their first shots, rolling forward with Judge. She slashes through the kneecaps of one officer before bashing Lumis' legs with her shoulder, knocking them both over. The last man standing empties his magazine into Karma's back and chest, barely able to keep his aim on such a swift target.

The trigger clicks helplessly, his eyes going wide as the crimson killer rises to her feet, seeing him as little more than an irritant insect. She turns to him, licking her lips.

"Let's try that again," Karma murmurs, pulling the taser out of her pocket. He turns to run, but she seizes him by the shoulder. He opens his mouth to scream, a fatal mistake. She forces the taser as far down his throat as she can manage, mercilessly lodging it in place. His body starts to jolt and dance like a mannequin on strings, his eyes bulging as he fries from the inside.

The other two scramble to their feet, literal shock and awe delaying their next attacks. Karma kicks the man to his knees, twirling Jury as she brings it down, bisecting the officer's head like a stump of wood. Fresh blood forms rivers between the deck's planks.

She snaps her head up like a hungering predator, bloodied mask daring the other two to make their move.

They do, raising their guns, the other officer shaking too much to make a solid shot. Lumis seems to keep his cool, several of his bullets tearing into Karma, one of them ripping through the side of her neck. She retreats, leaping over the bar counter and taking cover.

Her throat clogs, breaths hampered by the blood that gushes over her chest. She feels at her dirty skin, already healing back up, giving her back her flow of oxygen.

Good thing she racked up that kill count, too, she thinks, or she would've just bit it there. She rolls her shoulders, judges the approaching footsteps, waiting-

She reaches over the counter and grabs hold of the second cop, tugging him right over. He slams beside her, his dazed landing giving her the time she needs. Karma snatches a bottle of vodka from the endless supply around her, smashing it against the wall.

He reaches for his gun, fingers just grazing the trigger guard, eyes bulging as the murderer looms above him with her improvised weapon. She lets him desperately reach for his weapon as she pins him against the ground, teasing, teasing–

He grabs hold of the handle, and she plunges the sharp end of the broken bottle into his throat, covering his mouth with her other hand. He struggles and writhes like a fish over a fire, eyes as pale and cold as one. She feels something crack, wringing loose as much blood as she can from his erupting throat.

Before she can truly enjoy the moment, gunshots shatter bottles on the rack above her, showering her in alcohol. She swears as the next bullet nearly nails her in the head, ducking back down. Thinking quick, she traces the power supply for the speakers, clasping the cord and tearing it in half. It sparks and crackles at each end, clearly displeased with this arrangement.

"Hey," Karma yells, the next bullet nearly deafening her. "Hey!"

He stops for just a moment, maybe to reload, maybe to listen. Damned either way.

"Hey, Lumis?" Karma growls, reaching up and grabbing both speakers.

"If this isn't an admission of surrender, I will burn that bar down, do you understand me?!" He's yelling, the first time Karma's ever heard him do so. His voice wavers, his stony composure finally slipping.

"You wanna be a pig?" Karma asks, rising to her feet. "Squeal like one!"

She throws the speakers with all the strength she can muster, the first putting a vivid dent in his forehead. Lumis drops his gun, the second speaker slamming square into his chest. He slips at the edge of the pool, the speakers and their sparking cord falling with him. They land in the water, electricity rendering it lethal.

Karma rises, the stench of burning skin an aroma of arousing reward. She watches his body thrash and die in her improvised trap, a smile upon her lips.

"Guilty," she declares, leaping over the bar.

She retrieves her axes, twirling them in her hands. The smell of the alcohol that coats her is overpowering, but she manages to pick up Laurie's trail again.

Not too far off, and dressed in blood.

Karma stomps through the grass, making no effort to hide her approach, too confident in her own victory. Laurie's smell wavers, pervasive in one battered patch of grass, barely lingering anywhere else. Karma steps over a fallen trunk, entering the forest vast, sorting through the dozens of scents around her.

"Kora!"

Violet's voice, caught in the wind, hoarse and teary. Karma immediately starts running, following the screams.

She stumbles into a clearing, trampling autumn leaves, rain running down ragged trunks. The breeze smells of torn flesh. Finally, she comes to a clearing, discovering her partner in crime beside an ankle-deep stream.

"Vi, what's—" Karma begins, her masked companion uncharacteristically still.

And then she sees it, the steel bear trap clenched tight around Violet's crushed left foot. She drops her axes in shock.

"Oh, Jesus," Karma breathes, the crippling concern hitting her harder than anything else tonight.

Violet falls and Karma catches her, shushing her whimpers. "Ow, ow, ow... God, ow, please, K-Kora, fuck, this hurts, this hurts so much, please—"

"Hey, hey, hold on, I know how to use these, give me a second—" Karma pats Violet on the back, a rare attempt at comfort from a beast that's largely forgotten it. "Stand up. I need you to stand up, I can't do this with you leaning on me."

Violet nods, balancing on her good foot. Karma clenches one of her hands tight, nodding to reassure. "God, please don't tell me we're gonna need to chop my foot off, o-or something, I—" Violet moans.

"We won't need to amputate anything," Karma interrupts. "Shhh. Just let me do it."

Violet nods queasily, sweat and tears surmounting her mask. Karma kicks aside leaves and twigs, finding the trap's springs. Carefully pinning Violet still, she gently steps on both, activating the release mechanism. The trap springs open, ripping out of Violet's flesh. She cries out in agony, her leg shuddering as she tips over.

Karma catches her, stroking her back. "Hey, hey, careful," she soothes, gently helping Violet hop away from the trap, hobbling on her one usable leg. Karma grunts and leans down to scoop Violet up, trying not to disturb her oozing wound too much. Violet gasps, taken into a bridal carry, looking up at her fellow killer in hazy dissociation.

"What the hell happened?" Karma asks, stepping into the stream.

"Laurie, she…" Violet coughs hoarsely. "I found her crawling, I tried to shoot her… She grabbed me, I missed… Had no more ammo, but I wanted to… I guess to impress, or be helpful for once, I… She led me into t-that… ow… I don't know where she is now… I'm sorry…"

"It's fine. You're alive. That's what's important."

Violet giggles like a child, her cheek rubbing against Karma's chest.

"What?" Karma asks, raising an eyebrow.

"Just kind of ironic to hear that from the girl that's been putting Jason Voorhees to shame," Violet confesses, her voice wavering. "God, I feel like I'm gonna die."

"Your leg will be fine. It's probably broken, but it'll heal."

"I know," Violet murmurs, breathing slowly. "You got me."

"Damn right I do," Karma hangs her head. "Sorry this happened in the first…"

She trails off, the familiar stench of fire flaring up behind them.

"You know," Violet says groggily, clearly not all there. "You look kind of good all covered in blood—"

"Shit!" Karma curses, wary of a whistle in the wind. Without much other choice, she hurls Violet across the stream. The girl's startled scream cuts off as she lands in some leaves with a thump, avoiding any more significant damage.

Karma cannot say the same.

The Molotov cocktail shatters against her back, taking gleeful advantage of the liquor that's coated her. She hits the ground, another Molotov exploding against her side. She tries to roll into the stream, quench the flame.

"Happy Halloween, *freak!*" Laurie screams, stepping out of the trees. She hurls her third Molotov, nailing Karma in the chest. The killer trips over a submerged trunk, landing headfirst.

Laurie limps forward on her injured legs, wasting no time. She sluggishly leans over to pick up one of Karma's abandoned axes, admiring it for but a moment. The blazing killer curls up on the forest bed, flames taking their dance to the leaves.

"I had a whole speech prepared," Laurie pants, stumbling over. "But fuck that. You killed all my friends. You killed half the damn school, the entire police force. All that, and you ruined half of my favorite outfits."

She sways, raising the axe high. "Guess I really am your final girl, you *monster.*"

Karma thrashes in the water, the flame and her skin in an eternal game of give-and-take; fire attempting to ravage, healing factor attempting to restore. The agony is endless, unimaginable, and she prepares to embrace her failure, purpose lost in a sea of injury—

A large rock flies across the stream, crunching against Laurie's kneecap. She falls to one knee, crying out in pain.

Violet crawls forward, grunting through grit teeth. "I liked you a lot better when you were a cheerleader," Violet snarls, throwing another large rock at Laurie's chest.

Laurie doubles over, eyes watering in pain. She lurches forward, crawling towards her distraction, axe trailing through leaves. She dissuades Violet from collecting another rock by stabbing the ground between them, forcing the girl to back away.

Laurie wrenches the axe out of the dirt, heaving out broken breaths. "Vance, huh? Never would've taken you for the Ghostface type. Guess it really is the quiet ones, isn't it?"

Violet scrambles back through mud and dirt, nowhere near fast enough to escape the deranged blonde. Violet's eyes drift behind Laurie, a reaction the girl takes no notice of.

"I'm going to fucking hurt you, you know that?" Laurie growls. "You're just as guilty as her, you got that? You are *not* the heroes of this story, okay? You are *killers!*"

Laurie's shadow finds itself enveloped by another, illuminated in the raging flames behind her.

Laurie's eyes widen as she slowly turns, taking in the Shape looming over her.

"I couldn't agree more," Karma hisses, perpetually regenerating skin amidst the flame, the pain little more than a motivator. She shambles forward, picking up the discarded bear trap with ease. "I am no hero."

She steps forward, Laurie steps back.

"I am Wrath," Karma proclaims, eyes blazing with a ferocity that rivals the flames. "I am Wrath, I am vengeance, I am retribution, I am justice. You..."

Laurie raises the axe, but it disappears in her hands, obedient to one master alone.

"I loved you," Karma continues, something more than human. "No, I didn't. I loved the concept of love. I loved the idea of not being alone, no matter what form. I think I'd like to show you how that feels."

Laurie shrinks, nothing more than a helpless victim — the spitting image of so many people she thought little of walking over.

"I'll bring you back!" Karma roars. "I'll bring you back, over and over and *over*, and you will learn how it feels, and you will understand *pain*, and you will teach others to understand that same pain, until there is no hate left in this world, until there is no suffering left to dish out!"

Karma raises the bear trap, clubbing Laurie in the side of the head with it. The steel breaks her skull, the girl toppling into a pile of leaves. She rolls over with a wet whimper, a bleeding crater marring the side of her head, her treasured beauty stolen from her.

Karma drops the bear trap in the dirt, falling to her knees on Laurie's stomach. Laurie weeps and curls up as the flames lick her clothes, burning through to her skin. Karma leans down over her, the blazing butcher leaving her prey nowhere to go.

Karma plants her flaming fists on either side of Laurie's head, forcing her to lock eyes.

The flames crawl up Laurie's hips, the forest going up around them.

"Without judgment, Laurie, what would we be?" Karma whispers, examining the fruits of her inaugural hunt.

Laurie whimpers, no fight left in her, choking on boiling blood. "J-just... just kill me!"

"Oh, I will," Karma promises.

"Don't bring me back," Laurie sobs, screeching as her hand catches fire. "Please! God, don't... don't bring me back!"

"It's only what you deserve. I told you, we'd be alone together."

Laurie spits at the flaming shape above her. There is no achievement in the act, only the bitter end of a tapering rebellion.

"We don't deserve love," Karma muses. "People like us? We deserve to suffer."

She cradles Laurie's cheek, lovingly stroking it with one flaming finger. The inferno spreads, blanketing Laurie's screaming face.

"This world is hell," Karma says. "This world is hell, and people like us? We don't get out."

"Kill me!" Laurie screams, her skin blackened.

"I will, my love. I will show you so many things."

Karma tugs Laurie into her last kiss, her love's throat caving in beneath her grip. Laurie does not resist, the fight in her finally snuffed.

The flames clothe Laurie's bubbling skin, embracing her like they have her chosen nemesis, her remains kindling like a funeral pyre.

Karma bites down into her scorched lip, tastes the boiling blood. She wishes she could cry.

And then she screams and she howls, raising her blazing fists to the sky, looking to the outside observer like a wicker man in his final death throes.

"I won!" Karma screams, slamming her bloodied, scorched fists into the ground. "I killed her! You *fucking* hear me? I've killed them all!"

She doubles over laughing, giggles turning to tears, her kabuki mask surviving amidst the inferno. "Wrath will come for all, you hear me?" she promises, knowing Ira can hear her. "I will not fade away. I will *not* fade away!"

She flops onto her back besides Laurie's flaming corpse, the agonizing, impossible pain nothing more than a numb reminder that she's alive.

"I'll bring her to the lake," Karma whispers, watching smoke stifle the stars. "I'll survive for you, mother... I will."

She reaches over and squeezes Laurie's dead hand, lost in the moment.

The stars are so bright tonight.

And the lake laughs, the waves whispering woe.

Coda

...The National Guard arrived in Lake Leer this morning and have declared the area secure as of... six hours ago, is this right, Barbara? Yes, six hours ago. Authorities are reporting a total of forty-one casualties in the Karma killings, most of them high schoolers.

Jesus Christ...

Little is known about the killer herself, nor her motives, though most suspect this to be a spree of revenge killings. Lynch's father reportedly disappeared shortly after her identity was discovered, and he has yet to be found. No idea what's going on there, but I can't help but think it looks fishy.

What a horrible Halloween we've had this year, huh, Rob? Between this and the killings in Salt Lake City...

Oh yes, Barb, I almost forgot about that. Another gruesome story coming up in the last couple days — two young women in Salt Lake City, Utah, have reportedly fallen victim to another savage killer. Their bodies were found... Christ, this is unpleasant even without seeing the pictures... Their bodies were found "half-devoured". They have yet to be identified.

Jesus. Perhaps the Karma Killer has left Lake Leer?

The police seem to find that unlikely, Barb. Their M.Os do not seem to match up at all, and the Karma Killer was never caught eating people — but who knows, in these troubled times.

That reminds me, Rob — I'm sorry, I interrupted. What happened with the Karma Killer?

Oh, right. The National Guard are coordinating with the mayor as we speak. The locals are permitted to return to their homes again, it seems, and the National Guard tells us the situation is "under control".

So, they haven't caught her.

I'd assume not. They'd have said so if they had. However, it seems Lake Leer is safe enough for the time being, although the beloved Outlook Resort burned down in her latest spree.

Burned down? Really?

Yes, the entire resort and much of the forest around it. Firefighters reportedly have the situation under control now, but the blaze was raging out of control all night.

Good God. Let's hope the killer is captured soon, then. The entire country ought to be on high alert at this point. After all, we have no idea where the Karma Killer could possibly be—

"Can you turn that shit off?" Kora grunts. "Fucking talk shows think they know everything."

"Sorry," Violet mutters, glancing over from the driver's seat, the heat of the desert sun eliciting the fiercest of migraines. Kora leans back in the passenger seat, running a palm over her sweaty forehead. Her burns are far from fully healed, forcing her to hide herself under hoodies and long sleeves. Her mask, tucked away in the glove compartment, has not healed from its own scorched makeover, but Kora seems to think that it gives her proper face some more character.

"It's fine," Kora replies. "It's a nice car you got us. Drives like a dream."

Violet smiles weakly. "It's not mine."

"Of course." Kora nods towards the gas station they've parked at. "Gonna go get some food."

"You're wanted across the entire country."

"And you have a broken leg."

"Send her, then," Violet grumbles, nodding to the back seat.

Laurie Thompson leans in between them, discarding one earbud. She looks between the two of them, purple eyes wide and eager. "What's up, boss?" Laurie asks cheerfully.

"I told you not to call me that," Kora sighs. "Snacks. You're not a wanted criminal."

"Not *yet,*" Laurie corrects with a giggle, holding out a palm. "Cash?"

Kora sighs, pulling her wallet out of her pocket and leafing through that dead banker's dollars. She hands over thirty bills. "Get enough to last us a couple days. I don't want to stop this car any more than we already are."

"Where are we going?" Laurie chirps.

"I told you, I don't know yet. Just... somewhere that isn't on fire."

"This place isn't on fire."

Kora gives her a deadpan look, and Laurie nods. "Right," the girl says, clutching the wad of bills. "I'll just go get those snacks. Be right back!" She kicks open the back door of the car, hopping out into the sun.

Kora and Violet watch her cheerfully jog over to the gas station, money in hand. Violet shakes her head in disturbed bemusement.

"Are you sure this was a good idea?" Violet asks, giving Kora a wary glance.

"What do you mean?"

"The..." Violet gestures. "Making Laurie into... whatever the hell she's become."

"It's torture," Kora says, matter-of-factly.

"She seems to be enjoying herself."

"So do I," Kora replies. "Look, me and Ira know what we're doing."

"I just..." Violet sighs. "Is this really you trying to torture her? Or are you just too lonely without her?"

Kora scowls. "Lonely? What are you on about? I'm a serial killer."

"For someone so good at killing, it took you so long to murder this one. And then you took it back."

Kora gives her an irritated glare.

Violet shrugs meekly. "Maybe I was just hoping I'd be good enough."

"What? Do you mean to imply you're *not?*"

"I... never mind," Violet sighs, looking out the window.

"Violet, you're..." Kora pauses as she tries to find the words. She hisses through her teeth, frustrated with herself. "I'm not good at this anymore."

"It's just not right."

Kora stares at her blankly. "We just killed forty-one people."

Violet squirms in her seat, nothing more to say.

The bear awakens in the depths of his den, bone and skin caught between his pointed teeth.

His hand curls into a fist, water dripping from the ceiling of the collapsing building he's claimed. The sofa he's slept on is no more comfortable than it has been the last couple nights.

It all reminds him of where he came from.

Art sits up, groaning as the scars on his back ache with ignored pain. He rolls his shoulders, fingers feeling at his fangs. He picks at a fleck of dead skin, blood stained upon his lips.

Sunlight struggles to breach the planks of wood that board up the windows. Dried blood stains and half-eaten limbs stain the concrete floor, debris and glass scattered everywhere.

He turns up his nose, catching a scent that hasn't graced him in a very long time.

Art makes no greeting, simply turns to his visitor in dull surprise.

The little girl with blood-red eyes sits at the half-shattered dining table, sipping a cup of crimson tea.

He frowns and stomps forward, easily three times her size. The girl smirks, no older than eight or nine in appearance, brushing her short red hair.

"You never call," she says, flashing him an innocent smile.

He doesn't respond, throwing aside the chair opposite her. It quarrels with the wall and bursts into pieces, chair leg rolling across the tile. He plants both his fists onto the table, huffing out furious breaths.

"Talkative as always," the girl chirps, adjusting her black shirt. A silver, sparkling heart adorns the center. "It's been so long."

"It has," Art replies, clearly lacking the desire for conversation.

"Didn't I tell you little Karma would take after her father?" the girl smirks. "Didn't I tell you?"

"Didn't I tell *you* to stay away from my family?" Art growls. "I returned your mask. Who gave you the right to come back, Ira?"

Ira shrugs, even managing to intimidate in the form of a child. "I suppose no one did. But I don't see any reason not to take the things I want... I believe it's why we always got along."

"We never got along," Art grunts.

"Yes, you did take a chainsaw to me at one point. You don't have to be so bloody ungrateful all the time, you know. It's only because of me that your precious daughter's around at all."

"I am not going to talk about Kora."

Ira clicks her tongue, watching him with playful eyes. "But you gave up so much to get her..."

"I am *not* going to talk about Kora!" Art bellows, snatching a butcher's knife off the table. He stabs the knife into her forehead, the blade plunging all the way in. Blood bubbles around the hilt, trickling down her pale, deceptively young skin. Even as an apparent child, Ira betrays no pain or shock.

The blood runs down her face, and Ira catches some of it with her fingers. She looks up at Art with an amused glance, gingerly sucking her own blood. "Well, well, you've still got spirit."

"I didn't..." Art scoffs, slamming his fist against the table. "I didn't go through all the trouble of having a daughter for you to make her your plaything, Ira! Quite the opposite, really. But you couldn't find some other weapon of wrath—"

"I didn't make her do anything. I gave her an offer, and she accepted. Much like you."

He narrows his eyes.

"Maybe if you'd been there all along..." Ira whispers, the knife entombed within her forehead. "Maybe then, she wouldn't have felt the need to go so far."

"So, it's my fault, then?"

"No, Art, not entirely, but there's a reason a world like this keeps breeding killers and broken beasts. You can't blame me for taking advantage of such an advantageous situation."

"And you said karma comes for all," Art snorts, turning away.

"And I am prepared for it, when my time comes. Were you?"

Art runs his hands over his face, canines digging into his bottom lip. "What do you get out of this?"

Ira smiles. "If I told you, it'd be so much less fun."

"Or you fear the danger that comes with my understanding."

"No. I fear tedium."

He says nothing, hoping she'll simply disappear, like she has so many times.

"How did they taste?"

The bear turns, purple creeping into his blazing eyes. "Who?"

"You know who. The girls." Ira leans forward, tilting her head. "Any of them taste as good as the lovely little lady you used to be so fond of?"

"Damn you," Art says, defeated.

"No," Ira says, standing. "I believe damning is *my* job."

He digs his heel into the floor, refusing to face her.

"Wrath is a funny thing, my Bleeding Bear," Ira smiles. "It envelops everything, it consumes. Not just you, but everything you touch. It's like a raging fire, hungry and indiscriminate... you cannot fault me for allowing the choice. You cannot fault me for presenting you every option. You can only fault yourself for indulging."

"Yeah?" Art chuckles. "And what's gonna stop it from catching up to you?"

"Simple. I know how to trim excess down to necessity. There aren't very many heroes in this world, Art, but the best of us know the value that lies in dirty deeds."

She turns on her heel, skin dissolving into crimson. "One day, you humans really ought to teach yourselves a similar philosophy. Self-control, self-awareness. From where I'm sitting, you lot cherish the road to extinction... and what a petty extinction it will be."

The Lady Báthory fades away, no regret or remorse in her step.

If this novel moved you, please consider donating to Everytown for Gun Safety to help prevent further gun violence and mass shootings in America. Thank you.

More Resources...

Gun Violence Archive
https://www.gunviolencearchive.org

John Hopkins Center for Gun Violence Solutions
https://publichealth.jhu.edu/departments/health-policy-and-management/research-and-practice/center-for-gun-violence-solutions

Giffords Law Center
https://giffords.org

Everytown for Gun Safety
https://www.everytown.org

Brady United Against Gun Violence
https://www.bradyunited.org

Afterword

A lot of people ask me if Karma Killer is based on real life. I always answer "yes, but not really."

Yes, some scenes are loosely based on real things that happened (mostly to me) in high school. Some snippets of dialogue or some of the sins Karma surveys are based off real rumors and exchanges I've heard (generally, sadly, the most disgusting ones). Some rather obvious parts of this work are also based off real life mass shootings in America.

Ultimately, though, this novel is not really all that exemplative of life in America. This, really, is a sanitized depiction of American life, nestled right in the boundary between the tolerable and the undepictable.

When I went to high school, I was a sheltered kid with fundamentalist Christian parents who did their worst at "homeschooling" me. I was discovering my queer identity, I had been raised to be afraid of the world around me, and I had had my "first boyfriend" and first break-up barely a year or so prior.

He was thirty years old. I was eleven. What they don't tell you in all the true crime shit is how long it will take you to recognize something like that as a crime, and how much longer it will take to recognize yourself as a victim.

I was a self-taught, socially shattered, developing depressive when I got into high school. I had very little experience with people that weren't my abusive parents or my abusive "boyfriend", and my developing emotions were so twisted and mangled that there was no way in Hell I'd act relatively "normal".

I only made it into my high school because of an IQ test. That school was funded by and for elitists and rich kids, one a mangy little mutt like myself never should've set foot in. Practically everyone there was a white kid with wealthy parents and their entire life set out for them in a carefully curated checklist. I, meanwhile, had no idea what I wanted to do with my life except that I was learning firsthand what it felt like to be suicidal.

If the hell of my life before was the fissure, then high school was the tsunami that toppled the dam.

My bisexuality was a problem in such an overwhelmingly conservative establishment, and the mix of my autism and my trauma made me robotic, detached, crude, profane and openly suicidal. I was prone to fighting and even snappier with my mouth, and I was rather quickly othered to the darker corners of the school.

My first remaining memory of high school is being beaten half-to-death in the parking lot because I made a snarky comment about a classmate's ass. They valued their straight identity to such a degree that some parts of my body still don't work to this day.

Everyone just referred to me as the "psychopath". Few knew my name. My bisexuality, something I was never told I should keep secret for my safety, led to me being referred to in fleeting whispers and outright accusations as a pedophile and a rapist. Countless stories were concocted to support these accusations, and with all the mental breakdowns I had in class, all the visits I had to make to the fucking counselor's office, I was giving them all the satisfaction they needed to keep going.

I never did any of the things they accused me of, of course, but when you get abused so much on a daily basis by what is, in that moment in time, your entire world, you learn to accept that something must really be wrong with you. How could I have earned such treatment otherwise?

I quickly turned to drugs, alcohol, self-harm, casual sex, gambling, petty crime, everything I could think of to spare myself the pain of feeling. I was alone, so nobody cared I was destroying myself. I don't remember any of my lessons, because Ispent every day drinking whiskey out of a thermos and swallowing breath mints between class to cope. At lunchtime, I'd hide in a bathroom stall, cut open my arms and pray to die.

Of course, I was never a good Christian, so God never listened.

By the time I escaped that hell, I had been institutionalized for suicide attempts half a dozen times. I never attended my graduation. I'm sure nobody noticed. After my mother died, I inherited a lot of my own records, and I discovered that my teachers had characterized me as, essentially, a misanthrope and a danger to others. They made me sound like a school shooter waiting to happen, all because I couldn't rid my eyes of their violated vacancy.

I was nineteen when I wrote the first draft of Karma Killer. I'm twenty-two now as I write this afterword, and through all the change of the last few years, nothing has really changed.

I've gotten clean, but I haven't been able to keep a job under the weight of my trauma and freshly-diagnosed psychosis and **BPD.** I've bounced between abusive partners, replicating my childhood with every new household. I've been gaslit and manipulated and institutionalized and threatened with violence and worse over and over. Only now, after all this time, do I have some vague chance to start over.

America hasn't changed in any way that matters either.

As of this writing, there have been 2,280 mass shootings in America in the 2020s alone. 2,339 people have died in these shootings.

I watch these statistics grow with sickness and dread, always thinking back to my own suffering, absolutely repulsed that I was once considered a likely perpetrator of something like this simply because I couldn't hide my pain well enough to meet societal standards.

Even now, it's something that keeps me up at night. How many of these tragedies happened because of how callously America treats its children?

This month alone has provided a lot of reason to suspect America is at fault for many of them. Affirmative action has been declared unconstitutional. Student debt cancellation has been considered an overreach of executive powers. Businesses may be permitted to discriminate against the queer community on religious grounds. Federal prisoners belatedly found innocent will have to serve their full sentences regardless, all to fund a prison slavery system that elevates the elite even higher upon the shoulders of the broken.

The gap between the wealthy and the poor grows bigger and bigger. The rights of women, people of color and queer communities shrink day by day. Guns are still as easy to obtain as candy, all because the right-wing fund their political campaigns with **NRA** money. The disenfranchised are still trapped in catch-22s, unable to work without an address, unable to get an address without a job, unable to get a job at the living wage without college, unable to attend college without exorbitant debt.

When I first started to write in high school, I didn't write tragedies because I wanted to make people sad. I didn't write horror because I really wanted people to feel frightened. I don't take pleasure in putting people through pain, contrary to the claims of the people that haunt me at night.

I write these stories because I write what I know, and I'm not sure I'll ever get to write a happy one.

I write these stories in the vain hope that, if there's people out there like me, suffering in silence, that they'll see this and at least smile before they sink. I want to hold out a hand. That's what I wanted when I started writing — to reach out to the world and give it a shoulder to cry on.

I don't think I'm a good person. I'm told I must be because I want so desperately to prove I am, but I don't know if I can be. I don't know if I want to save the world for its sake or for my own.

All I know is that I don't want to be alone anymore, and I don't want anyone like me to be alone anymore.

My situation has improved, but this novel is a shot in the dark. I never got myself an agent, something I expected with my controversial proclivities. I'm self-publishing with the help of what are essentially loved ones and volunteers, people who just believe in what I have to say. I have no idea if this'll take me anywhere, or if I'll just keep spending my life despondent in a ditch.

I hope this isn't my only published novel. Looking back on it years later in my final revisions, I must admit I find it rather amateur, abstract and clumsy. My work since is much greater than this, and I've learned to develop some really nuanced, emotional, complex, sociopolitical stories. I hope to one day release them too, but I don't know how many will care to see them.

No one wanted to hear my story back then, but now it seems everyone does, so much so that they rallied around me when I just about gave up after a couple dozen agents passed me over.

Well, here it is. Here's a part of my story. It's a sad one, it doesn't really have a happy ending, and even its author is still a miserable old misanthrope. I have my dreams — a career as an author, a house by the beach, a woman across the sea I fear I won't live long enough to marry — but I have no idea if they'll make it to my final draft.

All I have is this, the malcontent memoirs of America's stillborn serpents.

If any part of this story has resonated with you, if you feel alone in this world, please know that you aren't. I've done all I can to survive, and I don't know how much longer I'll last, but I'll keep fighting so long as there's someone left to fight for.

I don't know why I fight, but if even just one person finds in me the inspiration to live, I think that'll have been good enough.

This world is often considered cruel, but it isn't. It's humanity that's cruel, and while me and my dearest one often debate in our contrasting views of humanity, I secretly hope that she's right.

I always argue that humans are inherently destructive, horrible creatures. She thinks they are, by and large, good and compassionate, crafted by circumstance and forever redeemable.

In this moment in time, I would love nothing more than to be proven wrong.

Be kind to those around you, no matter their differences, no matter their quirks and their pecularities. More than that, fight for what's right, fight for those who don't belong to you. Fight for every injustice you see, not just the ones on your doorstep. You don't need any reason, do you? Should anyone be in pain in this world?

Fight for what's right, and prove me wrong. That's all I want.

Acknowledgment

There are a lot of people to whom this book's existence owes its debt, and I fear I've forgotten some of them. If I have, don't take it personally.

First of all, a great thanks to A.A.H. and L.R., without whom I would be homeless, hopeless, and very likely dead. A further thanks goes to A.A.H. for drawing my profile picture on my socials and getting every aspect of my character down so perfectly.

One of my most effuscent thanks must go to S.G., one of the few people in high school who wasn't determined to make sure I was a corpse by the end of it, and, in fact, was quite determined to accomplish the opposite. Thank you. You're my best friend.

Much of my most heartfelt gratitude must also go to P.B., for giving my story a chance to breathe with the marketing acumen and business knowhow I most certainly do not possess, as well as their endless support as a partner and a friend.

Thanks to K.T. for drawing the cover art and in general enriching my life from pretty much the beginning, even at its darkest.

My deepest gratitude goes to my frostbite, who dragged me out of a ditch and taught me I could be seen as human even now.

My personal thanks go to my beta readers (of which there have been many), and even if they didn't criticize the work as much as I'd like, I guess not having much to correct is something to be proud of.

And finally, thanks to G. in Colorado, who sought my help and gave me the chance to prove to myself that I really can do good things for people in horrible situations after all. She loved this book, so the best I can do is repay this personal debt with an acknowledgement and a hope that a life made better stays better.

About the Author

Anathema Morgan is an Irish-American trickster deity moonlighting as a writer of fiction when it isn't too busy saving the world from itself. It goes by the pronouns it/its and presents feminine. It is a mouthy sufferer of a mix of Cluster **B** personality disorders as a result of its **DID**, as well as chronic fatigue/pain, severe agoraphobia, complex **PTSD** and some other lovely conditions that have endlessly enriched its life. Having spent 22 years walking the world alone and 8 of those years writing, it seeks to make sure no one ever has to feel the way it did again without a supportive voice and its trademark brand of realistic optimism for the future.

While Ana Morgan gets bored easily and never tends to write anything remotely similar once a project is done, it can assure you that pretty much all of its work will bear some sort of psychological & body horror element, unforgettable characters & diverse cultures, an emotional cocktail that hits harder than moonshine, enough radical anarchist politics to make a dozen bigots combust with every copy of its work sold, and tales so realistic that most would deem them not safe for life.

When it's not busy terrorizing the tyrants of our world and standing with scapegoats with its weaponized words, Ana Morgan has a number of unhealthy special interests, ranging from horror movies, metal & punk music, first-person shooters & roguelikes, history & mythology, culture, graffiti art, motorcycles & skateboarding. Feel free to ask it anything - it only bites a little.